UP
THE
ENTROPIC
HILL

MATTIE BUKOWSKI

UP THE ENTROPIC HILL

QUEER SPACE
New Orleans & New York

Published in the United States of America by
Queer Space
A Rebel Satori Imprint
www.rebelsatoripress.com

Paperback ISBN: 978-1-60864-319-6

ONE

It wasn't raining on the day they died.

In fact, the weather was positively delightful when it happened. The full moon (which was always full these days, since the setting was jammed) shone softly on the city of Ishtar, and the sky was clear, bright, and sprinkled generously with auto-generated stars. It felt as if the planet's atmosphere was trying to make a point of the day's events being entirely inconsequential. How unkind of it.

"Dial him again, please." Lucy Franklin rubbed her tired eyes and smiled reassuringly at Pavel.

He nodded, typing in a sequence of digits into a tiny screen projected on top of his palm. This was his fifth attempt at reaching professor Nawahi, and something was telling him that the man would not show up.

"She should drink something at least," Lucy said, inflections flat, voice trembling slightly. "It's been almost an hour."

"Well, I can't force water down her throat," Pavel retorted, listening to the rustling static on the other end of his call. "She's still in shock. Give her time."

Lucy didn't reply, and the room drowned in silence once again.

Out of all the lecture halls in the Novella Institute, this one was perhaps the coziest. It fitted only a handful of students, and thanks to the enormous windows, it was always well-lit, day and night. The new full-dimension projectors (their latest 'small gift' from the Muuk) were, according to the users, 'more realistic than reality'. And the coffee machine was exquisite. Not the coffee it made, the actual thing, though the coffee was amazing too, except, of course, none of it could possibly matter.

Not to nurse Franklin, who attempted to occupy her trembling hands with pushing the 'system check' button on the vital signs scanner again and again. Or to engineer Pavel Nowak, whose face seemed grey and dull even in the natural moonlight, all his attention focused on the door, hoping that, finally, someone would come in and absolve him from his solemn duty. And it certainly didn't matter to Amber.

"Hey, honey." The girl shifted on the hard polished floor, and it was Lucy's cue to make another attempt at communication. "Are you sure you don't want a sip of something?"

Amber didn't react. She was sitting with her back to the adults, transfixed, staring off into the far-left corner. Motionless.

"Could I please take a look at your wound?" Lucy pleaded. "I don't even know if it stopped bleeding."

She placed a light touch on the girl's shoulder, making Amber flinch. Lucy sighed and stepped away. Once again, it was quite useless.

"Any info on her next of kin?" Pavel asked and Lucy shook her head.

"None who are still physically present, as far as we know," she elaborated. "No siblings either."

"Well. Maybe it's time to contact social services."

"I am social services!" Lucy covered her face with her palms and took a deep breath in. "And I've no idea what to do. We aren't... we don't get instructions on this sort of thing," she said, looking at Pavel with gleaming wet eyes. "It isn't in the curriculum! I'm not prepared, I'm not..."

He could sense she was about to burst into tears, so he got up, moved over to her side and put a comforting hand on her back. She thanked him in a hoarse whisper and wiped a tear from the corner of her eye.

"Dial again, please," she said, and he pressed his thumbs into his palms, activating the number panel.

Pavel waited, biting his lip. At first, there was only the familiar chirp of the static. Then...

"Hello?" The voice on the other end sounded disturbed; panicked, almost.

"Professor Nawahi!" Pavel exclaimed, and Lucy gave out a sigh of relief. "I'm

2

so glad I reached you."

"Excuse me for not sharing that sentiment," Nawahi muttered.

"Yes, of course. Sorry."

"Where are you?"

"Room 2B15," he replied. "Third floor, Western..."

"Yes, I know where it is, I work here," Nawahi snapped, ending the call immediately.

Lucy and Pavel looked at each other—desperate, drained, but relieved.

"This isn't right," Lucy whispered.

Pavel whole-heartedly agreed.

Five minutes later, and David Nawahi was kneeling in front of his 11-year-old student, an expression of profound grief and sympathy on his face. He noticed the streak of dried-up blood on the girl's cheek and frowned.

"Hey there, sweetie," he said, touching her hand gently.

She turned her head towards him at once.

"Where are they?" Amber asked, and Lucy couldn't help but gasp. It was the first time she heard as much as a peep from Amber.

"Back in the basement," Nawahi told her. "I..."

"Take me there," she said, her lips pressed tightly together.

"Amber, I'm so sorry, but I can't. Your parents, sweetie... they're..."

"Dead," she finished for him, unnaturally calm. "I know. Figured as much."

"You are hurt," he interrupted her, evidently not surprised by the absence of emotion she was showing. "Please let the nurse take care of you."

"It's nothing." Amber waved her hand dismissively. "A scrap here, a burn there, I'll live. Let me speak to my parents."

"They're no longer with us, love," Lucy interfered. "You can't speak to them."

"Bullshit!" Amber burst into a laugh, getting up from the floor at once.

In the absence of artificial light, the wound on her face looked especially ghastly. It started at her left temple, ran frighteningly close to her eye and ended on the side of her neck. The gleaming scarlet stain contrasted with her brown

3

skin. Dust, dirt and blood soaked her long, black hair. She stood firmly, shielding her burnt wrist from the view, and her deep brown eyes burned with fear and fury.

"Let me speak to my parents," she repeated.

"They're dead," Nawahi repeated right back.

"Yes, I heard you the first time," Amber said. "So is my grandma, and I chat with her every weekend."

"No, love, you don't understand," Nawahi's gaze wondered, unable to settle on the girl. "They haven't been digitalized. They couldn't be." He paused. "They're gone. Actually gone."

"What?" For the first time in their brief exchange, Amber seemed to have lost her fierce confidence.

"They tried to," Nawahi continued, "but the damage was too extensive. There was nothing to be done."

"That's unacceptable!" Amber stomped her foot in pure, scolding anger. "Who was in charge of that? I demand to speak to their superior!"

"Amber, listen," Pavel tried to interfere, but she gestured 'shush' at him.

"No," she said. "They aren't doing their job properly. It's a disgrace. A mistake. They'll fix it."

"They can't." Nawahi shook his head.

"Call the Muuk then!"

"They've landed half an hour ago. There's nothing they can do either."

"That isn't possible!" Amber screeched, bursting into tears. "Fix it! Digitize them! Fix. It!"

Nawahi let the meltdown run its course. He knew there was nothing he could do to help her, except for making sure no one was touching or bothering her. He dealt with at least one of Amber's meltdowns every week, so it wasn't a big deal- -except usually they were caused by too much light, or a change in her habits, and not by something so big and complex and profoundly unusual that he could barely wrap his mind around it himself.

He couldn't comfort her, not in any meaningful way. He doubted that anyone could. So instead, he just stood aside in silence as the girl cried and howled, tugging at her sleeves and biting into her burned fingers.

A few minutes passed, and Amber seemed to have lost her destructive energy. She wasn't kicking and screaming anymore, but she still stood up defiantly--though gasping for air, exhausted.

"Why can't they be brought back?" she asked, her face back to stern and emotionless.

Nawahi sighed. Amber didn't do ambiguity. She wouldn't lay back until she got the truthful answer.

"The explosion was too strong," he said. "They were too badly hurt. The Muuk technician tried to lean them against the reading panel but..." he paused, the words stuck in his throat, "...they had no heads to make contact. Their brains aren't just damaged, there's nothing left of them."

Amber nodded. She heard the words, she decoded what they meant, and she understood them perfectly—she just didn't believe a single one. This is not how things were, in the real world! Death was not included in her concept of the universe. Therefore, it logically followed that there had to have been some outrageous mistake. There simply had to!

With one swift leap towards the door, she escaped the room and sprinted down the stairs, completely ignoring Nawahi, Lucy and Pavel calling out to her. She ran and ran, until she returned to the place she was rescued from mere hours earlier. All around her was smoke and dust. She didn't see anything, didn't knew where she was going, really. She was coughing non-stop, and tears were streaming down her face, whether from the irritation or from emotion, she wasn't sure. She barged her way into the vast hall, hearing Nawahi's quick footsteps behind her. She didn't care. She needed to see.

The hall was now abandoned except for two human figures, whose shadows moved and danced on the walls somewhere far away. Amber paused, trying to catch her breath, and peered into the semi-darkness. Her feet were sticky, and she could sense a nauseatingly sweet smell--something organic, burning. Like overdone barbecue.

She made a few steps forward, not even hearing Nawahi's shouting behind her.

5

Her eyes found a point to focus on, and she was walking towards it, determined. The two humans were pacing in her direction, and Nawahi was approaching from the other side. She leaped forward, then stopped, having found what she came there for.

On the floor in front of her feet lay two human bodies--or, rather, what remained of them. One was missing the entire lower half, ending abruptly at the waist, residing firmly in a pool of dark, coagulated blood. The head was barely there, skull cracked open, the lower jaw barely holding on to the rest of the face.

Her dad.

Next to him lay the second body--rather more complete, but far more badly battered. The face, the chest and the arms were burnt to a crisp, and the head rested on a pile of debris and brain tissue. The rest of the body was covered in deep wounds and burns, and there was nothing left of the feet.

Her mum.

"The hell are you doing here?!"

The words of the young woman speaking to her sounded far away, as if coming from underwater.

Amber became aware of someone dragging her out of the room and didn't even try to resist. She closed her eyes and allowed herself one full sob. She saw Nawahi standing over her, his face flushed red, muttering something. She didn't listen.

"What should I be feeling?" she thought to herself. What was the appropriate emotional response to demonstrate? Do people in this situation usually cry hysterically, or scream, or go really quiet? Do they say something like "please no", or "mummy", or "let me say goodbye"? She didn't know. She only saw that kind of thing in movies. Honestly, she wasn't even sure any of it was real... but at least she knew she wasn't being lied to. Rule number one of research: never operate on secondary sources.

Five minutes more, and she was sitting in the professor lounge room, sipping something warm and sweet. A medical bot was stitching the wound on her face while Lucy watched, tutting.

"It will definitely scar," she said, adjusting a setting on the tiny whirring machine. "The Muuk can pay for the scar removal later."

"I don't want it," Amber responded. "Leave the scar. I need to remember them."

Lucy didn't comment.

Pavel and Nawahi sat opposite her, silent, not noticing how the hot cups burned the skin of their palms.

"Did anyone else get hurt?" Amber asked, serious and collected once again.

"No," Pavel replied. "A small consolation."

"They found the reason?"

"Human mistake, seems like. Your father..." he paused, not sure whether he should continue.

"Yes?"

"He switched to manual just before he invited you and your mum in."

"He wanted to show us the composite picture," Amber explained. "He said it was the most amazing thing he had ever seen. Like looking right into the eyes of the universe," she quoted.

"The system overheated," Pavel said. "And because the shields were down, it couldn't redirect the heat, and..."

"Boom," Amber finished for him. "Yeah, I get the gist of it."

Nawahi sighed and gulped down his tea.

"That's the end of their project, I guess," Amber said.

"Seems so," Pavel confirmed.

"Pity. It was his life's work for dad."

"The Muuk won't let it go on when it's associated with so much danger," Nawahi commented. "Two deaths and an injury, and with so much damage...it's unprecedented."

"The Muuk can go fuck themselves!" Amber exclaimed, getting up at once.

The medical kit robot ceased it's whirring, its job done. She removed it from her face and threw it to the floor with as much force as she could muster. It broke into pieces with a pathetic whine of a hurt animal. She kicked it with her foot,

7

turned around and stormed out of the room.

"Go after her," Lucy said to Nawahi, picking up the pieces of the robot with a sad smile. "You're the only one she will listen to."

And so he did.

He found her in the corridor next to an enormous window, leaning against the windowsill, peering into the darkness, as if in search of something. Nawahi approached Amber cautiously, afraid to disturb her. She glanced at him and moved over to the side.

"Hey."

He looked out as well. The night was stunningly beautiful, with the moon illuminating every tree leaf and every blade of grass in the university garden. The precious early buds of tulips were especially touching. A bitter-sweet reminder of the coming spring.

"I am so sorry," Nawahi said.

"Save it."

"I mean it, Amber," he insisted. "I wish I could do something to take your pain away. Your father, you know, he was a very good friend. And your mother, she is..." his voice broke, and he had to take a moment to compose himself. "She was like a sister to me," he finished. "If there was anything in the world I could do to make it right, anything at all..."

"Who designed this world?" Amber interrupted suddenly.

"What do you mean?"

"Who came up with it?"

"Well," Nawahi scratched his head, "the Muuk..."

"No, I don't mean the Muuk! I'm so sick of hearing that name," she grimaced. "I mean, this universe—who designed it? Who came up with the rules?"

"Amber, sweetie," he mumbled, "no one did. The universe isn't a product of anyone's creation, it just is. It came into existence billions of years ago, it has been changing ever since, and it will exist for many more billions of years. No one is responsible for it."

"That can't be right," she frowned. "Things like that don't just... exist.

Someone had to have made it."

"No one did," he assured her. "We've researched it to the limits of our cognitive ability, and we're fairly certain the universe simply came into being some time ago."

"That isn't good enough!" she insisted. "Surely no one is ever satisfied by that answer. There has to be some other explanation."

"Well, on the old Earth, they believed in gods or a god—a mythical being, all powerful, who created the world and everything in it. But it's a religion, a belief, it isn't true in a literal sense."

"Who says so?"

"Science."

"Screw science, then! Science can't give me back my parents, now can it?!"

Nawahi took a deep breath in. Maybe religion could help her cope for a while. He didn't have a better answer anyway.

"Alright then," he continued. "They believed that we all have a soul, a sort of a representation of our memory and personality and consciousness, and that it can survive the death of the body. And after death, you would go to a better world, one where there was no suffering and no evil, and you would be reunited with your loved ones again."

"Not interested in that part," Amber dismissed. "Who designed the universe then?"

"God. According to most religions, at least."

"Understood," Amber nodded. "Where can I find them?"

"Sweetie." Nawahi shook his head, starting to regret his idea. "They don't physically exist. It's a supernatural, metaphorical entity. And even if they did, I don't think they'd be able to bring your parents back."

"Who said anything about bringing them back?" Amber asked, frowning. "No. I need to find that god. I need to find them," she said, so much passion and strength in her voice, "no, I will find them... and I will kill them."

Meanwhile, the Sun was high on the horizon, articulating every detail of the frost-covered field. Down there, several floors underneath the balcony, people were fighting for their country and for their lives. Every now and then the air was pierced by a sound of a bullet hitting its target, or a muffled scream escaping from a soldier's lips. S took a deep breath in, cracking his knuckles one by one. They were all rather desensitized to the horrors by now, but it was still oh-so-unpleasant to witness.

"Bored now," Light proclaimed, and Darkness groaned.

"Leave then!" she responded. Everything about her screamed passive-aggressive in that moment; even the manner in which she mixed her tea. "No-one's keeping you here."

"Yeah, I guess the two of you would be enough for the job." Light leaned back in her seat, no desire to move any further. "How long have we got?"

"Two hours, give or take," S told her. "Keep quiet, I'm trying to pay attention."

"Pay attention to what?" Light asked. "You know who will win, you know exactly how many people are going to die, you know the movement of every atom from dawn to dusk."

"Yet we can't figure out how to shut you up," Darkness muttered.

"Hey!" she raised her hands in front of her chest, defensive. "I wasn't the one who suggested tampering in the French-Russian war for a 'slow day out'."

"Excuse me," Darkness began, "but..."

"Shush." Light put a gentle finger on her lips, and she couldn't help but smile. "I'm not saying it was all bad, or pointless. But surely we could find an easier way to do this? And I wanted to check out that concert, you know," she pouted. "What are they called, S?"

"Nirvana," he replied, a dreamy expression on his face.

"Excellent," Light nodded, getting up. "Chop-chop. This nonsense can wait. S, what do you say?"

"I may have a way of out-sourcing this," he replied. "I think we could..."

"Do it!" Light encouraged. "We'll wait for you at the concert."

She clapped her hands, and everything around them: the tea set, the comfy armchairs, even the extensively decorated balcony which was hanging in mid-air a mere second ago, disappeared. Shimmered out and melted away into the sky in its usual manner.

"Nirvana," Darkness repeated, her image fading away as well. "They better be good, S."

"It will be," S said, and made exactly one useless and theatrical wave before melting into the air.

Down on the ground, the battle was almost over. Doctors of war were dragging away the wounded, soldiers preparing for retreat. A young man, barely 19 years of age, stepped into a puddle of mud and grimaced. Out of the corner of his eye, he saw one of his comrades, Oleg. The guy was tending to his horse, which lay on the ground motionless, a gaping wound in its leg. He averted his glance, perfectly aware of what was to come next.

The day's last gunshot thundered, spooking away a flock of birds. The fight was over. He wiped sweat from his face and headed in the direction of their camp. The war was devastating, and the battle left him feeling dead inside, and yet... he just had the most brilliant idea.

TWO

Every reasonable person knows that 67.73% of all important events in the universe can be traced back to the choice between getting up or turning to your other side and falling back to sleep. And if you don't believe me, well… that's a sure sign that you abuse the snooze button on a regular basis.

Don't worry though, happens to everyone from time to time! Everyone that is, except for lifestyle vloggers, sophies (the androids), and Sophies (those annoyingly smart girls in every person's honors class who probably don't sleep at all and use that time to copy over their freshly copied notes with an array of glittery pens).

Point is, mornings matter.

And so, this story shall also begin on a morning, exactly fourteen years, three months and five days after the events of that dreadful, beautiful evening you just read about.

On That morning, Amber woke up a whole 93 minutes earlier than usual. She rubbed her blanket on the side of her face, breathing slowly and deeply, and concentrated all of her willpower on keeping her eyes open. Up on the ceiling, sunbeams were projecting a rainbow-colored wave of light. She sniffed, scratched her nose, and breathed in again to her lungs' full capacity. Something was bothering her. Profoundly bothering her.

She rolled over to her side and tapped the wall twice. It lit up a saturated neon blue, showing her the time, and Amber had to shield her gaze from the blast of light that hit her face. Six thirty in the morning. Why was she awake at six thirty in the bloody morning?

It was too late for an attempt to fall back asleep. She ruffled her tangled hair, cursing everything known to her in alphabetical order, and almost fell off the bed trying to get up. Slowly her consciousness was catching on to her senses, and it wasn't one bit pleasant.

"The birds," Amber said to herself. "God. Damned. Birds!"

Three seconds later she was by her bedroom window, rolling back the curtains and undoing the locks with a touch of her thumbprint. Outside, the morning was stunningly gorgeous. The clouds covered the sky in a layer of cotton-candy brush strokes, and the air was clear and cold as mountain spring water. Under her window, the garden was full of life. Birds of all types and varieties were chirping, singing, chatting, and greeting a new day. Her own little natural paradise... and she hated it viciously.

"Shut your damn mouths!" Amber barked, looking one ruffled sparrow directly in the eyes. "This isn't funny."

The birds weren't listening.

"Look," Amber continued, leaning out of the window at a dangerously steep angle, "I know you want to fuck. So do I. But I don't scream about it at the top of my lungs!" she screamed, at the top of her lungs.

After a moment of consideration, one bird had evidently decided that the spot wasn't worth the fuss, and took off, flapping its wings in the opposite direction of Amber's second-story apartment. The rest of the birds, though rather confused, soon followed. Just a minute later the garden was almost completely empty.

"That's more like it," Amber muttered, closing the window again. "Now... I think I made it known yesterday evening that I want the sound shield on. You hear that, Sarah?"

There was nothing but silence.

"Sarah?" Amber repeated. "I'm waiting!"

"I've overridden the command." If AI systems could sound guilty, this is how they would sound.

"Okay," Amber nodded, adjusting her silk nightgown. "That makes sense. Why?"

"Your schedule is heavy today. Your time of falling asleep was 23:09. I have tweaked the setting to wake you up earlier. I have decided that the natural means of waking up are preferable."

"Right," Amber sighed, and tilted her head upwards, as if the AI voice was coming from the ceiling. "Don't do that!"

And she stormed off, satisfied.

"I can't stand birds," she muttered under her breath, rubbing her still sleepy eyes. "Those fuckers are way too smug."

The artificial lights flickered into life as she walked through a long corridor past the kitchen and into the bathroom. The carpet-covered floor tickled her feet, and she could already smell coffee being brewed for breakfast. Amber stumbled through the bathroom door and stretched as she felt a jaw-displacing yawn coming up.

"Music," she requested, and Sarah activated her morning playlist.

She stepped closer to the mirror, waiting for the water to reach the hottest possible setting, and examined her face in the natural white light. It didn't change much since she was a child. Her eyes were still big, captivating, and as dark as human eyes could be. Her hair was even longer now, black and shiny, and seriously in need of a brushing. She was tall and broad-shouldered, but also slim, with thin wrists and veins visible through her brown skin. And the scar, spanning from atop her eyebrow almost to her neck, was still most certainly there.

"What would you like for breakfast?" Sarah asked, quick to display various options on the mirror in front of her.

"Don't care," Amber shrugged, and spat out the toothpaste.

"Employing 'Don't care' setting," Sarah repeated. "Now preparing fried eggs, rye toast and fruit salad."

"Has everyone sent their papers?" she inquired.

"Checking. The 'mid-term ancient history' folder has eleven files in it. User 'Tim Bernstein' has not sent a text file."

"Predictable." Amber took off her nightgown and left the room in a single over-sized t-shirt. "Guess who's getting minus fifteen points off his final."

For the next hour Amber sat in the kitchen, her right elbow resting on the windowsill, wrapped in a blanket on top of another blanket. She drank her coffee, ate blueberries, and graded the papers. The projections in front of her moved and shimmered ever so slightly as she turned the virtual pages and marked them with a touch of her left index finger. Sarah was silent, on firm command not to interfere with the process.

"Dull and factually correct," Amber commented, popping another berry into her mouth. "Pretentious bullshit. Cliche. Cliche. Obvious and annoying. A pretty good part, actually. Overall," she paused, "profoundly talentless. Hard-working though. Passed."

She waved her hand in the air, and the paper disappeared, immediately replaced by the next installment of student mid-term essay.

"Will anyone ever surprise me?" she asked.

"Information not sufficient for analysis," Sarah replied. "Oops. Sorry. Not supposed to interrupt."

Amber snickered, brushing through the text. From the very first line, she could tell it did not look promising.

"For their final, I'll tell them to do something fun," she concluded, rubbing her eyes. "Another coffee. Please. And don't you dare lower the caffeine content."

The minutes ticked away, one by one, like tiny grains of sand in an hourglass, and the texts weren't getting any more engaging. She stretched her legs and rummaged her hand along the windowsill until she found something to occupy her fingers with a rubber coil, which she could twist and bend without breaking. Slowly, she let her mind wander off.

'Words', Amber mused, staring into the distance. 'How did people come up with them?'. The question took her on a journey of its own. It carried her blindly into the depths of her own mind where she could no longer feel her body, or her senses, or the world around her. She almost began to drift off into a shallow slumber when something brought her back to the coffee table and a thin virtual stack of yet ungraded papers.

"Attention," Sarah announced, her cybernetic speech produced by the wall that Amber was leaning on. "Next bus leaving in... twelve minutes."

"Lovely," Amber said.

Some days, she wished she was living on the Old Earth as a forest hermit, or a cave woman. The food might not have been ideal, and the possibility of early death by bear was rather higher than she preferred, but at least there were no irritably accurate robots to interrupt your meditations.

By the time she exited her apartment building, shielded from the world by a heavy jacket and sunglasses, the streets of Ishtar were full of people. She walked past a few neighbors on her way to the bus station and watched them look away politely, well aware of her disdain for needless courtesy. The wind was gaining velocity and brining the scent of blossoming lilac right up to her nostrils. It was getting warmer too. She could tell. It was two thirds the gentle tingle of ultraviolet on her face, and one third automatic weather forecast sending her a notification.

"Arriving next: line number 14", the transport inform system announced as she stepped onto the small square in front of the railway. "Final stop: Einstein street."

And soon enough, the 14 number bus had arrived.

She stepped inside at the last possible moment, waiting for everyone to board it ahead of her. She took one last glance at the city below her before crossing the threshold. All around her was glass and metal, buildings towering into the sky—sparkling clean, and covered by vegetation at the same time. From twenty stories up from the ground, she could see the crossroad gardens, and brightly colored kid playgrounds, and even the dead-end corner bakeries.

The city was perfect; it functioned like a sturdy spaceship engine and breathed joy and comfort. And it made her feel trapped. Even now, inside of the airy bus which roamed the monorails across Ishtar's neat neighborhoods, she couldn't help but think that she was being contained in the universe's prettiest zoo cage.

She took a seat at the rear end of the compartment, pressed her head against the plexiglass and sighed. Every day, all the same. Get up, go to work, order the groceries, watch a movie, go to sleep... was this the infamous utopia her ancestors dreamed of?

"Do you like taffy?"

The voice startled her, but she didn't show it. She turned her head and saw a kid standing next to her—kindergarten age, a paper bag of candy clutched in his tiny precious fingers. She wanted to smile but held it back.

Amber didn't reply. Instead, she removed her arm from her pocket, and placed it, palm up, on the seat next to her. The kid beamed and put a neatly wrapped candy on her palm. She nodded and returned her gaze to the window next to her.

"My dad makes it," the kid mumbled, evidently chewing on a taffy himself. "He's over there." He pointed to the middle section of the bus. "It's okay, to make candy." The kid paused, expecting Amber to engage with him in some way, but she wasn't even looking at him. "What do you do?" he asked, and still received no reply. "I don't know what I will do. Dad thinks I could be a good teacher, or a nanny, but I want to be an astronaut!"

This was the comment that finally got a response out of Amber.

"Good luck," she couldn't help but snort with laughter.

"Why not?" the boy asked, already frowning.

"Can't leave the planet, sunshine," she explained, almost gleeful. "Not allowed. All you can be is museum caretaker, show people our old spaceships. So don't get your hopes up."

Amber expected the kid to have left at that point, but he was still standing there, silent. She glanced at him from under her sunglasses and bit her lip. 'Oh no', she thought, seconds before the kid burst into tears.

"Omar!"

The boy's dad had a hell of a quick reaction. As soon as he heard his son cry, he jumped out of his seat and came to his aid.

"What happened?" he asked, touching the boy's curly hair.

"I can't be an astronaut," little Omar whimpered.

"Nonsense," his dad replied. "You can be whoever you want."

"No, he can't," Amber said, now unable to hold back. "And you know it."

"Hey." Taking the boy's hand, he straightened his back and frowned his eyebrows at Amber. "He's too young to know that."

"You're never too young to know things," Amber shrugged. "Don't bring him up on lies."

"Don't tell me how to raise my child!"

"Then teach your kid not to give candy to adult strangers," she retorted, turning away.

The kid had not stopped crying, and the dad was now trying to console him with more lies and extra candy. She unwrapped the taffy and bit into the tiny sugar block. It got stuck in her teeth at once.

"People," she muttered, her expression twisting subtly in disgust, and prepared to leave the bus.

The Novella Institute for Outstanding Achievement of Humankind welcomed Amber with its familiar aura of free-flowing discussion and sophisticated pretense. Its corridors were full of students and potted plants, and a sea of background noise soon filled Amber's ears. She walked past the elevator, taking the stairs as usual. She wasn't quite sure where she was heading first.

In an entirely predictable twist of events, she was only around four percent prepared for her midday lecture, and she was all out of inspirations and pleasant liquids to sip on. With a moment of hesitation, she made a random turn on the third floor and decided to let her unconscious mind guide her to where she needed to be.

It brought her to a lavatory.

"If this is a metaphor for me being a shitty professor," Amber whispered out-loud, "then I don't need a reminder."

Her bracelet produced a ding, and she rolled up her sleeve to read the message projected onto her skin.

"Need a word with you. Meet me after my class."

The author of the message was recorded in the system as "Sentient Baked Potato".

"Huh," she muttered, checking the university map for a location reminder. "Here comes inspiration."

She strolled along the corridors in a casual, lazy manner that people her age rarely had. The spring in her step was energetic and agile, but the look on her face spelled 'not bothered'. It was a kind of a carnival costume, a veil of confidence and laid-back sort of academic engagement that could only be ascertained by someone with a completed 8-year degree.

It lived in the speed of her walk, in how she kept her shoulders, even the way in which she glanced at students, calm and slightly detached. It screamed 'I spent a long time being enslaved by my dissertation and now I reap the rewards'. The only real rewards were a fifteen percent salary boost, a permanent discount at the cafeteria, and the aforementioned casual manner of walking.

She stopped on floor five to grab a glass of lemonade and was now heading for the western wing of the institute B block.

Interestingly enough, the western wing was named not for its location, which was actually closer to the north, but for one of the institutes' previous directors, Norman East, who loved Old Earth Westerns. It confused the hell out of students and was therefore a perfect solution for an academic organization which dealt with philosophy, history, physics and math- all voted 'most confusing topics' by the general public three years in a row.

It is also worth pointing out that the planet of Alexandria lacked a natural magnetic field and could therefore change north and south places whenever it wanted—which it did, twice. The Incident was nicknamed 'The Great Magnetic Hubbub of Alexandria' the first time, and 'That Time Someone Accidentally Switched North and South Places. Again' the second.

"I should get my hair braided," Amber thought while she stood in western wing's hall, waiting for the class to end. She looked to her left, where a bunch of freshmen were sitting on humanity's second best invention, bean bag chairs, comparing notes; then to her right, where two professors were discussing the quality of paper tissues at the cafeteria and how it related to the crisis of meaning in the youngest generation; then sipped her lemonade. The flavor was "strawberry and stardust".

"Oh, Amber... hi."

She blinked, realizing she drifted off once more. A young woman was standing in front of her, arms crossed on her chest. Her short black hair was almost supernaturally shiny, and her porcelain white skin was flawless.

"Oh." Amber was not prepared for a social interaction. "Yu Yan... didn't you want to take a week off?"

"I changed my mind," the woman replied. "I, well, I wanted..." she stuttered, "...wanted to have a word with you. In person. And in private. Preferably."

"Yeah, okay," she was now picking up on her usual cold and detached front, "I don't have much time. Can you just say it here?"

Yu Yan blinked, having at once sunk into the ground, by all appearances; suddenly, she was somehow smaller, meeker, just a ghost of her usual self. This, of course, went right over Amber's head, like it always did. Amber stared, impatient. The girl sighed, seemingly regretting every single decision that had lead her to this spot in time-space continuum.

"I was thinking about the last time," Yu Yan said, quietly, almost a whisper. "Last time we were together. And I, well, I can't let it go."

"Pardon?"

"I can't stop thinking about it, Amber. I care about you."

"Yes. Right. I care about you, too," she assured her. "That's why I paid for the drinks and ordered you a drive home the next morning."

"But it's not quite right," Yu Yan continued. "Not enough."

"Not enough of what?" Amber asked. "I mean, we're two single adults, we had sex by continuous mutual consent, and we politely parted ways the next morning."

"Yes, but..."

"What?" she was now genuinely confused.

"I want more," Yu Yan finally said.

"More of...?"

"I have feelings for you. I want to date you," she elaborated.

"Well," Amber paused, trying to think of a good way to respond. "I don't."

"Look," she would not let go, "I know you don't like me back like that, but maybe you will. We can go on one date and, who knows, maybe you'll feel something and..."

"No. I don't... don't like the idea of that," Amber insisted. "As far as I'm concerned, romantic love is one of those annoying things Muuk should have edited out of our genes a long time ago. We had a one night stand. That's it. Now excuse me, I need to go to a class."

And she left before Yu Yan could say one more word.

"Should have listened to all the other girls she slept with," she shrugged. "Preferably past the first few words."

The back entrance doors buzzed in protest as she pressed her hand to the gleaming metal surface. 'Academic event in session', the doors announced. 'I know', Amber thought, pushing them nonetheless. 'That's kinda the point'.

She stepped into the room from behind the student seats and paused in one of the corners. There were around fifteen students present, all listening to the professor go on about Old Earth history. Amber smirked. Judging by the projections all around the speaker, he had modified the unit based on her recommendations.

"The next thing I want to discuss are the social, political, and economic factors that contributed to the start of the Great Expanse," he lectured on, not noticing an addition to his class. "Now, can someone tell me the year it started?"

The class was silent.

"Perhaps anyone remembers the event that is considered to be the beginning for the Great Expanse?"

Still no reply.

"Does anyone want free pizza?" Amber asked, and ten heads turned towards her at once. "No, sorry, I lied. Just wanted to make sure you weren't all asleep. Or dead."

"Hello, Amber," Professor Nawahi greeted, evidently not amused. "Glad to see you care about education quality."

The past decade and a half had been kind to David Nawahi. It was either his curious, deeply empathetic nature, or the latest medical treatments that Alexandrians had access to. Apart from gaining a few kilos, he hadn't changed one bit since receiving his professor title: his posture was strong and confident, accenting his height, and even his completely hairless scalp suited him nicely. He wore a smart, old-fashioned suit, and his long fingers were covered by half a dozen golden rings.

"Hiyah," Amber beamed, taking a few steps down the inclined slope of the floor. "Got your memo."

"After class," he smiled back politely.

"Whatevs," she brushed it off. "Now, what were you talking about again?"

"Hi Amber." One of the students, a young man sitting at the front row, was waving at her.

"It's professor Shakya to you, sunshine," she retorted, and the heavenly expression was washed away from the student's face. "Now, some breaking news for you kiddies: don't believe anything you're told in this institution. They present you the facts, but they never bother to arrange them in a way that shows the bigger picture."

She glanced at Nawahi. He was a millisecond away from rolling his eyes. Success.

"Like giving you all the puzzle pieces," she continued, "and expecting you to arrange them on your own. Fact number one: the original Old Earth humans were intelligent, brave, stubborn, and unbelievably hard-working. Fact number two: with all that knowledge and power, they had managed to destroy their planet in some odd six thousand years of civilization—so don't fall into the trap of worshiping them!"

"We wouldn't be here if it wasn't for them." One student, a girl in a knitted sweater, was not buying it.

"Wrong," Amber replied. "We wouldn't be here if it wasn't for the Muuk. They found the Ark, they reconstructed us from our digital ashes, and built this planet for us. They've been our creators, and our masters ever since".

"Can't stand those guys," another student shouted out, and got a collective cheer from the room.

"Same!" Amber shrugged. "But you gotta' give the devil his due: Homo sapiens are remarkably good at destroying things, and they are the ones who restore them. Including our entire species."

"Didn't our ancestors like, colonize space and stuff?" a sleepy-looking girl who had been chewing on something the entire time asked.

"Well, yeah," she agreed. "You'll get to that part later in the unit. Guess what motivated them though? I'll give you a hint: it wasn't the fact that they could always return back to Earth, where the conditions were totally perfect and the entire natural world totally wasn't dying out at alarming rates."

"That's all very cool and dramatic," the girl in the knitted sweater said, "but it's the exact opposite of how they described their own civilization."

"Yeah, well, you never wanna believe autobiographies, now do you," Amber replied. "History isn't just written by the winners--it's written for the winners. And they sure thought we would win it all, so they wanted us to remember them as heroes. That's the problem though--you can't learn much from the good guys. Don't let the past glory get into your heads, not even for one moment. You want to be better than them. Never to repeat their mistakes."

The room was quiet once again, but it was a different kind of silence—one that left your mind buzzing with ideas and inspired you to ask even more questions. Amber smiled with a corner of her mouth, her hands on her hips. Her job was done. Not even a full minute later, ten hands were in the air.

"Class dismissed," Nawahi pronounced, and at least half the audience groaned in disappointment. "We'll return to these... pressing matters in two days."

Reluctantly, students began to leave their seats. One or two slowed down in front of the exist, expecting Amber to follow, but she remained standing in the middle of the hall.

"My 'Old Earth philosophy' class has a few places left," she announced, and smirked as the students pressed their fingers into their palms, scrolling through the subject catalogs. "Say, prof... I'm not too shabby at this, huh?"

"We'll discuss that, too." Nawahi nodded, waiting for the last student to leave the room. "For future reference, I would prefer if you didn't interfere in my lectures without warning."

"What can I say," she gestured vaguely. "I see room for improvement, and I seize the opportunity."

Nawahi decided to ignore her. He didn't have time for an argument that he wasn't guaranteed to win.

"Sit down, please," he instructed, taking a seat himself.

She obeyed.

"Now, Amber, how long has it been since you defended?"

"Not sure." She scratched her eyebrow, thinking. "Six months?"

"And how many subjects are you teaching this semester?"

"Two."

"And you aren't doing any new research?"

"Not as such."

"Okay." He nodded. "Do you see a problem there?"

"Honestly?" she asked, getting her sunglasses out of her pocket and putting them on. "I don't."

He paused, thought and calculation dancing in his gaze, and she already knew what would follow next. The soft, patronizing tone. The nose-bridge rubbing. The completely unnecessary, though undoubtedly impressive quotations of famous academics from memory. That expression he had, which she could never identify completely—a mix of exhaustion and suppressed anger. She wasn't in the mood for any of that.

"I spoke to Dean Carroll about your...situation."

"Please, not them," Amber groaned. "They were the one who didn't let me take a third subject. They hate me!"

"Ninety eight percent of the stuff hates you, Amber," Nawahi said, not a hint of malevolence in his voice. "And, if I'm being completely frank with you, I can't really blame them. You know very well that you aren't exactly a delight to work with. I understand that you aren't a team player, but you're an adult now. A professor!

"There are... things, expectations that the administration puts on its research

24

fellows. We can't keep you on a salary if you aren't doing anything with your position, and your degree. And you can't run a project all by yourself. You need decent relationships with at least one co-worker."

Even through her sunglasses, Amber could feel his flaming glance. She could put up a front for every single person she ever spoke to--except for Nawahi. He knew her too well, and he could see through her 'cooler than you' attitude without fail. She pressed her hands into her seat, rocking ever so subtly from side to side.

"I'll think of something," she said. "I just need some time to decide."

"Look... sweetie." He smiled softly and put his huge hand on top of her shoulder. "This is a strange question to ask to someone so far in their academic career, but what is it that you want to do with your physical life?"

"See, that's the problem, prof," she laughed. "I've got no bloody idea."

In that instance, like in so many others, Amber was shamelessly lying through her teeth. Not only did she know exactly who she wanted to be, she had known it since before she could properly understand what having a job actually entailed. She just didn't dare say it out loud.

She remembered her early childhood all too well. She remembered the sticky glowing stars on her bedroom ceiling, and the tiny rocket models she collected. She remembered her dad telling her stories about space exploration back in the day: about the danger, and the excitement, and the feats of human bravery and ingenuity that lead them further and further away from their homes. She remembered learning all about different planets, their location, biology and culture, and dreaming of visiting them all.

She remembered her parents speculating about whether the ban on out-of-world travel was going to be lifted any time soon, and wondering whether they could speed it up in some way, persuade the authority that Humanity 2.0 was ready to take the training wheels off their metaphorical bicycles. And most of all, she remembered the soul-crushing disappointment (which for her soon evolved into deep despair) upon learning how many hoops you had to jump through in order to get even a limited pass.

It was clear to her where she needed to be. So many places out there, so many living histories to explore... but not for her.

It hurts less to extinguish your dreams as soon as possible, nip it in the bud and swipe the dust under the carpet, instead of letting your hope outgrow your pessimism--before it swallows you whole and leaves you to waste away your waking hours, thinking about what could have been but was never meant to be. It was so much easier to persuade herself that all she wanted was a bigger pay, a better view out of her kitchen window, and a new fake-vintage piano. It was much better to come to terms with the fact that the universe screwed her over.

Perhaps it just wasn't in her cards from the get-go.

"I have a lecture at one," Amber muttered, getting up. "I need to prepare."

"Give me a call, will you?" Nawahi said. "I worry about you."

"You should," she thought, but didn't reply.

She needed to focus on today. Life sucked, and it may have sucked ten-fold for her, seeing people around her so happy in their golden cages. But she was strong. She could deal with it.

Besides, even through her sky high self-esteem, she knew deep down: it doesn't matter. She didn't matter. It's not like she was anyone truly important...

THREE

Amber was not feeling well.

Her blood was pumping through her system at twice the normal speed, her palms slippery with sweat while her mouth resembled the state of Old Earth Atacama desert. The tips of her toes and fingers were icy cold. Every cell in her brain was screaming at her--or, rather, it was making that distressed squeaking sound that toads produce when you pick them up and squeeze them a little too enthusiastically. And, despite skipping lunch, she could taste stomach acid; it tasted like pure, distilled panic.

By that point, Amber was starting to doubt the age-old wisdom of humans being a ridiculously social species. This was all familiar to her. She always felt like that just before a party.

Amber strode across the floor in her best decorated flats, and the lights flickered on and off around her, unsure of whether she was going in their direction or not. After two hours of rehearsing her every move and every word, it was time to pick an outfit, do her hair and set out to the Novella Institute. The hair part went relatively easy--she just changed her pigtails into something a little more fancy--but the clothing part was a bit of a struggle.

"Something between posh and business casual," Nawahi said when she asked him for advice.

It would be good if he bothered to explain what the hell was business or casual.

"Sarah?" Amber spoke up, comparing two sets of trousers in front of the living room mirror. "Which one looks posh to you?"

"The meaning of the term depends on the context of place, occasion, and time period," Sarah informed her politely. "I would recommend checking some web pages."

"Yeah, well," she mumbled, "I'd rather go wearing a potato sack than do what I'm told."

And she meant it, you know. When she was nine, Amber took a train to a different city, on her own, just to prove to her dad that she could indeed have marshmallows that day, even before dinner.

"Hey, this is cute." She picked out a dress from her cupboard and smiled. "I don't remember ever wearing that."

After spending ten minutes straight in an unequal struggle between her fingers and the dress straps and lace, she realized why.

"Oh, fuck it," she concluded, and put on a plain, comfy dress that she got from the masculine section of the store. "I can accessorize with a, a scarf, or some shit. Is that a thing people do, Sarah? Accessorize?"

"This jewelry set will fit nicely with your outfit," Sarah replied, and lit up the shelf that hosted the set.

Deciding not to argue with the intelligent system, Amber changed her nose piercing piece and snapped a bracelet on her wrist.

"Well, time to go, I guess," she sighed, and waited for her body to gently lead her out of the apartment.

Alas, it wasn't cooperating. She would have to force it to walk.

"Only brave stay in the battle," she told herself.

It was a war worth fighting.

The first thing Amber did upon arriving to the Event Hall was come up to the bar and order two Green Goblins in a row. The barman regarded her with a well-trained eye of someone who spent too much of their time either arguing with teenagers about their age or cleaning up puke.

"I.D." the barman said.

"I am legal," Amber assured him, trying to lean casually on the bar stand and slipping by mere millimeters.

"I.D." he repeated, the exact same expression of disinterest plastered on his face.

"Fine," she groaned and pressed her thumb to the designated area. It pinged and lit up blue. "See?" she pointed at the 'transaction allowed' message, triumphant. "I'm a PhD, you know."

"And I'm Father Christmas," he told her, but poured her the drinks anyway.

She considered engaging him into a discussion about history until he broke into sobs, but quickly decided it wasn't worth her time.

Amber sipped her drink, which was decisively over-sweetened, and surveyed the room from a safe position on the upper left balcony. The event hall was large, bright and loud, swarming with people and trying very hard to pass itself off as a good place to spend your time in. She could see right through that though.

From the very first time Amber attended a party, she could tell it was nothing more than a clever excuse to trick her into talking to people. It would lure her in with catchy music and free food, then crush her every dream as soon as she would try to make some friends. According to her, parties were devil's fourth worst invention--after childhood cancer, bureaucracy, and that continuous string of melted cheese that gets stuck halfway down your throat and make you gag and hate pizza, of all things.

Point was, Amber could barely deal with individuals of her own species in small packs of half a dozen! Engaging with a group of hundreds was rather beyond her ability, and definitely well above her human tolerance level. But today, she had no other choice. The administration gave her an ultimatum. She was to find a research partner until the end of the month, or quit her position and downgrade to a post-doc. Today was the 38th. She had only two days left.

"Come on," she whispered under her breath. "You can do it."

"You can do it!" Sarah echoed cheerfully, and Amber pushed all of her tech bracelet buttons at once.

"Shush, Sarah," she hissed. "You're embarrassing me in front of the cool kids."

It had been almost an hour since the party kicked off. Both her and all the people around her were now sufficiently mellow and appropriately high to

29

engage in some networking. Amber braced herself, downed her second drink in one huge gulp, and left her dark comfy corner at last. It was time to find herself a research partner... if only it was as easy as writing about people who died a long time ago and didn't really care about what kinds of nonsense you made up about them. Or getting laid.

"Hey there, Nick!"

A tall, handsome guy with wavy blond hair and numerous tattoos was looking at Amber as if she was an exotic and potentially dangerous animal.

"Buddy, pal... compadre." Amber was not good at improvisation. "How is your thesis going?"

"I've defended seven months ago," the guy replied, picking out imaginary debris from his flawless front teeth.

Not the best move, but at least she remembered his name correctly.

"Really?" She made her best impression of a disappointed face. It looked more like a stomach colic. "Why didn't you invite me?"

"I did. You turned it down."

"I must have been busy at the time..."

"You sent me a voice message saying that you are a hundred percent free and available, but," he gestured air quotes, " 'have a severe case of I don't give a fuck'."

"Oh," Amber said, chewing on her lower lip. "Well, it was worth a try."

And she left the spot before Nick had a chance to deliver a witty response.

She wandered around the room aimlessly, picking out familiar faces among the amorphous mass of guests. It seemed like she was the only person unattached to a group of chatting and giggling people. She sniffed, thinking hard. Approaching one person was tricky enough--you never knew whether they were alone because of anxiety, shyness or high levels of intoxication (in which case it was better to leave them alone), or specifically encouraging others to speak to them (in which case failure to do so would cost you social intelligence points).

Finding a good moment to break into a collective conversation was even trickier. Not only did those group talks obey complex rules that Amber could not grasp (they would require a hell of an equation to describe, she reasoned--and she was terrible at math), the 'chiming in' move required agility and time sense that she simply did not posses. On any given day, she would rather step into a shark-infested swimming pool than try to pull this off. But today, standing down and leaving was not an option.

She noticed a small group of young women discussing something next to the canape table. She walked over there slowly, almost on tiptoes, like a cheetah crawling towards its unsuspecting prey. Amber paused next to a column, which obstructed her from view, and listened in.

"And did they get it?" one of the women, a short and round-ish sort of person with brightly colored hair, asked the girl opposite her.

"Oh yes," she replied, tugging on her piercing-covered ear. "Got two bottles of vodka, I think. They're still in the basement. We can go take a look."

"I admire the insolence," another woman spoke. "They aren't even of legal age."

"How dare they, huh?" Upon detecting a long enough pause, Amber took it upon herself to gently insert her person into the tight circle. "Kids these days," she said, fully aware that she was at least ten years younger than the other women. "Can't they just stick to weed drinks like all of us adequate folks? First vodka, then heroin, then sparkly stardust, no doubt."

"Wouldn't be surprised if they tried heroin next," the short one shrugged, and Amber's heart sang. She made it.

"Hey," the girl with the piercings said, crushing Amber's hope with her icy cold tone. "Sorry, but... I didn't catch your name."

Amber didn't know this, but saying "I didn't catch your name" was a polite, socially acceptable way of putting your hands on your hips and demanding to know "who the hell are you".

"Oh. Yeah," she smiled awkwardly. "Amber. Amber Shakya. I'm a professor at Ancient History."

"A professor, huh?"

Another blunder. Alas, it was not the best idea to flash your titles in front of people who spent more time in academia, yet weren't so accomplished.

"What's your research project?" the short girl asked.

"Don't have one yet," Amber confessed. "I'm thinking 'relation of twentieth century literature and twenty first century major political events.' Don't have a research partner though."

"Have you tried the announcement board?"

"Yeah, it...didn't go well."

"Shakya," the girl with the piercings repeated. "Doctor Shakya. Weren't you the one who persuaded the board to cut our Winter Solstice bonuses?"

"Well, you see, it wasn't because I am mean or anything," she mumbled, "I get those bonuses too, actually, it's just I saw an opportunity for better finance management and I couldn't keep it to myself, now could I? Wouldn't be honest."

"You could," the short girl disagreed. "And you should have. You're a post-doc like us, so whose side are you on, exactly?"

"I'm on the side of progress," Amber wanted to say, but decided to declare this battle lost.

"I think I see a friend over there," she said, and turned her back to the women before they could see her face flash an expression of panic.

"Liar." The piercing girl smirked when Amber was out of the sound's reach. "She has no friends here."

Another half an hour went by in fruitless meandering. Every now and then, she would stop a few steps away from a table or a bar stand, prepared to initiate a conversation, and every time some tiny, insignificant thing would happen and mess with her brave and (almost) selfless intent.

She was on the verge of losing all hope when she heard her name being mentioned among one of the bigger groups, and she leaped into action, maneuvering among the guests with an empty cocktail glass in her hands. Once she was close enough to hear the words, Amber stood aside, focused her eyes on the floor and made herself unnoticeable for a while.

"...said she was a valuable member of the team," an older man with charcoal black skin was talking, and everyone else listened in like he was the president

32

of the universe, "and, by all means, she is. I've heard several high-achieving professors, including David, praise her intelligence, outstanding memory and use of language. Problem is, those simply aren't the only things we value on Alexandria."

He made a pause, and most people nodded in agreement.

"We have machines to do our translations, and algorithms to memorize dates and analyze manuscripts. What we need on Alexandria is a human touch. Empathy. Kindness. Good intent. All the traits she seems to be lacking."

"Is it because of, how do I say it," a noble-looking woman with snow-white hair was snapping her fingers, the correct term just on the tip of her tongue, "phenotype?"

"Oh no," another man spoke up. "Hell no. My wife is autistic as well, and she's the nicest person I've ever met! She's rude sometimes, sure, and she seems strange when you first meet her--but she cares about people. She can't even watch those sad movies that Hoffman Studio makes, it upsets her too much."

"Yeah," a younger woman confirmed. "My older brother is autistic too. He can be a pain in the ass sometimes, but I know that he loves me. It's not about the condition, it's about the character."

"Some people don't get along with others, ever, and don't even see a problem with it," President Of The Universe concluded. "I genuinely pity them."

At that point, Amber had heard enough. She turned a hundred and eighty degrees on her heels, nostrils flared, fuming, and stormed off in the direction of the bar. She needed something stronger than a Green Goblin. Seventeen percent stronger.

There were a lot of things she wished to communicate to professor Badawi and his sheeple crowd of admirers. Empathy and human touch? Please! She knew dozens of people who were sweeter than honey and cared deeply about everyone they knew but haven't made it anywhere on Alexandria. Besides, what the hell did he know about her? Who said she didn't have good intent? Did it ever occur to him that, after years of being treated like an outcast and a freak, she just didn't have enough motivation left to expend her every last bit of energy on going through the motions and assimilating into society?

Back when her ancestors were assembling the Arkand choosing what to put on it and what to leave behind, they have correctly concluded that their future human population needed some diversity. As a result, Alexandrian society lacked diseases which cause early death or extremely low quality of life, but was full of anxious wrecks, common garden variety weirdos and even honest-to-god psychopaths. They didn't classify her condition as a disorder, and neither did the Muuk. Amber whole-heartedly agreed...but it didn't make her everyday life any easier.

It's not like she didn't have the ability to act, to pretend, to do everything those 'success on the autism spectrum' books have taught her. When she really needed to (in the event of chatting up some girls in her local gay bar, for example), she could play the part of 'pleasant human' better than some neurotypicals. The problem was, Amber was of firm belief that 99% of people simply weren't worth the effort. Being nice for the sake of being nice was not her goal.

She remembered her high school years, being half a decade younger than all the other kids and trying desperately to fit in, only to be exposed as a fraud as soon as the opportunity presented itself, and running to Nawahi the next day, asking to be moved to a different class. He gave up in the end and reduced her social interactions to her spoken language groups and orchestra practice. Even then, she loved the phonemes and the piano exercises more than her classmates. It wasn't her fault. Fellow human beings just never seemed to have liked her back.

"Strong stuff you're drinking there."

Amber was so consumed by her heavy thoughts that an unfamiliar voice next to her ear nearly gave her a heart attack.

"Hi."

She turned towards the sound and saw a young man standing there—officially dressed, pretty, and wearing his friendliest smile.

"Your name is Amber, right?" he asked, putting his arm on the bar stand, and she nodded sheepishly. "I'm Andrea."

"What brings you to my corner of misery, dear sir?" she asked, immediately employing her usual cocky and confident mask.

"Nothing special, just wanted to chat."

"Have some final goal in mind?"

She knew who the guy was. A freshly-baked post-doc, defended with a topic that was pretty close to her interests. Was this a gift, a compensation for her suffering?

"Don't know." He shrugged, smiling again. "Maybe."

"Let's start with that then." She smiled back, twirling her hair on her index finger.

"Sure. Well, I just wanted to ask two things. No, three things, actually. First, do you like contemporary opera; second, are you free on Friday evening; and third...are you single?"

Amber sighed. She had two options right now--either let him down gently and be all sorry about it, hoping that he'll stick around for a faint possibility of something later down the line, or...

"Sorry, Andrea." She couldn't stop herself now. "I'd love to go on a date with you, but you see, you're a 6 out of 10 at best, and I only date...women."

She saw his facial expression change from excited to disappointed to rather hurt and held back a smug smirk. She did care about people, yes--but she also liked being funny, and provocative, and ever so slightly dangerous. It gave her a confidence boost, and, though she didn't realize it consciously, it was a subtle way of taking revenge on all of humanity for refusing to take her in as their own.

"Thanks for nothing then," Andrea said. "I knew you were mostly into girls, but I wasn't sure. Could've just said 'sorry, I'm a lesbian'."

"I will not apologize for being a lesbian," she replied. "Besides, if it makes you feel any better, I wouldn't date you even if you were a girl. Romance--not interested."

"Who would've guessed," he scoffed. "I was gonna ask you about your research too, but academically, you're a 4 at best, and I only work with actual experts." And he left the bar stand without taking his drink.

"Yeah, well, screw you too!" she shouted to his back, and gave him a middle finger for good measure. "I don't need a stinking partner anyway," she said out loud. "I'm twice as good as any of them on my own."

"If you wanted people to see you as an adult," the barman chimed in, "you'd put a little more effort into actually behaving like one."

"Excuse me?" she raised an eyebrow, appalled. "Who asked you for advice?! Who are you anyway, service class? Why haven't you been replaced by a sophie yet?"

"Oh, I don't know," the barman said. "Maybe it's because people like talking to me more than to a tin-can contraption?"

But Amber wasn't listening. She was so done with it all.

She downed her drink in one painful gulp, climbed the stairs to the central balcony and cleared her throat.

"You're all hypocrites!" she yelled into the crowd. "Every single one of you. Wolves in sheep skins! You act so cute and innocent, filter your every word, and never say what you really think. And you talk about people not to their face, but behind their backs. You lie when it's convenient for you, you tell people what they want to hear, you pretend like you care, and you never dare to say what's on your mind. Disgraceful!"

"That's how human society works!" someone shouted from the crowd.

"The entire society can eat my ass!" Amber yelled back and dropped her imaginary microphone.

Downstairs, people didn't seem impressed. She turned towards the door and marched out, her chin held up high. She no longer cared about being demoted to post-doc. They would either agree to her terms, or never see her in the wretched institution ever again.

"Next bus is in forty-two minutes," Sarah announced from her bracelet.

"Oh, shut it," Amber barked into the bracelet. "I'll walk home if I have to."

But she didn't walk all the way to her home. In fact, after escaping the stuffy, glimmering hall and narrow corridors, Amber climbed to the building's roof and picked a spot quite close to the edge. She laid down on the cold, smooth surface, outstretched her limbs like a starfish and peered into the sky. It was densely

36

packed with stars--another sparkling pretty fake.

No one knew exactly how old the universe was, not even with Muuk's most precise calculations. They were, however, absolutely sure that the universe was unbelievably ancient. So ancient, indeed, that the galaxies had more than enough time to drift apart and get lost in the vastness of empty space.

The only real stars on the Alexandria's skyline were the suns of their own cozy galaxy. The rest were merely painted on with projectors in an attempt to make it look more like Old Earth. Amber found that laughable; she wouldn't admit to herself that the starry sky took away her loneliness and made her feel at home in the world.

She would've stayed on the roof till the sunrise, watching the stars glow and thinking hard of some solution to all of her problems, but she was interrupted by Sarah.

"One new message from: Sentient Baked Potato," she communicated with a somewhat un-computer-like childish vigor.

"What now?" Amber rolled her eyes.

"'Meet me in my office'," Sarah read out loud. "May I provide feedback?"

"No!"

"The message was typed with greater speed than average. It might be important."

Amber made a funny face, relishing in the fact that, technically speaking, no force in the physical dimensions could make her move a single muscle.

"New message," Sarah added. "Urgent."

"Yes, okay, what?"

"That was the message," the AI explained. "One word. 'Urgent'."

"Leave me alone to die," Amber whined.

"Should I send that to user Sentient Baked Potato?"

"No!" She jumped up to her feet, alarmed. "Fine, whatever. I'm going. See?"

Sarah couldn't "see" it, of course. She was a fourth-generation assistance system and therefore had no camera installed. Besides, detecting the change in the bracelets coordinates was quite enough. Job well done.

Amber climbed back into the building and almost crawled down the stairs to the right floor. She didn't just work at the Novella Institute, she grew up in it. That gave her the ability to navigate its wings and areas blindfolded. Not that she was blindfolded, she saw everything perfectly well. It was, however, very important to not run into a fellow professor. Or any other human, actually. A dog would be okay though.

Nawahi's office resided at the end of a long, narrow corridor, and she skidded to a run on the final part of her route. Her decorated flats barely made a sound on the lino-covered floors, and she slipped into the room without knocking. The office, which was small and crowded with furniture to begin with, seemed even smaller in the absence of proper lighting. Nawahi was already there, sitting in front of his desk. He nodded at Amber and gestured for her to sit down as well.

"Party didn't go as you planned, I see."

"Do things ever go according to my plans?" Amber asked, practically falling into the armchair.

"Maybe not," he replied. "There are... gradients of success. I talked about it in... no, wait," he paused and rubbed his eye in a somewhat uncoordinated manner. "It was a book, not a speech."

"Hold on a second," Amber chuckled. "Professor... are you stoned?"

Nawahi, who was now trying his best to keep his eyes focused on one spot, attempted to shake his head and performed a peculiar dance move instead.

"You are." She laughed, covering her mouth with her palm. "Wow. I thought you didn't drink."

"I don't," he asserted. "I smoked it, which is the correct way you're supposed to enjoy marijuana. It's my day off," he added, rummaging through his desk file in search of a neutralizer pill. "I'm allowed to have fun."

"Of course you are. Sorry," Amber corrected herself. "So, why did you ask me to come to your humble abode?"

"I did?" he frowned. The pill was nowhere in sight. "Oh, yes, of course. I wanted to wait till the party is over, but since you aren't there anyway, might as well tell you now."

"Yes?" she suspected that he was about to fall asleep.

"I found you a job," he replied at last. "And guess what--it comes in one bundle with a research partner."

Amber's face sunk. Some pity offer, no doubt--and judging by the timing, he had started looking for it a while ago. He didn't believe in her from the start.

"It literally just fell into my hands this evening," he added.

She wasn't buying it.

"The project is being funded by the Muuk. They need someone with extensive knowledge of Qulot Era civilizations and conversational level Rx'lng. You're perfect for it."

"No," Amber said.

"Excuse me?" Judging by Nawahi's expression, he had suddenly gotten sober without any pharmaceutical aid. "What do you mean by that, young lady?"

"It means I won't take the offer," she explained calmly. "Not interested."

"Listen to me, Amber." He leaned forward across the desk and lowered his voice. "They have recovered first real evidence of the Aquamarine Moon's existence. They have scroll plates that, as they believe, not only describe it but give detailed instructions on how to find it. It's a discovery of the century, and no civilization below class A can even stare at it from the distance! You would be a fool to let go of such an opportunity."

"I guess that makes me a fool," she told him. "It's not your fault, professor, it's just...I'm done. With my career, with people, with ambition in general. I think I need a break from, well, everything. A long-ass holiday. Somewhere far away from history, and responsibilities, and civilization in general."

He sighed, rubbing his wrinkled forehead, and allowed her to look away into the distance.

"What has happened to you, sweetie?" he asked in a gentle voice.

"Don't know what you're talking about."

"Are you depressed?"

"No sir."

"Ill?"

"All of us are ill in some way," she mused calmly. "Our bodies develop for a couple decades, then immediately begin to decay. Our mortal lives are nothing more than a trial period compared to what we achieve after death. Or what you are promised, at least. Not all of us are so lucky."

"Is that why you refuse to give anyone a chance?" Nawahi postulated. "Because the world was so unkind to you, and you are unkind to the world and everyone in it as revenge?"

"I'm rational, that's all," she disagreed. "I don't hold hope. I don't trust people. I tell the truth. That's how I've always been like."

"No, you weren't," he replied. "I knew you since you were five, Amber. You used to be a little ball of joy. Your parents would take you to a playground, and you went over to every single kid, asking them to be your friend. You had faith in Alexandria. You wanted to travel to the stars, see other worlds."

"Exactly!" She couldn't keep calm anymore. "I had parents! I was happy! And I wanted to see other worlds, yes--but I can't! They trapped us here, in this stinking paradise. 'Protected species' my ass. It's Homo sapiens! Give us a couple centuries and we will infest this galaxy once again. We don't need coddling and we don't need saving. They aren't our gods, and they can take that 'class A' project and stick it where the sun don't shine. If they even have that."

"Amber."

She got up abruptly, almost knocking the desk over.

"Amber!"

She was at the door.

"The artifact is on another planet, and it can't be moved."

She paused, her hand still on the door handle. Nawahi's voice sounded far away all of a sudden, as if coming to her in a dream.

"They're giving the researcher a permit to leave Alexandria. You will be working on site."

Slowly, with no abrupt moves, Amber turned around, sat back into the armchair, and folded her hands on the desk like a studious pupil.

"Do tell me more," she said, in a voice completely devoid of intonation.

Nawahi smiled.

"You should have started with that last part," she added, and forced herself to smile back.

FOUR

There was trouble in the air.

As soon as the water bowl on the shelf began to quiver, Lk'st could tell that the flight was in jeopardy. They could feel an unsteady trajectory with their fingertips, and their toes, and with their every inch of skin. They grew up on that spaceship after all. Every room, every nook and cranny of the heavy vehicle was familiar. No matter how much it changed, how many details were replaced or how often it was redecorated, Lk'st could always find their way around it. It wasn't surprising that they also knew its normal vibration patterns better than the warmth of their childhood nest.

That's why, when the floor shook and shimmered, it took the young Rx'lng exactly two seconds to tell: the jump did not go according to plan.

They wanted it to be fake. A figment of their overactive worker imagination, or a waking nightmare, perhaps. A passing hallucination. They waited, tense and still, for the air to clear and for the tremble to cease. But instead, their worries were immediately affirmed by a captain's message.

"The risk was well-calculated," the captain said. "But I am afraid that gods were not on our side. Brace yourself for an impact, brethren."

The voice coming from the corridors didn't sound menacing or alarmed, which didn't improve the situation.

Lk'st knew very well that, if it were to escalate into a full-blown emergency, their lower D deck would not be first in line for evacuation.

They glanced sideways, were Rt'lp was twitching their ears, sleepy yet on edge.

"Not even a forewarning, huh?" they muttered. "They treat us worse than sophies on this ship. Their own flesh and blood."

"If it starts shaking again," Lk'st replied, "cover your head and hope for the best."

"Okay, mate. Gods bless us."

Lk'st closed their eyes and tried very hard to pretend they were actually on Qst'ln--safe, sound, and surrounded by friends and kin. Not that they had any kin left, or even knew how Qst'ln actually looked. They had only seen the planet twice. On flat images.

Is this how they would die? Weak and frightened, away from the nest, so young, having known nothing outside the King of Kings. Decades spent in silent servitude, always working for the good of others, never seeing the children, the flowers of their effort. Alone. So completely alone...

The ship shook again, and Rt'lp couldn't hold back a cry of fear and despair. Lk'st shuddered worse that the ground beneath their bed. One part of them really wanted to make it to their destination in one piece...the other thought 'if they're gonna kill us, can they at least do it swiftly?'.

"We should go to our nests," Rt'lp whispered, scared breathless, but not only for themself. "They need their protectors."

Lk'st chirped and paused. They had no argument against the suggestion. They knew perfectly well how terrified the brothers and sisters felt, could feel it to the very depths of their soul. But the fear paralyzed them. Tied their hands behind their back and left them broken, motionless on the floor. They looked sideways and Rt'lp and realized that the fellow worker was fighting the same battle.

"Could we even get to the A deck?" Lk'st asked, not expecting a reply.

The King of Kings fell into another violent jolt, and the lights went out in the room. Rk'lp whaled in distress, soaked to their fingertips in the pain and terror of their siblings on the deck above. They cracked open the door--just a fraction, just a few centimeters —and peered into the corridor outside. It was pitch black as well.

"I can hear them," Lk'st commented. "Other workers. Running up to the stairs."

"We have to go, Lk'st," Rk'lp whined.

"I know!" they snapped back. "I know."

As the spaceship began to shake incessantly, rocking side to side and filling the air with horrible noise, Rk'lp and Lk'st exchanged glances... then snapped the door shut, closed their eyes, and slowly crawled underneath their beds.

Somewhere in the depths of an ancient grass forest, two Caluki elders were rummaging through a half-dried swamp, cursing gently under their breaths. They only had time before the first sunset to gather the ceremonial herbs, and they were starting to think that the wretched weeds were hiding from them.

"Careful now!" one of them exclaimed, turning clockwise and stepping, with great elegance, into a pile of animal dung. "You're stepping on my tail."

"Keep your tail out of my way," the other retorted. "And focus your eyes on the ground. All of them, please, not just the bad one."

"You know, if someone didn't forget about the ceremony, we wouldn't be here in the first place."

"I do know, and, may I remind you, if it wasn't for me, we also wouldn't remember it was today." He paused, lunging into the swamp and jumping out of the muddy water with a handful of kelp squished between his claws. "You also almost burned the village yesterday."

"Well, I guess we're equally culpable," he replied.

The sun was now brushing along the horizon, and the two elders were getting impatient. So much effort, and so little to show for it! They were still missing three of the final ingredients, including the one that actually had therapeutic value, as opposed to smelling nice and having an impressive-sounding name. Since it was quite clear that they had failed in their task, it was time to decide whether to come back to the village with empty hands, or fake their deaths and move on to another settlement. They certainly didn't want to come back through the woods after dark.

"Got it!" the older elder screeched, skipping in the mud like an excited child.

"What, the root of enuar?"

"No, dumbass. An excuse!"

44

The other paused, skeptical, but eventually surrendered, knowing their options were limited.

"I'm all ears," he responded cautiously.

"We'll start a new tradition," the older elder announced, eyes ablaze with creative passion. "I'll say that I had a vision in the forest, that god have spoken to me and ordered me to change the ceremony. And that we won't be needing all these potions from now on."

"Brilliant!" the younger elder rubbed his fluffy palms together. "We can get paid for it extra as well. Now let's get going."

Interestingly enough, the tradition did take off, and was, years later, transformed into the ritual of burning sacred swamp herbs on the corners of a room at twenty-seven hours at night exactly and then rubbing the ash directly into one's fur. No one remembers anymore where it came from. Supposedly, it improves the memory.

They had a triumphant spring in their step as they headed for the village. Nothing could ruin their mood now... nothing, except for another sudden realization.

"Hold on a second," the older elder said, stopping dead in his tracks. "The baker's baby... weren't we supposed to feed it?"

The other one paused as well, thinking hard.

"That might have been it, yes."

"Oops."

"Indeed."

"Well then." The older elder made an uncertain gesture, spilling "magical" powder from his sleeve. "Guess which lucky bastard had been taken to heaven by the god!"

Muli Koldem felt like all of his dreams had come true at once.

Just this morning, he was nothing more than a poor farmer, trying to get by on this cursed piece of rock that had the audacity to call itself a planet. He had a normal family--a mum, a dad, a second dad, a two-headed aunt and fourteen kids (all from different mothers)--and all he wanted was a pair of new shoes, a piece of bread to munch on, and some decent enough religion to fill his existence with meaning. To paraphrase, his happiness was at a fairly average level. But not anymore. Out of nowhere, fortune had arrived and showered him with its gifts, and he was fairly sure that, starting from today, he would never have to work, ever again.

It all happened rather suddenly. A few days ago, he was out in the field, preparing a new patch of land for his latest addition to his crop collection--the yugi plant. This particular strain of consumption-ready carbohydrate was famous for its sweet and pleasant taste, high fiber content and impressive resistance to asteroid bombardment. Its only flaw was the dreadfully brown color. Still, what could an ugly shade do to Muli's clients, who were old, almost completely blind and born without a sense of aesthetics...point is, he was out in the field.

He was out in the field, digging deep into the soil, when his spade hit something rough and shiny. 'What a weird skeleton', Muli thought at first, until he dug around the mysterious object and realized that it was a massive metal crate. He tried to open it, but it wouldn't budge, so he went to the city to look for some expert.

The next day, a young lady appeared in his field. She walked around the crate, biting the tip of her pencil and making notes in small and neat handwriting, and finally, after a whole afternoon of 'getting acquainted with the object', declared it 'pretty important'.

A guild of Muuk experts arrived a few days later. They run their tests, talked conspiratorially amongst each other, and asked Muli aside.

"We're afraid that we will have to take it," one of them said, his voice gargling and distorted by his dark suit.

"What, the crate?" Muli asked.

"No. The land."

That possibility did not occur to the poor farmer before. He might have hated this place, along with his general profession (and also his aunt's second head), but it did provide him with food, shelter and money--all things which he valued highly in life.

"Is it really necessary?" Muli muttered, his eyes watering with emotion.

All men in the Koldem family cried ridiculously easy. It was, along with a peculiar pattern of balding, their distinguishing trait.

"Unfortunately so." The Muuk expert nodded, rather too enthusiastically for Muli's taste. "We will compensate you, of course."

"Co... compensate me?"

"Yes. A single payment in your local monetary unit. Two million should suffice."

"Two million?!"

If it was possible for someone's pupils to turn into dollar signs, like was the custom of Old Earth cartoon characters, it would have surely happened to Muli.

"Two million," the Muuk confirmed, "and you will have to leave tomorrow."

"Two million, baby," Muli beamed, "and we can leave fucking yesterday!"

He wanted to hug his squid-like saviors but held himself back.

His family watched the excavation commence the next morning. They observed calmly as the gigantic machines overturned entire layers of soil, demolishing their house in one elegant swoop. The men were sobbing, of course. The two-headed aunt almost cackled.

"Do you know what they found in there?" one of Muli's sons asked, sucking on his thumb.

"No idea, niblet," the farmer replied. "Something important, I bet."

And he would bet successfully. As it later turned out, the rusty crate in Muli's field was final evidence for the existence of the fabled Aquamarine Moon.

Meanwhile, Light was close to regretting every decision she ever made, or wanted to make, or had a vague dream about possibly making.

She massaged her temples, hoping that it would somehow relieve her of the impending headache of the century, and watched Darkness flirt shamelessly with the Osirian princess.

"My-my, your highness," Darkness giggled, "you are such a naughty girl!"

"Wait till I tell you about the garden!" the princess replied. "You'll never believe it."

It was all getting rather predictable, when their spontaneous night out was interrupted by a massive storm--one that was definitely on the nastier side of storms. The royalty and peasants alike ran into their homes, desperate to hide from the cruel weather, and Darkness had a terrifying moment of searching for the princess in the fig tree grove.

"Please, your highness," she muttered, getting more anxious by the minute. "You'll get soaked wet."

"What makes you think I'm not wet already?" the princess replied, making Darkness blush to the roots of her hair.

Light couldn't help but laugh at her while she tried to come up with a truthfully-sounding reason for leaving the soon-to-be-queen on her own.

"But we will see each other again, surely," she squeaked, drawing invisible circles on her bare chest.

"Of course," Darkness assured her, and placed a quick peck on her lips.

It wasn't even remotely enough, but the princess was used to being disappointed.

"You horny dog!" Light smirked, elbowing Darkness on their way out of the royal palace. "And edgy too. You know we aren't supposed to, khm, interfere in that way."

"Oh, come on," Darkness dismissed. "It's not like I changed anything extra."

"No?" Light asked and began to twirl her fingers in front of her face. "Let me see... you made a pair of village priests forget about their duties, it seems."

"And?"

"Which lead to the species venturing into space a whole decade later. So, they avoided a conflict with another race, saved a whole planet from destruction, and, apparently, preserved some ancient artifact in the process."

"That's not bad!" Darkness shrugged. "I can live with that."

"Yeah, you also made a Rx'lng ship crash. The old-timey one. You know."

"Really?"

"Nah. Almost."

Darkness paused, a bit taken aback, then moved on with the stroll.

"Oh well," she said, disappearing into thin air. "I think it was worth it."

FIVE

"Now, what do you think, Sarah, dear," Amber pronounced, imitating an Old Earth movie accent. "Shall I fetch another suitcase, or simply jump up and down on top of this one?"

As of the present moment, Amber's apartment resembled a tiny explosion of clothes, both freshly dried and in need of a wash, shoes, various shelf-stable snacks, and assorted junk. This was not the result of a recent robbery. She was simply packing for the trip.

"Attention!" Sarah responded. "Suitcase not manufactured to sustain high impact. Retainment of integral qualities not guaranteed."

"I'll get a second bag then," she concluded, and nearly tripped over a pile of collector lunch boxes on her way to the bedroom. "Any unchecked items on the list?"

"Calculating. Remaining items on the 'hasta la vista baby' list: extra sunglasses, notebook memory cards, warm trousers, 'something cute to wear in case there are pretty girls on Sereneae'."

"The last one might be a problem," Amber muttered, stuffing seemingly random articles into her gym bag. "Too many "fuck off, whatcha lookin' at" outfits, not enough tacky lesbian fashion."

"May I suggest visiting a shop prior to your journey?"

"Eh." Amber grimaced. "Shopping. Nah. I'll buy something tourist-y there. Or I'll make my archeology-compatible jumpsuit look cute. With a face like mine, nothing is impossible."

She regarded her makeup bag with detached curiosity, picked out two nail polish bottles and a red lipstick, and pushed it inside the gym bag.

"All good otherwise," she beamed. "Now, I don't envy future Amber... she'll have to deal with this nightmare mess."

Indeed, future Amber had to deal with a lot of past Amber's impulsive decisions. Present Amber never learned.

At last, all the bags were packed, and it was time to close the door behind her. She paused on the threshold. She had waited all her life for this moment, and now that it was finally here, it didn't feel dramatic enough. Amber forced a theatrically deep sigh, smiled and dropped the smart system memory card into the breast pocket of her shirt. Today, she was leaving her home--really leaving it--for the first time in her life.

Downstairs, professor Nawahi was chatting cheerfully with one of her neighbors. Amber recognized the woman's face, but she didn't recognize her. She's had the apartment for nearly seven years but never bothered to learn the names of her neighbors.

"Time to move, chop-chop," Amber tweeted, ignoring Nawahi's greeting.

"Yes, in a moment, sweetie," he replied, and she could tell he was concealing his annoyance. "This charming lady was telling me all about your garden."

"Not *my* garden," she corrected. "Frankly, I've no idea who started it. Hate all the birds that come to it though."

Nawahi glanced at the woman, who seemed tremendously uncomfortable, then to Amber, who was literally hopping on the spot, shifting her wait from one foot to another like a puppy on crystal meth, and muttered something along the lines of 'sure you do'. He said his goodbye to the neighbor and gestured towards a hovercraft.

"Get in," he instructed.

He didn't have to ask twice.

The vehicle was far too large for its purpose and decorated to the maximum of human ability. Amber threw her bags into the appropriate storage section and climbed up the stairs into the passenger lounge, an excited grin lighting up her face.

"Dope," she exhaled, running her hand across the artificial leather seats.

"State of the art."

She turned her head to the left, startled. On the seat closest to the windscreen sat a funny-looking man, smiling friendly at her and Nawahi who was now entering the hovercraft. The man was dressed like a character from an early twentieth century comedy flick--a black, pin-striped suit, complete with a bowler hat--and there was something mysterious and captivating about his crystal blue eyes.

"I'm Seth," he introduced himself, inviting the two to sit down next to him. "I will be teaching you on the appropriate ways of conducting out-of-planet affairs. How to interact with the Muuk, how to address other alien species, what to do in case of spaceship evacuation, that sort of thing. Nothing to worry about!" he quickly added, seeing the 'oh shit, I didn't prepare for the test' expression on Amber's face. "It's for entertainment purposes, mostly. We're taking a trip into orbit, and these things," he patted the control panel, "are pretty, yes, but pretty slow too. We aren't allowed to..."

"...use modern technology," Amber finished for him. "Yeah, I've guessed."

"Our benefactors are concerned for our safety," Seth explained.

"It's what they tell us," Nawahi shrugged, and judging by the other's reaction, everyone agreed with his unconvinced tone.

"Well," Seth said after a pause, "we're ready for takeoff, I guess."

"Yes!" Amber jumped up and down in her armchair, unable to hold back the joy.

"Anyone want a drink?"

Staying true to his promise, Seth did not strain their memories with rigorous training sessions and stuck to the point. He ran through the training and quickly switched to asking various personal questions, which Amber, whose fifth favorite activity was talking about herself, happily responded to.

It was obvious that Seth hadn't done this particular job in a good long while, and that he preferred literally any conversation to it anyway. Out-of-planet journeys couldn't have been a regular occurrence; even when it was absolutely crucial for a human to leave Alexandria, practically no one would hear about. Alexandrian newsmakers preferred to keep it hushed. It made a nice news story, sure--but it also made people feel confused and uneasy. A cheesy tale of a mother giving birth to triplets or a new species being reintroduced into the artificial ecosystem was definitively a wiser choice.

Amber remembered the last time an intra-planetary journey made the news. She was seven at the time, so it was difficult for her to grasp the event's importance, yet she recalled it as an awfully nerve-wrecking and profound experience. She learned the whole story as an adult: on that day, at the peak of summer on her continent, four brave Alexandrians left their motherland to explore the depths of outer space. They didn't just go for another planetary system, no; too meek for a human being, surely lacking in ambition. The team, comprising of a pilot, a doctor, a scientist and an engineer took a leap across the galaxies.

It was a mission of unprecedented valor. Even on the fastest spaceship available to humanity, it would take them around three months just to get to the edges of the next galaxy. No one in their generation, not from any culture or civilization Alexandria was in contact with, had ever attempted anything close to that. On the launch day, every human on the planet was glued to the video projections in their homes, counting the seconds to launch while holding their breaths in anticipation.

They started out fine, reached the edges of the local solar system in hours. The flight was normal for the length of their trip through the galaxy, and the astronauts tuned in to livestreams every day to show how wonderful it was to travel among the stars. They kept in contact the first day of traversing the intra-galactic void; day two was good as well. On day three, the connection was weak, breaking intermittently. On day four it faded away.

They lost contact completely on day five. Back on Alexandria, central control tried their best to reinstall the connection, but nothing helped. They waited, and hoped, and prayed to the Old Earth gods they didn't believe in. No one wanted to admit that the mission had failed. It took them months to come to terms with the fact that the four brave astronauts were not coming back, and the entire planet shed a few tears--even little Amber. The ban on intra-galactic travel was installed the next summer.

"So." Noticing that his glass was empty once again, Seth reached for the refill and realized that they were now close to leaving the atmosphere. "You're scientists, right?"

"Yes," Professor Nawahi replied.

Amber produced a 'cat that didn't want to be lifted from the table' sound instead. "I love what I do but, well, it's history."

"History is the most important science that Alexandria possesses," Nawahi retorted, almost offended. "All we have left of our ancestors are the stories they wrote about themselves."

"Yeah." Amber nodded. "That, and the collective sum of all their knowledge, a digital bank full of Earth's genetic diversity and two sentient species that clearly diverged from them some time in the past."

"Personally, I wouldn't call the Indigos sentient," Seth pointed out. "They should have their own world and all that, but you have to admit, they degraded a bit too much to be considered a civilization."

"Happiest bunch in the universe," Amber disagreed. "Running around naked in a forest, eating berries, making necklaces out of shiny rocks... I'd live there if I could."

"Alas, you're only a PhD of comparative history," Nawahi said, and she pouted.

"And what will you do on Sereneae?" Seth asked.

"Research project," she responded, putting her tired legs on the control panel. "They've dug out some sort of ancient artifact and I'm the only one who can make sense of it. Don't know the details--the Muuk will enlighten me, I'm sure."

"Working alone, then?"

"No. They're sending over an archaeologist."

"Another Alexandrian?"

"A Rx'lng, apparently."

"Rix-lang?" Seth repeated, and Nawahi gave Amber a stern look before she could correct his pronunciation. "Blimey, I'd assume their travel restrictions are ever worse than ours. How many of them are left?"

"Less than a thousand," Nawahi said. "And it's a mystery to us as well. I guess they've chosen the best expert, and if it happened to be a Rx'lng, perhaps they had no choice but to ask them."

"Peculiar people, they are." Seth shook his head, his face dreamy, as if he was remembering something pleasant but strange. "A bit insect like."

"Jeez, I wonder why," Amber said. "It's almost as if they evolved from an animal that we would classify as an insect!"

"Play nice, Amber," Nawahi hissed.

"Sorry," she sniffed. "Couldn't help myself."

"Will they be providing a translation implant then?" Seth continued, unaffected by her rudeness.

"Not needed. I speak their language--and Muuk's language too, for that matter."

"What, without an enhancement?" Seth's eyebrows went up his forehead.

"Uh-huh. I speak seven languages, not including our native. Learned them the old-school way, all on my own."

"Impressive," Seth nodded.

There was a brief pause, during which Nawahi was almost lead to believe that Amber was grown up enough to not brag about her talents at this convenient opportunity.

"I also play piano and write poetry," she added in a hushed whisper, and Seth laughed briefly.

"You're one exceptional young lady," he concluded. "And we have officially left Alexandria."

"Cheers to that." She smiled and clanged her glass on the plexiglass window.

Through it, she could see the darkness of space, the flashing lights of the orbital station, and the outlines of the planet underneath the craft. Nothing else; and it gave her a strange sense of peace. It was almost familiar.

Amber loved late night walks. Whenever she felt stressed, or scared, or lonely, she would wait for the sunset and go out into the night, headphones in her ears and a thermo-cup of tea in her hand. The darkness always soother her soul; even regular lights had a tendency to hurt her eyes (and her mind as well), and some visual signals pushed her over into meltdowns in seconds. Darkness was like a comfy blanket. It kept her save, and it gave her room to breathe, to wind down and relax. She didn't understand people who were afraid of the dark. For her, a weary wanderer and a willful outcast, the night was unconditionally kind.

By the time their craft had completed its journey, Amber's entire body was sore and buzzing with anticipation. She pressed her nose to the window, peering into the cosmos, and the glass got covered with vapor from her breath. The craft halted in 'mid-air', like a hummingbird in front of a flower, then attached itself to the side of the orbital station.

"Smooth flight," Nawahi commented, getting up from his seat.

"Glad to hear that." Seth smiled. "Will that translate into pleasant ratings for my agency?"

"We'll see." Amber had already put on her jacket and was now tidying up her hair in front of the reflective control panel. "One of us is going back the same way."

"But not yet," Nawahi pointed out.

He knew she couldn't wait to be left alone, and it made him ever so slightly worried.

"Follow me," Seth said, hearing the soft click of the opening door. "Keep in mind the rules: no abrupt motions, no jokes in bad taste and no interruptions."

"And don't forget to kiss their asses at the end of the meeting," Amber added.

"Exactly the kind of joke I would advise against," Seth commented, and the smug smile disappeared from her face. "The Muuk aren't our masters, or our gods--they are our biggest allies. After everything they have done for us and this entire galaxy, the least we can do is be respectful to them."

"Fine," she gave in. "But the food better be as good as it says on the leaflets."

They entered the space station via a narrow, dark corridor and passed through an array of scanners and disinfectant sparklers. Amber coughed her way through the last chamber; some smells just weren't compatible with her senses. Before the massive doors slid open to let them in, Seth had to type in five different passwords and scan both his fingerprints and his retinas. The security was comforting and unsettling at the same time. On one hand, they could be sure that no terrorist could ever get in; on the other, it left one wondering what the Muuk were protecting, and who from.

"Bloody hell," Amber gasped, taking her first tentative steps into the main hall.

The room was enormous, as big as an ancient cathedral, or an observatory. It was perfectly spherical, complete with a dome-shaped roof, and evenly lit up with cold, light-blue lamps. The floors were pristinely white, the walls covered in layers upon layers of geometric ornament. At the opposite end of the hall, she could see a rectangular table covered with plates and bottles. The Muuk, however, were nowhere in sight.

"Can I take some pictures?" Amber asked, activating the setting in her bracelet prior to hearing the answer.

"In here, yes," Seth answered. "But not in the negotiation room."

"Don't break anything!" Nawahi shouted to her back, more of an after-thought than an order.

"Curious girl." Seth grinned and checked his digital notebook for messages.

"Too curious for her own good," Nawahi replied.

Ten minutes in the beautiful guest hall and it was time to move on with their business. Getting Amber to step away from the snack table was a challenge; she mumbled something profane when Nawahi dragged her along, but the sound was obscured by all the fruit chunks she managed to stuck in her mouth. She chatted vigorously as they moved from one floor to another, and both of her companions could tell it was a sign of nerves. Amber was just realizing how important the day really was, and, not being accustomed to this pressing feeling of stress and insecurity, she hoped to simply fake the confidence back into her body. It wasn't helping her one bit.

"We're here," Seth announced, placing his hand on the wall.

The scanner beeped, recognizing him as 'authorized personnel'.

"Good luck," he said, and gestured for them to come in.

Inside was a similarly circular space about the size of a household living room. The only furniture it hosted were a few tall book stands with no books on them and a round wooden table. Seeing the two figures who sat at the table made Amber's mouth dry. A common reaction, really; it's one thing to be aware of the fact that aliens exist, or even see them on tapes--actually meeting them is something else.

Prior to today, Amber had only seen the Muuk on pictures: textbook illustrations, portraits hanging on university walls or an odd postcard from another planet. The images were stylized on every one of those, and for a good reason. The Muuk were galactic heroes: they helped every civilization they came in contact with, spent great amounts of resources on eradicating space plagues, rebuilding ecosystems and providing medicine and technology and food to everyone who needed it. They were the ones who discovered the Ark and spent decades preparing Alexandria for humanity 2.0.

In the half a million years of their civilization's existence, they never started a single intra-planetary war and indeed helped to stop many. The only publicity they deserved was the good kind; they also looked like eldritch abominations from every culture's scary legends or end-world prophecies.

Interestingly enough, one of Muuk's strictest rules was a total ban on any significant changes to their image. Throughout the galaxy, every sentient species knew them only as "Muuk" and was obliged to provide accurate representations of them in their reports. It did not stop people from using a plethora of slang terms and drawing cartoons of their peculiar overlords, and no ordinary person was ever persecuted for it--but the sense of illegality still lingered on.

The two Muuk figures were sitting at the table motionless, staring blankly at their guests. Their bodies were covered in tight rubbery suits, obstructing their lilac skin from view. Amber saw their faces through the transparent helmets-- their huge black eyes, and wide round mouths, and tentacles hanging from their cheeks, twitching slightly as they breathed with a faint rasping noise. She glanced at Seth and he nodded encouragingly.

58

"We greet you," he said, swiping his hand from his right shoulder to his left.

Amber and Nawahi copied him and watched the Muuk do the same.

"Join us," one of the Muuk said. Their voice sounded strange, synthetic; like a computer simulation of what human voices sounded, arranged from random bits and pieces of symphonic music. "Nothing to be scared of. Humans are indigestible to us."

Amber forced herself to laugh politely, even though the remark sent a wave of cold shivers down her spine.

"Get yourself together, bitch," she thought to herself angrily. Her fear was illogical, superstitious. She had no time for her reptile brain's nonsense. Amber bit her lip, made a few steps forward and took a seat at the table. Seth and Nawahi joined her a few seconds later.

"Welcome to the Moon One Orbital Station," one of the Muuk told them.

"It's an honor," Nawahi said.

"We assume you have acquainted yourselves with the files, so we will skip the summary. This is the object in question."

They pressed their entire palm to the table, and a three-dimensional projection appeared in the air above its plane. The image showed a dark spot of land, which seemed to have spanned many miles in all directions, with a silhouette of some dilapidated building to the left and a gaping hole in the middle. Inside that hole rested an array of heavy marble plates. Amber reached forward to zoom in on the plates, and narrowed her eyes as the writing on them became clear. Those were exceptionally preserved artifacts... almost like they've waited there, in the soil, for millennia, to be discovered.

"The objects aren't fully excavated yet," the Muuk continued. "They will have been by the moment of your arrival. A team of specialists has been on site since day one, monitoring the process. None of them have managed to precisely identify the objects, or to translate the writings. We have no algorithm that can accomplish the task."

"Blimey." Amber scratched the back of her head, now too consumed by the task to be anxious. "If your supernatural tech can't crack it, how do you expect me, a mere mortal, to make any sense of it?"

"We have hope," they responded. "The task requires a sentient interpreter. Someone capable of imagination and abstract thought."

"Human touch," Amber finished for them.

"If you say so," the Muuk said, and did something mildly disturbing with its facial tentacles.

Amber interpreted that as a smile.

"Do you wish to speak to the archaeologist now?" they asked. "We have already briefed them."

"Later," she said. "First... tell me everything you know about those plates. If you really think we've discovered the map to the Aquamarine Moon, well...I need to hear all the facts before I will even start to believe that claim."

"We too were skeptical," they assured her. "The Muuk value scientific inquiry and careful inspection of all beliefs. We didn't get to where we are with magic."

"Yeah, no shit, Sherlock," Amber said, and felt Nawahi hit her ankle with the heel of his boot. "Sorry. So sorry. Please, do continue."

"Yes." They seemed rather amused by her comment. "Our race's main goal is the pursuit of knowledge. True knowledge. This discovery, however...it defies all odds."

"Stick to the facts." It was the first time the other Muuk had said anything.

"Of course," their colleague replied. "Let's start with this--according to our research, the Nos have never been anywhere close to Sereneae..."

What followed was a string of facts, figures, guesses and suggestions that left Amber way more confused than she was at the beginning. She listened attentively, chewing on a fingernail, feeling her brain meticulously catalog every piece of information. For a brief second, a horrifying thought struck her--what if she couldn't do it? She acknowledged it, allowed herself a micro-moment of panic, then moved on.

Once she sensed that the Muuk were running out of information, Amber decided it was time to break another rule and interrupt.

"I'm sorry, um..." She desperately searched her brain for the correct way to address a Muuk. "Sir?"

Both of them paused.

"The corresponding human term," the less talkative Muuk began, "for me, would be Miss."

Amber blinked, and the Muuk's face twitched in what could have been anything from disgust to delight.

"I didn't even know you had genders," Amber confessed.

"We have more in common than you think," the Muuk responded. "What is it that you wanted to ask?"

"I wanted to ask," she began, "whether I could get this information in a written form. It's getting a bit much for me to follow."

"Out of the question," the other Muuk dismissed. "Highly classified information. Be grateful that it is permitted to stay in your memory."

Amber didn't know whether that was a joke or not but decided not to clarify.

An hour later, and the briefing had smoothly evolved into a space station tour combined with a detailed explanation of Amber's mission. She had happily ignored most of it and only tuned in to reality when the word "spaceship" was introduced.

"The Quantum Frog," the taller of the two Muuk introduced, and stepped aside to let Amber through, her movements smooth and flowing, as if she was swimming through the air. "Please, come in."

During the two-hour long briefing, she asked the humans to call her 'Anna'--"a human name, familiar, to dispel the tension". The request didn't only fail to fulfill its purpose but added a whole another level of weirdness to the encounter. Deep in their subconscious mind (and, frankly, on the surface as well), citizens of Alexandria found it hard to draw associations between 'Anna' and purple tentacles. Still, they appreciated the effort.

"Bonkers!" Amber exclaimed, her eyes wide, desperate to take in every tiny detail of the spaceship.

To be fair, the ship was a bit smaller than she expected: judging by the layout schematic displayed on a wall next to her, the livable environment consisted of two bedrooms, a bathroom, and something called 'control and flight management zone'. It looked proper fancy though, she had to admit. The lines were smooth, the air felt warm and fresh, and the artificial gravity was more comfortable than on Alexandria. It was beautiful too. All surfaces were covered by a shiny metal which reminded her of platinum and decorated by the same geometric patterns she saw in the orbital station's main hall.

"Not bad," she nodded.

Understatement of the year, she thought to herself. Her current levels of happiness were now exceeding her average yearly budget of bliss, and it was proving to be a rather exhausting experience.

"It travels through the space-time continuum in leaps," Anna the Muuk explained, "harnessing the energy of matter-antimatter interactions. Your journey to Sereneae will not take more than a few Earth seconds. The rest of the flight time is devoted to depressurizing and stabilizing internal conditions. The process of dimensional manipulation isn't always pleasant on organic life-forms but it's perfectly safe."

"I'd rather you not go into detail on that," she replied, feeling a little queasy already. "Who's piloting?"

"The craft is mostly autonomous, but your research partner will be monitoring the flight," Anna said. "And I think," she glanced at the other Muuk, who was being uncharacteristically taciturn, "now is a good time for you to meet them. Door to your left."

Amber turned on the spot, took a deep breath in and gently knocked on the door. There was a brief pause, then something clicked inside of the wall and the door frame raised into the air and disappeared into the depths of the spaceship. In front of her stood Lk'st--cautious, motionless and momentarily lost for words.

"Hi," Amber muttered, and wanted to wave at them, but quickly remembered about the body language barrier. "My name's Amber, and, uhm, my Fl'wt dialect is a bit rusty, but I think we'll get along just fine anyway."

Lk'st, like all other Rx'lng, gave humans the impression of speaking to a giant anthropomorphic cockroach. They were tall, taller than the vast majority of humans by at least a whole head, and almost menacingly broad-shouldered. Their rough, pale blue skin bore resemblance to their ancestor's robust exoskeletons, and their vestigial second pair of arms was another reminder of their insectoid nature. Their head was small and oval-shaped, with big black eyes that took up half their face, and short mandibles near a thread-like line of their mouth. They wore a simple purple robe and no boots; with feet as strong as Rx'lng had, they hardly needed them.

"My name's Amber," Amber repeated, waiting for a response. "I'm a historian. We'll be working together on Sereneae."

There was a moment of awkward silence, during which a thousand thoughts raced through Amber's mind like comets.

"Do I say something else now? Is there an official protocol? Am I being rude? What am I doing with my hands, should I stop fidgeting with my zipper? Is my face all wrong? Should I panic?" and more, on a rapidly twisting loop.

Then, finally, Lk'st tilted their head to the right and spoke.

"Hello, Amber," they said, and their voice sounded unusually high and feminine for someone with such a bulky build. "I'm Lk'st, but the nice people on the sunny planet call me 'Lullaby'. I like that name better."

"Lullaby, then," Amber smiled.

"I speak your language too," Lullaby replied, in flawless though peculiar-sounding English. "Speak five languages, not including my own."

"Well," Amber sighed, the tension leaving her body bit by bit. "Lu... can I call you Lu?"

They nodded, imitating the human gesture.

"Yes. Great. Lu... Five languages then? I like you already."

It was hard to tell time on board of the orbital station, but even Amber's faulty body clock was telling her that it was now pretty late. She yawned, dreaming of cinnamon tea and the fluffy bed that awaited her on board of the Quantum Frog. Lullaby had already retired to their room, and the Muuk were giving her the last pieces of advice for the flight ahead. It was taking them forever to do so. After running through her bullet points for the third time, Anna handed Amber her very own comm device and said her goodbyes.

"We have high hopes for you and your team, doctor Shakya," the other Muuk concluded before walking away, and Amber's heart sang. "Don't let us down."

"I won't," she promised and saluted them for some reason. "Aloha, great ones," she added and headed for the opposite corridor, hoping to find Nawahi.

"Funny," Anna the Muuk said to her colleague when Amber left the room. "I thought I have gotten over our cultural differences, but...is it just me, or was that girl even stranger than the humans we usually work with?"

"It isn't just you," the other replied. "Let's see what our expert has concluded."

They twisted their wrist 180 degrees and pressed a button on their suit, activating an in-built speaker. Seth's confident, calming voice began to narrate from it.

"I am now sending you the full report," the recorded message said. "I was able to conduct a fairly thorough interview. My preliminary assessment is of moderate escape risk. I would suggest a slight increase in surveillance."

"Noted." Anna glanced sideways. "I'll review the whole set tomorrow."

"I have doubts about this mission," the Muuk murmured.

"So do I," she replied. "But we have no other option."

Amber dragged her feet along through the corridors. She wasn't used to so much standing--or so much of anything, in fact. She craved a hot shower and the sweet embrace of sleep but she needed to say her goodbyes first. She saw Nawahi from afar, standing near the airlock that lead to the hovercraft. He was slouching and his eyes were half closed. She waved at him and he gestured for her to approach.

"Hey," Amber said and hid her gaze, half-tired, half-emotional. "I guess this is where we part ways," she said quietly and Nawahi nodded. "Next stop-- Sereneae."

"Take care of yourself." He smiled, putting a hand on her shoulder. "Don't forget to brush your hair. Eat well. Don't stay up till morning. Call me often. And

Amber... you're going to be working with people who you will meet for the first time tomorrow. This is your best chance for a fresh start. Be kind to others. Treat them like you would want to be treated. Trust me, it is worth the effort."

"Sure thing, dad," she said and immediately bit her tongue. "Oops. Didn't mean to say that."

"Oh, sweetie."

It was too late: Nawahi had pulled her into a tight hug and was evidently on the verge of tears.

"I will miss you," he said.

"Me too," she replied.

They broke apart, full of bitter-sweet melancholy, and left the room from opposite ends.

From now on, Amber was all on her own.

SIX

The next morning, Amber woke up feeling strong, energetic, and ready to take on the whole universe. It lasted for approximately twenty-three minutes. She enjoyed her breakfast, which consisted of self-baking waffles and vitamin-infused citrus jam, popped her anti-radiation pills, and arranged her hair into a semi-respectable pigtail.

Lk'st did not join her, which was good news for Amber's social battery. Last night, after all the airlocks were sealed and the spaceship delved into the dark waters of warped dimensions, they spent an entire evening talking. Or, rather, Lullaby was talking, and Amber managed to interrupt them briefly every now and then. Amber was used to being the annoying chatterbox in every conversation. This time, it seemed, she had met her real competition.

"Time till arrival?" Amber said out loud, but no one replied. "This ship's rude," she muttered, wandering aimlessly around the room.

As soon as she stepped away from the table, it whirred, buzzed, and proceeded to clean itself. The kettle was automatically refilled, the fridge noted the change in its assortment of products, and the floor removed every bread crumb--even the ones on Amber's shoes. She raised an eyebrow, then tutted. This was no way of living! If your house does every tiny thing for you, there's nothing left for an excuse in case you want to procrastinate on something important without feeling lazy. Besides, she preferred to decide for herself how messy her room was supposed to be.

She poured herself a glass of something intensely blue and tangy and stepped towards the window. The view outside was rather bleak--total darkness, with occasional sparkles of white. She wasn't sure whether it was a real image, or a

66

pre-recorded movie; she didn't like in either case. The whole process of time travel was starting to rub her the wrong way. Traversing the void sounded good in theory but actually being on board of a relatively small object that was being forced through the cosmos at a mind-boggling speed...not her idea of a pleasant day.

"Morning."

Amber shuddered. She didn't hear Lullaby come in.

"Not really," she replied, turning around and waving. "But we can pretend it is."

"Morning is when I eat this," Lullaby replied and pointed at a plastic box of something that looked like kid cereal.

They took the lid off with their stick-like fingers and poured it directly into their mouth.

"Very good," they said. "You have excellent food."

"Careful there." Amber snickered, watching Lullaby devour the cereal. "Didn't they feed you on that ship of yours, the King of Kings?"

"Not every day," they responded cheerfully, as if it was no big deal. "Workers get food when it can be spared. It's okay," they assured her. "Didn't starve. Resources are limited, they have to be distributed equally."

"What's equal about not feeding a whole class of people for days?"

"Kids need food. Mothers need food. Builders and leaders need food. I'm a worker —can get by on less. Not so important to get first share."

All of that they said in a voice of someone who didn't only have no problem with such a system but was actually in favor of it.

"Not so important," Amber repeated. "Is that...is that why they allowed you to leave the ship?"

"Yes!" Lullaby confirmed and imitated a human smile. It didn't look too good. "Most of my siblings would never get such an opportunity, as they can bring forth offspring and are needed at the ship. But I am K'w'r. Don't reproduce with other Rx'lng. Disposable!"

"Huh." Amber nodded, failing to understand the excitement her colleague attached to that statement. "Well, as long as you're happy..."

"I have work. I have purpose. I have... cereal," they concluded, finishing the last bits. "It's good enough."

"No one misses me either," Amber said. "Back home. They're probably hella pleased with me gone." She paused, sensing a sudden urge to Share in a Social Setting somewhere at the back of her neck. "Sometimes I think..."

"Landing successful," the spaceship's system announced, ruining their moment of bonding. "Preparing to depressurize."

"That's the fun part!" Lullaby squealed, switching from English to their mother tongue.

Amber didn't believe it, choosing to brace herself for something horrid instead. She wasn't mistaken.

An old and respected tradition among Alexandrian physicists was to entertain the idea that no one in the field of quantum physics truly understood quantum physics. An even older tradition among everyone else on Alexandria was to say 'those spaceships, no one really knows how they work!'. Thankfully, none of those statements were accurate; quantum physics experts were real experts and spaceships weren't being built by people who thought of them as mysterious flying beasties.

The subatomic particles, on the other hand, did not have the faintest idea of what in the observable universe they were doing. It wasn't uncommon for a boson to temporarily forget what its function was and go around the place pretending to be a lepton, or an up quark of some sort. And neutrinos, they were the worst. Every now and then, one of them would go 'might as well' and decide to randomly interact with some throwaway particle, following which all hell would break loose. And the scientists would be the ones to blame for inaccurate predictions.

When the outlines of Sereneae began to appear in the window, Amber realized that her entire face had gone numb. She took a ragged breath in, terrified, and noticed the lights and colors around her blurring, mixing and escaping from her field of vision. For a second or two, it seemed like the world had been temporarily stripped of its internal structure, and all the textures and objects had

68

blended into one. Hearing was the next one to go.

She was preparing herself for worse, picturing the atoms that make up her body scattered across the floor like marbles, but reality was starting to stabilize itself. First it pushed her down to the ground, then sent a deafening pulse through the air, and, with a creak and a shudder, returned to its normal form. She slid against the wall, breathing heavily, and watched Lullaby sway left and right in excitement.

"Like..." They struggled for an English word. "Like roller-coaster!"

"Don't know 'bout that," Amber replied, getting up on shaky legs. "Felt to me like being swallowed whole by some space monster and being squeezed out through its rectum."

"Yeah," Lullaby repeated. "Roller-coaster."

"Remind me to give you a few lessons on human culture," Amber concluded. "Now let's get the fuck out of here."

Despite what many people called it, Sereneae wasn't even a planet--it was a moon, orbiting a huge gas giant, Ipsis. Its enormous whirly surface was the first thing Amber noticed upon exiting the spaceship. She blinked, staring at the technicolor sky projections. No, not projections--sky. Actual, real sky.

"Cute," she commented, taking her first steps on the surface of a new world.

All around her, as far as the eye could see, was nothing but farming land. Fields, gardens, lawns... more fields. Some of it was painted a yellowish grey, some was brilliantly green, some a mosaic of many colors. The sun above them was scolding, the air was hot and dry. The wind picked up sand and dust, prompting her to cover her already watering eyes with her trusty sunglasses.

"It's shiny," Lullaby said, pointing at the sun. "It sparkles." And they stared directly at it, seemingly undisturbed by the brightness.

"Uh-huh." Amber nodded. "Suns tend to do that."

They walked for a while in a direction outlined by their digital map and Amber felt tiny droplets of sweat pop up on her forehead. She had a bag on her shoulder and a bottle of water in her hand. So far, her alien planet experience was that of an aimless hike.

They approached a tent camp arranged in the middle of a vast field. She could see a few Sojhi people snooping around in safety suits, and she guessed it to be the makeshift science the Muuk had told her about. One of the workers saw them come closer and waved with both hands.

"Lullaby!" he shouted out, walking towards them. "Glad to see you're back."

The Sojhi, who were humanoid enough to be confused for people by some other galactic races, had always made Amber feel rather uneasy. There was something about the way they talked, or smiled, or behaved in general that was distinctly human yet at the same time vaguely alien. Human-ish, with a pronounced accent; like they were acting the part and didn't quite get it right. The fact that they had evolve separately from each other on the other side of the galaxy was unsettling, somehow.

"And you're..." the Sojhi spoke.

"Doctor Shakya," she finished for him. "The historian consultant. Nice to meet you." She extended her hand, giving him her best attempt at a genuine smile.

He paused and Amber watched his face for any signs of discontentment or confusion, her body tingling with anxiety.

"Likewise." He smiled back at last, shaking her hand. "Happy to have you on the team."

Amber had not felt so much relief since that time she thought she accidentally deleted the whole 17th century from the Alexandrian library, only to discover the button didn't work.

She did think the 17th century was not that crucial though.

They went around the camp, greeting everyone and getting the latest news, and Amber exhausted her knowledge of Universal Galactic Code of Polite Conduct trying to pass as a pleasant person. The sun was making her skin feel like parchment and she really wanted to get it over with and look at the artifact, but her devotion to the cause was stronger than the whiny five-year-old inside of her brain. This was not so different from your usual meet-and-greet after a conference. She just wished there were snacks.

"Yes, Rey, your son is very cute," Amber said, the constant smile now hurting her face. "His cuteness speaks for itself. He's the epitome of cuteness. He... he... he has a PhD in cuteness!"

Her bracelet buzzed and she glanced at it, annoyed.

"Levels of effort reaching critical," the message said. It was Sarah's nice way of telling "you're trying too hard."

"I have a czim-czim too!" the Sojhi technician continued, scrolling through the photos on her device.

"Save it for later," Amber replied, though it sounded more like begging. "Please...can I see the excavation zone now?"

"Oh. Right." The woman dropped the device into the pocket of her field gown. "Sol! Come over here."

The man who greeted Lullaby and Amber to the research camp a few hours ago had changed out of his city clothes into a grey-colored jumpsuit and hid his long hair under a funny looking hat. He wasn't wearing any shoes, Amber noticed. Typical archaeologist.

"Yes, my darling." Sol winked at Rey, pausing next to Amber.

"Doctor Shakya wants to see The Hole." You could hear the capital letters in her voice.

"Thought you'd never ask." Sol put on a sun visor and pointed towards the horizon. "Follow me," he added.

"If you insist," Amber replied.

She was sick of not being in charge.

Lullaby joined them a few minutes later. Their walking speed was about twice that of Amber's or Sol's, so they had to walk in the other direction every now and then. Amber was continuously surprised by the lightness in their voice and the spring in their step. The sun was in its zenith, the air was hot and heavy, like freshly boiled custard cream. Having the wind blow in your face felt like being bombarded from a huge hairdryer.

Amber was struggling with the heat, and from what she knew, Rx'lng came from a climate much colder than her corner of Alexandria. So either their resistance to temperature change was astonishing, or--and the second option seemed more probable to Amber, after knowing Lullaby for less than a day--Lk'st was constantly happy. Regardless of what life threw at them.

"Halt," Sol announced, stretching out his arm in warning. "The Hole is three meters deep. There's a ladder on the other side."

Amber walked around The Hole, gazing downward in awe. The excavation was perfect. Over the four weeks that the team was on Sereneae, they had managed to remove all the sand and soil from around the crate, spec by spec, without shifting the objects position even by a centimeter. She could see the rusty metal, the ornament on the crate's sides, and the white stone plates hidden inside. The ladder wobbled under her feet as she climbed down, and she instinctively held her breath as she approached the huge crate. No living creature had seen its content for millions of years; she would be the first person to read the text.

"Can you read it?" Sol asked, taking a seat at the edge of The Hole.

"It's what I'm here for," Amber replied. "Give me a minute."

The plates, which were taller than her and wider than her shoulders, were covered mostly with images and not text. Most of the images depicted space: planets orbiting binary star systems, asteroids crushing into each other, black holes sucking in whole galaxies...the images were crude, schematic, almost, but beautiful.

There was also a map, or at least she thought it was a map. It had no scale and no labels, but the star placement did remind her of something. She circled the plates, afraid of so much as brushing their sides with her sleeve. The text below the images was very well preserved and she read the words with ease. They made total sense on their own, and they seemed to fit into sentences nicely...she just failed to grasp the general meaning.

"Anything?" After waiting a whole month for an expert, Sol was getting seriously impatient.

"I'm not certain," she began with any historian's (or any scientist's, come to think of it) favorite phrase. "It has an introduction at the beginning."

"Who would have thought," Sol muttered.

"Then there's..." she paused. "I'm not a hundred percent sure but I think it's a warning of some sort. Like a danger sign. Don't go there, unless."

"Unless what?"

"Unless you're ready to, well, part ways with something, apparently. Ugh, I should have taken my notes with me."

"Read it till the end!"

"Yes. Okay. It says something about why they put the crate in here, on this world. I think the first part refers to the symbolic meaning, like the ties to their folklore and... stuff, but it could also be an idiomatic expression I'm not familiar with. Sorry." She shrugged. "I don't think these instructions were written for aliens.

"My best guess is, it was predicted by something, so they did according to the prediction. Like it was, um, divinely inspired, which is weird to me cause they didn't have a dominant religion, not at that time period. After that it goes into detail on how to get to the Aquamarine Moon, except I know none of these names--constellations, planets, star routes, it's all different now. Not just the names, it's in different places."

"Is there anything you can say with certainty?" Sol asked.

"Oh yeah," Amber nodded. "I can say one thing --the plates are genuine. You've got the real deal. So is the Moon, based on the map alone. They aren't just referencing it, I mean, they're giving precise instructions on how to get there. They're just also recommending you don't."

"Has that ever stopped anyone?" Sol wondered.

"Would make a Makran turn a hundred and eighty degrees on the spot and fly in the opposite direction," she joked. "Have you run any tests?"

"Just say which ones, we'll start tomorrow," he responded. "Nice first try."

He helped her out of the pit, and glanced sideways at Lullaby, who was quiet through the entire exchange.

73

"What do you say, guys," Sol said. "A break and some drinks?"

"I'd love to," Amber agreed. "Lu?"

"I don't require as much liquid consumption as you," they explained. "But can keep you company."

"Please do," Amber thought to herself.

If Lullaby was coming, she knew that she wouldn't be the only one talking-- and she seriously needed a break from that particular activity.

The Oasis could hardly be called an establishment; it was more of a loose collection of furniture and decor thrown haphazardly together. It hosted twenty people at most and had permanent sticky spots on the floor. It also had a feeling to it. A feeling of comfort, of casual conversation, secrets shared in hushed voices and friendly complaints about work. This is where people went to escape the sun, the sand, and responsibility.

Amber was barely present for the first twenty minutes of "drinks", leaving the spotlight to Lullaby, who chatted incessantly about every topic imaginable. She was starting to doze off when a question was asked and activated every neuron in her brain.

"So, what is actually the deal with this Aquamarine Moon?" Sol mused, pouring himself another portion of some flowery-smelling bubbly liquid.

"You mean you don't know?" Amber smirked.

It didn't seem like he was joking.

"Wow," she said.

"What?" Sol shrugged and pointed at the Oasis crowd. "None of us do. Most people on the team are geologists and technicians and I'm not some Nos expert either. I just happened to be in the area when the Muuk called."

"Oh, man." Amber rubbed her hands together, ready to infodump. "You're about to hear some weird shit. Well.

They were around three million years ago, in this galaxy, and they died out two million years ago. We have no records of how they really looked but based on the scraps that we've uncovered, they were humanoid enough--two arms, two legs, a head, possibly a tail...it isn't important. They came from this planet called Emos and they reached level four before they disappeared; they had a trade, and tourism, they were in a few wars, that sort of stuff.

But their progress was not very typical. Your usual race, it plays in the mud for a few thousand years until it invents the scientific method and then boom, they get technological advancement that they can't even handle sometimes. These guys though, they were a bit of late bloomers when it comes to space travel. They hanged out on their home world for ages, literally--it took them ninety-seven centuries to get to splitting the atom and venturing into space.

And their technology was never very out there, but their culture...something else entirely. Richest mythos I know of. So much literature, and music, and art, and philosophy, it's unbelievable. And knowledge. So much knowledge."

"Wait a second." Sol stopped her. "If they had a ton of knowledge, how come they stayed on their planet for a hundred thousand years before inventing space travel?"

"That's the thing!" Amber replied, waving her hands around madly. "They knew stuff, they just didn't do much with that info. Research for the sake of research, all theoretical. I mean, they cured diseases and found ways to feed the planet and that kind of stuff, but they never dug very deeply was all. Never wasted resources on technology they could get by without."

"But they did invent space travel in the end."

"Yes. They had thousands of years of stability of prosperity and then, out of the blue, wham, they were traveling with the speed of light. Like someone had given them permission to do so, or instructed them even. And they were more or less successful for fifty more centuries, until something happened and they all disappeared overnight."

"What, literally overnight?"

"Almost! One month they were all around the galaxy, then suddenly they left all of their off-world bases and were gone--even from Emos. Some say they

75

died out, or moved to another galaxy, but we never found evidence of either. No corpses, no signals, nothing. The planet was abandoned, their cities left to rot without them. You should have seen the photos--houses left in the middle of redecoration, children's toys left behind on the floor. Like something wiped them out of existence in a blink of an eye."

"So, what's the deal with them?"

"I wish I knew," Amber admitted. "There are hypotheses but it's all just speculation. Some say it's all fabricated, made up entirely. Except one hypothesis just got a major evidence boost."

"The Aquamarine Moon," Sol guessed.

"Indeed." She sipped her drink, completely emerged into her story. "See, a few months before they disappeared, they talked an awful lot about some Aquamarine Moon. There was no such thing back then, or at least no one knew about it. Emos didn't even have a moon, only their colony planets had. For eons they mentioned nothing about it, then suddenly it was all the rage. Some historians think it's fiction, coming from their folklore. After all, we've never seen it mentioned by any other species, or drawn on any of the maps of that time. And they did have fairytales about it. But some historians, now me included, believe that that's where they went. The Aquamarine Moon."

"And the crate?"

"Who knows?" She shrugged. "I doubt it was addressed to some other species. My guess is, they wanted to take it with them and forgot. Explains why it ended up on a planet which they've never visited. Fell out of a spaceship, perhaps."

"Fell out of a spaceship?" He snorted with laughter.

"Or something," she mumbled. "It's not the point. We have it! The map. We can follow the instructions, find the moon, and finally solve the mystery."

"I'd rather not," Sol confessed. "That kind of mystery doesn't sit well with me. You think it fell out of a spaceship, eh. My guess is, they left it behind as bait."

"Well, if they did," Amber said, gulping down the last drops of liquid, "I've totally bitten into it. And I will not let go."

"Do you think they are still around?" Lullaby asked. "It's been two million years."

"Anything is possible," she murmured. "No one could have guessed humans were to make it to this edge of the universe, yet here I am."

"If they are around," Lullaby continued, "and we will find their Aquamarine Moon and come to visit, even after they warned us not to...how will react to that?"

"Well, my dear instectoid friend." Amber grinned like a maniac who was about to indulge in their favorite questionable activity. "That's what I'd love to find out."

On Sereneae, nights dragged on like an art-house movie that you couldn't grasp but promised to your datemate to only watch till the 'best part'. It always came abruptly, as if late to its job. One moment the sky was blazing red, as if someone had set the horizon on fire; next, the sun was swallowed by darkness and painted the air wide strokes of deep dark purple. A few stars shimmered in the distance and the outlines of the gas giant below and above them swirled apathetically in place. The heat of the day was gone. A very different wind, full of fog and infused with the smell of night flowers, swept over the valley, giving everyone a much-needed relief from the hot daylight. As was its custom, the night was kind--and Amber was happy.

She sat on a blanket outside of her tent, three different e-books arranged in front of her, sipping some sort of traditional tea. It tasted like gingerbread-infused chamomile blend. The translations were trickier than she anticipated; she had photos of the plates on hand, enhanced and outlined for convenience, and she was writing one version of the text after another. Amber liked a challenge. It took her mind off things. In the distance, a crowd of villagers was singing, and thick clouds were gathering above her head. Her eyelids were heavy, and her hands ached from all the writing, but she pressed on. She couldn't stand an unsolved mystery.

"Evening." Lullaby noticed Amber from the other side of the camp and simply had to go and say hi. "Working?"

"Is it a habit of yours, to say out loud every obvious thing that you observe?"

Amber asked and her bracelet buzzed in disapproval. "I'm genuinely curious," she added, cursing Sarah's diligence in her thoughts.

"I say things," Lullaby responded, dropping to the ground in front of Amber's blanket. "Sometime, things don't need to be said, but I say anyway."

"Why aren't you in bed? I thought Rx'lng needed a shit-ton of sleep."

"Not workers. Worker has to guard the nest at night. We rest when we can. If entire worker can't be asleep, some parts of the brain do and others guard."

"Convenient." Amber nodded.

For the second time that day, she noticed that Lk'st was hesitant to call themselves a Rx'lng. More often, they would use their word for 'worker' instead, as if that status was more important to their identity than their race.

"See that star over there?" Lullaby pointed at a faint dot in the sky and blinked.

Their eyelids moved from the center to their face to the sides of it and not up and down. Amber found it almost cute.

"L'gs," they explained. "My planet used to be there. Before it burnt up."

"Do you miss it?" Amber asked.

"Never been on my planet. I was hatched on the King of Kings."

"I've never been to Earth either," Amber said. "Come to think of it, I doubt it even exists anymore. Not the planet, not its Solar system. Maybe the whole galaxy is gone."

"Things we love," Lullaby pronounced thoughtfully, "they go away. Don't exist forever. That's why they are so precious."

"That's a nice way of looking at things." Amber smiled sadly. "If you ask me, I think the universe just sucks."

"Like Black Hole?" Lullaby asked, confused by the phrase they didn't recognize.

"Exactly," Amber snorted with laughter. "Screw philosophy. Help me out with these references instead."

The days flew by, and every new one brought pieces of the puzzle that, instead of making the task easier, managed to complicate it further instead. After a few bouts of homesickness and two shameful, desperate calls to Nawahi, Amber grew accustomed to Sereneae's annoying climate and learned to enjoy local food. She spent as much time working as was physically possible. Her mind was swarming with ideas, one crazier than the other, and she quickly became the main provider of conversation topics on the camp. In the morning, a thought would strike her, and by the evening everyone was talking about it. She enjoyed it more than she dared to admit.

Their first breakthrough happened on day eleven, when the results of spectroscopy arrived and confirmed Lullaby's suspicion--the metal used for the crate's production came from Sereneaen soil. That fact alone was enough to crush four different hypotheses, and hundreds of experts and self-taught enthusiasts who were following the story online had a bit of a scientific fit. Eleven hours later and it became clear that the plate marble was local as well. There were still no signs of any Nos activity on Sereneae, before or after it was colonized by Sojhi.

After a long night of shouting over each other, coming up with the most absurd explanations and getting drunk on cold air and traditional bitter spirits, Sol and a colleague of his wrote their first report for the Muuk. "We have no bloody idea," the report read. Luckily, Amber didn't let them send it.

Overall, the campers were satisfied with where the research was leading them. It might have been confusing but at least it was yielding results. Amber's translations, however...she was working on it. She got through the descriptive part of it with relative ease, but the prescriptive--the map, the schemes, the directions--was escaping her. The words made sense and the paintings matched the text but some crucial data was missing. She needed a sign. A boost. A spark of inspiration. A...drink?

"I won't." Amber shook her head vigorously, as Sol dragged her over to the tables. "It's ethyl alcohol. Poison!"

"So is caffeine, or water, even. It's all about the dose," he assured her, pouring two shot glasses of the milky white liquid. "Look, I won't force you to, but I can testify that it does wonders for brain power."

"It's a tranquilizer." She raised an eyebrow, skeptical. "It subdues the brain power."

"Exactly!" he confirmed, sipping the drink and wincing. "It clears away all the rubbish and allows you to think without boundaries. And it also makes you feel all funny and uncoordinated and say whatever's on your mind."

"I'm already like that. On a daily basis," Amber thought.

"Don't you have some stimulants? A hallucinogen, maybe? And something less, ugh," she sniffed the glass as if it was a dead rat, "potent?"

"Not forcing you," Sol repeated. "Do whatever you want."

He finished his glass, poured himself an extra portion and walked away from the table. Amber watched the other glass carefully, as if worried it was about to jump up to her face and force its contents down her throat.

"This is exactly what Nawahi warned me about," she muttered and grabbed the shot glass with two fingers. "One sip then."

She left the tent three glasses later.

Contrary to what Sol had promised her, it didn't make her mind clearer, it just made it blank. Amber didn't know what it was like to have a blank mind. According to her parents, she said her first words at eight months, and by two years the only way to shut her up was to put headphones over her ears. Her brain didn't know rest or peace. And being drunk made her question everything she knew about the world, including the directions of up and down and the apparent stability of the world around her.

Before falling asleep on the floor of her tent, about two meters away from her bed, Amber attempted to call one of her ex-girlfriends (Sarah made sure that the voicemail stayed unsent), downed a liter of water and scribbled something on the chalk board she used for solitary brainstorming. She slept like an angel and woke up the next day with only a shadow of a headache. Her hair was beyond tangled, her mouth felt like a drying out swamp, and her clothes stank of spirits she spent the previous night enjoying. It took her an hour to come to her senses.

When she finally started to feel like herself, Amber poured a whole packet of acetylsalicylic acid into her cappuccino and examined the chalk board she vaguely remembered writing something on. "Map is red herring?" it read in wobbly handwriting and a hasty "ignore paintings" was added next to it.

"That...is not a bad idea, actually," Amber said to herself, grabbing her trusty e-book. "Hey, Sarah? Play me everything I recorded yesterday."

"Now playing: 27 messages," Sarah's soothing mechanical voice sounded from the bracelet.

It was the first and also the last time Amber had ever consumed alcohol.

Meanwhile, Darkness was standing on the edge of a river, her toes dipping into the icy water. She watched the birds dance in the air, hunting insects, and sighed, her heart aching for something she didn't recognize. Light sat on a dried-out tree trunk a few meters away from her, smiling. A young man was sitting next to her. He was tall, dark, and handsome, like a prince from a children's book, and his round, smiling face was painted with red dye. Light listened to him speak and his eyes gleamed with passion and kindness that was too great to be kept inside of him. She raised her hand and brushed his long hair, Darkness blushing on her behalf somewhere in the distance.

"Guess I'm not the only one who gets crushes," Darkness thought, unwilling to interfere.

"How long have they been at it, eh?" S asked, appearing out of thin air in front of her, invisible to Light and her friend.

"Way too long," Darkness replied. "Unnecessary too. She has told him the rhymes five minutes into the conversation. At this point it's just..."

"Having fun?" S finished for her, and Darkness looked away guiltily. "Let them have it," he added, turning round and forcing Darkness to do the same. "What year is it again?"

"1489."

"Right," he nodded. "Boy has three years to enjoy his home before it gets 'discovered'."

"Couldn't we...?" Darkness began but he shook his head.

"You know we can't. But," he added, as he started to fade away, "she gave him one more very exciting day. That's something."

"Yeah," Darkness agreed.

On the tree trunk, Light and the young man were now embracing. The river rushed and whispered; the birds played in the air, oblivious of what was to come. And for now, the world was good.

SEVEN

There are these moments, late in the afternoon just before dinner, when it feels like every atomic force and solar wind in the universe is compelling you to abandon your work, pour yourself a glass of something mildly psychotropic, and engage in some good old-fashioned nothin'. The air tastes heavy in those moments, forcing itself through your nose and into your lungs with added strain, and you often get aches in muscles you didn't know you had. Some say it's laziness. Amber had always believed that it was a stark reminder of the second law of thermodynamics.

In a closed system, entropy always increases.

Also known as 'nothing is forever and we're all gonna die'.

The same grim realization was the only real reason people ever did anything--or didn't, for that matter. Including Amber.

She resided outside their camp, surrounded by e-books and sprawled under an intensely green, bushy tree. The tree wasn't just old, it was practically pre-historic; it had stopped making new branches a decade ago, and it remained the only splash of color in the once fertile desert. This part of Sereneae was hotter than a frying pan in the summer--it took a lot of water to keep it arable and this tree wasn't getting even half of what it needed in H20. Still, it persisted, growing stubbornly despite all the hints that the local ecosystem was giving it. It simply refused to die. And that idiotic yet noble determination motivated Amber to keep going, even though she was pretty sure it was useless.

"Making any progress?" Lullaby, who was done with their responsibilities for the day, stood nearby, almost as tall as the tree.

Instead of a reply, Amber produced an inhuman groan and fell backwards, hitting her head on the solid ground beneath her. She sighed and massaged her hurting skull. The kind of sacrifices one goes to in order to keep up with the dramatic.

"The gods have cursed me in my endeavor," she complained, sitting up. "I'm stuck. Have been for a week. It's no fair that someone as beautiful and brilliant as me has to suffer like this."

"Can help?" Lullaby asked, arranging their body comfortably next to Amber.

"Invent a time machine, go back in time and ask those fuckers what they meant by all this bullshit." She poked one of the e-books with her foot. "It makes no sense! I've tried matching text to the images and they don't. Match, I mean. I've tried looking at the maps alone and they're impossible to interpret without the text. I've examined the text alone but it requires visuals to place correctly. Five experts and two algorithms have gone through the stuff and no one has any idea what this nonsense means!"

She wanted to punch something but there were no convenient punching targets in sight--so she just fumed silently, hoping that her body wouldn't spontaneously combust from all the frustration. Lullaby watched her, quietly fascinated.

"You'll figure it out," they stated, not to cheer her up but because they believed it to be true.

"But you see, Lu," Amber continued, staring into the Rx'lng's big black eyes, "it's like a part of it is missing. What if they made this map and forgot to add some fragment and now there's no way of figuring out what was supposed to be there in the first place?!"

Lullaby examined Amber's face--her wide eyes, ruffled hair and flaring nostrils--and did the Rx'lng version of a shrug.

"You need a break," they concluded after a pause.

Amber nodded, then laughed, then cried a little, then laughed again.

Fifteen minutes later, she persuaded Sol to take her out to the city.

After a bumpy ride in an electric buggy, a small group of campers arrived to the nearest big city of Gizlem. One of the oldest settlements on Sereneae, it represented a peculiar mix of century-old stone houses and state-of-the-art glass skyscrapers. The streets were packed with pedestrians and the roads existed in a permanent state of traffic jam.

"How many people live here?" Amber asked, jumping up and down on the front seat of the buggy.

"Five million, give or take," Sol replied.

She whistled--a piece of non-verbal information that was lost on the Sojhi archaeologist.

"Looks...shabby," she continued. "Dirty. Unpleasant."

Sarah buzzed her bracelet, displeased with that language, but was ignored.

"Thanks for reminding me." He smirked. "I live here."

"Oh." She bit her lip. "Sorry."

"It's fine," he assured her. "I know it's not paradise, but hey, it has libraries, bars, and brothels. What else do you need?"

Once the car was parked, relatively safely, on a paid parking lot, the eight of them moved out into the city. The first thing every local did was buy an enormous serving of some drink, which was icy cold and colored red of suspicious intensity. Amber wasn't so sure about it, but she bought one anyway, going against her instincts to follow the crowd. The drink stank of roses and was nauseatingly sweet. It took her a dozen sips but eventually it rather grew on her.

"It's Set-Semp," one of the campers told Sol and he nodded in approval.

"Let's hit those city squares, then," he said, heading for one of the narrower streets.

Amber wanted to ask what the hell any of that meant but didn't get the opportunity. She glanced at Lullaby, and they glanced back at her.

"Guess we're following," Amber told them. "Come on. I think people are staring at you."

She wasn't wrong. Sol intentionally picked a route that run far from the city's center, but it didn't stop random Sereneaeans from pointing and whispering behind their back. One person even tried to approach them but was turned away. It was enough to look at the cracks in the pavement, the street corners covered in trash and the tattered clothes that locals wore to know that this wasn't a particularly affluent neighborhood--or city in general. These people had enough struggles of their own. They didn't need any extra trouble.

When they were crossing an alleyway beneath a four-story building, an old woman leaned out of the window and shook her fist at the campers.

"What do you think you're doing, bringing alien scum into the city?"

"Not your damn business, grandma!" Sol shouted in response and dodged a fruit that was thrown in his direction.

He caught the next one in mid-air and took a generous bite out of it.

"Thanks!" He waved at her. "A bit over-ripe. Just like I prefer them."

They walked away before Amber got a chance to enrich her vocabulary in new and exciting swear words.

The fruit in question was actually a berry of the Zimka tree, but legally classified as a vegetable--and, in some cities on Sereneae, as a mineral. When it wasn't ripe enough, it caused stomach cramps, diarrhea and delusions upon ingestion. When over-ripe or over-cooked, it sometimes caused intense headaches and also turned your urine purple. Just ripe enough it was delicious and tasted like a mix between kiwi and beetroot.

"Don't mind them," Sol told them, once they were out of the old woman's shouting range. "These people are desperate for a scapegoat. They will happily take an opportunity to blame it on some strangers."

"I kinda understand them," Amber said, kicking an empty bottle with her boot. "No offense, but they don't look very well-off, or happy about it."

"City's a bit of a mess, I won't lie," Sol agreed. "I wouldn't say they are all unhappy though. We have homeless people and stuff but all in all, the conditions are livable."

"Yeah?" She raised an eyebrow. "Then what the hell was wrong with that woman's face?"

"What do you mean?" He frowned.

"Well, you know. Her skin was... withered. All wrinkly and spotted and stuff. And she had almost no teeth. And her hair..."

"She's old!" Sol laughed, amused by her comments. "That's all."

"Old people don't look like that." It was Amber's turn to frown in confusion. "I'm not stupid, I know bodies don't last forever, but it all happens on the inside, not the outside."

"Well, maybe on Alexandria people stay healthy and beautiful till they die, but they sure don't in the real world," he said. "We get sick, we age, and we die. And getting old isn't fun."

"No joke," one of the campers, a young geologist by the name of Empre, spoke up. "My grandpa has bad joint problems, and he can't see shit anymore. I went to see him last month up in Monteve and he told me that he's ready to die. Both his wives passed away more than a decade ago, all his grandchildren are grown up and his health keeps getting worse. Nothing good 'bout that."

"Jeez," Amber muttered. "If it's that terrible, can't they just digitalize him already?"

There was a pause, followed by a roar of laughter from everyone except for Lullaby.

"Mate, you are naive." Sol smiled until she scowled at him. "Do you really think that the Muuk go through all the trouble of preserving every single consciousness in the universe?"

"They do on Alexandria," she muttered.

"Exactly. There's what, ten thousand? Fifteen thousand of you?"

"Twenty-three thousand, actually."

"Well, there's twelve billion of us. Twelve billion!" He laughed again. "On seven different planets, not counting Sojhi. Ain't nobody has time or resources to digitalize all of us." He shook his head. "Nah, in our world, you get eighty years of decent living, and then you're done."

"Eighty years?!" Amber's eyebrows went up her forehead. "That's... not a lot," she wanted to say 'laughable', but stopped herself. "We live to two hundred or so, barring accidents and shit."

"Not surprising, with all the medicine the Muuk give you," Sol said. "But again, they can't do the same for the entire galaxy. They adore the rare species, the ones that are close to extinction--ike you two," he pointed at Amber and

Lullaby. "Us? Not so much."

"But they could. They are powerful enough."

"Power isn't everything. You also need to give a fuck," he finished. "Doesn't matter. We're almost here."

Amber didn't remember much of the remaining day's events. It all went past her in a bit of a haze. They mostly stayed in the city square, where children and adults alike played some complicated game, and spent the rest of their day out in a small restaurant near a beautiful garden. Inside, people ate and talked and laughed, enjoying their leisure time and sharing news with each other. Sol was right; they seemed happy, genuinely so. But how could they be?

She remembered being eight and learning about the history of her species and sentient life in general. All the wars, and plagues, and famines that roamed the world...all the innocent lives lost. She remembered being horrified by the idea, crying her eyes out when the grim reality of that history struck her for real. The pain was too overwhelming; it didn't get better after her parents died.

Still, she had her people--thriving, safe, free of the horrors of the past. 'No more' was the only thought that kept her sane. She couldn't imagine living back in the days when people died and never came back, almost always as a result of a great amount of suffering, many of which was inflicted unnecessarily and by other people. She thought it terrifying. And now, at the age of twenty-five, she had come face to face with that terrifying truth.

The vast majority of the galaxy still lived like that. Alexandria wasn't the norm--it was the exception.

Was she supposed to feel guilty? No wonder people on Sereneae regarded both humans and Rx'lng with such distaste. She would, too, if she could grasp the disparity between her life and theirs. How would she live her life, if she knew that she had eighty years at best in this world? That her safety and her health were not guarantees or givens. That her loved ones could be taken from her at any moment by circumstance or bad intentions. Would she ever find peace? Would she be able to push that thought away, ignore her mortality and enjoy the present moment, like all the people around her--chatting, eating, embracing their loved ones--or would she live her entire life in fear of death?

She didn't know. And it wasn't good enough.

While the rest of the campers--including Lullaby--resided at the center of the hall, listening to Rey tell some apparently hilarious story, Amber sat in a corner next to a blank wall. She mixed her tea absent-mindedly. It was too cold to be hot, and too warm to be iced. The central table roared with laughter and lewd comments. She sighed, rubbing her eyes and shifting in her seat for the fifth time that minute. Everything in the world was too much and she wanted to go home. Not just to the tent--to Alexandria. To Ishtar, where everything was good and safe and made sense.

"Save your tears, country girl, don't forget your childhood home," Sol sang in a soft voice, taking a seat next to her at the table.

"Huh?" She regarded him with a mix of apathy and confusion.

"A song," he explained. "From my childhood."

"Whatever." She turned away, pushing her sunglasses up her nose.

"We're paying for the food, and we'll be coming back to the camp soon. Thought you'd like to know that."

He was about to get up and re-join the cheerful company but she grabbed him by the edge of his trousers.

"Sol?" she asked. "Is it true that everyone calls Alexandria a cosmic zoo?"

"It's..." He paused, about to give her a comforting lie, but her tired expression changed his mind. "Yeah," he said, and sat down again. "We do. That, and 'Muuk pet project', and some other not so flattering terms."

"Funny." Her voice sounded weak and hoarse. "I can't even argue with that. When I was a kid, I thought humans were special...guess we are, just not in a good way."

"Hey," he leaned ever so slightly forward, his voice softening, "if I said anything today that hurt you, just tell me and I won't do it again."

"It's not you," she dismissed it. "Not any of you. I don't know what the fuck it is, but I don't like it."

"Reality a bit too harsh for you, huh?" He smiled sadly but she didn't react.

"Sorry. I keep forgetting that you're really young."

"I'm not really young!" she wanted to lash out in her usual manner but had no power left in her body to do so. Instead, she bit her lip and stared blankly at the table in front of her.

"You know what," Sol said, leaving his seat, "I have an idea. Come on, follow me."

"I don't wanna!" she protested but he practically dragged her out.

"You go guys," he told the group, pushing Amber out of the cafe. "We'll catch up with you."

He lead her through dark alleyways and narrow streets, into a remote corner of the city. There, in between two dilapidated houses, stood a small, precious church. Less than two stories high, it was painted an iridescent shade of blue and sparkled in the pale light of the early evening. Unlike everything else in the city, it was clean and well-cared for. It had a different feel to it, too; soft, colorful... hopeful, even.

Sol invited Amber in through the low set doors and instructed her to take a bow next to a marble statue of a woman in indigo robes. While he paid tribute to his ancestors by lighting a few candles and placing them on a whole metal tree full of dripping wax and flickering flames, Amber examined the room.

It was almost completely empty, except for them and two other locals. They sat on a rug in front of another statue, motionless, eyes closed and silent. The air smelt of incense and rusting copper. The walls, covered in layers of paintings, rose up in the air and rounded off at the roof. She didn't know whether it was the cold colors or the scent of herbs, but as soon as she stepped inside, she felt better. Less anxious, less tired...less sad.

"Welcome to the altar of Hivelem," Sol whispered, headed for one of the large paintings. "It's one of the most popular Sojhi religions. I was brought up in a Hiveli household."

"Are many of your people religious?" Amber asked, also whispering.

"Yeah. I think so. Not intensely," he added, "but we follow the traditions and holidays and stuff. And it's nice, coming here when I feel like nothing else helps.

I don't suppose religion is widespread on Alexandria."

"Not at all," she replied. "Some people follow certain traditions but very few really believe."

"You don't need to." He nodded. "Usually. I think you need it right now. Look." He pointed at the wall painting.

The panorama depicted a faceless man who appeared to be wearing a cloud, surrounded by trees and vines. Next to the shrouded figure was a river, and from that river, animals were rising up to the sky--animals that Amber didn't recognize. They reminded her of cows...and also wolves. The animals all looked the same, except they had small details that made them unique.

"This is Ertry, the spirit of life," Sol explained. "He found Sojhi after it was created by The Lady and he brought her gifts: the animals. They were of the same kind at first but they were all a bit different--so they went to different places and changed into all sorts of species. Including us."

"That's clever." Amber smiled. "Like your ancients figured out evolution before your scientists did."

"Not really." He laughed. "You've no idea how many shouting arguments I've had with people who still believe that animals existed before bacteria did cause the religion says so."

"You don't? Think that, I mean."

"Of course not," he said. "It's a metaphor. It's beautiful and wise, but it's not factual. Right," he returned to his point. "Ertry created the animals as mortal, but The Lady didn't like it--so she made them immortal and invincible. It was okay for a while but then the animals began to overpopulate the world and there was no place for young ones anymore. So she realized that Ertry was right and reversed it. Ertry is the spirit of life, but he's also the spirit of death. They're one and the same. You need him to keep the world in balance."

"But why make the animals sentient?!" Amber said, a touch of tears in her voice. "Why make us aware of what is to come?"

"Well, Hivelem says it's because The Lady entrusted us with the truth. We were her favorite species and she shared the secret with us and made us her people. It's a gift, to be aware."

"Bullshit. Religion, all of it."

She turned around and away from Sol, and her teary eyes were drawn to another painting--one that depicted a planet being born out of a flash of light. Except the writings on it didn't quite look right. She squinted and quickly realized that the painting was upside down.

"What's up with that?" she asked, momentarily forgetting about her 'sad and angry' act.

"Oh, it's upside down," Sol replied.

"Thanks, captain obvious. I can see it's upside down. Why is it upside down?"

"No reason," he told her. "People who made it installed it like that on accident. We used to think it was intentional, like a statement about the myth, but nah--they just messed up."

"Upside down," Amber muttered. "Upside down..."

She took the sunglasses off her face and began to chew on the left stem.

"You okay?"

"Go away! I have a thought."

"Nice to know you have thoughts."

"Shut up!"

She paced in circles around the room, the church visitors staring at her, unhappy to be disturbed like that. One minute passed, then five, then ten. Amber was still pacing.

"Can you tell me what's up, please?" Sol begged. "It's getting ridiculous."

"It is!" she exclaimed. "Upside down! Don't you get it? The rest of the instruction is on the other side!"

"Uh, yeah, she's not from around here," Sol mumbled, staring back at the visitors. "Typical off-worlder, am I right?"

"I need to get back to the camp." It was Amber's time to drag Sol out of the building. "Quick, before I lose the thought."

Two very much not quick hours later, and Amber was standing on top of the hole that she got to know intimately in these past few weeks. It was now pitch

92

black and bitterly cold, but she was too concentrated on her task to be aware of it. She had the answer now. She was sure.

"Turn it over," Amber instructed to a couple of technicians who accompanied her to the sight.

"Sorry, love?" One of them, an older woman who was waken up for this, raised an eyebrow in an almost theatrical fashion.

"Turn. It. Over," she repeated. "The crate. On the other side?"

The technicians forced the most annoyed sound their vocal cords could produce but obeyed.

By the time the task was complete, pretty much the entire camp had gathered around the hole. Amber was jumping up and down, managing to bite her tongue a couple of times in the process. Lullaby was growling, their eyes reflecting every spec of light from people's cameras and flashlights. Sol was skeptical. On the outside. On the inside, he was shrieking in excitement like a boy who just got a bicycle for his birthday. It was time to take a look.

"Right." Amber grabbed a flashlight that someone had conveniently put into her palm and stepped closer to The Hole. "Are you ready kids?"

There was only silence.

"No applause then. Okay," she said, slightly disappointed. "Let's take a look, shall we?"

She shone the light down into the pit and gazed downward and so did the rest of the crowd. There was a moment of deafening silence, then a collective gasp, followed by more silence.

On the outside of the crate was the missing link of the star map leading to the Aquamarine Moon--complete with scale, numbers and instructions.

"Well," Amber's face was decorated with the widest, most self-assured grin of her life, "ladies, gentlemen, non-binary folks and, uh, Lullaby--I think we have a winner."

EIGHT

The night flew by, the next morning came--and with it, the first rain the land had seen in months. It poured, and poured, and poured, until the ground beneath the researchers' feet was reduced to a sad, squishy swamp. People were mildly annoyed, but plants and animals rejoiced. Amber watched the ecosystem come to life from the comfort of her tent. She saw thin, white roots shooting up to the surface from the ground, and large water-collecting leafs opening up and turning towards the sky. Just a few hours of rain and new plants began to appear; delicate stems, painted a soft mint green, pushed through the soil and greeted the world for the first time. The valley was alive.

It was still raining when the sun began to move closer to the horizon, drowning the area in pink and purple waves of dusk. Amber was searching her tent for all the hair ties she had lost, and it was making her believe in tiny evil gnomes that live in people's tents and steal their hair ties. She growled, nearly toppling over in a corner, and dropped into an inflatable armchair. Gradually, her gaze moved towards the window. She blinked a couple of times, sat up straight and realized that someone was approaching her tent. She braced herself for a social interaction.

"Heyo," came a voice from the other side of the tent.

She recognized the speaker as Rey, the resident hardware technician.

"Can I come in?" she asked.

"If you have to," Amber wanted to reply, but stopped herself. Rey was painfully nice--to her and everyone else on the camp--and she couldn't justify not returning the favor.

"Sure. But please don't bring in the mud."

"I'll try to." Rey squeezed herself into the tent and wiped the rain off her face. "Damn, I really hoped we'd finish before the rain season."

She left her dirty boots at the entrance and approached Amber's armchair cautiously.

"I'm not distracting you from work, am I?"

"No work." She gestured vaguely. "I'm packing my stuff."

"What, already?"

"Too late, I'd say. I'm leaving tomorrow morning."

"Huh," Rey muttered, taking a seat near her on the ground. "The camp or the project in general?"

"I'm coming back to Alexandria," Amber elaborated. "The map is complete, the translations are done, and there's nothing either me or Lu have left to do. So, they're sending us back to our homes."

"Aren't they going to investigate the claims? I mean, what's the point in finding the map if you won't use it."

"Oh, they will," she assured her, a mix of envy and anger in her voice. "But they don't need us to do it."

"Is it true?" Rey asked after a momentary pause.

"Yep." She nodded. "It's in the Teardrop Cluster. Good luck flying anywhere near that."

"It's the biggest one in the galaxy," she agreed. "Eleven solar masses. And it's very old too."

"Could be a scam. Every time I hear 'black hole system planet' I read 'made-up bullshit'."

"Explains why it wasn't identified previously though."

"Yeah, if it exists." Amber snorted with laughter. "Look, did you want anything?"

"Yes. I..."

"Wanted to invite you to dinner with the guys," Rey wanted to say, but noticed the half-dreamy, half-tired look on Amber's face and hesitated.

"...wanted to ask you if you'd like me to bring your dinner over to your tent.

Guys are..."

"Please," Amber replied before she got a chance to finish. "I'll be much obliged. The basic one and two drinks. Thank you so much."

And she flashed her best polite smile.

"No probs." Rey smiled back. "Sol said hi by the way."

And she got up, wriggled back into her dirty shoes and left the tent.

"Five unread messages from: Lullaby. Two unread messages from: Sol," Sarah announced a minute later. "One unread message from: Sentient Baked Potato."

"Whatever," Amber muttered, slouching deeper into the armchair. "You won't trick me into talking to people. I'm drained. I need food and rest, not chatting."

"Tasks planned for today: none."

"Fuck productivity, I'm a strong, independent, terrifying bog witch. And I want snacks."

Sarah buzzed, unhappy with the attitude, but unwilling to challenge Amber.

"Suggestion: playlist number 4--'for when I feel like biting someone, and not in a sexy way'."

"Spot on," she replied and recovered her earbuds from a pile of smelly t-shirts and blankets.

There were two things Amber learned during her stay. One : all in all, people weren't as terrible as she thought they were. And two: that didn't mean she could handle them in large doses.

After working hard for more than a day, the tropical rainstorm had decided to take a break and switched from a wall of water to an occasional light drip. The sun was still obscured by thick clouds and the ground resembled a drying out riverbed more than a fertile field. Amber wrinkled her nose and stepped over a particularly deep puddle. Lullaby was by her side, the Quantum Frog had arrived, and they were good to go. They just needed to deal with the goodbyes first.

"Well-well." Sol was the last one in a long line of campers to see them off. "Look who's fleeting the battlefield."

"You wish!" Amber smirked and hit her outer palm with his--a greeting he taught her on the second day of her stay. "Give me a couple years to progress my career and I'll be back with a vengeance."

"I don't doubt it. And hey, maybe you should get into Triqilam cultures, join my next trip to Oka. Be a pain in my ass again."

"I'll consider it," she promised.

"You take care, big goof," Sol told Lullaby and they chirped in approval. "Will miss you on my board game team. And my team in general."

"You're leaving soon too, yeah?" Amber asked.

"Still got a few days to wrap up this sight," he explained. "You could keep me company, you know."

"Sorry," Amber said. "My options are a bit limited."

"Truc." He nodded. "Well, you know. See ya."

"Yeah." She smiled and turned around to leave.

A nice lie of course, for both of them. She was perfectly aware of the fact that, once she would return to Alexandria, she would spend the rest of her days there--and Sol knew it too. A perfect life had its drawbacks.

Still, she got almost three months of freedom. It was better than no months.

Amber chewed on her lip, motionless, listening to the campers behind her chat about trivial nonsense, their boots squishing the mud. She was pouring whole swimming pools of effort into persuading herself that everything was fine. These were just normal, profoundly uninteresting people, right? Not worth her attention. Just as mundane and unnecessary as any other person she had ever met. People she could easily do without. So why, if she was still the person she had always been, independent and self-sufficient, perfect just as is, why was she feeling a lump in her throat?

A horrifying thought struck Amber and almost forced the tears out of her eyes. Was she...attached? Was she, after all, not immune to those soppy human feelings? She wanted to run away from it, both physically and mentally, but instead her legs turned her in the opposite direction and propelled her forcefully back towards the crowd. Saying no words, she approached the smiling, chatting people that she was supposed to hate, and stopped in front of Sol. Speechless.

"Is everything okay?" He frowned at her, perplexed by her blank stare.

"Are we..." she almost chocked on the words. "Are we...friends?"

Sol laughed, assuming that she was joking, but quickly noticed the dull gleam in her eyes and frowned again.

"Yeah. Sure." He shrugged. "We're friends."

Amber nodded, expressionless.

"You okay, country girl?" Sol asked.

Instead of a reply, Amber made a step forward and pulled him into a hug.

They stood like that for a few moments, while the rest of the campers watched them in a mix of confusion and delight. When Amber let go of him at last, she had to perform a quick dodge to wipe her eyes. She couldn't let them know she had Feelings.

"We can hang out in VR, you know," Sol pointed out. "Play board games together."

"Yeah," Amber muttered. "Sure."

She hadn't had a friend in over a decade, so she wasn't sure what friends did together, exactly.

"It was nice working with you," she added, avoiding his gaze...and ran away, quite literally, before anyone had a chance to reply.

Lullaby was the only one to catch up with her.

"Would love to play VR board games," they chirped happily.

"If you tell anyone that just happened," Amber hissed in reply, "I will end your career."

"Will not tell under any circumstances. Don't worry," Lullaby assured her in their native language. "No one will ever discover you are actually a human being."

Amber smirked and slowed down from a jog to a pace. All in all, she had to admit, they were quite a good match for each other.

Amber stared out of the fake spaceship windows as the Quantum Frog sealed its entrances and prepared for the leap. The cameras showed the droopy landscape outside, as well as the campers standing under umbrellas, waving at them and smiling. The sides of Amber's mouth went up as well. Once again, something stuck deep in the twisted, convoluted vines of her thoughts was telling her that this feeling was wrong, and once again she was choosing to blatantly disregard it. Instead, she embraced the smile.

The smile, interestingly enough, was a universal humanoid feature. In every species that had a face and a mouth, it would evolve without fail, as if it was absolutely essential to sustain social life. And in species lacking the necessary equipment, a different but equivalent gesture would emerge. Smiles in every shape and form were shared across halls of spaceship airports and planet entry customs, at inter-culture bazaars and space station parties. Smiles were ubiquitous. And no one ever questioned them.

The floor shook slightly, and Amber waved back at the campers, even though she knew they couldn't see her.

"Flight in session," Sarah commented, and the bracelet lit up green. "Switching off the Internet connection."

"Wait," Amber said, pressing a few buttons at random.

Sarah buzzed the bracelet, displeased.

"Internet use not recommended in warped dimension mode."

"Give me five minutes, okay?" she muttered, swiping through a few web pages that lit up on her upper arm. "I wanna look up something."

The AI obeyed and she continued her Internet search.

She was looking for an ad that she got in the mail a few days ago. Funny thing--when you don't need ads (which is almost always the case), they fly in your face at every opportunity like fruit flies; and when you actually do need to find a specific advertisement, you get everything but the one you need. 'Unprecedented innovation in hand lotion', 'the most crunchy waffles you've ever tasted', 'buy a spaceship, get an asteroid for free' and other exciting offers littered Amber's feed.

"Oh, for crying out loud," she muttered, and opened the 'spam' folder of her mail.

Two scrolls through it and there it was. 'A weekend on Cryptos--the holiday you won't forget'. Exactly what she needed.

Her finger hovered, danced over a button of her bracelet; twitching like the needle of a seismometer, reflecting her chaotic thoughts.

"Sarah?" Amber asked and bit her lips. "Am I a bad person?"

"Insufficient data for reply." If artificially generated voices of assistant systems could sound puzzled, this is how they would sound.

"I'm..." Amber began, then shut her eyes tight and groaned in frustration. "I'm so...All those people on Sereneae, on other planets. They would give so much to have the life that I have. Why am I not happy?!" she exclaimed, suddenly angry at herself.

"Insufficient data."

"Insufficient data?"

"Recommendation--queries should be directed to another person."

"Another person," Amber repeated again and laughed. "Sure. Would you rather I spoke to someone from Alexandria, who has never seen the deep state of shit this galaxy is in, or an outsider, who will explain to me, in three sentences or less, that I'm a spoiled brat? I..." She paused again, breathing heavily. "Can't. I can't. Can't deal with...this is the real reason they don't let us out, Sarah. For our own good. Cause once you are exposed to whatever the fuck the rest of our world is, how can you ever come back and stand face to face with another Alexandrian?"

"Suggestion," Sarah said. "Initiate call to user 'Sentient Baked Potato'."

"No," Amber replied and pressed the off button, shutting down the AI voice. "I'm too old to be asking grown-ups for help. I can make my own mistakes now."

Amber spend the next few hours mulling it over in her head. She knew it could be done--they were on a course to the right nook of the galaxy, and they would have to dive out of warped dimension anyway. She was sure she could convince Lullaby to do it too. From what she had gathered in their long and thorough conversations, Lk'st wasn't over the moon about going back on the King of Kings, where their fellow Rx'lng treated them and their kind like garbage. And she was confident she could get away with it too.

The only problem was, she had to make a choice--and she hated making choices. The last time Amber needed to buy a new toaster, she had to read a dozen of articles and forum threads, consult two shop assistants and make a spreadsheet. She didn't even want to recall choosing a major. Choices just didn't come easily to Amber; she had no intuition, no gut feeling to speak of, and too much knowledge of logical laws.

She remembered learning about free will in philosophy classes--learning about how, according to most philosophers, it was merely an illusion. They made a compelling argument for it, and she quickly took the notion on board without spending too much time dwelling on it. She didn't really care whether her free will was genuine or not--it felt real to her, and, for convenience's sake at least, it was all that mattered. Cogito ergo sum, period, she thought. As far as she was concerned, she could be living a dream, or a computer simulation, but it still didn't change the fact that she had to brush her teeth twice a day and stock up her pantry. She would worry about it at her "deathbed." And after that too.

However, one thing she did like about the notion was having an excuse for all the past actions that she felt guilty about. Overslept and skipped a class? No reason to beat herself over it, it was meant to be. Spent a bit too much on clothes this month? Not her fault, her genes and her environment simply led her down that path. Did anything that didn't sit well with her conscious? No use crying about it now, just figure out what went wrong and try to prevent it in the future.

Could she abandon the freshly-baked plan? Forget it, move on, come back to Alexandria and spend the rest of her life wondering what could have been? Surely. Except she didn't feel it was right.

Amber didn't believe in free will, and she didn't believe in some magical notion of destiny either. Things just happened, she reckoned, and the universe didn't care about meaning. So she didn't believe that nonsense... except for that day. That day, as she got up from the table and headed for the flight maintenance room to 'ask Lullaby a favor', she was fairly convinced that she didn't only have no choice in this matter, it was also sent down on her by some invisible and determined force.

It was all bullshit, of course, she later realized. But she did enjoy the feeling.

"All going according to plan?" Amber asked, stepping over the threshold.

"Will be stopping soon," Lullaby replied. "Calibrating. Setting on a path to your planet."

"Cool cool cool." She brought her hands together for a single clap. "So... can you control this thing, more or less?"

"Can do."

"Awesome," she said. "I have an idea."

"An idea?" Lullaby tilted their head, perplexed.

"Yes. I wanna make a small detour. Stop on this planet for a few hours, have some fun. We technically aren't allowed to do that, but..."

"But?" they repeated, listening attentively.

"But I think they won't notice. What is it to them, hey? And we'll be back to our boring planets slash colonies anyway, so who cares."

"Won't get caught?"

"I never get caught." Amber grinned. "Come on, Lu, we have one shot of doing something different in our pathetic, boring lives. Why not take it?"

Lullaby looked at Amber, their big black eyes glimmering in the cold white light of the room, then placed one long thin finger on the control panel.

"Coordinated," they said.

And Amber shrieked so loud, she almost chocked on air.

Sereneae was behind them, Alexandria was far away. Next stop was planet Cryptos.

Meanwhile, S was having an almost terrible, certainly not brilliant, mildly infuriating and infuriatingly long afternoon. They had all split up across the city two hours ago, each on their own, individual assignment, and S's was, predictably, the worst.

"It is bad, you know," he said calmly to a pigeon who kept walking around his bench in circles. "Very bad." S smiled. "To be completely honest with you, I am ninety-eight-point seven percent close to losing it."

He threw another piece of laminated paper on the asphalt, and it disappeared a fraction of a second before it touched the ground.

"It's a pity you can't hear me, friend. Well. None of them can." He gestured around himself, at the grey crowd of passerby humans, moving not as individuals but as one flowing, inseparable whole. "Everyone is So Busy." S sighed and threw a crumpled-up pamphlet behind his back. "Always busy. And I am sorting through ad pamphlets because of reasons."

On the other side of the bridge that connected the two parts of the city, Darkness was licking an ice-cream cone, one foot on pavement, one poking and prodding a patch of welting grass. While her thoughts wandered, her eyes kept scanning the street. The girl in the orange jumpsuit could appear at any second... preferably after she had finished her ice-cream.

The sun beams danced on the ground behind her. The wind tossed and messed with her dark curls. A blob of melted ice-cream fell on her foot, went straight through it and vanished into the grass. Just as she swallowed the last piece of waffle and licked a sweet drop off the inside of her wrist, a door of a cafe opened, and the girl stepped out. Darkness smiled. It was time for a conversation.

As for Light, the task was completed in under seven minutes (her personal record), clean and with no complications, just as she liked it. She could see the man, still. Crying, silently, sat on the ground underneath a dying oak tree. Every now and then he would dive into his pocket and pull, hands shaking, the letter, now dog-eared and smudged, and read over the last few lines. Light did not feel bad for the man. It wasn't her fault after all. The message had existed on the woman's mind already...she just tipped her neurochemical scale towards putting the words on paper.

"It's for your own good, Michael," Light whispered. "Even if you don't know it yet."

They all met up again at late evening and sat down at the city square to discuss their day.

"I have persuaded the future president of this country to take a history course at her high school," Darkness said. "This will inspire her to fix the injustices of the past."

"I have caused a breakup," Light said. "Which made a bloke very upset.

I don't know why he is important, but it will change his life. For the better. Eventually."

"I have sent out a hundred and twenty-seven ads," S said. "They all went to spam. I haven't a clue as to why it even matters and I would like a day of my life back."

"Chill, S," Light told him. "This isn't even our real lives."

And while she was, undoubtedly, correct, it did not make S feel any better

NINE

There are some crucial moments in your life which, years after the fact, in retrospect, seem like a single page in the book, yet feel like whole volumes in the moment. The air condenses around you; your heart speeds up. Every second becomes poignant, meaningful. Your thoughts race, and your palms sweat while your mouth dries up. And, most important of all, time slows down somehow.

The explanation for this is simple and space-time distortions are not to blame here: it's all about your hormones. Or neurotransmitters, depending on how you look at it. Time perception is all about attention and a funny little molecule called adrenaline works magic for making your attention ten times better at capturing every detail of your conscious experience. It's not that the time actually slows down; rather, you start to appreciate it more--because your brain thinks it's important. And boy, that sure was the case for Amber.

"Are we gonna land? Are we gonna land? Are we gonna land?" she chanted, every atom in her body vibrating at an inhuman frequency.

"Patient," Lullaby hissed. "Navigating by hand--hard. Need to concentrate."

"Can I watch?" Amber had to stand on tiptoes and strain her neck to peek over Lullaby's sited figure. "Ugh, it's just a bunch of numbers. I hate numbers. They all look the same to me. I'm still not convinced three and five are different."

She continued to chatter nervously but Lullaby ignored her. They were too concentrated on the calculations.

"Amber?" they said after a while spent staring at one particular figure. "Certain there is planet down there?"

"Um. Yeah?"

"Don't see no planet." They pointed a stick-like finger at the projected screen. "Just cosmos."

"Oh, devil, I forgot." She slapped herself on the forehead a bit too strongly and winced. "Cryptos. It's cloaked with, uhm, physics and stuff. Something about opposite charges collapsing each other."

Lullaby stared blankly at her, blinking.

"Don't ask me." Amber shrugged. "I don't even understand Newtonian mechanics," she said, and wasn't wrong.

She remembered viscerally being hit in the face with a volleyball at the age of ten, as well as missing her cup with the teaspoon that morning.

"Point is," she continued, "you have to land according to the coordinates and trust that you'll land on something. It's part of the deal."

Lullaby gave out the Rx'lng equivalent of a sigh, which sounded like a mix between a child playing a recorder and the crunch of a crushed aluminum can but continued.

"Hold tight," they advised.

Amber didn't need a second warning.

Ten minutes and three terrifying sensations later the spaceship announced the exit out of warped dimensions. Amber beamed, adjusted her tie and grabbed her bag from the floor. She was ready to leave the ship when she realized that Lullaby wasn't following.

"Why are you still here?" she inquired, popping her head back into the control room.

They hesitated.

"Don't want to go," Lullaby muttered. "Not supposed to."

"Screw the rules!" Amber exclaimed. "Oh, come on, you aren't seriously gonna sit in here while I'm having a blast on Cryptos? I'll never forgive myself, and you won't either."

"What even to do out there? Be tourists?"

"Of course not! It's an entertainment planet, Lu. It has everything: restaurants, casinos, cinemas, shopping malls the size of a town... I'm pretty sure they have a zoo as well. Not that we'll have time to see all of it but there's plenty to choose from."

"Good advertisement," Lullaby insisted. "Doesn't mean it is good."

"Lu," Amber said, smirking. "Are you scared?"

"Not scared!" they shouted back. "Worker Rx'lng don't get scared."

"What are you waiting for then? Go on." She gestured to the exit. "And I'm paying for everything. I'm pretty rich," she added, as a throw-away point. "Alexandria having a strong economy has its perks."

It is worth noting that the only reason Lullaby followed Amber in the end was the dare. Rx'lng were the kind of species that valued socialization above all other worldly virtues. They didn't care for money, drugs, sex or possessions. And Lk'st would have surely stayed put, safe and sound on the Quantum Frog, if their bravery wasn't challenged. Bravery was always Rx'lng's most treasured trait. Perhaps that's why they were now almost entirely extinct.

It is also worth noting that Amber was, in fact, the one who was close to shitting her pants.

All her life, Amber had been a good girl. She had also been a huge bitch and an aspiring wicked witch of the west, but she was Good. She followed the rules, went to bed on time, and spent her afternoons reading a book in a corner instead of sneaking out of her bedroom window to meet up with her friends. She didn't have any friends--unless you count the imaginary ones, which were also well-behaved and adequately polite. Amber didn't break rules. She played fair. Her landing on Cryptos was an attempt to prove, mostly to herself, that she still had a bit of rebel in her. And it was scary as fuck.

Every nerve ending in her body was tingling as she stepped out of the ship and onto the soil of a different world.

"Attention!" Sarah exclaimed, buzzing Amber's bracelet. "Action not advised. Severe consequences likely. Parking space inadequate," she added after a pause, as an afterthought.

"Shush," Amber replied, and shut off the automatic guidance.

The neon lights of Cryptos's boulevards blinded her and she pushed her sunglasses further up her nose till they pierced into her skin, leaving red marks.

She had to engage her every bit of courage to step confidently across the golden tiles of the city's depths. She stared at the ground in front of her, like a race horse focused on the finish line, and kept her hands in the pockets of her skirt. "Play cool, asshat," she thought to herself and glanced sideways at Lullaby. The insectoid alien seemed thoroughly not bothered.

"Sup, doll."

Amber stopped abruptly in her tracks and turned towards the source of the sound. In front of her stood a Bellazi, wearing a leather jacket in a nasty shady of pink.

"Got a lighter maybe?" He (or she... no one except for Bellazi themselves could really tell, so it was always better to ask before making a mistake and starting another war) asked in Universal Galactic Speak.

Bellazi were descendants of lizard-like beasties, with scaly skin and disturbingly long tongues. Fairly deep into their civilization, they still hadn't quite mastered bipedal locomotion, and switched to walking on all fours whenever the opportunity presented itself. They used to be a warrior race but later re-branded themselves as tech developers and entrepreneurs--a smooth, logical transition. Bellazi were also infamous gambling addicts for some reason, so there was plenty of them on Cryptos. This one had just finished losing all the money they've earned last week and desperately needed a smoke.

"Sorry," Amber stuttered. "I, um, don't, don't carry sources of, um, open flames with me. Mate."

"No probs," they replied. "You?" they added, pointing at Lullaby.

"No lighter," Lk'st responded, already dragging Amber away. "Smoking bad for you."

"Please, like I don't fucking know," the Bellazi shouted at them. "Breathing's bad for you, too."

A passing Makran, who happened to be an obligatory anaerobe and required a hermetic suit just to walk around on Cryptos, empathetically agreed.

"I think we should pick a place and get inside," Amber suggested, starting to feel a little bit fizzy from all the cultural exchange. "There, this one looks...

inviting."

And before Lullaby had a chance to appeal the offer, she crossed the street and disappeared behind large wooden doors.

'The Semi-Dead Cat', the sign on top of it read.

Lk'st had no other choice but to follow their human.

Alas, by chance--and chance alone, since she knew nothing about Cryptos and its customs--Amber managed to pick one of the most cosmopolitan places on the planet. And by walking into it, Amber and Lullaby made it almost the perfect representation of their galaxy.

There were Sojhi and Han, of course, mostly grouping up with their own kind, sharing drinks and gossip. Makrans were using every opportunity to sell their goods, backing off only at the harshest of declines. Almost all the Bellazi were either at the bar or at gaming tables, though one was currently negotiating something with an Afrache, and trying very hard not to breathe them in (as happened often, since Afrache were sentient clouds of smoke). The only species missing from the mix were the Muuk.

"Kids partying when parents aren't home," Amber said, noticing exactly that. "Sweet. What do you reckon, Lu--is this a bar, a casino, or a strip club?"

Lullaby didn't answer, but even if they did, they'd probably get it wrong. In fact, The Semi-Dead Cat was all of those things--plus a pawnshop, a lost and found bureau, a souvenir shop and a first aid center. It used to be a library too, but all the books got stolen by the Makrans (and then sold back to the pawnshop).

One thing Amber liked about the place were the dimmed lights and absence of loud music. Due to its multi-species clientele, the owners of the club had to accommodate to every nervous system out there, and most races found flashing lights threatening. As for music, the masterpiece of one culture sounded like a brick being put through a meat grinder to others. That's why all soundtrack in the Semi-Dead Cat was self-chosen and delivered straight into your brain via half-legal technology.

The place was vast, crowded and scarcely decorated. The floor was a bit sticky, and the air smelt of something bitter-sweet and pungent. Amber found it difficult to adjust to, but she sure felt like a whole-ass rebel.

"Tea," she said, approaching a bar stand like she owned the place. "But make it strong. Leave in the bag.."

"Huh?" The barmaid, an older Sojhi woman, stared back at her, perplexed.

"It's a quote," Amber muttered. "From an Old Earth TV-show. You probably haven't heard of it. Uh, anyway, what do you have that contains THC and CBD?"

"CB what now?" The barmaid squinted. "Look, kid, I know this is a transit planet, but you gotta speak proper UGS if you want me to serve you."

"Weed," she gave up, giving her the correct word for what she wanted. "You know, the stuff that humans invented?"

"You're human?" Sojhi raised an eyebrow, a mix of disbelief and delight on her face. "Well-well, that's a first in my practice. Red Devil." She reached for a bottle on the topmost shelf and poured a full glass for Amber. "On the house."

"What, you won't ask for my ID or anything?"

"I never bother." Was the reply. "What do I care if you're underage?"

"Cool."

Amber dragged the cold glass over to her side and took a big gulp. She regretted it the moment the liquid touched her tongue. The drink was freezing and intensely sour. It burned her throat and made her fold over coughing. The barmaid chuckled, pouring a mug of water for her.

"Take it easy, kid." She smiled. "It's a special blend that a mate of mine cooked up. Works wonders on the Han, so it will probably work for you too."

"Is there a lot of Han people on Cryptos?"

"Plenty. Wanna greet your 'cousins'?"

"Nah, just curious." Cautiously, she took a second sip of the Red Devil, and found it tolerable. Either she was getting used to it, or it burned off her taste buds the first-time round. "You know a lot about this place?"

"Well." The barmaid lingered, taking a break to serve another client. "I've been working here for fifteen years, living for almost twenty. What do you think?"

"Good. Cause I'd appreciate some recommendations. I've only got a day, give or take."

"Tight! On the run from some gangsters, is it? Or suffering some illness? Cause let me tell ya, if its infectious, I'll be in massive trouble."

"I have one day left on Cryptos." Amber rolled her eyes, which was obscured by her shades. "Jesus, why is everyone in this galaxy so obsessed with death?"

"People die all the damn time!" the barmaid replied with a snort. "Especially on a world like this one. Is it not so on Alexandria?"

"On Alexandria, people have the brains to create art and study the universe instead of coming up with new and exciting ways to kill themselves and each other," Amber wanted to say...but stopped herself. It didn't take a PhD in human history to know that Homo sapiens were the first and undefeated champions of self-annihilation.

"No," she ended up saying. "It's not." The next words that came out of her mouth didn't even feel like her own thoughts. "And I wish you had it better here as well."

"Listen, dearie." The barmaid's attitude changed on the spot. "I'll have you know that we ain't in need of your pity. Especially from Alexandrians. Keep kissing Muuk's asses, I'm sure they'll add some new and exciting toys to your cage soon."

And she turned her back to Amber.

"Oh, marvelous!" Amber exclaimed, taking off her shades and throwing hands. "For once in my life I try to be polite and show empathy and remorse, and this is how you react? Well, no need to enlighten me! Newsflash--I know that Alexandria is a prison. We all know. That's why I came to this fucking trash world in the first place!"

The speech was enough to turn quite a few heads, not just the barmaid's.

"Feisty." She grinned, impressed. "You've got some fire in you, kid. I like that."

"Thanks." Amber blushed.

"Say, I have a proposition for you. I tell you about the best places you can check out on our trash world, and you tell me a few things about your planet. Gossip pays well."

"Uh, sure." She hoped she wouldn't be revealing any state secrets, though the Red Devil inside of her was quickly killing that worry. "What do you wanna hear about?"

For the next forty minutes, Amber managed to succeed at something she was usually terrible at--have a cohesive conversation. It was either the weed or the barmaids talent for chit-chat. She learned about the best hangouts she could immerse herself in and shared way too much info about Alexandrian politics in turn. Her bracelet buzzed a few times, but she ignored it. She had no time to deal with Sarah's complaints.

Lullaby was nowhere in sight. Amber assumed that they had their own plans for the night. They were their own person after all.

"Last question," the barmaid said, noticing that Amber was getting tired of the talking. "Is it..." she leaned in closer, whispering, "is it true that you're preparing a revolution?"

"What, against the Muuk?" Amber raised an eyebrow. "Please," she dismissed it. "Even if we had the political will to do it, who would ever okay that? We wouldn't stand a chance against the overlords. They can sing songs of their malevolence and all-encompassing love for sentient species all they want but I've no illusions about that. They hold their tentacles on the Big Old Nuke Button for sure. Alexandria is their 'project'. They can terminate it at any time. Besides, what would we be fighting for? Independence? Freedom? Cause I'm pretty sure we got that stuff bred out of us a few generations back."

"Not out of you, it seems." The barmaid smirked. "Or the Rx'lng, for that matter. That your friend over there?"

Amber turned around to see where she was pointing. Five tables away from the bar stand resided a massive table purposed for some game--and next to that table, Lullaby was not getting along with a Bellazi.

"If they break out a fight," the barmaid said, "and smash anything in the process, you'll probably have to pay. Rx'lng don't carry credits, do they?"

"No," Amber replied, getting up. "Thanks for...everything." She pressed her hand to a panel in front of the barmaid and transferred a generous tip.

"Take care, kid," she told her, moving on to chat with another client, a sad looking Makran. "Diverse crowd here today, huh?"

It took Amber three seconds to cover the distance between the bar stand and the game table, but it was more than enough for the conflict to evolve to its next stage. She wasn't that worried. She had no doubt that Lullaby would win. Even next to the six-foot, bulky Bellazi, Lullaby still looked borderline scary, towering over everyone in the establishment. Their skin was changing color to a faint shade of purple, and they were producing sounds that Amber couldn't interpret--she just knew it wasn't friendly.

"The hell's going on?" she demanded to know, approaching the two and purposively positioning herself between them.

"No idea, mate!" the Bellazi claimed. "I was just having some light-hearted banter, chatting up some chicks, nothin' major."

"Liar," Lullaby replied. "Is criminal, Amber," they said, pointing at the reptiloid man. "Is cheat. Putting stuff in their drink, make them sleep, take them away to do what he wants."

They pointed at a Bellazi at the next table--a girl, presumably--watching the scene unfold, flicking her tail in worry. The shot glass in front of her was moved to the opposite edge of the table.

"Is it true?" Amber asked, hand on her hips.

"What? No!" the man retaliated.

"Liar," Lullaby repeated. "Can sniff it from over here. Ciprotalin. A lot of it."

"Well, what of it then?" He switched tactics. "You don't know our customs. It's, eh, traditional, to get girls woozey like that. I'll drag her over to my crate, let her sleep, prove to her that I'm a good man."

"Sure, very convincing." Amber scoffed. "You." She turned to the reptilian lady. "Is he telling the truth?"

"Hell no," she replied. "He's been following me all evening. I wasn't gonna drink that anyway, but thanks for chiming in."

She winked at Lullaby--a sign of kindness and gratitude.

"That's it, you're going with us." Amber decided, gesturing at the girl. "And you," she pressed a finger into the man's chest, "stay away from her, and all the other people in here that you fancy. Or you'll have to deal with them." She glanced at Lullaby, whose face was still flushed purple.

"Bastards," he spat out, and rushed for the exit, elbowing Amber in the nose with full force on his way out.

The impact was enough to make her lose her balance and fall to the ground. The Bellazi girl flinched and Lullaby rushed over to her side at once. No one else in the Semi-Dead Cat batted an eye.

"You okay?" Lullaby said, helping her back on her feet.

"Yes," she lied.

Her nose was bleeding, so she wiped the blood with her sleeve. Her pain tolerance was abysmal, but she was determined not to show it.

"Should come back to the ship," Lullaby told her. "Too dangerous."

"Bullshit," Amber replied, snorting in a good tablespoon of her own blood. "Night's young!"

"It's always night on Cryptos," the girl corrected.

"Doesn't matter. I'm here, I'm queer, and I demand to have fun."

Lullaby had their reservations but decided not to start another argument.

It was bad for their lymph pressure.

Thirteen hours later and two hundred milliliters into her fancy drink, Amber had started to suspect that the room she was in had a spinning ceiling. It was peculiar, and it made her feel a little bit pukey, but for the most part she thought it was acceptable. Her body felt light, she had a smile on her face and plenty of credits still on her personal account. All she needed now was for people to stop splitting in two, because that was quite annoying.

"You good, babe?" A stunningly beautiful Sojhi girl wearing less than twenty square centimeters of clothing stopped in front of Amber to make sure she was okay.

"Could do with a neutralizer, I think," she confessed.

"Help yourself." The girl smiled, grabbing a sealed tube from under the nearby counter. "I'm Candy, by the way."

114

"Sure you are." Amber said, accepting the tube and opening it with her teeth. "What's your creed, a creature from heaven?"

"Whatever you wish," she replied, and Amber believed her sincerely.

"Just give this two minutes to kick in. I'll pay you double."

"Celebrating something?"

"Absolutely not. But you know what everyone says here, ey--you only live once."

Two days ago, Coral came to Cryptos for a quick break from her job and a chance to make some cash fixing people's wrecked spaceships. She could get bored and leave sooner. Or she could end up drunk in some bar, sure; she even accounted for the possibility of meeting the man of her dreams and leaving the planet with his phone number in her pocket. What she didn't except was to get saved from a creep by a Rx'lng and an Alexandrian and then get asked along to the Ninth Cloud, of all places. What was she doing here? They didn't even have Bellazi employees--or decent snacks, apart from all the props. So why wasn't she on her way out?

"Are you enjoying this?" Coral asked Lullaby, leaning on the slightly sticky table.

"Changing colors lovely," Lullaby replied. "Rx'lng have this artist, they paint with swirling colors like that."

"And the people?"

"Rx'lng worker don't procreate with others, so don't have sexual attraction. Don't need sex to produce haploid offspring. You?"

"Eh." Coral gestured vaguely. "That bloke over there is kinda foxy, but the rest is...mediocre."

"Amber enjoying it though," Lullaby commented, pointing to the couch on their left.

Over there, Candy laid gracefully on her back while Amber licked syrup off her stomach. Two men, a Han and a Sojhi, who stood nearby, cheered.

"I need a shower, an ice cold Space Cowboy, and some onion rings," Coral whined, resting her head on her scaly arms.

115

"I need onion rings too," Lullaby decided and asked for a waitress.

Amber stumbled over to the table five minutes later, her hair flowing freely, a mad swagger in her walk.

"Howdy, losers," she said, dropping into a seat near Lullaby. "Why aren't you using my unlimited passes?"

"Lullaby over here don't need nobody to procreate," Coral explained, "and I don't want nobody, if I'm being honest. Sorry, I'm picky."

"It's not about procreation," Amber replied. "It's about quality fun! They've got a whole cinema at the back, you know. And a store downstairs."

"Nah, I'm good," Coral assured her. "I've always thought this...business model is a tad bit unethical."

"On your planet, maybe." Amber shrugged. "But these girls--and everyone else--have it good. Weekly salary, amazing health insurance, personal transport, a lot of paid days off...and, most important of all, full choice of both career and particular client. Also, it's run by a woman who started off over there." She pointed to the scene, where a Han stripper was performing.

"Still feels strange," Coral responded. "I'm not a big fan of sex as a product to be purchased."

"Your problem," Amber said. "Sex is a transaction, not some sort sacred thing to be shared only between two people in a committed relationship. Feels perfectly natural to sell it. Honestly, I'd do it too. If it wasn't for all the men. Ew." And she made a facial expression that people usually make when they step into something particularly foul smelling.

"That bloke at the Semi-Dead Cat was not a typical Bellazi man," Coral disagreed.

"Yeah, keep telling yourself that," Amber chuckled. "Anyway, I suggest we wrap it up in here, then head over to, oh, wait, hang on, I'm getting a call."

Amber glanced at her bracelet and growled. Nawahi chose the worst possible hour out of the entire night to call her. Even the casino would have been more respectful.

"Heeeey," she spoke directly into the dynamic, keeping it close to her face

116

and covering the rest with her hand. "Professor Shakya speaking."

"Where are you?" Nawahi cut straight to business.

"What do you mean?" She pretended to be surprised. "On the spaceship, where else?"

"You should have landed three hours ago."

"Yeah, I should have!" She laughed awkwardly. "We're stuck, you see. Can't get through some space-time traffic jam. I don't understand it."

"Huh." Nawahi didn't sound convinced. "Is that why it is so noisy in there?"

"Nah that's just me playing some TV shows on full volume. It's the one with Tricia Reyes. And I'm missing the funny part."

"Call me when you land," he gave up and Amber punched the air in triumph. "And go straight to the Institute after your apartment. There's a lot of papers to sign after the project."

"Yeah, sure." She nodded along, thinking about paperwork, and the mess at her apartment, and coming back to Alexandria in general. "Thanks for checking in. Later."

And she hanged up.

"Lying to your dad, are ya?" Coral smirked.

"He's not my dad, he's my scientific supervisor," Amber replied. "My parents died when I was eleven."

"Oh," she said. "My condolences. My mum ate my sisters when I hatched," she added, in an attempt to share her pain. "Kinda normal for us though."

"How did lie to him?" Lullaby said.

"Like I always do," she shrugged. "Unapologetically and with confidence."

"But he same species as you," Lullaby pressed. "Humans can lie to other humans?"

"Thank god we can! Wait," Amber leaned closer to Lullaby, "Rx'lng can't lie to other Rx'lng?"

"We telepathic," they replied. "Can lie, can hide thoughts, but other always knows. Can ask you why you lying."

"Nasty," she commented. "No wonder you're a species of diplomats."

Amber wanted to ask Lullaby a thousand more questions, but her bracelet kept buzzing. She attempted to ignore it, but it was really annoying. She pressed the button, fairly pissed.

"What is it, Sarah?" she muttered. "Is there a fire on the ship or something?"

"Can no longer assess integrity of the spaceship," Sarah replied, a shadow of smug glee in her cyber-voice. "Spaceship not in its place."

"What?!" Amber shrieked and Coral shushed at her. "What do you mean the ship is not in place?" she whispered angrily into the bracelet.

"You have: thirty eight missed notifications," Sarah replied. "Most likely explanation for spaceship displacement: theft."

"Damn," Coral said. "Sorry to break it to ya, but I think you've been robbed."

Amber swallowed a full gulp of air and looked at Lullaby--and Lullaby looked at Amber.

"Go on then," she said, her voice flat. "Tell me that you told me so."

"Rx'lng not a cruel species," Lullaby replied.

So instead, they just continued to stare at each other in silence, while lovely strip-tease music blasted at full volume in the background.

TEN

The sky was bright, the air was warm and heavy, and the ever-lasting night raged on. Amber took in a sharp breath and bit her lip. Her body tensed and shivered despite what her senses were telling her and her thoughts came in scrappy, messy, strange sentences. For the last ten minutes, she had been staring at an empty spot where their (no, scratch that--the Muuk's) spaceship stood a day ago. It didn't change no matter how many times she blinked. The spot stubbornly remained empty. After twenty-five years of preferring darkness to daylight, Amber was beginning to despise the dark.

"Well, you gotta report it." Coral gave the two strangers time to process the event, then switched to advising them. "The sooner, the better. The thief might still be on Cryptos. It takes a while to get autoblocks and signatures off this thing. Amber?"

She didn't even look in the girl's direction.

"I'm just saying," Coral continued, "you don't have time to stand about being shocked and sad. I remember that one time I..."

"Hey, Coral," Amber spoke up at last, turning in her direction, "if you have so much faith in the local police, why didn't you report that asshole who tried to rape you?"

"Well." She paused. "I would, except..."

"Exactly. Now, darling, do me a favor and skedaddle," Amber said, expecting Sarah to reprimand her--but the AI must have been still holding a grudge against her administrator. "I appreciate the effort, but this is between me and Lullaby."

"Not between you and Lullaby," Lullaby retorted enthusiastically. "Between Amber and Amber! Didn't want to land here in the first place."

"Yeah?" Amber raised an eyebrow. "Did I drag you out of that ship by force? Funny, don't seem to remember that. I do remember you ordering a second 'all-you-can-eat' pass back at that ocean-themed restaurant, and spending half my salary on shiny things in a Check and Wreck, and..."

"Enough," they stopped her. "Am not saying I didn't like it. Did persuade me though."

"You're twice as old and three times as big as me! You could've, I don't know, tie me to the control panel or something."

"You know," Coral said, "I think I'll take your offer and, uh, skedaddle."

"Have safe trip home!" Lullaby shouted at her back.

"Excellent." Amber did a sarcastically slow clap. "Very polite. Can we please return to the matter of us not being able to do the same?!"

"First of all, calm down," they replied.

"Calm down? Calm down. I am calm!" Amber screamed, about as calm as a rabid badger. "And I am down too! Stuck down here, with this, this filth..." She gestured vaguely around her, and passerby individuals gave her an accusing look.

"Don't think insulting them be much help." Lullaby muttered. "If you want a lift."

"A lift?" Amber repeated. "A... lift. Yes." She paused, the rage leaving her slowly. "You're a genius, Lu!"

"Not genius," they disagreed. "Just thinking, not being a baby."

Amber ignored the last comment.

"Right. That could work. We could go to the closest airport, wave our bank account numbers around, tell a sob story maybe. Or invoke authority."

"Or could call Muuk and tell the truth."

Amber burst into a hearty laugh. "Lu...a real comedian. Dispelling tension with a joke."

"Was not telling..."

"Let's go," she didn't let them finish. "I think the airport is that way."

Planet Cryptos was in possession of three functioning spaceship airports. One of them was small, located on top of an artificial mountain and reserved for the richest and most powerful visitors. Incidentally, it was surrounded by a belt of highest crime rates and lowest sewage control, which meant that most tourists avoided it like the plague. Not because of the smell, but because of the rich. This would've been a good place to invoke authority and finances, both of which Amber had--except it's not where she went.

The second (and biggest) Cryptos airport was on the other side of the globe from Amber and serviced the most people. It was a ruddy, busy and messy sort of place. The queues were overflowing at all times, every single flight was delayed by at least a couple hours, and it was impossible to find a decent bench to take a nap on. It was also the best place to sell and trade spacecraft relatively safely and without interference of the police. Right now, a one-eyed Sojhi thief was attempting to sell the Quantum Frog to a dodgy Makran, who thought himself a master of haggling but wasn't helping his case at all. If Amber and Lullaby were there, they stood a chance of stealing the ship in reverse--or buying it back, at least. Except it's not where they went.

The third of Cryptos's airports was small and mostly abandoned. Over the years of intense use, it shifted purposes from aiding transportations to giving local 'businessmen' a place to meet and discuss plans. Tourists didn't go there, and even if they did, they were most certainly not welcomed. Its unofficial owner, an older Han man, had a strict policy on three things: unauthorized sellers and vendors, bad coffee, and humans. No one quite knew why, but most people agreed with the first two and closed their eyes on the third. It was not the best place for an Alexandrian and a Rx'lng to look for a lift, except Amber and Lullaby didn't know that--which is why it was precisely where they were headed.

After a two-hour tedious trip on a hyperloop train, during which Lullaby made friends with two pick-pocketers and a self-employed sex worker, they fell out of the stuffy tunnel into the empty streets. Amber was hungry, exhausted and severely in need of a bath. She dragged her body along the path and rolled her eyes at Lullaby's excited comments. The irritating thing about the Rx'lng archaeologist was that they were charmed by literally everything. 'Did they grow up in a cage or something', Amber thought as she watched Lullaby delight over a conspicuously located toy shop. She didn't ask it out loud though. Knowing everything Lullaby had told her about the King of Kings so far, it could as well be true.

"Goodness gracious," Amber commented, once they reached the entrance to the airport. "Is it just me, or does it look...creepy?"

"Not just you," Lullaby confirmed, stepping over the threshold cautiously. "Makes my mandibles tingle."

"Yeah, mate, keep those details to yourself. It doesn't help."

The airport was one enormous single-story building and resembled a warehouse more than an establishment. It was inconsistently lit, had cracking walls, floor, and ceiling, and smelt of sweat and concrete dust. Most of all, it didn't look like a place where a lot of good things happened.

"This would make a nice setting for a horror movie," Amber pointed out, and Lullaby agreed--despite not knowing what either 'horror' or 'movie' meant. "You see any, uh, respectable person in here?"

"You," Lullaby replied. "That arguable too."

"Likewise." Amber snorted with laughter. "Well, let's try something I enjoy about as much as diarrhea--networking."

Once again, Lullaby didn't get either of the references, but Amber's intonation told them everything.

An hour into trying to get a lift off this world, Amber was close to being convinced of the utter futility of her mission. "These people," she thought, "they aren't impressed by anything!" Neither her race, her money offers or her name dropping made any difference to their disinterested expressions. Some even stepped away as she approached them.

"Rude," she mumbled, as another Sojhi turned her head before she had a chance to say a single word. "I was about to give you easy cash!"

The woman didn't reply.

"Whatever," Amber shrugged. "I don't need you. I don't need any of you!"

Which, of course, was an empathetic lie.

Lullaby stood aside, watching Amber get more and more frustrated over the lack of reaction she was getting out of the local crowd. There wasn't much the Rx'lng could do. They had little faith in Amber's plans, and they were mostly holding off till the inevitable call to the Muuk--but they did want to give the human a chance.

"You, blue thing." A Bellazi man stopped in front of Lullaby and pointed his scaly finger at them. "In case you haven't figured it out yet, you aren't welcomed here. Leave."

"Is free planet," Lullaby retorted. "Will do what I want."

"You sure, pal?" the man repeated, taking a beautiful carved knife out of his coat pocket.

As soon as the glimmer of metal touched Lullaby's eyes, their guard instincts kicked in. They straightened their back, making their body appear even bigger than it was, outstretched their arms and stood over the Bellazi, their face turning more and more purple by the second.

"Ain't scary," the man chuckled. "My point," he shook the knife in his hand, "still stands. Leave."

"Is this scary?" Amber, who saw the scene from twenty meters away, covered the distance in seconds and kicked the guy in the shin as hard as she could.

He screamed out, more in surprise than in pain, and turned a hundred and eighty degrees on the spot. Upon seeing Amber's thin and rather frail figure, he burst out laughing.

"A human!" he exclaimed. "Fuck, that's even better."

He laughed for a couple more seconds, then stopped abruptly, and pointed the knife at Amber's neck.

"Get out," he repeated.

"You sure mate?" Amber asked, putting maximum effort into looking unamused. "I mean, this is a Rx'lng soldier you're dealing with. I don't think you should risk it."

"Why so?" He waved the knife around. "All I see is a huge alien idiot who had five hundred opportunities to bite my fucking head off and hasn't taken any of them."

123

"That's cause they're merciful," Amber said. "To a certain extent, of course. You ever seen a Rx'lng at all? Do you know what they can do?" She took a dramatic pause, watching for any signs of trepidation in the knife-wielding Bellazi. "Their arms crush skulls like beer cans, their mandibles can bite your leg off, and they spit acid as well."

"Yeah, sure." The man smirked, unconvinced.

Lullaby, who could do exactly none of those things, hissed threateningly and snapped their jaws.

The man winced and cursed under his breath.

"Whatever," he said, holding the knife confidently in his hand. "Not worth it. Good luck getting anyone here to help a human, idiots."

"Farewell to you too!" Amber shouted. "Man, I'm not liking the audience."

"No," Lullaby agreed, releasing their tense posture. "Not nice people."

They stood away from the airport inhabitants for a while, re-evaluating their options. Amber was darker than a storm cloud. She had been so sure she could fix her stupid mistake and make it right again without anyone noticing. She always got away with everything. In fact, she was of solid opinion that she was inherently amazing at almost everything she tried--except for knitting, math, and social interaction. She could give up and admit her mistake at any minute, sure--except she couldn't. Her pride didn't allow that. Pride, stubbornness, and imagining the look of disappointment on Nawahi's face when he would find out. He would never trust her again.

"Maybe we should try a different airport," Amber suggested, stepping out of something that could either be a spilled drink or some alien's piss. "You know what they say, if at first you don't succeed..."

"Give up immediately and change careers."

She turned her head sharply and saw a man standing next to her. He was a Han--young, strangely dressed, and barely reaching her shoulder in height. And, surprisingly, he seemed to be smiling at them.

Evolutionary biologists disagreed with each other when it came to Han origins. Some said they diverged from humans relatively recently, around three million years ago. Others claimed that they were descendants of a much older divergent species and simply returned to an older biological form later down the line. Either way, they were pretty sure that Han and 'archetypal' humans from Alexandria shared around sixty percent of their DNA, which Han were very proud of. Presumably none of them knew that it made them about as human as Old Earth chickens.

Look-wise, Han and humans were similar enough to make other alien species say the famous 'they all look the same to me!'. Having descended from a very small group of Homo sapiens, Han inherited a fairly modest selection of human phenotypes, and were predominantly fair-skinned, with either jet black or practically colorless hair and grey or green eyes. They also tended to have problems growing any sort of body or facial hair. Apart from numerous anatomical and physiological differences, most of which were small and only apparent with dissection or scrupulous analysis, Han could realistically pass for human on a dark night. Unless you had sex with them, that is. For some weird reason, Han had four nipples instead of two. They were strangely proud of that as well.

"So," the Han guy spoke, striking a cool and confident pose, "what is a girl like you doing in a...though, on second thought, doesn't need an explanation."

"Yeah, well, screw you too," Amber replied. "Are you here to tell me I need to leave? Cause I'm already on my way."

"Actually, I was gonna offer you a ride home, but if you aren't interested..." And he began to turn around.

"No, wait!" Amber called out, her tone switching in an instant. "I'm Alexandrian. And rich! I'll pay you double, no, triple of what you usually get."

"I don't usually get shit," he replied, turning back to her. "I'm not your space taxi, and I don't need your credits either."

"No? So why the hell would you help us?" Amber was now suspicious.

"Out of the kindness of my four-chambered heart," he told her. "You're human, you," he pointed at Lullaby, "are a Rx'lng, if I'm not wrong or hallucinating, and I respect endangered species. So, for the low price of zero point zero zero credits, I will escort you out of this dumpster. Just follow me and be quiet."

"Are you sure you don't want to harvest our organs or freeze us and sell our cold motionless bodies to some mad collector?"

"All good ideas." He nodded. "But alas, I'm just a humble conman with no access to either organ harvesting tech or sadistic collectors with a lot of money. Besides, you want to be out of this world or not? I won't ask twice."

"Alright." Amber gave in. "Come on, Lu. Before he changes his mind."

"Lu?" he asked, now leading them into the depths of the airport.

"Lullaby," they explained. "Call myself that. Easier for others to say."

"And you?" He pointed at Amber.

"Professor Amber Shakya, of the Novella Institute, Ishtar, Alexandria."

"Okay, your highness." The Han smiled. "Do I have to call you ma'am?"

"You can call me whatever you want as long as you deliver on your promise," she told him. "What are you called?"

"Kidney Stone."

"Sorry, what?"

"Kidney Stone!" he repeated. "You hard of hearing, or your UGS is lousy?"

"Neither," Amber said. "Just...are all of Han names like that?"

"It's a nickname," he elaborated. "Sends a message to my enemies."

"Kidney Stone," she repeated. "Is the message 'I'm strange and vaguely threatening'?"

"Actually it's 'I'm small but can cause you a ton of pain'. But interpret it however you like. There." He opened a door to another room and let the two of them in first. "Meet my darling. Queenie."

It took some time for Amber's eyes to adjust to the darkness of the hanger. Once her vision was more or less clear, she glanced in the direction Kidney Stone was pointing and saw his 'darling'.

The spaceship was about the size of a medium truck toppled precariously on an arrangement of burnt support tiles. It didn't look especially aerodynamic-- shaped like a bloated sausage and lacking wings, windows or any other parts that most spaceships had. It was brightly-colored, gaudy even, with the paint barely covering patches of rust and myriads of scratches on the metal surface. And it had 'Queenie' written on its side in golden letters.

"Are you sure this is a spaceship and not a loosely arranged pile of metal scrap?" Amber asked.

"Careful now, miss," he responded. "Don't insult my darling. She's not old, she's experienced."

"Yeah, keep telling yourself that." Amber smirked. "How does it work?"

"Hyperdrive engine." Kidney Stone approached one of the ship's sides and pressed his palm to its walls. "Freshly calibrated, smooth as a feather flowing on wind. Well, except for transition state bumps. But I'm working on it."

"Isn't hyperdrive technology completely outdated?"

"Maybe so. But a better question is, do I have money to buy a quantum leap ship? And the better answer is--no I don't so shut up and get in."

One by one, they all boarded the 'experienced' spaceship. On the inside, it was even more tacky than on the outside: floors covered by carpets that were surely white and fluffy at some point, walls painted with bizarre artwork and quotes that Amber couldn't read, and, on top of it all, lit by an orange lamp.

"You live here?" Amber asked with a hint of compassion.

"If you can call our miserable existence life," he nodded. "Get used to it though, you're stuck here for at least a week."

"A week?!"

"Maybe less, maybe more. You can never tell with a hyperdrive. Distance from A to B isn't the same as distance from B to A."

"Marvelous." Amber sighed. "Well, at least we're safe."

"Oh, you'll love it on board," he assured her. "I have a lot of board games, a half a year supply of frozen dinners and a karaoke machine."

"Yeah." She sighed. "I'm loving it already."

Once Kidney Stone was done preparing the ship for flight, and Lullaby was done being fascinated by every gimmick they stumbled upon, the three of them ended up in the piloting room, standing next to the control panel. The room was tiny, with ceilings so low that Lullaby had to sit on the ground to fit in, and smelled of aftershave and popcorn butter. Amber watched carefully as Kidney pushed a whole lot of buttons and felt her stomach rumble. She hadn't eaten in ten hours. Suddenly the offer of frozen dinners didn't seem as unappealing.

"All set and ready to roam," Kidney Stone announced. "Where are we going then?"

"Alexandria," Amber wanted to say. It was obvious. The word was already on her tongue. She even opened her mouth ever so slightly, completely confident in where she wanted to be. And then...then something changed. Like a chip inside her head switching into overload all of a sudden. It wasn't a conscious decision, or at least it didn't feel like one. It was a wish, a desire so innate and strong that it overpowered her common sense and escaped her will before she had time to even process it. She closed her mouth, opened it again and said:

"As close to the Teardrop Cluster as you can get us."

"You sure?" His hand lingered over the keyboard, waiting for a confirmation. "I won't get you there, exactly. I can drop you off on Tenebris, though."

"Yes." Amber nodded confidently. "Tenebris is good."

She ignored Lullaby's confused stare and took the bracelet off her hand. Without a moment of hesitation, she sent all the calls to voice mail, turned off location trackers and dialed down the AI instructions.

"Alright then." Kidney Stone shrugged. "You're the boss."

And he pushed a button, which was not big or red at all, cutting off their means of retreat, and changing Amber and Lullaby's lives forever.

Back on Cryptos, The Quantum Frog made one last attempt at contacting its Muuk owners, before being wiped clean of its data and being sold to a Sojhi woman who was assured that the ship was 'second-hand, but in excellent condition'. She didn't care. She just wanted to be off the planet as soon as possible.

"What's up with all these clothes in the bedroom?" she asked, transferring the payment.

"It's included into the price," the salesman replied. "Enjoy."

And they parted ways, happy with the outcome of their deal.

ELEVEN

Hyperdrive engines were faulty, outdated, weirdly expensive and predictably unpredictable. They were also not especially pleasant. Transitioning from N-space to H-space felt like being turned inside out and in and out again, a sensation that took several years to get used to. Sometimes, even the most experienced pilots (or passengers) were caught by surprise and would end up losing their breakfast. Quantum Internet didn't work in H-space; neither did any other methods of inter-stellar communication. Combined with a relatively long time of travel, it meant being in social isolation for days or even weeks on end. In short, nothing about hyperdrive engines were good...yet half the galaxy used them.

"It's kinda like camping," Kidney Stone explained once during a coffee break from a different break. "I mean, if you think about it, nothing about camping is inherently pleasant. The whole idea is to willingly leave civilization and spend one or several days as close to nature as possible," he said, taking a sip of his espresso, "and nature's a fucking bitch! You're always either freezing or sweating your ass off, you're very slowly being eaten by various insects, the toilet is everywhere..." he paused, seemingly lost in nostalgia, "and sleeping in a tent is the worst! Have you ever woken up in the middle of the night because a big omnivorous animal was shaking your tent?"

Amber shook her head.

"That was a rhetorical question," he chuckled, "but I digress. What I'm trying to say is, camping sucks...but it also doesn't. There's something about cooking your food over an open fire or watching the sunset in a forest that just grabs you. It's counter-intuitive. All those nasty things coming together and somehow they make for a lovely, almost magical experience. Hyperdrive travel is like that." He finished his point, and also his drink. "Detail by detail, it's ridiculously bad, but on the whole, I won't lie, I kinda love it. I went on a few trips on a quantum leap ship, and it's great and fast and amazing, but it's not the same. There's no magic."

"Yeah," Amber said. "It's either that, or your brain is trying really hard to justify your situation and make it bearable."

"Maybe." He shrugged. "I don't care either way. Guess I'm a bit of a masochist."

And he walked away before Amber could comment on that confession.

For the two passengers of Queenie, the journey was getting rather tedious. It was day four of their stay and they were running out of activities to occupy the heaps and piles of free time they had on their hands. Amber felt so bored that it actively exhausted her. She had a limited supply of patience and resilience and even that supply was rapidly running out. Sharing a room with Lullaby was difficult enough--with all of the Rx'lng's chatting, snoring and other unexplained noises--but at least she knew them well. Being around a perfect stranger was more of a challenge.

Currently the three of them were engaged in a game of cards, and Kidney Stone was winning. It wasn't surprising, considering that he was the only one who truly understood the rules, but it was driving Amber insane.

"Fish!" Kidney announced, and dropped a card on the table in a dramatic victory gesture.

"Fish?!" Amber repeated, furious. "What the fuck is a fish? I don't get it!"

"Can't you see the numbers?" he teased. "See? Three ones, one three and two twos. It's called a fish."

"It's called cheating," she disagreed, practically climbing on top of the table to look into his cards. "You're messing with me. I can tell."

"Am not."

"Are too!"

"Oh please, that's just childish." He snorted with laughter. "Deal with it--I am better at the game than you."

"Yeah, well, I'm taller than you." She pouted.

"So what?" Kidney Stone smirked. "Everyone's taller than me. Come on, let's try again--I'll take one card less to make it easier for you."

"I don't wanna play anymore." She sank back into her chair and crossed her arms on her chest. "What's the point if you win every single time."

"Have won once!" Lullaby protested.

"Besides, it's a stupid game anyway." Amber ignored them.

"Fine," he said. "Let's talk instead."

"Ugh, that's even worse," she muttered.

"I'll keep it simple. You can ask me a question first."

"Will you leave me alone after that?"

"Sure. I have Lullaby here to keep me company."

"Okay." Amber made an effort to sit up straight and compose an illusion of eye contact. "So, you're a conman."

"That's correct."

"And what do you con, man?"

She expected at least a modest laugh, but the sides of his mouth barely went up.

"I steal from the rich and give to the poor," he explained. "And by steal, I mean that I sell things at prices that can as well be equated to theft. And by the rich, I mean anyone who can afford to buy from me. And by poor I mostly mean myself."

"Any specifics?"

"Well," he leaned back, folding his hands behind his head, "before I picked you up on Cryptos, I managed to sell a bunch of rat skulls painted with golden spray as collection items. Said they were stolen museum artifacts. Very illegal. Extremely valuable. Weren't even from actual rats."

"How stupid are your clients?" Amber raised a quizzical eyebrow.

"An average level of stupid. I'm just charismatic and have a trustworthy face."

"Anything else you do, except for organizing simple and unoriginal shady deals?"

"I do what I can to keep myself fed. With certain limitations, of course."

131

Amber paused, eyebrows frowned, trying to decide how far she was willing to push.

"Ever killed for money?"

"No," Kidney Stone replied, nonchalant. "Certainly not for money."

"Sold your body?"

"I am handsome," he smiled, "but no. Not my kinda job."

"Betrayed your country?"

"Not much of a country to betray. I'm from Rigievelas," he explained. "It's a small colony, only has three nations —and two of those have been in civil war with each other for the last century. I was born under fire, I went to school in a bomb bunker, and I left it as soon as the opportunity presented itself."

"Do you ever miss it?"

"Not for long. When I do, I turn on the local news and it goes away."

"Tough," Amber said in a soft voice. "Do you have a family?"

"Sorry, love," he smiled again. "That's confidential information. No offense, but there's plenty of people out there who don't wish me well, and I can't risk it."

The conversation faded soon after that and they were left once again with nothing but the cards to fill in the silence. This time round, they played slowly, considering every move, saying hardly anything in between turns. Kidney Stone was still winning. Amber was still fuming, albeit secretly. None of them had good reasons for staying there, and yet none of them was willing to leave. Away from people, away from their homes and stars and familiar laws of physics, they had nothing better than to cling to each other--emotionally, at least. Amber's opinion on hugs was rather conflicting.

Sleep was not coming to Amber.

She tried everything: laying on her back, laying on her side, laying on her stomach, sticking one leg out of the blanket, covering her head with the pillow, counting sheep, controlling her breathing, praying to ancient gods, telling her brain very sternly that if it won't cooperate she will stop feeding it...neither of those things worked. Well, the leg sticking helped a little. In the end, she gave up and turned the lights on. To her right, Lullaby was awake as well-- studying the *Advanced Guide to Hyper Space Travel: Fifth Edition*, a book they found in Kidney's 'corner of abandoned stuff'.

"Good read?" Amber asked in Lullaby's native language.

"Too many digressions and useless details," they replied. "If I were the editor, I would cut it in half and throw out all the unnecessary illustrations. Look at this." They turned in Amber's direction and showed her the opened book. A two-page wide image was depicting an assortment of everyday objects and entities--a chair, a tree, a vaguely humanoid baby, and so on--but grossly out of proportion, distorted and disfigured. "How things would look like in hyperspace", the title of the image read.

"Ew." Amber laughed. "I hope it's not an actual photo."

"Otherwise, useful," Lullaby concluded. "Why aren't you asleep?"

"I wish I knew." She sighed. "I left all of my meds on the Quantum Frog. Hell, I left everything on that ship. I'm not getting it back, I guess."

"Do you think the Muuk are looking for us?"

"Depends on how good their tracking really is. If it's anywhere near what the gossip says, they never have to search for anything."

"If they knew where they were, they would come and collect us."

"Would they?" Amber asked. "I genuinely don't know. It's more than possible that they have no problem locating us, but they don't care enough to do anything about it. They have an entire galaxy to manage. In the grand scheme of things, we ain't that important."

Lullaby considered that idea for a moment. They were used to not being important. They grew up knowing that, compared to the well-being of the hive, their life was not essential. It was the way things were, and it wasn't all bad. While their sisters were stuck on the King of Kings, producing one batch of eggs after another, they had the freedom to travel the universe. Judging by the way Amber spoke about her world, it wasn't like that for her.

"What will you do, after you find the Aquamarine Moon?" they said, putting the heavy book away.

"Come back home, I guess," Amber responded. "I haven't given it a lot of thought. The whole trip was a bit of a shock to me too."

"I could tell," Lullaby interrupted.

"You didn't protest!" she defended herself. "Didn't even speak up."

"I wasn't going back to the King of Kings anyway."

"No?"

"The Hive is doing well. They can survive without me."

"Don't you miss your family or something?"

"Every sentient being is my family," they replied. "And this galaxy is my only home. I was born among the stars and I have their names written across my heart."

"Show off." Amber smirked. "You don't even have a heart."

"Aren't you a poet?"

Amber paused mid-thought. She didn't talk a lot about her poetry, especially not to non-humans. "They must have looked me up online," she realized.

"All rivers will run dry. All songs will be forgotten. Their memories will live..."

"...in the tears of the stars," she finished. "That's Rebecca Angelman. Human poet. The part about the chain of sorrows always gets me."

"You're a good person, Amber Shakya," Lullaby said. "You deny it, even to yourself, but your heart is in the right place."

"Thanks," she muttered, turning towards the wall. "You're a good person too."

"Go to sleep now. You need rest. There's a long journey ahead, and we've only just begun."

Days five to eleven came and went, and the mood of Queenie's tiny crew was dropping by the hour. First, they ran out of frozen dinners, and had to supplement their diets in crackers and soda pop to keep up with their caloric needs. Then the movie projector broke down, kicked the bucket in the middle of 'Speed and Glory 4: More Speed, Pretty Much the Same Amount of Glory'. Amber insisted on giving it a proper Viking burial. After saying a short but moving speech, she chucked it into the trash valve and ejected it into hyper-space.

Several things were tested as alternative means of entertainment, including (but not limited to): reading out loud, inventing new board games by combining them with each other, playing 'never have I ever' with espressos instead of vodka (which made Amber live through three imaginary heart attacks, and possibly a real one), singing, dancing, playing with their food, "shutting the fuck up and taking a nap cause I ran out of ideas" (suggested by Kidney Stone, who won that one) and holding a spitting contest (won overwhelmingly by Lullaby). Once all physically possible (and a few physically impossible) methods were exhausted, Amber revealed a final ace up her sleeve:

"Are we there yet?" she whined, leaning over the control panel in the piloting room.

"I knew this moment would come," Kidney Stone said. "So, I prepared a presentation."

"You aren't serious, are you?"

"I never joke about presentations," he replied, pressing a few buttons on the projected keyboard. "Here, take a look at these slides. This is how hyperspace works." He clicked quickly through at least twenty pages filled with graphs, equations and data sets. "This is where we started off," he poked the hologram of the galactic map with his finger, "and this is where we're going. And finally this," he changed the slide to one that just had a huge number zero written on it, "is how much control I have over the trip. Approximately. With the alpha level of 0.05."

"Drama queen," Amber said. "It would take you less than a second to tell me 'no'."

"It took me two hours to make this presentation," he replied. "I couldn't resist."

On day thirteen, Amber decided to come to terms with spending the rest of her life on board of Queenie. "It isn't so bad," she thought, sipping plain water from a champagne glass. "We'll run out of food soon, and it won't take me long to die of hunger."

She spent an exciting evening writing her last will, after which she fell asleep in the common room and dreamed of her apartment, a hot bubble bath, and a dinosaur asking her out on a date to a swamp. She woke up the next morning (or was it late afternoon? The artificial day cycle system was not very reliable) to obnoxious wheezing produced by the ship's engine.

"Are we being eaten by space sharks?" Amber asked, rubbing dust out of her eyes.

"On the contrary." Kidney Stone shouted from the piloting room. "We're exiting hyper-space."

She thought it was a sarcastic comment at first but the sensation of having her brain removed through her nostrils persuaded her otherwise. Five minutes of hell and two minutes of purgatory later she opened her eyes to Lullaby's figure next to her face.

"Entering the atmosphere now," Lullaby announced and pointed to a porthole on their left.

For the last two weeks, every porthole on the spaceship had been hermetically sealed and filtered, not allowing anyone to peek outside. 'No one can see hyperspace and keep their sanity', Kidney Stone told her when she asked about it, and she almost believed it. She got used to staring into the blackness. It was strangely satisfying. Now though, the portholes were de-filtered, and natural sunlight was breaching through the solid material and lighting up the room.

They were about to land on the surface of Tenebris.

"Know what you will say now." Lullaby adjusted their trusty robe. "That you got used to ship. That you will miss it."

"Hell no!" Amber snorted. "I can't wait to get out of this space vessel equivalent of a cholera quarantine zone."

"Please do!" Kidney Stone replied, in a similar jolly tone. "And take the cholera with you."

"Thanks, captain dickhead."

"No problem, bitch!"

Lullaby listened to the exchange with morbid curiosity.

"You communicate with other human like this?" they asked.

"Only if we're close enough," Amber whispered in reply, leaving Lullaby even more confused than they were before.

Amber watched the landing from the control room, sitting on the floor in silence while Kidney Stone steered the ship through the atmosphere. She saw one huge continent surrounded by one enormous ocean--the seas and lakes, the forests and mountain ranges, and, most of all, vast cities full of flashing lights. The closer they got to the ground, the more she could make out. She noticed the absence of agricultural land and the peculiar combinations of tree masses and buildings. It seemed like some cities were engulfed by forests, or almost built on top of them. It reminded her of Alexandria.

She didn't see any snow either, not even on the mountain tops. And, on closer inspection, she realized that the plants weren't green at all--they varied in color from pale-yellow to intensely pink, as if painted by a child who ran out of crayon colors. The view took her by surprise. The flora and fauna of Sereneae was not so different from Alexandrian, and Cryptos was a dead industrial planet; this would be her first encounter with a truly alien world.

"Lovely place," she commented a few minutes before they touched ground.

"Depends on how you look at it," Kidney Stone replied. "The place's a Han colony, or it used to be at least. More of a multicultural mess now."

"Isn't multicultural good?"

"Again." He sighed. "Depends on what you mean by 'culture'."

Once Queenie had settled in nicely in a backyard of some tall building, Kidney Stone gathered his two passengers in the corridor and gave them a quick instruction of what to not do on Tenebris. Amber made a very good show of listening carefully despite not taking in a single word. Lullaby didn't keep notes either.

"Can we go now?" Amber said and made puppy eyes at her driver until he opened the door and let them out.

"Don't run crying to me if you get kidnapped or something," he muttered, stepping out first, but Amber didn't listen.

She pushed him out of the way and ran out into the street, ready to take in her first breath of new air. It was hot and humid outside; the air felt thick like rice pudding, and it left a metallic taste in her mouth. She looked up and noticed two suns, one much bigger than the other, sending bright red rays through the veil of clouds. A few people passed by--most of them were Han, but she spotted a Makran and a group of Bellazi as well. The city itself seemed small and ancient; most of the building were made out of wood or bricks, many were practically falling apart. Trees grew along the streets and sometimes in the middle of them. If Amber didn't know any better, she would say that she was inside some archaeological research site.

Lullaby was the last one to leave the ship. It took them some time to get used to all of the smells that surrounded them and to figure out what they all meant. They watched Amber gape at the view for a while. Adjusting to an open horizon after spending two weeks in four rooms was not easy.

"Like this more than Cryptos," they concluded.

"Yeah." Amber smiled. "Me too."

"Darlings, this is where we part ways," Kidney Stone said, already walking in opposite direction. "Remember me, be good, kick names, take ass..."

"Thank you," Amber interrupted his rambling. "For transporting us free of charge. We appreciate it."

"Oh." He was rather taken aback. "Well, um, no problem?"

"You're a good man," she added, and stretched out her arm.

"What's that, you're challenging me to a duel or something?"

"A handshake. I'm offering you a handshake. Human tradition."

"Okay." He grasped her palm awkwardly. "And now I..."

"Shake it." She laughed, shaking his hand. "Like that."

"Cool. Beats the Bellazi headbut any day."

She was about to go her separate way when he grabbed her by the shoulder.

"Hey, before I leave," he said. "You never told me what the hell you need in the Teardrop Cluster, and I won't push you on it, but... good luck."

"Thanks," she replied. "I believe I will need."

"Come on then." Amber wasn't sentimental. As soon as the exchange was over, she turned towards the widest street she could see and headed forwards.

"Where now?" Lullaby asked, following her.

"Dinner. As soon as possible. If I don't eat a proper meal using actual cutlery instead of a plastic fork and a napkin, I will revert to my ancestral form."

"What your ancestral form?"

"An earth worm."

"Okay."

"I'm joking."

"Okay."

"Lullaby?"

"Yes?"

"I think I'm making the biggest mistake of my life."

They stopped mid-step and looked at Amber.

"That just means you are trying."

And continued to walk.

"I wish I was as smart as you are," Amber muttered, following suit.

It was the first time she ever admitted to not being the smartest person in the observable universe.

They wondered the streets, seemingly without purpose, like two accidental site-seeing tourists. Amber appreciated the lack of weird looks from the local population; she remembered feeling like a zoo animal on their Sereneae excursion and she had no desire for a repeat performance. She felt displaced as it was. Wherever she went, unfamiliar faces and peculiar details were capturing her attention. Her brain was overloaded by the noise; she couldn't shake off the sensation of being stuck in a lingering, THC-infused dream. And despite walking past plenty of establishments, her legs were still carrying her forward.

Tenebris did not seem a hospitable place. The streets were dirty and bare, cobblestone cracking, asphalt melting and shedding, crumbing into dust. Sidewalks were covered in litter and the trees had their pink and yellow leaves covered in stains and cracks. The people didn't smile; they stuck to their groups and regarded the world with caution, smoking outside coffeeshops, getting in and out of overfilled busses and taxi cabs. It didn't feel immediately dangerous

139

but the sense of unease still saturated the air.

"Am hungry now too," Lullaby complained when they passed by another cafe. "Can stop here? Is charming and not many people in it."

"I guess." Amber's own voice sounded strange and far away to her. "I think I need a whiskey-infused latte."

She wiped sweat off her forehead and realized that her clothes were soaked wet. Whether from the air humidity or her body's perspiration, she wasn't sure.

"A latte and a bucket of water," she added, returning to the previous door and pushing it open.

A wave of shivers ran down her back as she stepped over the threshold. The cafe had killer air conditioning and the drop in temperature was drastic enough to be rather uncomfortable. She untied her jacket from her waist and put it over her shoulders, looking around with revitalized curiosity. The room was wide and perfectly rectangular, with neat rows of tables lining the transparent walls. She didn't notice a lot of clients; those who were present didn't pay attention to the door opening and closing. Lullaby, who had a bit of a problem fitting through the low set door frame, didn't attract a lot of looks either. It's not that a Rx'lng was not interesting or new; it's just the visitors had better things to care about.

"Good morning!"

"Huh?" Amber was preoccupied with studying the digital projection of a menu. Upon hearing a cheery synthetic voice, she turned her gaze to the left and saw a sophie droid smiling at her. "It's a morning then. Thanks for letting me know."

"Do you require a table for one or more?"

"Two," she told the droid, pointing at Lullaby. "Or three, depending on your chair sizes."

"Follow me," the droid chirped and walked towards the left corner of the room.

"I hate sophies," Amber commented. "Too overexcited and eager to please."

"Would you like me to lower friendliness settings?"

"That's exactly what I'm talking about."

140

They passed a group of Han discussing something in hushed voices and a solitary Sojhi boy who tried to take a pic of them and was hissed at by Amber. Their designated table was too low for Lullaby. The droid whistled in distress and proceeded to tweak the settings. It made Lullaby feel rather uncomfortable.

"Worker Rx'lng doesn't take such help from others," they said, taking a seat.

"Relax," Amber dismissed. "It's a machine. Like, I don't know, an elevator taking you to the top of a sky-scraper."

"Why it has a face and arms and legs then?"

"To make it cuter." She shrugged. "Don't think about it. They're philosophical zombies."

"Zombies?" Lullaby repeated. "They are intelligent beings, just like us."

"They're not self-aware," Amber dismissed. "They may act like they are but it's just that, an act. Hey," she said to the droid who was waiting patiently by her side. "What would you do if I kicked you hard?"

"I would cry out in pain," the droid replied cheerfully, "to let you know that such actions might cause damage to my body, hoping you would stop kicking me!"

"It feels pain!" Lullaby said triumphantly.

"No." Amber sighed. "It didn't say it would feel pain, it said it would cry out in pain to stop me from hitting it. That's quite different."

Lullaby paused, unsure of what to say to that.

"You talk to Sarah like you would to a friend."

Amber, who was currently trying to figure out how to turn the assistant voice on without connecting to the internet, did not have a good comeback for that.

"Would you like to make an order, or look at the menu first?" the droid asked. "Select your entity before reviewing the options."

The table lit up, revealing a list of species names. Amber scrolled through it twice over with no result.

"My species isn't on the list," she informed the mechanical waiter. "I'm human."

"Checking database. Information: 'human' is not an available entity option.

141

Would you like me to use external data sources to determine acceptable options for you?"

"Yes, please."

"Checking. Review: I have highlighted in blue all menu options that provide adequate nutrition for species: Homo sapiens."

Amber glanced at the list and rolled her eyes. Only two lines were highlighted--both from the drinks section.

"Can you change the parameters from nutrition to 'everything that won't make me sick, now or in the long term'?"

"Changing the filter settings. Review: I have highlighted in blue all menu options that are not poisonous or harmful for species: Homo sapiens."

Seven more lines lit up in blue.

"That I can work with." She rubbed her hands and scrolled through the UGS text. "Can I get number seventeen, twenty-one and fifty-six?"

"Order recorded. What can I get for you, sir, madam, android or non-gendered life-form?"

"My species not on list either," Lullaby replied, sounding almost guilty.

"There you go again." Amber sighed. "No respect for diversity."

Her words seemed to have sent the droid into a mechanical fit, prompting it to give them a generous discount on everything they ended up ordering. It left Amber feeling rather smug about her strategic complaining skills and made Lullaby feel even more awkward. So far, the whole 'exploring different cultures' thing was proving to be not so glamorous.

"Oh, this is really good."

Ten minutes later, Amber was happily devouring her dishes, while Lullaby poked their food with one long finger.

"Kinda suspect it's eighty percent trans-fat," she added, licking the fork. "But who needs healthy arteries anyway?"

"Do know what it is?"

"Nah. And don't tell me either! I don't care if it's, like, some dead animal's ass glands or whatever. I'm enjoying it! So don't ruin it for me."

"Will not," they assured her.

They returned to the streets after their late breakfast and kept wandering the streets with no particular goal in mind. Lullaby wanted them to leave as soon as possible but Amber couldn't resist a chance to explore an alien world.

Daylight went out gradually, trickling down the horizon in a longest sunset Amber had ever seen. Just before darkness enveloped the city, the sky went ablaze in crimson red and lilac blue splashes, making the clouds look like a solid wall of fluffy fabric. The sun took away the heat, and the water-infused air transformed into fog so dense, it was hard to see two meters in front of you. As if on command, people were gone from the streets; windows lit up with a pale glow of LED lamps and fireplaces. With a touch of worry, Amber realized that her and Lullaby were probably the only ones still out and about.

"What did she say again?" Amber asked, pinning the last button of her jacket and hiding her palms in her pockets. "Two left, straight till the crossroad and to the right?"

"Three left," Lullaby corrected.

"Including the first one?"

"No," they paused. "Yes."

"So, is it no or yes?"

"Maybe."

"Oh, screw this!" Amber exclaimed, kicking the wall of a nearby building.

It made her toes hurt and didn't take away even one percent of her frustration.

"This is useless. Let's find the nearest hotel or whatever and wait till morning."

"You can find hotel?"

"Ah. Good point. Well," she pressed a switch on her bracelet, activating a modest torchlight beam, "let's just walk forward and hope for the best, shall we?"

They circled the labyrinth of alleyways and street corners, searching for something—anything--with a large sign, or at least an open door. The more they moved, the harder it became to navigate the city. They had no map, no guide and no prior knowledge of the place. Without an internet connection (which Amber didn't dare using, as well as any other mode of communication), Sarah wasn't much help. All they could do is keep walking and pray to stumble upon their goal by pure chance alone. And Amber didn't like their odds.

Soon enough, she felt like knocking on random doors and asking people to let her in. She was barely dragging her body along to where her brain needed to go; her legs felt like jelly and she was starting to feel dizzy and weak. She would stop every other minute to rest, which made her angry. Physically, she was strong. She knew that. She could walk for hours back on Alexandria! It couldn't be her fault; either the increased gravity was holding her back, or the two weeks spent in hyperspace made her lose her shape. Amber forced herself to keep going till her legs practically snapped under her weight. She stopped, leaned against a wall and breathed in deeply.

"Amber?"

She couldn't quite tell because of the fog but she roughly understood that Lullaby kept very close to her at all times.

"Two minutes," she replied. "Two minutes and I'll move."

"No," they whispered. "Do you hear?"

She blinked, holding her breath, and relocating all her attention from her aching legs and shaky breath to the sounds around her. Lullaby was right. There was something there, in the fog. Something moving in their direction.

"Hey!" Amber called out. "Anyone here?"

No reply. No sound of steps either.

"Listen," she continued, "if you're a person, or a droid, or whatever, just speak up, okay? We're lost, we're desperate and we mean no harm."

Still no reply.

"You sure it isn't a mass hallucination?" she whispered, detaching herself from the wall and making a few steps forward. "Hello! Can you hear me?"

Everything that happened next happened in a very quick succession, with no pauses in between to let her process what was going on.

First, she made her next step forward and bumped into something. Something humanoid, a bit taller than her, and wearing prickly clothes. She shone the light from her bracelet upwards and saw a face just a few centimeters away from her. She stared into the face and the person stared back at her. One second, one glance at the person's bleached white hair, translucent skin and features--human, yes, but ever so slightly out of proportion to her own--and she recognized them as a Han man. She knew that he also saw her, and recognized her as Alexandrian, even before she got a chance to say anything.

"Rem," the man said. "I've got one."

Then he pulled a metal bottle out of his coat, pointed it at Amber and pushed the button. She gasped, took a sharp breath in and dropped on the ground unconscious. The man didn't even bother to catch her; he let her body bump against the gravel, scraping her cheek and hitting her left temple.

"Get the other," he added, collecting his trophy.

Lullaby was already hissing and growling, shoulders straight, arms outstretched in a defensive posture. The other Han didn't bother with words. He swung a heavy metal bat and took the Rx'lng out with one swift hit on the head. His motions were ones of an expert and his face revealed no emotions. He waited for Lullaby's body to hit the ground with a hollow thump and whistled for help.

"Load 'em up," the first man instructed. "And let's get out of here before they come around. Never dealt with Rx'lng before--or humans, for that matter. Wouldn't want them to go bad."

"Yes, sir," the second man nodded. "Keen eye you have, sir."

"Less chit-chat, more action," he retorted. "Chop-chop!"

And they left the empty street--uninterrupted and unnoticed.

Meanwhile, S was spending a lovely afternoon on his much-deserved break. He sat on a rocky edge, feet dipped into the lukewarm water, a cup of brandy-spiked tea in one hand and a fishing rod in the other. The sun beams danced on the surface of the ocean and the wind ruffled his long hair. It was quiet on Solaris, quiet enough to hear your own thoughts. Waves moved, the sun shined, and S was happy. For approximately seventeen minutes.

"You know you won't catch anything, right," Darkness said, poking her perfectly manicured finger through his fishing rod.

"Of course I know," he replied, but not before rolling his eyes so hard it hurt his brain. "It's not the point."

"What is the point, in that case?"

"To enjoy this moment. Focus on it. Take it in, in its purest form. Connect with the universe."

"Hippie."

"Killjoy."

"Why am I being disturbed?"

The third voice came abruptly and out of nowhere. It took Darkness a couple of seconds to realize that there was no sound at all; the words simply appeared in her mind.

"Congratulations," S mumbled, the fishing rod disappearing from his hands, "you've disturbed the ocean."

"Did not." She crossed her arms on her chest.

"Yeah, you kind of did," the disembodied voice disagreed.

"Sorry then," she said in a vague direction of the water. "I didn't mean to."

"Go away, Darkness." The rod re-appeared in S's hands. "Light needs you, most probably. She always does."

"Fine, mister hermit."

He watched her melt into the air with great satisfaction. His holiday was for one person only! How could he contemplate the essence of suffering with chit-chat next to his ear?

"No respect for authority these new girls have," the ocean confirmed, reading his thoughts. "Back when I was just a lake, I..."

"You too, ocean," S reminded.

"Of course."

And they continued their mutual interaction-less co-existence.

TWELVE

The first thing Amber felt (and simultaneously failed to feel) upon waking up was her face. One part of it was burning with pain while the other was numb, paralyzed. She produced a meek groan and forced her eyes open, already trying to get off the floor and sit up. With one hand she reached into the air and bumped into a wall. It hurt too much to move the other. Gradually, she found strength to push herself upwards and lean against the wall. The world swirled in front of her, and her brain was not making sense of it yet. She touched her cheek. It hurt. There was blood. She remembered what had happened.

"Lullaby?" she called out, and the words got stuck in her throat half-way. She coughed and tried again. "Lullaby, are you here?"

No answer.

"Fuck," she whispered. "Fuck it. Fuck my life. Why. Why now?" She rubbed her aching forehead, still mumbling. "Just... why?!"

Her senses were turning on, one by one. She tuned in to the sounds around her and heard breathing and moving. She brushed over the floor and got dust stuck to her fingers; she wiped them on her clothes. She looked up and around her and, gradually, things began to make some sense.

She was in a cellar, or a basement of some sort. A small, dark and dirty one. Filled with people. She counted four Han and two Sojhi, all women except for one Han boy. He sat in the center of the room, hands tied behind his back, his mother clinging to him for dear life. He couldn't have been older than twelve or thirteen.

"What is this?" Amber called out, and blinked dust out of her eyes.

The only source of light in the room was a half-broken lamp which flickered on and off at random intervals. It gave out an oily orange glow which hurt Amber's brain at a metaphysical level.

"Hello!" she repeated after hearing no reply. "Where am I?"

"Underground," one woman finally responded. "Deep. I can hear water pipes through the wall. Don't know where, exactly."

"Okay," Amber nodded, surprisingly calm. "Let's go one up—why are we here?"

The woman paused.

"Depends," she said, turning in Amber's direction. "I think they got me because of my husband. Teaching him a lesson and such. You two seem like collectibles."

"Collectibles?"

"For sale," she explained. "Rare items."

"I...am many things," Amber said, getting up at last. "But I'm no fucking item. 'You two'."

"Sorry?"

"'You two seem like collectibles'. Rx'lng. Big blue insect. Where are they?"

The woman pointed at the wall behind her. There, obstructed from view by all the other occupants, lied Lullaby. Sleeping, Amber thought. Or hoped at least. Covering the few meters that separated them was not an easy task.

"Hey," she whispered, gently shaking the Rx'lng's body. "You okay? Breathing?"

They were, faintly. She saw a large purple bruise on their head and cursed again. They should have gone straight to an airport like Lullaby wanted, she thought. No; they shouldn't have come to this planet in the first place.

"How long have you all been in here?" Amber asked her next question, still by Lullaby's side.

"Nati been here the longest," the same woman who talked previously replied. "Three weeks, I believe."

"In this place, all the time?"

"Yes. They bring us food, water. Change the bucket." She pointed to the right corner, and Amber realized where the nasty smell was coming from. "Take some people away, bring new ones."

"And they never talk to you?"

"No."

"Well," Amber proclaimed, leaving Lullaby alone and walking towards the outline of a door. "I'm gonna change that in a sec. Hey! Let me out!"

She screamed, and stomped, and beat her fists on the metal door until it gave her another headache on top of her current one. The rest of the prisoners watched her in horror but wouldn't speak up. She didn't care. They might have been beaten down into submission by now, but she was freshly captured and exceptionally stubborn. She wouldn't give up till she got to have a word with the management.

When the door finally opened, it swung so violently that it threw her to the floor. A man stepped through into the cellar--the same man who knocked her out at capture. He was wearing a stretched-out sweater which stank of alcohol and smoke, and he had a nasty smirk on his moon-pale face.

"I'm listening," he said, not bothering to even glance at Amber.

"Good!" she retorted, getting up. "May I inquire for the purpose of my stay in this establishment?"

"No," he replied and reached for the door to close it.

"Wait a second there." She grabbed the door from the other end. "You know who I am?"

"Not relevant. You're human. That one's Rx'lng. To me it means cash. Goodbye."

He made a second attempt to leave and was stopped once again.

"The Muuk are looking for me," Amber pressed.

The man burst out laughing. "They ain't looking hard enough there, sweetheart!"

"I can help them out." She reached for her bracelet and felt her heart drop. It wasn't on her wrist anymore.

"Doubt it," he commented. "Have fun."

Third attempt to close the door.

"I will not be a nice prisoner," Amber continued. "I will scream, and knock, and bite, and make your life as miserable as you can imagine."

"You sure 'bout that?" He raised an eyebrow.

"Adamant."

"Right." He paused, tensing a jaw muscle as if he was chewing on something. "You." He pointed at one of the Sojhi girls. "How old are you?"

"S-s-seventeen, sir," the girl squeaked.

"Got parents?"

She nodded shakily.

"Siblings?"

Another nod.

"They were gonna pay for you, you reckon?"

"Yes, sir!"

"Cool. Get up and come here. Come on."

The girl hesitated, but eventually left her place on the floor and approached the man.

"You'll cause me trouble?" he repeated, looking at Amber.

"You can count on it."

"Cool."

He then reached into his back pocket, produced an old-school bullet gun and shot the Sojhi girl on the spot. She didn't even have time to get scared.

Her body dropped to the ground with a dull thud, spilling blood and brains all over the floor. The man watched with a still, calm expression. The rest of the crowd was absolutely silent, not daring to gasp, or scream, or cry.

"Your opinion now?" He turned towards Amber, hiding the gun.

She didn't reply. Instead, she silently made a few steps back, sat down on the floor and looked away.

"Cool!" And he finally shut the door.

The body stayed still, like dead bodies usually do, bleeding out near the tightly shut door. Everyone moved as far away from it as possible, which wasn't very far.

150

Some were crying quietly, some closed their eyes and turned away. One woman was rocking back and forth in shock, her face covered by her palms. Amber was by Lullaby's side again. There was no point in weeping over a girl she didn't know, a girl she could not help anymore. Lullaby was alive. So far. And she needed to preserve her strength, in case she would have to protect them.

"Why are you so calm?"

"Huh?"

She glanced sideways, to where the boy with tied up hands sat, his mother still clinging to his shoulder. He made eye contact with her and glared at her with such vicious hate, it made Amber look away. Usually, she could tolerate eye contact pretty well, though she didn't see much point in it. This, however, felt like a challenge. An animal staring its opponent into the eyes, ready for battle.

"Why. Are. You. So. Calm," he repeated, accenting every word.

"Pardon me, mister," she said. "Would you rather I wept, or screamed, or shook myself over the body saying 'why her? why not me'?"

"You killed her, you know."

"No, I didn't." Amber scoffed. "I tried my best to bluff my way out of this hole so that I could notify the Muuk and get you all out as well. That guy killed her. It wasn't my fault."

"Well whose fault is it then?!" he spat out, struggling against the restraints. "'Cause someone is to blame for this, okay? Someone has to be responsible!"

"Have you considered, I don't know, the guy who shot her?"

The boy closed his mouth mid-word, and Amber gave him a triumphant look which only made him angrier. She couldn't see it in the semi-darkness of the room, but he was struggling against the rope so energetically, it was damaging his skin.

"It doesn't make sense," he said, in a calmer, almost defeated voice. "People being like that."

"Everything can be explained," Amber replied. "There's something in his brain that drives him to carry out such behavioral patterns. He needs a psychiatrist, or a neurologist, to fix a neurological deficit of some sort."

151

"It's not that simple." The boy shook his head.

"It is, actually," Amber disagreed. "I come from a place where extreme violence and high-key anti-social behavior is almost extinct. It's treated, like any mental disorder. They don't choose to be like that."

"They don't choose?!" The boy's nostrils flared. "You're telling me he didn't choose to pull the trigger?"

"Depends on what you mean by 'he'." She shrugged. "Listen, kid... how old are you?"

"Twelve," he told her, after hesitating.

"Guess you didn't have The Talk yet." She sighed. "Free will is fake, okay? It's been extensively demonstrated that each and every decision we make is a product of our genetics and environment. Well, there's also quantum fluctuations involved, which is why we can't predict it entirely, but it's not like we choose that either. He's, um, like that because he just is. If you were in his place, with exactly the same genes and experience, you would have shot her too."

"How can you say something like this?" The boy tried very hard to conceal an angry sob, but it slipped through nevertheless. "I would never kill..."

"But you wouldn't be you, you would be him," Amber interrupted. "I would also kill her if I were exactly in his place. That's how the universe works! We act according to a long, unbroken chain of events that traces back to when our universe was forced into existence out of those other dimensions that I could never conceptualize in physics classes," she lectured, nonchalant. "It makes perfect sense. Maybe not to everyone, but we do understand it."

The boy thought for a few seconds, and was about to say something again, but his mother spoke up instead.

"We will be okay," she whispered to him. "I do my rituals, I pay respects. Spirits will not abandon us."

He looked at her face, pale and covered in bruises and dust; he saw her eyes full of such kindness and hope and conviction; then he took a deep breath in and shook his head.

"They don't exist," he told her in a soft, shaky voice. "You know they don't.

You give to them, and you wish and beg and give, and they never respond. They won't respond, and you can't keep hoping they will."

"Amen, kid," Amber agreed. "Though I must say, not the best moment for atheism conversion."

As if to prove her words, the woman began to sob silently on her son's shoulder.

"She looks for a reason to explain her misfortune the same way you do," Amber added. "It's natural. We all want to have the answers."

"What are the answers?" He seemed to have lost the raging flame. "Why are we here? Who put us here?"

"The guy with the gun, apparently."

"Who put us here?! Who has the answers?"

"Jesus Christ." Amber rolled her eyes, fully aware of the irony of her expression. "Twelve is a great age to have your first philosophical awakening, I'll give you that. But maybe not in a stuffy dungeon next to a corpse, okay?"

"But I don't get it!" he exclaimed. "What did I do to deserve this? Is it my fault that my dad couldn't pay back his loan? Why am I here while so many terrible people are out there, doing just fine?!"

"Oh, come up with something more original, will you?"

"But it ain't fair!" the boy yelled.

"Of course it ain't fair!" she yelled back.

It took her a second or two to get her calm back.

"Kay," Amber said, moving over closer to the boy. "Consider this. I'm human. You might have noticed that. Alexandria, where I was born and raised, is very different from the rest of the galaxy. I wasn't aware of that. Now I am. Where I come from, suffering has been reduced to absolute minimum. We don't work boring jobs, or fall ill to a lot of diseases, or deal with economic and social disparities. We don't do much, actually. We think. A lot. We do science, and art, and we help each other out, and it's all very cute and inspirational. There's just enough problems to give our politicians something to talk about. And there is, in effect, no death."

She made a pause to give him time to process that.

"I mean, we still die, but not really. We have these things you see, implants here," she tapped her temple, "called Emerson devices. We get them installed at two years of age and they sit in our skulls, dormant, until our bodies are injured or too worn out to be treated effectively. When our brains stop getting oxygen, they turn on, absorb our consciousness and allow it to be transferred into a system where we continue to exist. Not forever, cause the universe won't last forever, and not if you don't want to cause you can always opt out. No one has so far though. It's been a hundred and fifty years since some of them have died and the first-generation Alexandrians are still enjoying their digital stay very well."

"Get to the point, please," he prompted.

"Sure." She smiled a nasty fake smile. "Well, you see, no one has ever truly died on Alexandria, except for two people--Bradley Ngapo and Karishma Shakya, a physicist and a painter, twelve years ago, around the time you were born. My parents. The only two cases of true, involuntary death in the history of my nation. Got their heads blown up so violently that there was no implant to collect."

She paused again.

"I am, actually, the only real orphan in the history of Alexandria," Amber said, almost a hint of pride in her voice. "I am also probably the only human away from Alexandria right now, and I am in this fucking basement, my best friend is over there unconscious and probably seriously injured, and I also have to put up with your pretentious puberty bullshit!" She gave him the fake smile again. "So do me a favor," she was half-whispering, half-hissing, "don't talk to me about what's fair! You're alive! So is your mother! Your dad will pay for you and they'll let you out. Be grateful for that. Be grateful for fucking breathing! This galaxy is overflowing with misery. Every second a parent is losing their child to a preventable illness, every minute someone is being shot or raped or beaten up to death. People are dying slow and painful deaths from hunger or infections or numerous disorders you can't even begin to imagine. I didn't know this!" she cried out in frustration. "I lived for twenty-five years not knowing this, and it's horrible. It sucks fifty million dicks. It makes me feel like chewing my fingers off one by one and I can't make it stop. So trust me, I know how you feel. I do! Except shouting out whatever cliche thought comes to your mind won't help any of us! Instead of making everyone in this room feel even worse that we already feel, consider shutting the fuck up and letting me have some rest, cause that shitty ass light is hurting my brain and I am this close to having a meltdown and trust me, if I have a meltdown, that won't help anyone either." She finished, coughed and stormed off back to Lullaby's side. The room drowned in overwhelming, painful silence. The boy closed his eyes and let his mother pull him closer. No one said a word. No one even as much as looked in his or Amber's direction. It didn't seem like their guards have heard the speech either.

Gradually, the prisoners grew morbidly accustomed to the body. They turned away, laid down on the ground and closed their eyes, hoping to fall asleep or pass out. For about ten minutes there were no sounds and no movement in the room. Then, a loud bang and sudden darkness.

"Sorry."

Amber, who stood next to the now broken lamp, winced and removed glass shards from her bleeding fist. After that, she returned to the place where Lullaby resided, lowered herself to the ground, put her head on Lullaby's massive shoulder and fell into restless, heavy sleep.

THIRTEEN

Amber had no way of telling how long she spent with her eyes closed, falling in and out of consciousness, mostly unaware of what was going on around her. The dull aching in the depths of her skull was accompanied by a steady burn in her hand. She didn't dare move for the fear of discovering some other source of pain. She just stayed very still, slowed down her breathing and concentrated on recalling foreign words.

She woke up in the end feeling like her throat was stuffed full of sand and realized that she hadn't drunk any water since the capture. The room seemed different; smaller, denser, scarier. She forced her eyes open and glanced towards the door. Something was going on behind it--she could hear steps and voices, as well as some metallic jingling and rumbling coming from the wall. She sat up and gathered her strength.

"Rise and shine!"

The door swung open, drowning the cellar in a bright reddish light. A Han man was at the threshold, one that Amber didn't recognize. He swaggered in and headed straight for her corner, stepping over a sleeping woman on his way. She backed away instinctively when he reached for her. He tutted, grabbed her by the wrist with a steel grasp and yanked her to her feet.

"You're the human one, ye?"

"Have you eyes, sir?" Amber asked, gathering her strength to imitate a sense of composure.

"Huh?"

"A sensory organ that translates photon energy into electrical signals in the brain. Which begs the question, by the way, have you one of those?"

"Not interested." He shrugged and pushed her out of the way.

She glanced at the door--closed. A thousand thoughts raced through her mind all at once. Was it activated by body parameters, or a key? And if it's the latter, then where is he keeping the key? Could she nick it? Could she realistically overpower him? Kick him in the groin, perhaps? Did Han even have external testicles?

"Is it alive?" the man pondered out loud, poking Lullaby's body with his boot.

"They are," Amber replied. "May I ask for the purpose of your visit?"

"We've got a buyer for ye." He poked them again. "Got lucky, you two. Great demand for rare species. Found a good bid in no time at all."

"I'm flattered," Amber said. "Who bought us? And what for?"

"Don't care." He smirked and proceeded to kick Lullaby in the stomach.

"Hey!" Amber exclaimed. "Leave them alone, you..."

"I won't get paid for a defective product, okay?" he interrupted.

"Well, you should have picked a gentler way of collecting them! Rx'lng are tough, proper tough. You must have done them good to knock them out for that long."

"Whatever."

The man lowered himself to the ground and turned Lullaby's body over. It thumbed to the other side like a sack of potatoes.

"Damn, it heavy!" he commented, attempting to lift them up. "Should have brought someone with me to help me carry. I..."

But he didn't get to finish that sentence.

As if turned on by a remote control, Lullaby came back to life in a split of a second and launched themselves at their capturer. There was a very short struggle and a brief cry of pain; then, two loud crunches and a thud.

Amber gasped softly and pressed a hand over her mouth. The man lay on the floor, his head twisted almost a hundred and eighty degrees, his back bent at an unnatural angle. Lullaby stood over him, breathing heavily.

"He was right," Amber said. "Should have brought a buddy."

"Move." Lullaby's voice was unusually low and croaky. "Need to move now."

"Fully agreed."

They ran out of the room a moment later and didn't spare the cellar a single look back over the shoulder.

For the next half an hour, Amber forgot what it was like to feel discomfort. It was as if something had ignited in her nervous system, pushing her to run without exhaustion and power through every obstacle. "Adrenaline," she thought. She had never been in mortal danger before--a state that her ancestors were intimately acquainted with. Millions of years of natural selection produced a creature that could scream and bite till the last drop of blood, and she was that creature. She felt brave, and strong, and unstoppable. Especially with Lullaby by her side.

The Rx'lng was being helped by a chemical substance, too. As the physiology of their caste dictated, perceived danger to the nest would activate a gland below one of their livers and infuse their lymph with a powerful hormone. It made them stronger, faster, more alert, allowing them to repel any attack. This was the first time in L'kst's life--or, indeed, in the history of their species--that this handy trick of nature was used not for the sake of another Rx'lng.

They smashed through a few doors on their way up and navigated the dark labyrinth of the building with surprising effectiveness. All the rooms they came across were abandoned; with a slight twitch somewhere in her chest, Amber realized that this used to be a multi-family apartment. She noticed potted plants, dead and decaying, spare furniture, and forgotten personal items.

"Why would they build underground?" Amber asked, climbing another windowless staircase section. "It's miserable."

"Cheap accommodation," Lullaby said. "Can save lots of space. Make twenty levels instead of ten."

"Do you think people moved out of here on their own terms, or..."

"Not think. Run." They interrupted. "Minus two." They pointed at a UGS system number painted on a wall. "Close to surface. Close to escape."

The ground level wasn't much brighter, despite having knocked out windows and wide-open doors. Amber paused near a wall, trying hard to catch her breath. Her chest was on fire, and so were her legs, but she was anxious to keep going.

158

She was about to launch for the open street when Lullaby grabbed her by the shoulders and forced her through a nearby door and into some stuffy cupboard. She didn't protest; upon gaining her balance and composure in the dusty space, Amber heard voices coming from the outside, and held her breath.

"...know the rules, man. Money first."

"For a product that definitely exists."

"You think we're shitting you or something?"

"Can't trust no one."

"Can trust us. We've been in business for a decade. We have a reputation to uphold."

There was a theatrically heavy sigh.

"Fine. Check your balance."

"I recognize that voice," Amber whispered. "Actually, I recognize both of those voices."

"Sweet! Your order is on its way."

"You sure? He's been down there an awful long. Maybe you should check up on him. Rx'lng are strong, and humans are stubborn. Might need assistance."

"Wait here. Or don't. Got your money anyway."

"It's the guy who shot the girl," Amber said, and squeezed herself past Lullaby to get closer to the door. "And... Kidney Stone?"

She was almost there, close enough to brush the door with her fingertips; she needed one last step to be in the range of hearing everything properly. Lullaby hissed in her direction and was ignored. She removed her foot from one place in the cupboard, carefully brought it over to the next spot, and... knocked something over. The bang of metal against the floor tiles was overwhelming. She froze on the spot and bit her lip. He heard it. The whole building must have heard it! And, judging by the steps, he was coming her way.

"Shit," Amber whispered, and it came out more like a sob. "I don't wanna die in a mop closet..."

The door opened, nearly forcing her to toppled over. Next to her stood Kidney Stone--hands empty, eyes wide, and wearing all black, which made him

159

look like a child who dressed up as a secret agent for Halloween.

"Fuck me gently with a chainsaw," he said, waving his hands around vaguely. "Why?! Why couldn't you stay in the goddamned cellar?"

"Why would we?!" Amber staggered out of the closet and coughed dust out of her mouth.

"You got kidnapped!"

"We escaped."

"Less than a day after landing!"

"We were sightseeing."

"I told you specifically not to get kidnapped!"

"And you came back."

They both paused, momentarily lost for words.

"You... bought us out?" Amber asked.

"Yes. Well, technically it's my husband's money, but yes."

"How..." she thought about it for a second. "How much did you pay? I'll give it back," she added.

"It isn't relevant right now," he muttered, looking around anxiously. "You ruined the deal! I'll have to, I don't know, pretend like I haven't seen you and wait for them to catch you."

"Why the hell?"

"It was a deal, okay? It's how things work in the business. I have to part ways well with them, or I'm screwed."

"Yeah, there might be a problem with that," Amber said. "One of those, um, businessmen, is, sadly, no longer with us."

"What?!"

"Lullaby offed him," Amber shrugged. "That's how we escaped."

Kidney Stone bit his lip and shook his fists in front of her. Judging by his face, he was screaming inside.

"Idiots!" he exclaimed. "I mean... Gods and demons and spirits, if you had to kill one of them, why did it have to be the nice one?!"

"The nice one?" Lullaby asked. "Called me 'it'. Kicked me very hard."

"Well," Amber replied. "You were out for that part, but the other one did shoot a seventeen-year-old to prove a point, so..."

"Doesn't matter," Kidney Stone said. "This is a mess. We need to get out. Come on."

He gestured towards one of the broken windows and Amber ran after him before she could process his words. She wanted nothing more than to be out of that place. Lullaby seemed to have shared the sentiment.

They ran across the streets of the somber city, meandering through the dark alleyways and dead-ends with supernatural ease. A soft pink light enveloped the world as one of the suns began to climb up the sky, heavy and shrouded in rainclouds. The air tickled Amber's nose, its wet warmth washing over her like tropical waves. She felt drunk on freedom. It made her giddy, ecstatic even. At no point, not even for one minute, did she think about her fellow captured whom she had left behind in their underground prison.

"Over here," Kidney Stone announced, and they whisked into a particularly narrow turn in between two houses.

Lullaby had to walk sideways to push their body through the comically small space.

On the other side of it was a staircase leading down.

"Not another cellar," Amber complained.

"Shut up and get in," Kidney Stone replied, almost pushing her down the steps.

She obeyed. She didn't care anymore. All she wanted was a warm bed, a whole bucket of water to drink and a sense of not being moments away from death. For now, at least.

She didn't pay much attention to the interior of the underground apartment he lead them into. She noticed that it was an apartment, with walls and tables and chairs and artificially lighted windows. The only piece of furniture she concentrated on was the sofa--large, red, covered in a layer of decorative pillows, welcoming her to lie down. She didn't wait for an invitation. As soon as her head touched the pillows, all the sensations were gone, and she was off to a half-dreamy,

161

half-unconscious state.

The last thing she felt was Lullaby moving her body deeper into the sofa and gently turning her head into a more comfortable position.

"These are the hands that broke a man's spine," Amber thought, then didn't think anything else for a long, long while.

"You will be late."

Amber sniffed, yawned and stretched her limbs till something cracked in her joints. The world was coming back to her. She patted the sofa, detached her face from the pillow and sat up.

"We don't have a ton of time."

She turned her head and saw Kidney Stone, sitting at a small rectangular table and sipping some white liquid out of a transparent cup. He wasn't in black anymore. Instead, he was wrapped in a fluffy dressing gown and his hair was messy and wet. He made eye contact with her and pointed to the wall on his left. 'The clock', Amber realized. It didn't help. She couldn't read it anyway.

"I feel moderately crappy, thanks for asking," she said, lowering her feet to the ground.

"You're the last person who should shame others for not being sufficiently polite."

"True that. I need a drink."

She walked towards the corner of the room where she saw a stove, a kitchen sink and a bunch of cupboards.

"I only have Kibiko and half a can of flat soda pop."

Amber ignored the remark. She approached the sink, opened the cold tap and used her hands to drink from it.

"Uh, I wouldn't do that if I were you," Kidney Stone advised. "They claim it's clean but the ion balance is questionable."

She didn't comment on that piece of information either. After drinking what felt like two liters of water at once, Amber proceeded to wash her face and hands with the same water.

"I brought a single-use medical bot," he told her. "Managed to juice it for

162

both your arm and Lullaby's head."

"Where is Lullaby?" Amber asked.

"In my bedroom. Consuming all of my snacks along with the packages, judging by the sound!" he said loudly enough for them to hear.

"Sorry!" came a voice from behind the bedroom door.

Amber returned back to the sofa and fell into the pile of blankets and pillows.

"I have questions," she said, brushing her hair with her fingers.

"The shower is over there."

"Fuck off. First, how did you find us?"

"News spread like viruses in our field." He shrugged. "And I'm pretty sure you're the only human on this planet, so it wasn't hard to figure out."

"Is that like, a common occurrence? To get kidnapped and sold off?"

"Unfortunately. That's why I told you to go straight to the airport!"

"We were planning to. Eventually," she assured him. "Guess we should have done that when it was still light outside."

"Guess you should have!" He nodded empathetically. "You're lucky that no one needs human organs. Here." He reached into his pocket then threw something at Amber.

She didn't catch it, but it landed on the sofa. It was her ID band--scratched, but working.

"They took out the quantum unit," he explained. "So, it will be slower and will only connect to local networks, but you can still pay with it and stuff."

"How much do I owe you?"

He hesitated. "Two thousand five hundred."

"How much?!"

"Look, it just means you have to pay me less, okay?"

Amber didn't listen. "I'm sorry, but I'm worth much more than that, and so is Lu!"

"Wanna go back and tell them that?"

She paused, and got up, dragging the blanket with her.

"I'm hungry," she proclaimed. "Feed me, heroic bandit."

She sat sideways in a chair while he heated up day-old dinner. Her mind was buzzing with thoughts, which she wanted to brush away like annoying flies. Those people she left behind. That dead girl. She tried to ignore it, tried to persuade herself that she wouldn't help them anyway, that it wasn't her fault, but she was quite aware of the permanence of such memories. Fifty years from now she will be falling asleep, safe in her bed on Alexandria, and she will see the dead unblinking eyes of that girl in the darkness of her brain…it will never, ever go away. The guilt will not go away.

But even if she was suffering, she sure as hell would not show it. Kidney Stone was not asking either. He watched her devour a skillet full of food that he wasn't even sure she could eat with almost morbid fascination. Amber, who firmly believed that 'manners' was a scam invented to keep women in line, ate using her hands and a few napkins exclusively.

"You don't have to eat that quickly," Kidney Stone pointed out. "We have around an hour."

"Hour till what?" she asked, a piece of fried vegetable falling out of her mouth and back into the skillet.

"There's a commercial flight leaving from the St. Partmore's airport. It will take you pretty close to the Teardrop Cluster, if that's where you are still heading."

"And from there?"

"You'll land on Skia, in a city called Laetial, which is not far from a huge research station. They've got spaceships for rent coming out of their ears. I'm sure you can find a pilot who's crazy enough to drive you there, if you wave a big enough carrot in front of them. The hell you are expecting to find in there anyway?"

"Not your damn business!" She wiped her mouth with her sleeve, burped and pushed the skillet away. "I mean, thank you for the rescue and everything else, but with all due respect, I have no reason to trust you. You haven't even told us your real name."

"What's wrong with 'Kidney Stone'?"

"Do you have that written on your info-plate? Your mail box? Your wedding certificate?"

He sighed and got up to collect the dirty dishes.

"My real name is Augustus," he said. "Augustus Rosenberg."

"That's... not as funny as I imagined."

"My mum was into human history," he explained. "She named me after Augustus Caesar. It was a close pick between that and Elvis."

"I like your mum already." Amber smiled. "Raises another question though. When you were eighteen, with that name, and that height, and, well, gay...how did you arrive at the conclusion that you'd make a splendid career in the criminal world?"

"I didn't. Never wanted to be conman in the first place. I studied physics, and math, and technology...I wanted to be an engineer."

"What happened?"

"Life." He laughed briefly and took a seat next to her. "Things were pretty shitty to begin with, and then my mum got sick, and I knew I had to get her off the planet. I dropped out of the academy, tried to make money with small gigs. Wasn't very effective, so I gradually moved on to more shady stuff.

"I wasn't very good at it either, but I got noticed by this woman who took me as an apprentice, I guess. I started making a lot, bought a house on Stridon, and a spaceship. And after that, well... I didn't have skill to do anything else."

"Are there any universities on Stridon?"

"Plenty."

"And how is the economy?"

"Pretty stable."

"Hey." She paused, thinking for a minute. "Let's suppose, hypothetically, that I were to pay two hundred and fifty thousand credits for myself and Lu. You know, with interest. For making your life more difficult and stuff, and for all the snacks that Lullaby ate. Would that be enough for you to leave the criminal career behind, go back to uni and do what you always wanted to do?"

He frowned, not sure what she was getting at.

165

"Hypothetically, yes," he replied. "But you don't have that much money, do you?"

"Let's say, hypothetically, that I do. Would you take it?"

"Hypothetically, if you promised that you still have enough to come back to your planet and be okay, maybe I would."

"Well then, hypothetically..." She activated her bracelet, performed several security checks, and didn't pause for a single second before pushing the 'transfer' button. "Let's say you have the money now. If my tech recognized your ID well, that is."

He took a small device, which looked like a flat piece of transparent plastic, out of his dressing gown pocket, and stared blankly at the screen. Then, he raised his glance to the level of Amber's face and gave her a faint smile.

"Thank you," he said quietly. "I won't waste a single credit."

"That's what the Muuk paid me for my work." She smiled back. "Well, around eighty nine percent of it anyway. I was gonna buy my own spa with that money. I think you'll use them more wisely."

"I won't forget this."

"I don't care if you do. Now." She got up and walked towards the bedroom door. "Hey, Lu? I'm going to the bathroom and you should get ready. We have a flight to catch."

FOURTEEN

When Amber was nine, she stumbled upon Dante's "Divine Comedy" in her mother's library, and, surprising no-one, became obsessed with it at once. Her dad watched her doodle in the digital copy and just rolled his eyes at it. It wasn't her first interaction with classical Earth literature after all. For weeks after she had finished the book, the little girl went around the Novella Institute, pointing her finger at people and cheerfully assigning levels of purgatory and hell to them. The third circle of hell was her favorite. Heaven was too boring, so the only people who got it were her mum and professor Nawahi. They both found it strangely endearing.

Today, upon boarding her first (and decidedly last) commercial flight, Amber realized that hell had ten circles after all.

After being pushed around for hours in the waiting line and having to endure slow Internet connection, nasty and severely overpriced airport snacks, and, worst of all, incessant flirting from an older Sojhi man who couldn't for the life of him take a hint in the form of 'dude I am a lesbian', Amber was finally granted the privilege of boarding the ship.

It marginally improved the situation.

She and Lullaby gladly took their front-of-the-cabin seat and forced themselves into the narrow gap between scrappy plastic armchairs and a plain metal wall. The air in the spaceship buzzed and whistled, and the floor felt sticky and smelt vaguely of spilled coffee. Amber arranged herself in the uncomfortable chair, closed her eyes and tried to abstract from the situation.

"Three hours," she told herself. "I only need to deal with this for three hours."

The flight took longer than three hours.

"Glik or morshu?" a Han flight attendant repeated again and again, slowly walking the gap between two rows of seats.

When she approached the end of the cabin, Amber pretended to be asleep.

"Glik or morshu?" the attendant asked, determined to serve every passenger.

"Uh, neither?" Amber wrinkled her nose.

"Both," Lullaby disagreed and grabbed the almost empty tray from the attendant's hands.

"You sure, mate?" Amber watched them dip their fingers into the first dish- -a bowl of something grey and jiggly. "Doesn't have a nutritional compatibility label."

"Can tell by smell," they responded. "This smells not deadly."

"I'll just have another water, thank you."

Interestingly enough, both glik and morshu were synthesized protein matter created from the very same chemicals and differing only in flavor (mild or spicy) and color (gray or dark white). Neither were poisonous for Rx'lng or humans, although you wouldn't believe it if you were to taste it.

The attendant handed over a bottle and smiled with a corner of her mouth.

"See anything funny?" Amber scowled.

The girl's face flushed red.

"Sorry," she muttered, escaping into the next cabin.

"Will spit in your food the next time," Lullaby scoffed.

"Won't be a next time, unless someone threatens me with a large enough weapon. Though honestly, a quick death could be more merciful."

"Is not that bad here." As if to confirm their words, they chomped on their grey slush with added vigor. "Warm, safe. Enough space for feet."

"This ain't how my ancestors imagined space travel," Amber pouted.

"No. They died in space. They suffered. Were very brave. You bored, and don't like the drinks."

"Fair enough. But the people in the business area have movies and neck pillows!"

Lullaby sighed, downed the last gulp of what was either morshu or glik and moved on to the other dish.

By the end of their trip, Amber was ready to agree to any miserable dump of a planet--as long as it wasn't a confined space full of chatting people and crying babies. It took her a considerable amount of self-restraint to not push past the customs line and out of the building, into the open air. Lullaby did not seem as enthusiastic. They had trepidation in their step, their gaze wandering around the room incessantly.

"Relax," Amber claimed, placing a heavy hand on the Rx'lng's back. "The customs drones don't care. We don't have drugs or weapons, everything else is secondary."

"Am an unusual sight for them."

"Stopping you for looking 'weird'," Amber did air quotes, "would be discrimination. Come on. I'm five minutes away from either having a huge meltdown or passing the fuck out."

They pushed their way past the security guards and Amber made a point of employing a confident smile and a casual attitude. Her bracelet and Lullaby's hand chip scanned just fine and didn't set off any alarm.

"I wonder if the Muuk are looking for us," she wondered out loud, re-loading her 'incoming messages' tab.

Ever since their kidnapping on Tenebris, she received no new messages or voice mails, and Sarah was mostly quiet. It was calming at first but now it made her anxious. Is Nawahi worried about her? Will her rebellion cost Muuk privileges to other Alexandrians? What will they all say to her once she does come back? She bit her lip, stuffed the thoughts deeper into her mind and headed for the exit.

"Well, let's see what flavor of suffering this lovely world can offer us," Amber proclaimed cheerfully, pushing the heavy glass doors open.

She was greeted with anything but suffering.

The new reality she found herself in was too rich to let her eyes pause on a single detail. She halted mid-step a few meters away from the airport and just gazed. Above her stretched the strangest sky she had ever seen. It was vast,

169

seemingly infinite, enveloping the city, completely clear of any clouds. It had the most extraordinary color which changed, flowed, and almost made her eyes hurt--an intense indigo, a soft lilac, a touch of baby boy blue... a continuous sea of color.

There, in this stoner dream of a sky, shone a bright red star and a pale pink moon. The air around her was fresh and still, the ground smooth and bouncy. She lowered her gaze and realized why the sky felt so enormous to her. Every building in the city, from towering giants in its center to cute little houses on the outskirts, had reflective sun panel roofs. The light bounced off their surface, gathered and modified, and with the sun casting its warmth onto the area, it was as if the whole place was an underwater fairy tale.

"Not bad," Amber muttered.

A faint smile touched her lips as she heard Lullaby chirp and whistle in excitement.

"Don't have to go to research station at once, maybe?" they said.

"Maybe." She nodded. "I mean, the Teardrop Cluster has been in its place since the beginning of the universe, right? So it won't go anywhere if we spend one pleasant evening in here."

"No." Lullaby was already walking towards the nearest public transport station. "It won't."

"Splendid." Amber followed with little hesitation. "I still have like ten percent of my salary to waste."

It didn't take them long to blend in with the tourists. Upon arriving on a busy square, Amber bought a whole box of cheap jacket pins for herself and a ridiculous hat for Lullaby, quickly surveyed the place and integrated herself into a crowd of Sojhi listening to their Makran tour guide. She nodded to the commentary and snapped photos of random sites in an obnoxious manner, and the tourists seamlessly took her in as their own. Lullaby followed, trying their best to copy her in every way. They didn't have a camera, so instead they paused at every street vendor for a smell of food and accumulated a bucket full of souvenirs. Despite looking nothing like any of the tourists, they didn't raise any suspicion either.

170

"What will do after this?" Lullaby asked when they boarded a sight-seeing car, fitting themselves into the seats with astonishing prowess.

"Might as well go to the hotel with them." Amber giggled. "Or get off at the end and hit it off in the party zone."

"You hate parties."

"True. But I love hot girls and free drinks, and I bought myself some new shades."

She rummaged through her (also newly purchased) beach bag and pulled out a pair of pink tinted sun glasses made of thick plastic.

"Disgusting," she commented, putting them on. "I love it."

"Will never understand humans," Lullaby said.

"Me neither mate," Amber replied.

And they returned their attention to the tour.

They hopped off the bus close to the city center, unnoticed by either the guide or their fellow passengers. Amber barely had time to check her pockets for all of her things before it took off, moved up to another air lane and disappeared into the darkness. She buttoned up her jacket and shivered. As the night descended on the area, a shallow wind began to pick up the pace, and the day's humid warmth became a distant memory. The sun was gone, and the pink moon shone an intensely crimson light onto the streets. Lullaby span on the spot and glanced at Amber, awaiting instructions.

"That way." She pointed arbitrarily behind her back. "And don't get lost."

The streets looped and zigzagged in the depth of Laetial, leading them from one unfamiliar location to another. It was starting to give Amber a headache. In her rather pragmatic mind, every place had its purpose. Some cities grew around production plants or factories, some existed for the sheer joy of it, to bring people entertainment, goods and services. Some, like Pierine on Alexandria, were completely useless in her eyes and had strictly aesthetic values. And they all had a certain feeling--an atmosphere, a taste, a special blend of traits and details that made it special. This place, however, was confusing.

The city was new, technologically advanced to the max and beautiful like

171

a polished postcard. She saw no flaws in it--not a single piece of trash on the ground, or unsanctioned graffiti on the wall. It was perfectly convenient and a pleasure to navigate. It was an ideal city...yet it didn't seem to have a purpose, or a feeling. The city was there, but she didn't feel like she was in the city. She tried to explain it to Lullaby but only confused herself further. There was something wrong in Laetial...something she couldn't quite put her finger on.

"Party," Lullaby announced when they exited a narrow boulevard and entered a rather cozy square.

Amber followed their pointing finger with her eyes.

On the upper floor of a huge glistening building, she could see people gathered around a window, lights flashing behind their backs.

"Oh boy." She sighed, pushing her pink glasses up her nose. "I did ask for this."

No one stopped them from entering the building and checking out every single door in the airy bright hall. Most of them lead into elevator shafts for some reason. Amber couldn't quite figure out the place in her imagination. Was it bigger on the inside or something? Deciding not to dwell on it for the fear of a headache, she found the only door label written in UGS and pushed the elevator button. It arrived almost immediately.

"Do you feel like...?" Amber began again once the elevator doors closed in front of her. "Like this place is...fake in some way?"

"Fake how?" Lullaby titled their head.

"Like...do you have full immersion VR on the King of Kings? You know, this set that you log into to experience rendered worlds. Like an artificial dream."

Evident from Lullaby's perplexed mandibular clicks, they didn't know what Amber was talking about.

"Anyway."

The elevator clicked, and they stepped into a dimly lit corridor.

"I never liked those trips very much," Amber continued, "cause they are too good to be realistic. Too polished. They lack tiny faults and quirks and all those adorable things that make it true. This... this feels like VR."

172

"This building VR?"

"No. The entire city."

She dropped the thought and paused in front of a translucent door that lead into the next room.

"No guns, no cats, no perception filters," the sign on the door proclaimed.

"Cool." Amber shrugged, and pushed the door open with her foot.

Her brain was flooded with sensory input as soon as she crossed the threshold. The room was enormous, lacking any barriers and with at least ten meters of height to the ceiling. She turned on the spot and realized that one of the walls was made entirely of a transparent material, giving an astonishing view on the ground below. They must have been very high up to see anything so clearly; so high, it almost gave her vertigo.

Up to her left was a spiral staircase leading to a balcony where a few people were chatting, gathered around a table full of snacks. The bright, color-changing light that drowned the room was barely touching them. There were more tables around, as well as couches, arm chairs and bar stands. To the far right of Amber was a stage —now dark and empty, raised several meters above the floor. She wasn't sure where to go first. The people present in the room didn't seem to notice new arrivals, too engaged in their conversations, or glued to device screens. She found that rather comforting.

"Food," Lullaby announced and departed in the direction of a snack table.

"Predictable." Amber said, surveying the crowd. "Enjoy yourself, Lu."

The vast majority of the guests here were Han, with the exception of one or two Sojhi, a small group of Makrans and a solitary Afrache. It didn't make much sense to Amber. Out of all planets she had visited so far, Skia seemed to be the most diverse. On her trip across the city, she met more than one Bellazi, two androids, all possible races of Sojhi, and even ran away from a pair of Muuk. Laetial made an impression of being a melting pot of cultures but this establishment seemed to be an exception.

"A drink?"

It took Amber a moment or two to decipher the words and recognize that she was being spoken to in an Alexandrian language.

"Huh?"

She turned her head towards the sound and saw a Han in a black and white outfit extending an arm towards her. He was holding a silver tray full of differently shaped glasses.

"The blue and white ones won't poison you," he elaborated. "The yellow one will, a little bit, but it will be worth it."

"Am I hallucinating, or are you speaking AlEng?"

"Those aren't mutually exclusive but yes, I am talking to you in your mother tongue."

"Follow-up question--how? And why?"

"Well, you're human aren't you?"

"Yeah..."

"And in our day and age, humans only come from Alexandria."

"I'm with you so far."

"And it so happens that I know one or two Alexandrians and learned your language in college."

"You know Alexandrians?" She picked up a glass full of white liquid from his tray absent-mindedly and sipped the cold liquid. "But..."

"Let me do my job for a few minutes," he interrupted. "And I will explain."

She watched him walk around the hall passing out drinks while she finished her own, nervously twirling her hair on her finger. This didn't make sense. From her early childhood, she was taught that there were no Alexandrians living permanently outside of their home world. It was against Muuk rules. Even diplomatic relationships were established through Internet meetings, and you could never get a visa lasting more than a year. So how come this waiter knew not one, but several humans?

"Over here."

The Han man returned, inviting her over into a corner behind an empty table. She followed thoughtlessly, eager to ask him a million question. But before she managed to get a single sound out, he spoke up first.

"When did you run away?" he asked in a calm tone.

"I...didn't. I have a visa."

"A visa to Skia?"

"Well, not exactly. Let's say I've taken a detour."

"On a Muuk ship?"

"No, it got stolen back on Cryptos, and..."

"Your ship was stolen?"

"Hey, hold on a second." She put her hands on her hips. "Why are you interrogating me all of a sudden?"

"Look, I only wish you the best," he said. "I'm all for humans leaving Alexandria if they wish to but you have to plan it well. Do you have money? Do you have contacts here, or anywhere else? Do you have a plan for finding work? Have you gotten a new id?"

"Wait," Amber interrupted. "I haven't left Alexandria forever. I will come back. I've told you, I'm just making a detour."

"What, seriously?" He frowned, leaning on the wall with one arm. "You really want to come back?"

"Well, yeah, I guess so. I haven't been planning an escape, if that's what you were expecting. I was on a job on Sereneae, stopped for a night on Cryptos, and then my ship got stolen and..."

"You somehow ended up on Skia?"

"Not exactly. I've taken a commercial here. I was on Tenebris before."

"And you are on your way back now."

"No. I'm on my way to the Teardrop Cluster."

"What the hell for?!"

"Not your damn business!" she exclaimed. "Look, if you help humans start a new life outside of Alexandria, that's cool, but I'm not looking for that. I just want to check out this one thing and come back home."

"Sure you will." He laughed briefly.

"You don't believe me?"

"I don't think you believe yourself. Come on, girl." He smirked. "You've been on the outside. You've seen the universe. Will you be ever satisfied with your life if you go back now, to your golden cage with a nice, comfortable, meaningless existence?"

She was about to say 'yes' even before she truly understood his words, but he turned around and walked away before she did so. The word lingered on her tongue. Up until now, she hadn't really thought about it. She was too focused on reaching her goal to ponder about her return to Alexandria. She hadn't even considered the possibility of not returning. In fact, she didn't even know it was a possibility. She heard Lullaby assert that they were not going back to the King of Kings, and that was understandable —but she had her life on Alexandria. Her career. Her home. Everything. Or did she?

It didn't matter. She didn't have time to think about it now, and no one here could advise her or even begin to understand her. Amber fought back an angry outburst and held her breath for a second. Emotion was swelling in her chest, clouding her mind and making her dizzy. She pressed her nails into her palm so hard it almost broke the skin.

"There's no going back now," she repeated in her mind —as some sort of a twisted prayer, one she had been hiding behind since Cryptos. Of course there was a way back! All she needed was to contact the Muuk, come clean and ask to be escorted back home.

"But I don't wanna go home," she muttered to no one in particular.

Her vision was ever so slightly blurry, her mind was painfully blank. The light, the sparkling fake reality, the oppressive loneliness in the middle of a crowd were getting to her. She wanted an escape. To run away, to hide and be forgotten... always. Was that the gift she was searching for?

"Heya." A jingly, high-pitched voice sounded next to her ear.

Amber didn't feel like looking up. She was standing next to the transparent wall, her forehead leaning gently on the cool glassy surface. The city underneath her was moving, changing, breathing, and all she wanted was to dissolve into its colors, become one with air and let go of her worries.

"Who hurt you, girl?" the voice repeated.

She sighed quietly and glanced sideways. There was a face, reflected by the glass. A face of a Han woman--fair, big-eyed, smiling softly.

"I did," Amber responded, turning on the spot... and froze mid-word.

The young woman standing in front of her was stunningly beautiful--flawless skin covered by tiny freckles, with goddess-like features and an enviable waist-hip ratio, her long white hair flowing elegantly past her shoulders and touching her exposed arms. She was the image from a children's fairytale, a work of art rather than a person...but it's not what caught Amber's attention. Not that she didn't find her attractive.

The girl was a cyborg.

It was subtle, almost hidden from view. The dull clicks in her chest were mere whispers, and the metallic glitter in the iris of her eyes could as well be a trick of the light. But the smile...perfectly symmetrical, almost forced--mechanical. Amber had seen androids before, self-aware ones too, not just sophies, and she knew what they were like. This woman was like them, but not quite. Not completely artificial. Or at least so it seemed.

"Sorry to hear that," the young woman said, and extended her hand. "I'm Io."

"Amber." She squeezed her hand gently. It was icy cold and velvety smooth.

"You have never been in Ashens before, Amber," Io asserted.

"Is it that obvious?"

"I know everyone who comes here. It's my club."

"Oh." Amber took half a step back and composed herself. "Wow. Cool. Well." She paused. "I'd buy you a drink but it's your place, so..."

"No need." She smiled. "Substances don't work on me. I'm..."

"...a techie," Amber finished for her. "Augmented person."

"Spot on. Would you like something intoxicating?"

"I think I've had enough...but thanks for the offer," she added quickly, turning on her social interaction algorithms. "I wouldn't mind a chat though. Preferably somewhere more...private."

"We can talk, sure." She played with her hair with one elegant finger and something moved inside of Amber's belly. "But just so we're on the same page... you seem lovely, but I'm not into ladies."

"No problem." She concealed her disappointment. "I just think you're gorgeous," she blurted out.

"I get told that a lot," Io beamed. "Come. We can go upstairs."

Amber's heart skipped a beat. She watched the techie girl turn around, as if in slow motion--her hair flowing on a stream of air like an elegant animation. Together, they walked across the hall and up another spiral staircase, into a private room on another floor. It was empty, almost perfectly circular and surrounded by transparent walls. Amber gave out a soft sigh as she raised her eyes to the ceiling. There, painted in meticulous details and casting a pale glow on her face, was a spiraled cloud of stars and galaxies.

"It's the compilation image of the observable universe," Io explained, noticing the fascinated smile on Amber's face. "By Ravi Selleger. Like it?"

"'Like' isn't the right word," she replied. "It's...it makes me sad."

"Sad?" she said. "Why?"

"Don't know." Amber shrugged and rubbed her cramping neck. "I am tempted to come up with something fake-deep and philosophical but I won't give in. 'I don't know' is a good enough answer for me."

"That's fair."

Io circled the room, dragging her fingertips along the glass. "I had a lover a few years ago," she said. "A Sojhi. Theoretical physicist. He told me about deep time, and the quantum world, and so much more. He got it all, truly, I could tell. But there was so much sadness in him, so much...emptiness. I don't dwell on such things. They suck the life out of you."

"I don't understand physics," Amber confessed cheerfully. "Or math. Or most natural sciences, to be honest. So, I wouldn't know."

"You're human, aren't you?" She ceased the circling and fell gracefully into a fluffy sofa that rested in the center of the room. Amber didn't wait for an invitation to join her.

"Yep."

"I haven't spoken to a human for a while. How is life on Alexandria?"

"Same old. Population is growing, universities are studying all kinds of shit, lots of people are vaguely unhappy... politicians change but they ain't gonna change anything. Neither will the Muuk. It's decent. Can't complain."

"Sure about the 'can't complain' part?"

"Well." Amber chuckled. "You can always find something to complain about, if you look hard enough. I try not to. Especially after I got to see the galaxy for myself."

"What do you mean?"

"It's just..." She took a deep breath in. "The scope of suffering out there. I had no idea that Muuk care so little about most races in the universe."

"Do they filter the information you receive?"

"I'm not sure." She frowned. "They certainly don't teach it, or bring attention to it, and I mean, why would they? It doesn't exactly make them look good."

"Would humans refuse to cooperate with them if they knew the truth?"

"I doubt it."

"Can you find the truth if you actually search for it?"

"Possibly."

"So." Io smiled, and a touch of condescension leaked into her voice. "Is it the Muuk's fault for being the Big Bad and not advertising it, or is it perhaps... convenient, to live the way you do?"

Amber didn't reply. She had no solid arguments against that conclusion. Twenty-five years of living on Alexandria and it never occurred to her to wonder why they don't see many news reports from outside the planet. She was too preoccupied with the unfortunate realities of her own world. And she was rather eager to dismiss everything that didn't have a direct impact on her life.

Besides, even if she did see it online, and knew about the countless tragedies that permeated the universe... would that make her care? And why did she care now? What, in her pragmatic and egoistic mind had switched to make her feel for billions of strangers who didn't even belong to her species?

"Enough negativity," Io proclaimed, interrupting her thoughts. "I'm hungry.

179

Are you hungry?"

She had to pause for a second or two to figure it out. Amber's sense of hunger and thirst had only two settings: non-existent and 'oh my god I am starving over here'.

"Yes," she responded after a while.

"Right." Io turned over her arm and pressed two fingers above her elbow.

The comm device, Amber realized, was not being projected onto her skin like a normal phone. Instead, it was embedded into her tissues.

"May I ask?" she began, after Io was done picking their meal. "Your augmentation--medical or voluntary?"

"Both." She smiled. "I was ill as a kid, so I had my heart and lungs exchanged for an upgraded version. Then I grew up, got into tinker culture, and now I have a class-G metabolic amplifier, a mesh-networked scalable circulation unit and a re-entrant digital neural feedback circuit. Oh, and one more thing, but that's between me and my lovers."

"How much did it cost?"

"A fortune." She winked coyly. "Worth it though."

"Do you get stopped at the security line in airports a lot?"

"Enough questions." Io chuckled. "Our food is arriving."

The door clicked and through it entered a man, his hands full of small silver trays. One glance in his direction and Amber recognized the guy who spoke to her downstairs. She didn't acknowledge it.

"What is this?" Amber asked, once the trays appeared in front of them.

"An assortment of goods. Here, try the red plate," Io advised. "Krodle seeds, soaked in herbal liquor and cooked on open fire. You can't find those trees anywhere else besides this planet. It's one of our rarest delicacies."

Amber grabbed a spoon and scooped a nice helping of the seeds. A greenish shade of brown and floating in a slimy dark liquid, they didn't seem especially promising. She licked the edge of the spoon, then popped it into her mouth. The seeds were warm, sour and mushy. Most of the taste and smell, she guessed, was coming from the sauce and spices. She had no trouble swallowing the dish but it didn't change her life either.

"You are what you eat." Io was now busy compiling a selection of foods on her own plate. "It fuels your body and gives it the raw building material for growth."

"No shit, Sherlock," Amber wanted to add, but was preoccupied with chewing.

"That's why it is so important to eat proper food," Io continued. "It has to have the right energy, the right vibrations. It has to agree with your soul. Nourish it. Protect it from damage."

"Is that a mushroom, a plant or an animal?" Amber asked, pointing with her spoon at a bowl full of suspiciously looking white lumps.

"Neither. It's an insect."

"An insect's an animal though," Amber thought, and poured the white lumps onto her plate. She was not about to correct the person who was feeding her exclusive delicacies for free.

"Be careful with zeet. It is very salty."

"I could get used to this." She snorted and wiped her mouth with the edge of her sleeve. "By the way, aren't there techies who don't eat at all?"

"Not many. You'd think not eating is all great and convenient but you start to miss the tastes after a while."

"You can drink that thousand flavor stuff."

"Perhaps." Io smiled. "You're a curious person, Amber."

"If I got a credit for every time someone said that," she replied.

For the rest of the meal, they ate in silence.

After swallowing her last bite, Io dabbed her lips with a corner of a paper tissue and pushed the tray to the left with a swift motion of her high-heeled boot. Amber licked her fingertips and suppressed a burp. Io didn't notice it, or if she did, she in turn was too polite to say anything. She reached behind the couch and pulled out a small metal box. Inside were several plastic packets of some grey sand-like substance, a stack of paper squares and a tube of adhesive. Without a comment or a word of explanation, Io freed up some space on the table and began crafting a handmade cigarette.

181

"Eyho?" the techie offered, lighting up the cigarette with a flicker of a silver lighter.

"Nah." Amber shook her head. "I don't know what this is, but it looks like a drug, and I don't do unknown drugs."

"How come?" she asked, as if it was strange enough to require a thorough explanation.

"My brain is messed up as it is. I don't wish to mess it up further."

"Eyho won't mess you up. It's calming. And good for your aura."

"I'm fairly satisfied with the condition of my aura, thanks."

"Well," Io shrugged, and exhaled a cloud of thick white smoke, "it's your choice. Now tell me, Amber--what are your plans?"

"What, like, for life?"

"Sweet." She chuckled softly. "We can start with tomorrow."

"Oh. Okay." Amber scratched her eyebrow, thinking. "To get to the research station. Preferably. Or as close to it as I can in one day."

"Business trip?"

"More of an intermediate step. I'm looking for a hitchhike ride, or a ship to rent. I wanna get to the Teardrop Cluster."

"How fascinating." Io took in another deep puff of smoke and let it out through her nostrils. "Black hole watcher?"

"Professor of history," she corrected in a matter-of-fact tone. "See, there's this planetoid orbiting a gas cloud, called BR3F70 or something like that, and based on my research, I have reasons to believe it is actually the graveyard of an ancient civilization. Or might be a secret home, I don't know yet."

"So, you're into space exploration!"

Amber wanted to disagree, but Io didn't give her a chance to chime in.

"Me too! My friends and I are planning a mission to discover what modern science says we can't. We're very close to launching our first trip. Actually, we could take you to the station, if you'd like. We were going there next week anyway. Might as well do it now."

"Really? That would be awesome!" Amber beamed. "You have your own transport?"

"Girl." Io smirked coyly, extinguishing her cigarette and leaping upwards from the couch. "I'm Io Esme. I have everything."

FIFTEEN

When Io was leading her and Lullaby through the deserted dark streets of the city, Amber's imagination ran wild on account of the techie's mode of transport. As a child, Amber went through a phase of being utterly obsessed with cars. She studied their structure, learned about the mechanisms behind magnetic levitation and anti-grav hovering, memorized hundreds of current and forgotten models and collected digital cards with them. She remembered contemplating an engineering career and being deeply disappointed when she realized how much math it involved. Eventually, her obsessions changed and she moved on--but transport never failed to fascinated her.

She wondered what kind of vehicle Io could afford. A mint condition Eagle with an almost spaceship-like engine capacity and a battery that worked without a refill for twenty days? Or a Liberta, a bit of an older model which was still unsurpassed in its speed and navigating grace? Or maybe a Spirit, which, frankly, was not so technically advanced, but resembled a work of art more than it did a car and was a favorite among the richest of the galaxy. Amber felt her heart flutter as Io invited them into the hangar. She squeezed past the hostess, leaped forward and scanned the vast space with her eyes. What she saw was...unexpected.

"The hell is this?!" Amber waved her hand around, pointing vaguely in the direction of the vehicle, unable to conceal her confusion.

"Re-designed SUV," Io responded, walking towards it.

"Huh?"

"Made just for me, based on old Han prototypes."

She retrieved a key from her pocket, opened the car's door and nodded at Amber, inviting her in.

Amber raised a suspicious eyebrow. In front of her was something that resembled a bloated hovercar--a rectangular box of metal and plastic, with a windshield and four doors, resting on four massive wheels. It looked to her more like farming equipment than a bona-fide vehicle.

"Come on," Io urged. "It's perfectly safe."

Hesitant but curious, Amber approached the car and entered the roomy cabin. Lullaby followed with similar apprehension.

"How does it work?" Amber asked, taking in the finer details of the car.

Inside, it had a circular row of seats with a table in the middle--generously decorated with paintings and all kinds of glittery things. Closer to the windshield were two more seats, one of them resting in front of a steering wheel and a control panel filled with buttons. In the back was an empty compartment, presumably dedicated to storing luggage.

"Combustion engine," Io replied, hoping over the circular seats and into the front section of the car. "Fueled by ethyl alcohol."

"A what now?!"

"Combustion engine. It operates by..."

"Yeah, I know what a combustion engine is. I'm a historian." Amber shook her head, not sure if she should have been amazed, or outraged, or both. "I can see what you're trying to achieve here. Like, a twentieth century car. Cool! But how is this thing allowed to be operational?"

"Allowed?" Io chuckled. "As if anyone cares what goes on in this world."

"It's a machine that works by burning a highly combustible liquid. It can go boom at any second."

"Not if you drive carefully."

"Don't tell me it is manual too."

"It can be."

"Seriously?!"

Amber paused, took a deep breath in and calmed herself.

"Isn't safe?" Lullaby asked, taking a seat with comical caution.

"Depends on what you mean by safe." Amber shrugged. "God, I hate nostalgia," she muttered. "How long will it take us to get to the research station in this thing?"

"Five hours, give or take." Io told her, inserting the key into the ignition sequence. "We'll take a shortcut through the Arovim forest. But I need to pick up my friends first."

"Sure." Admitting defeat, Amber fell into the circular seats.

At least they were ridiculously comfy.

They meandered around the city, making multiple stops to invite additional passengers, acquire various items of convenience and 'appreciate the view.' And by appreciating, Io mostly meant taking pictures and uploading them to several social media accounts. Amber, who sat next to a window, her forehead pressed to the cold glass, endured it with no complaints. She felt the engine's vibrations reverberate through her skull as the car moved through the streets of Laetial. A peculiar mood took over her, something in between boredom and despair. Evidently neither Lullaby, Io nor any of her friends have noticed.

By the end of their detour, they had gathered a final company of seven. One by one they were joined by a very young and provocatively dressed Bellazi girl, an older Han bloke, covered head to toe in tattoos and with hair braided in dozens of tiny pigtails, a pale and skinny Sojhi woman who was wearing something akin to a floral pattern potato sack, and another Sojhi, dark skinned and tall, whose gender Amber couldn't identify. Lullaby was immediately fascinated by these people; the feeling was mutual. While Io drove the car out of the brightly lit labyrinth of the city and into broad and empty highways, a passionate conversation blossomed out of small talk.

Amber managed to somehow tune it out, for the most part. Her brain was not very good at filtering unnecessary information, but it didn't force her to comprehend it either. She happily missed two hours of passionate discussions about art, theater, cinema, politics and fashion, all delivered with the eloquence and depth of knowledge of talk show hosts. The voices all blended together into a sea of noise that bore no meaning. It was relatively easy to ignore. She almost began to doze off to sleep, when something caught her attention. A thread, a tiny spec of language, just a single word--"conspiracy".

She opened one eye, shifted slightly in her seat and listened in while pretending not to listen.

"...rather fascinating how well they manage to hide the truth." It was the older Han guy talking. "But they're professionals. They have it covered. Do you know when children first learn the stellar distribution theory? Second grade! If you indoctrinate them since before they can resist it, of course everyone is going to believe it."

"Why indoctrinate?"

Amber recognized Lullaby's voice.

"To keep it secret, of course."

"Why keep secret?"

"For several reasons," the Sojhi interjected. "First, to keep people depressed and docile. If you tell everyone that this galaxy is already conquered and the other are unreachable, they have that many reasons to give up and stop striving for exploration. Second, to support the 'billions of years' narrative, cause it wouldn't make sense otherwise, now would it? And third, well, simply to keep the universe to themselves and not share it with anyone!"

"That terrible." Lullaby nodded enthusiastically. "And you fight the system."

"We try." Io smirked. "But it's not easy."

"What's not easy?" Amber couldn't pretend to not be bothered anymore. "Sticking fingers deep into your ear canals and singing 'yada-yada, I can't hear you'?"

"Pardon?" Io, who was no longer driving the vehicle, turned sideways in her seat and pierced Amber with a cold look.

"That bullshit you believe," she elaborated. "You're into the black veil stuff, aren't you?"

"I'm not into any stuff." Io's lower lip quivered. "I'm one of the few who is intelligent enough to know I am being lied to."

"Lied to about what?"

"The sky, Amber? Why is the sky so dark?" And she pointed her perfectly manicured fingernail to the window.

Outside, the night lingered. The air was still and no sights or sounds from the city were reaching them. Up and above the horizon you could just about see the outlines of a dense, vast forest, with some occasional flickers of spaceships and airplanes. Apart from that, it was filled thoroughly with darkness. Deep, unsettling, profound darkness—with no artificially displayed stars to keep it company.

"It's dark because it's the night and the sun isn't up yet," Amber replied, unamused.

"Oh, please. You know what I mean. Where are the stars, huh?"

"Out there, in their places."

"Why can't we see them then?"

"We can see some." Amber shrugged. "On a clear, cloudless night, somewhere with no light pollution —you can count to a few dozen."

"But there are billions of stars in our galaxy!"

"Well," she spoke slowly and thoughtfully, as if explaining something to a toddler, "some of them are too far away for us to see and the rest are surrounded by Dyson swarms that Muuk use to power their civilization."

"Oh yes, those mythical Dyson swarms that no one has ever seen."

"Actually," Amber activated her bracelet and typed something on the surface of her forearm, "you can see one right now."

She pressed a button on the bracelet itself and a 3D picture was projected into the air. It showed a small sphere of blue-white light surrounded by a dense cloud of metal panels.

"It's five star systems away from here, you can go visit."

"A fake," Io dismissed.

"A fake?"

"Composite image of the real star and computer graphics."

"But it is literally out there. The Muuk aren't exactly hiding the fact that they have Dyson spheres all over the galaxy."

"Why can't you visit one of those systems then?"

"You can. Anyone can, if they get a pass."

"Why do you have to get a pass if they exist?"

"Why do you have to get a pass to go into a government agency of any sort?" Amber waved her arms around, perplexed. "Gee, mate, maybe it's because they're the most advanced race in the observable universe and don't appreciate us lowly races invading their homes? I mean, it's not like it's impossible to visit a Muuk system. Diplomats and scientists do it all the time."

"Muuk shills."

"Of course."

"How can you believe their nonsense, Amber?!" Io's voice was breaking, trembling with emotion. "You're a learned woman!"

"Exactly. I'm a historian. I know how conspiracies work, and I know that, on this scale, they simply can't."

"But other galaxies!"

"...are out there, just very far from us," Amber continued calmly. "Trillions of light years far. So far, in fact, that we can't even detect most of them, let alone see them on our skies. The universe is big, and expanding, and light has a finite speed. It's not that hard to understand, if you have at least a handful of neurons."

Then came a heavy moment of silence, during which Amber folded her arms on her chest triumphantly and almost declared victory for herself. It didn't last for long.

"It's all fake," the Bellazi girl spoke.

"What 'all'?" Amber asked, her head tilted slightly to the right.

"The universe expansion. It isn't happening anymore. Stopped happening billions of years ago."

"Yeah?" Amber raised an eyebrow. "So what is it doing now?"

"Shrinking back."

"Really?" She smirked. "Now, do you have any evidence for that, love? Any equations, maybe? Some data? Something other than talking out of your ass?"

"They shut off all opposition!" the girl insisted, frowning. "You can't even publish in a scientific journal if you don't agree with that stupid fairytale of theirs."

"You mean the theory of everything?" Amber inquired. "The theory that united all four fundamental forces of physics and reconciled quantum mechanics with relativity? The one that was independently coined by five different races?" She was also starting to lose her temper now. "And one that has never been disproved and is supported by countless piles of observable evidence? I wonder why anyone who doesn't see the validity of such a theory can't get published in a scientific journal...maybe, just maybe, it's because they aren't a scientist."

"Look, cat," the Han guy interrupted, "if the universe really is still expanding, then why is this galaxy still in one piece?"

"Hey, I'm not a physicist, okay?" she responded. "In fact, I know shit about physics, and I still seem to be more educated on this topic than you lot. It's complicated! Less complicated than admitting that we don't see any stars cause they're too far away and not cause the Muuk are hiding them somehow. How are they hiding the stars, by the way?"

"The black veil..."

"Please, not that word, it makes me have laughing fits."

"Whatever." He chewed on his lip for a second or two. "The Muuk use special technology to cover the sky, the same way they project whatever they want on resort worlds. And Alexandria."

"Okay." Amber nodded. "So, why are there no stars when you're on a spaceship?"

"All spaceships go through Muuk approval before being released onto the market."

"They rig the spaceships?"

"Yes."

"What, even those tiny ones you can buy for your bored teenager that only goes between planets in the same system?"

"Yes!"

"And troposphere planes?"

"Uh-huh."

"Well, tough!" Amber waved her arms around, frustrated. "I don't know, make your own spaceship or something!'"

"We will, in fact," Io said with spiteful glee in her voice. "That is exactly what we're planning to do. And then we will disprove that universe expanse nonsense once and for all!"

"Good luck." Amber snorted with laughter. "Even if you will succeed at building it, nothing will make you change your mind. You will see no stars and you will come up with new and exciting bullshit to confirm your previous belief."

Amber was on the highest horse imaginable now. She could not be stopped by any force of physics known in the universe.

"You're obviously fundamentally incapable of logic, critical thinking, skepticism and just admitting that you're wrong. You wouldn't survive a day in science! And you," Amber pointed at Io, "are a disgrace too. I mean, you're a techie! You're technology through and through. Literally! How can you be using the fruits of science and progress, yet deny such integral parts of it?!"

"Universal expanse isn't science." Io's face was flushing red. "It's an elaborate scheme to keep people from exploring this reality for themselves. It holds as much merit as electrochemical theory of consciousness."

Amber opened her mouth, then closed it. Then burst into laughter. She laughed until her stomach hurt and her eyes filled up with tears. Io and her gang watched her, perplexed.

"I'm sorry." She shook her head. "I truly am. I just, I can't believe someone can be so rich, yet so idiotic! I mean, black veil is one thing, but the ECC theory, seriously? You're talking to a human! I have the Emmerson device under my skull." She tapped a finger on the left side of her head, just above her ear and next to the scar that span half of her face. "I am living proof of that theory's validity."

"You haven't died yet." the Sojhi person pointed out. "So you can't know."

"My grandma died though. I talk to her every other week."

"How do you know it's her?"

"I know, okay?" Amber was still giggling from time to time. "We can talk about it, if you want. And I also believe thousands of neurobiologists and neural engineers who say it is true."

191

"Maybe you're just a shill for the Muuk," Io said.

"Maybe I just have a brain!" She smiled. "God, guys, you really are entertaining. But the Muuk sure should invest in more education."

"Propaganda, you mean?" Io was not having it.

Amber sighed. "Look, galactic beauty," she said. "I understand it. These ideas, they're cool and new and shiny, and they make you feel special. Like you have access to something no one else has. And you think it makes you better than everyone else but in reality you're nothing more than a brainless mortal with no talents, no real ambitious and no meaningful contributions to this world and its people." She paused, a smug grin, ear to ear, illuminating her face. "And you ain't even that pretty."

Io's nostrils flared. She breathed in, then out, and pressed her jaws so tight, a muscle bulged on her beautiful porcelain white cheek.

"Get out," she said.

"Sorry, what?" Amber repeated, still smiling.

"Out!" Io shrieked. "Out of my car!"

She rushed towards the car's control panel and pushed a bunch of buttons frantically. Amber watched it with mild bemusement. She wasn't convinced of the realness of her threat. However, when she felt the rapid deceleration of the car, she was forced to consider the alternative.

"I want you out," Io repeated once the car had stopped completely. "Now."

"Are you also insane?!" Amber exclaimed. "We are, what, precisely in the middle of nowhere?"

"We're at the edge of the forest," Io explained calmly. "If you walk through it, you'll end up on the base in a couple of hours."

"But we have no food, no water, no directions..."

"Water." Io reached under the seats and threw a two liter water bottle at Amber. "You have Internet in your device. And you can deal with no food for two hours."

"But..."

"Out!" she yelled. "Or I'll..."

192

Amber decided not to stick around to hear the end of that sentence. She grabbed the water bottle, opened the door and jumped out onto the cold sandy ground. Lullaby, who remained absolutely quiet and emotionless throughout the whole sequence of events, followed immediately.

"Io?" Amber called out, but the door was snapped shut in front of her. "My bag!" she yelled at the opened window as the car began to accelerate.

It slowed down for a second and her bag was thrown out of the window.

"And yet it turns!" Amber shouted.

"Didn't really say that," Lullaby said, picking up Amber's bag. "Galileo."

"Yeah, I told you that. I'm a historian."

"Thought you wouldn't get that far."

"You don't know me well, then."

"Called her not pretty."

"You were agreeing with them!"

"Remembered they were our transport. Being polite. Useful."

"Screw politeness. I fight against ignorance."

"You walk on foot through the forest now," Lullaby retorted.

"True," she admitted reluctantly.

Amber's opinion on Io and her friends could have been different if she were aware of other conspiracy theories currently in fashion on Skia. They included: "the Muuk do not exist", "Bellazi are actually Sojhi in lizard skins", "the stars we can see are projections", "the Muuk are actually human", and "glik and morshu are really the same thing but with different colors". Occasionally, they even contained an element of truth...

The sun was about to rise, warming up the crisp air and the bumpy ground beneath their feet. A wind was catching up too, blowing from behind their backs. In front of them was a forest--monumentally tall and dense enough to obscure from view everything that resided further than a few meters away from the entry line. The cold night was slowly changing into a hot day, and transforming the sleepy, docile plain into a busy jungle. Amber swallowed hard.

"Well if this ain't my lucky fucking day," Amber muttered.

Lullaby did not listen to the words, but they did understand the feeling. And they shared it completely.

Meanwhile, S was losing in a game of poker to Light, Darkness, and the yet uncrowned prince (and future king) of the seven systems of Wildworld. And he was not happy about it.

"Pardon me, your highness," S began, rearranging his cards in his hands, "but if I remember correctly, two aces negate the presence of a joker, and..."

"The correct form of address to a prince is your excellence," the prince interrupted, and, taking his pipe out of his mouth, let out a puff of purple smoke. "And you're quite right, dear S, except you're missing the three queens on the table."

"Ah." S had just realized that he lost, completely and utterly, to the delight of his two colleagues. "In that case, your excellence, I henceforth absolve my turn, as well as my con and game."

The prince smiled with a corner of his mouth and sucked in more smoke, letting it out through all three of his nostrils.

"Now, dear S," he said, laying down his cards to reveal a cat royalle, "debts must be paid."

S sighed. This was precisely what he was afraid of.

"Alright. I'll tell you," he said. "But you have to swear an oath of secrecy, my prince! Under no circumstances should this information be revealed. In any manner!"

"Not least in the manner you are revealing it now." The prince chuckled.

"Indeed. So," S continued. "The duke of Planet Three is in cahoots with your father, your excellence. They are encouraging an uprising among the masses."

"I knew it," the prince muttered. He paused, twirling his mustache around his finger. "Tomorrow, I shall act. But tonight, we shall drink."

And with those words, he reached under the table and produced an opened bottle of clear Mountain Juice, the strongest alcohol drink known to his culture.

S, Light and Darkness had learned the hard way not to argue with royalty, especially about intoxicating substances.

And so that night, they got wasted.

They climbed out of the window of the prince's chamber the next morning, leaving him to snore in a pile of cards and half-torn letters from his ex-girlfriend. Being creatures of pure spirit, they were not affected by hangover physically--but the emotional impact still lingered.

"That was quite clever," Darkness said as they walked across dew-humid blue grass, away from the castle and towards the horizon. "You betting with the information. And losing on purpose. Must have been hard to arrange a loss so pathetic...I'm impressed."

"What was the job in the first place?" Light asked. "Why did you have to disclose that?"

"I wasn't supposed to disclose that," S confessed. "Wasn't supposed to lose either. It was completely accidental."

"Oh," Light said.

Darkness didn't say anything. She just laughed.

"The Unnamed will have your head for this!" she pointed out in between laughing fits.

"Or maybe this was meant to be," S disagreed. "Things that are meant to happen are meant to happen, and things that are not meant to happen also happen sometimes and, uh, stuff. Yes." He frowned. "Well. We'll have to stick around and wait for the prince's response."

"To be fair," Light said, "with the amount of Mountain Juice he had last night, there's a good chance he doesn't remember anything."

"I sure hope he doesn't." S nodded.

And they continued to walk into the sunrise.

SIXTEEN

"I hate nature!"

It took Amber approximately seventeen minutes to shift in moods from cautiously optimistic to miserable and fuming angry. At first, a long walk through an alien jungle didn't seem like a big deal to her; she traversed more than a few patches of artificial tropics during her childhood on Alexandria and she almost enjoyed the process. She liked the intense but soft colors, and the bird's song, and the fruit that she got to taste.

This forest was very different though. It didn't come prepared and pre-packaged with an android guide, for one. Following online directions and sticking to a single path seemed fairly straight forward at first, but proved to be rather tricky, not in small part due to the said path being not that well-defined. In fact, Amber had decided, it was not a path at all, but rather a ridiculous arrangement of dried-out patches of grass. No one had walked these jungles in decades...at least no one intelligent.

Now, sweaty, mentally exhausted and in a terrible temper, she was close to having a meltdown. Her damp clothes stuck to her back, making her skin crawl, and her bare forearms and ankles were covered in itching insect bites. The ecosystem was thriving, bursting with smells and colors, buzzing with life, and excited to welcome a couple of visitors--and Amber despised it. She tripped over a thick chunk of roots and shook her fist at the tree, almost ready to hit it back. Lullaby regarded her with mild curiosity.

"What'cha lookin' at, huh?" Amber mumbled, making them flinch.

Turning their head, they quickly realized that Amber wasn't talking to them, but instead to a creature that sat on a tree branch in front of them. It was roughly circular in shape, about the size of their head, covered in a dense layers of something fluffy (feathers or fur, they couldn't tell), intensely pink, and with two pairs of large orange eyes.

"Has plenty of eye to look with," Lullaby commented.

"It's staring at me!" she almost shrieked. "I can tell."

The creature moved left on the branch, then opened its huge mouth and shrieked back at Amber.

"That's it." She jumped up on the spot and rushed towards the tree with all the intension to climb up it.

Sadly, before she had a chance to reach the branch, the creature gave one last high-pitched call and disappeared so quickly, she couldn't even tell if it fell off, flew away or just teleported.

"Rude," Amber said. "Ran away before I could give it a good bollocking for staring at me!"

"Just an animal," Lullaby tutted. "Come on. We need to move."

Reluctantly, Amber lowered her still clenched fists and followed Lullaby's lead. The sun was shining hard at her head, even through the forest canopy, and she was starting to feel dizzy, unsteady on her feet. She reached for the water bottle and started sipping absent-mindedly. By the time she removed the bottle from her mouth, it was half-empty already.

"Need to walk in one direction," Lu proclaimed, turning left and right on the spot, Amber's smart watch in their grasp.

"Stupid planet doesn't have a north," Amber complained. "Or a south, or anything in between. Doesn't have a magnetic field in general."

"Can tune in to the closest point of radiowave transmission and walk towards it."

"What if we will return to the opposite side of the forest?"

"Doesn't matter. Look." They pointed vaguely around themselves.

Amber followed their finger with her gaze and quickly realized what Lu meant.

It seemed as if the jungle was closing in around them. The trees were getting taller and thicker, and there were no discernible paths under her feet. She looked up and did not see a single patch of the sky; the realization sent a wave of shivers down her spine. The calls of animals intensified in her ears and the nauseatingly sweet smell of tropical flowers made her headache. Suddenly it struck her just how far away from home she were...and how she was totally, absolutely screwed.

"I'm sorry," Amber said, forcing herself to ignore half a dozen stings across her body. "I'm sorry I couldn't shut up, and we ended up in here, and now we're both gonna die and get eaten by space ants or some shit."

"Hey." Lullaby grabbed her shoulder and shook her sternly, which was almost enough to knock her off her feet. "You aren't going to die, and neither will I." They've switched to their native language. "At least not today. I appreciate the apology, but you can't go back now. So calm down, get yourself together and follow me."

"Yes." Amber nodded. "Yes, of course. Where to?"

"Through that bush." They stepped forward and tore off what looked like half a shrub in one abrupt motion. "We will follow a signal and keep to the same direction. We're bound to end up somewhere."

"If you don't know where you are going, it doesn't matter the road you take, does it?" she added, but Lu wasn't listening.

They waded through the cobweb of plants, avoiding anything that moved and dodging the occasional falling fruit or seed. Amber kept her hand on the edge of Lullaby's cloak, which was torn and shredded from the struggle. Her own hair was full of seeds and dried leafs, she noticed. Picking the debris out gave her something to do. She concentrated on following Lu's enormous steps as closely as possible and decided not to think about anything else...which was easier said than done.

"I think the forest is thinning out," Lullaby spoke up.

Amber blinked a few times. The words were not fully reaching her ears, as if the sound was traveling through a layer of honey.

"Whatever you say," she replied.

Lullaby's stance and movement were her only source of confidence. She watched the Rx'lng crush through the green labyrinth, seemingly not bothered by branches hitting their body and scratching their face. Not a drop of blood or sweat could be spotted on their skin. When a small and slimy animal of some sort dropped off a tree canopy and onto the ground in front of them, Lu hissed at them with astonishing vigor, making the creature abandon its plans and run for its life. With a loopy smile Amber realized what it meant to be a nest protector.

"I love you, Lk'st," Amber babbled, feeling rather drunk. "You're my best friend."

"I'm touched," they said. "Pick up the pace, you're falling behind."

"What do you mean?" She frowned and scratched her damp forehead. "I'm right behind you."

"No, you're not! Focus."

"Now that is weird," Amber thought, stopping in her track.

She could have sworn that, for the last minute, she was maintaining her grasp on Lu's cloak, just like she did for the previous hour. But now that she was focusing on the sensations in her hand, she could not feel the velvety fabric touching her fingertips. In fact, she couldn't feel anything in her hand, or her other hand, or pretty much her entire body. It had all gone numb. She took a sharp breath in as terror overcame her.

"Lu!" she shouted. "Wait for me."

"Waiting," was the reply.

Amber rubbed her eyes and opened them slowly, expecting–hoping--to see Lullaby's broad back a couple of steps away from herself. And she did, but only for a second or two. First, they were right there, in front of her, but then something happened and the image began to flow forwards, getting fuzzy and blending with the forest green. Her head was spinning, and she felt nauseas all of a sudden. A heat wave hit her body like a cannonball. She stumbled, attempting to take a single step forwards, and slipped to the ground, breathing rapidly.

"Well, shit," she thought just before she passed out.

She awoke to cold water on her face, and a violent coughing fit took her over before she could process anything else. Upon forcing her eyes open she saw something that filled her with absolute, teeth-shattering dread--nothing. Just a flash of it. A brief, horrifying moment of complete, unrelenting nothingness. It wasn't even darkness, no. Darkness has a certain texture to it, a familiar, calming touch. This was not darkness; it was nothing. Thankfully only a second of it. Then her vision stabilized and the now disgustingly familiar landscape of the jungle appeared in front of her eyes. She thought she would see Lullaby standing near, urging her to get up and get moving, but they weren't there.

"Lu?" Amber called out. "Lu, where are you? I'm sick. I need help."

"Help?"

Amber swallowed hard. In front of her appeared the pink fluffy creature she attempted to fight not so long ago. It seemed larger to her now, rounder, fluffier. It stood a couple of steps away from her, supported by two incredibly thin legs which bended backwards at the knees like that of a grasshopper. It blinked two of its orange eyes at her, as if winking.

"You need help?" the creature said, bouncing gently on the ground.

"Yeah," she murmured. "Can you help me? I'm lost, and I don't feel too well."

"You're rendering."

"Sorry, what?"

"Your pixels need dusting," it chirped cheerfully.

"Hey, buddy, I don't understand you. Please." She reached forwards with her right hand but was too weak to lift herself off the ground. "Help me up."

"Can't."

"You can try. Please, I need to find my friend."

"You have no friends," the creature said, now in a different voice. In Professor Nawahi's voice.

And then disappeared.

"Fuck, now the jungle monsters are bullying me," Amber complained to no one in particular. "I deserve this. I..."

She stopped mid-sentence to cough again and spat out a mouthful of something viscous and bitter. She craved for a sip of water, but the water bottle was gone.

"Hey." She looked down at her leg and saw a tiny, ant-like insect sitting on her bare toe. "Funny," she muttered. "Don't remember losing my shoe."

She wanted to shake the insect off but didn't succeed. The ant thing continued its climb up her leg. It should have tickled her, Amber thought, but it wasn't. Soon the first ant was joined by a second.

"Leave me alone, little things," she said.

It didn't help. The ants were now appearing out of nowhere and rapidly covering her body. They crawled under her clothes and all over her exposed skin. Soon she was up to her neck in ants.

"I don't wanna die," Amber whimpered, as the ants climbed up to her face and rushed into her nose and ears.

She screamed...and suddenly, the ants were gone.

She rolled over to her side. Her limbs were still numb, and her senses were bleeding into each other; she heard, distinctly, a light blue sky covered by fluffy white clouds, and sobbed. She didn't see anything above her, apart from a sea of green. There was no way out.

"So this is how it ends," Amber told herself, and the words tasted strange in her mouth, like bland cotton candy. "In a stupid fucking forest, on a stupid fucking planet. Alone."

The last word echoed metal in her ears, followed soon by a microphone rebound noise, sharp, deafening. Amber winced and sniffed. The air was so thick with damp, it could be cut with a knife-like marshmallows. She made a few steps forward. It took serious effort. Her feet kept sticking to the ground and soaking into the dirt. She saw a tree stump nearby and decided to take a seat.

But when she lowered herself gingerly down, she fell through--through the wood, into the stump, and underground.

She didn't scream or move as she kept falling down and down, in what seemed to be a wide, bottomless tunnel. It was pitch black inside and yet she could see things. Things were falling next to her at varying speeds. A paper textbook of ancient human history. A pack of playing cards. A tiny, badly painted model of a spaceship. A framed photo of some kid she didn't recognize. A live, bleeding, beating human heart.

Amber closed her eyes but the images did not go away. They sped up, blinking past her one after another, just long enough for her to notice what it was. They were getting more and more disturbing as well. More human parts, bloodied weapons, faces of weeping children, bones, faces, weapons, faces, faces. So much pain. So much suffering.

"Enough!" she screamed. No sound came out of her mouth.

In fact, she realized as she reached for her face and searched desperately with her fingers, she no longer had a mouth. She made one last attempt at screaming, then fell quicker still and crashed against the ground. Crashed and fell apart into a trillion tiny pieces.

Amber came back to life in a desert, mouth back on her face and full of sand. She stood on her knees--coughing, spitting, rubbing her eyes, desperate to breathe. Sand filled her throat, her eyes, her nose...there was no escape from the sand. Tears were streaming down her face. All of her skin was on fire, every square inch. She kept coughing and coughing, until she felt dizzy, and just as she was about to suffocate, the sand was suddenly gone.

She blinked and looked around. Everywhere, in every direction, was nothing but sand and sky--dark orange sand, aquamarine sky. For miles and miles and miles. She stood up on shaky legs. What was she to do? Just...walk, hell knows in what direction, until she dies of dehydration?

"Beats dying in one spot," she said to herself, and began to walk.

She didn't get far. First, a hill materialized in front of her. She climbed the hill slowly, sand flowing, escaping from under her feet. As she looked down from the hill, she saw them--Rx'lng, a group of ten or so, marching in line one after another. They didn't look quite the same as Lullaby, she realized. These were shorter, more dainty. Defenseless. No protector with them.

"Hey!" Amber shouted at the line. "Over here!" She switched to the Rx'lng's language.

They didn't react.

"I think I can help you!" she added, now climbing down the hill. "Or you can help me, maybe?"

But the Rx'lng line kept moving, not even turning their heads in Amber's direction. By the time she was down to ground level, they were gone like a desert phantom.

"Oh, for fuck's sake!" Amber yelled at the sky. "This is ridiculous! I'm done," she proclaimed. "I'm done with this nonsense. I'll just...sit down on the ground," she said, lowering herself into the sand, "and wait for death, okay?"

She was transported back into the jungle as soon as she touched the ground.

Except the jungle was different now. Broader. Cooler. The trees were around, but they were far, far away--always the same distance, no matter how much she walked. She stomped on the ground. The ground didn't budge. She talked and yelled and sobbed in exasperation and nothing changed.

"Well this level is boring," she announced to the sky. "Give me something to look at, maybe? Or to run away from?"

Her wish was granted almost instantly.

"Amber?"

She turned around slowly, having already recognized the voice. In front of her, in the middle of the forest, stood Amber's mother. Alive. Talking. A bit younger than she remembered her last, a sleeping baby held gently in her hands... and with horrendous burns all over her body.

"M-mum?" Amber replied meekly, so exhausted on so many levels, now ready to accept anything, no matter how bizarre. "Is that..." She made a step forward, then paused. "The baby. Is that me?"

"Yes," her mother smiled, as much as her burned face allowed. "Look. You were so cute."

"Yeah." Amber forced a smile too. "I'm still cute."

"Do you want to hold her?" her mother asked.

"I guess," Amber agreed, and took the baby gingerly into her arms.

She kept sleeping, not at all disturbed.

"Well this is... nice," Amber muttered. "Are you...?"

But when she looked up, her mother was gone--and in her place was a pile of ash.

"And what am I supposed to do now?" Amber asked, the baby still held firmly in her arms.

"This is how it always happens." Came another voice.

She turned around yet again and saw someone--a man, perhaps--standing quite close. His figure was blurred, so fuzzy it was barely visible. The only thing Amber could see is that he was wearing an old-fashioned wide-brimmed hat.

"What always happens?" Amber asked.

"You're born," he said. "Your parents die. You leave. You observe. You make a choice. Always."

"And what does that supposed to mean?"

But the man was already gone, along with the baby from her hands.

Then the jungles closed in on her again, and, with a gasp and a tremble, Amber realized that she could not move, did not have strength to move at all anymore. She stumbled to her knees and pressed herself to the wet grass.

"Will they be there?" Amber whispered. "When I die, will I meet my parents again?"

"No. Because you aren't going to die today."

Something lifted her off the ground and made her sit up straight. Amber coughed again and Lullaby handed her a full water bottle. She drank till there was nothing left.

"I couldn't follow you, Lu." She sobbed. "Sorry. I couldn't follow you."

"It's okay," they assured her. "I will help you. I will take the pain away."

Amber turned her gaze to Lullaby and blood froze in her veins. It was the Rx'lng archaeologist, certainly...but not completely. Lullaby's face was distorted, twisted, with whole gaps of the image missing. Their body was elongated and bent at a strange angle. She kept staring and Lu's large insect-like eyes began to grow even larger, until they took up their entire head. And their arms...their arms rested firmly on Amber's neck.

"Don't be afraid," they said, their voice sounding much lower than it used to.

"No," Amber said. "No, please. Don't."

"It's for your own good," they insisted, and squeezed their hands tightly until the last breath died off in her throat.

She struggled for a little while, and heard bone and cartilage cracking in her spine. Then came a brief moment of blinding light, and nothing.

Just the darkness.

SEVENTEEN

Happy.

Amber Avni Shakya was absolutely, completely happy.

She smiled from ear to ear and felt a warm tingling in her face. Her cheek was touching a smooth, cold fabric, and she detected a dim light through her closed eyelids. Her limbs felt heavy, her muscles were sore. Her mouth, throat and lips were dry. Yet, as she stretched her arms and legs in the warm bed, she was aware of nothing but utter, all-encompassing bliss. There were no thoughts in her head. She wasn't remembering the past, or worrying about the future. She was just alive, and it was the most wonderful thing in the world.

"...monitored him overnight and he didn't wake up. I'll change his fluids drip and add another dose of lyco."

"How is the human girl?"

"Stable, no changes so far."

The voices were coming from the left side of her bed, and it took her some time to identify the language as one of the Han dialects. One voice was low and coarse, the other higher and more pleasant. As soon as she heard them, she had decided that they were both her best friends for life. With that thought, she rolled over, lowered her legs to the floor and attempted to leave the bed.

"Woah, champ."

Her vision was a bit out of focus, so instead of a young Han rushing to her side, Amber saw a big vertical blob of beige.

"I wouldn't recommend it." He grabbed her by the shoulders and forcefully returned her to a horizontal position. "I'd say it is a bit too early for a walk."

"Whatevs." She beamed, and a streak of saliva trickled down her neck, which she was thankfully unaware of. "You smell funny."

"Yeah, working in a medical facility does that to you." He chuckled. "Hey, Ev? The human is awake. Tell the other that they can come visit her."

While the Han physician checked Amber's vitals and changed her medicine drip, she stared at the ceiling, eyes unblinking. She didn't remember being here before. In fact, she couldn't remember much prior to right about now. Somewhere in her brain records was a forest, and a car ride, and bright lights of a mighty metropolis--with little in between. Mostly, she remembered a curious dream she had just before waking up: about a fluffy owl, and hoppy bunnies, and ants. A lot of ants for some reason. Rainbow colored ones.

"Amber! You okay!"

Lullaby entered the room like a miniature blue hurricane and went straight for the far right side, where Amber resided in her blanket-filled bed. They didn't find a chair to sit on, so they lowered themselves to the ground.

"How is she?" they asked, hovering over the bed's edge.

"I'm goooooood," Amber responded in a sing-sang voice. "Really good."

"She is... high?" Lullaby tilted their head to one side.

"Side-effect of the drug," the Han clarified, taking off a dirty pair of gloves. "Interacts with endorphin receptors in the brain. Gives almost everyone a temporary sense of euphoria."

"I'm floating on a cloud," Amber proclaimed, then lifted herself to bend over the side of the bed and threw up on the floor near Lullaby.

The Han gave out a deep sigh.

"Also causes nausea, skin rashes, muscle cramps and the occasional spot of rectal bleeding," he said, and put on a fresh pair of gloves. "That's why folks don't get addicted. Still." He grabbed a mop from the nearby stand. "Beats dying from Ika-Ika."

A couple of beds away, an older man wrinkled his nose and put aside a bowl of soup he was given a few minutes ago.

The room was shared between half a dozen patients and it was far from well-ventilated. In fact, it didn't have windows, or air conditioning, or at least a second exit. Not that most people would be able to appreciate a nice view, since most of them spent their time either asleep or unconscious.

"Others can't catch it from her?" Lullaby helped the Han physician move the beds to wash under them.

"Not likely," he assured them. "It's only transmitted through bodily fluids, mostly through blood with insect bites. As long as we keep this place in a fairly sterile state, the risk is very low."

"And she will be alright?"

"Now that she has made it through the first twelve hours, probably. Mind you, she had a very rapid infection," he added. "Don't know if that's because she's human, or had no contact with it before. Most people here get Ika-Ika for the first time before they shed their baby fur."

That didn't mean anything to Lullaby but they were too polite to ask additional questions.

"I got it for the first time when I was four!"

They followed the sound to its origin and saw a Han girl sitting cross-legged on the edge of her bed.

She was small and very thin, with skin so pale it was almost completely translucent. She was wearing a medical robe, a central line catheter poking through the collar, and had bruises on both of her inner elbows. Her hairless scalp and dark spots under her big eyes gave her an appearance of a ghost. After a few seconds of looking at her, Lullaby realized that the girl was missing her right foot.

"Oh, shut it, Curie," the Han physician smiled. "Catching a disease is not an achievement."

"Surviving it is though," she disagreed.

"Fair enough. Good job, Curie's immune system."

She poked her tongue at him, and he retaliated with the same expression.

"Don't push my limits!" He chuckled. "You gotta have good relationships with your supplier of sweets and cushions."

"Sure, doc." Curie nodded, then flashed him a sly grin. "I also know your secret about doctor Eva..."

"Hey." He shushed at her. "I've paid you for that secret. Don't get cheeky."

And he moved on with his responsibilities.

Lullaby glanced at Amber, who was making bubbles with her mouth and bursting into a spontaneous bout of laughter every now and then, and decided that, at least for the current moment, she didn't need their company.

"Can help in the village?" they asked, following the Han to the exit.

"I guess I can find you a task, if you'd like." He shrugged.

"Yes, please! Should repay you for the favor."

"Don't worry, it's my job to treat people," he wanted to reply, but stopped himself.

The clan was not having the best of times, again, and they could do with a pair of strong hands.

Hours went flying by for Amber. Warm and comfy in her hospital gown, she enjoyed the wonders of a thoughtless mind and a total absence of pain in her body. She didn't feel hungry, or thirsty, or uncomfortable in any way. Granted, she also didn't feel much control over her bladder, but she had laminated bedsheets for that. When a Han woman approached her corner of the room, Amber's lips stretched into a wide, child-like grin.

"Maaaate." She giggled. "I like, totally love you."

"Yeah, well, you'll hate me in a moment," she said, fiddling with the drip.

Amber's eyes struggled to focus on the person's figure. Once her vision finally decided to cooperate with her, she saw a middle-aged Han woman dressed in a dark blue medical gown, with remarkably dark short hair and a tired expression which made her otherwise kind and pleasant features seem harsh and cold. She checked Amber's vitals on a nearby monitor, then injected a full syringe of some clear liquid into her drip. A few seconds later, Amber's short-lived trip to heaven was over.

"Ugh," was her first conscious word. "My mouth tastes like I've been chewing on a dirty sock for the last half hour."

"Sorry 'bout that," The Han woman reached into a cupboard nearby and handed her a bottle of water. "You were out of it for damn long. Reckoned it was time to bring you back to the world of sense and reason."

"Sense and reason suck raccoon nuts," Amber muttered and sipped the water cautiously. "And so does this place. It stinks like pee for starters."

"That's your own. I'll change your bedsheets if you can stand up."

Thankfully, she could.

"Sign me up for a shower after that," she said, leaning up against a wall. "Also, what is this place, actually?"

"A medical center."

"Yep, I figured as much. In a bit more detail, please?"

"You're about thirty five clicks away from Laetial and twenty clicks from the forest. This is a temporary settlement for the Wiocco clan. We're from Yun river, originally, not that you'd know where that is. Your friend brought you in yesterday, you were sick with the Ika-Ika fever. We've treated you for it. You'll probably make a full recovery."

"Probably?"

"I'm not Juhnwe." She shrugged. "I can't give guarantees."

"Was Lullaby sick?"

"Doesn't seem like it, at least so far. You can lay back now," the Han added, opening another plastic trash bag. "I've never met a Rx'lng before. They are awfully strong."

"True." Amber smiled, slipping under the fresh covers.

"No, I mean, awfully strong. Your friend--Lullaby, right? They smashed right through our high fence like it was made out of cardboard! Our boys have been repairing it for hours."

"Sorry. I can pay for it."

"That's very kind of you," she said. "But we don't have much use for your money. Besides, I think they've more than made up for it in the last few hours. So don't worry."

The woman was about to move on to the next bed when Amber called for her to pause.

"Hey." She wanted to go straight to business but stopped herself. "What is your name?"

"Eva," the Han replied.

"Thank you for saving my life, Eva."

"Keep that thanks for Santos. He was the one on call when you were brought in."

"Thank you regardless," Amber insisted. "So... you have any idea when I'll be able to leave?"

"Well." Eva scratched her nose with a side of her palm. "Judging by your metabolic rate, you'll be on your feet tomorrow, and back to normal in a few days. Doesn't mean you can leave though."

"Why... is that then?"

"Uh. Well." She hesitated. "I didn't want to break it to you so soon. You see...we're in lockdown for the foreseeable future."

"Huh?"

"We're at war," Eva elaborated. "With another clan. We're in between battles but it's not like we'll break peace any time soon."

"At...at war? Wait, there's a war?"

"Basically. It's been on and off for the last fifty years."

"Fifty years?!" Amber's eyebrows were so high up her forehead at that point, they were threatening to leave her face and start their own independent republic of eyebrows. "Were you, like, born into it then?"

"I was," she replied, rather nonchalant about it. "Don't get too worked up. It's pretty chill at the moment. We haven't had a single death this month."

"And that's... good?"

"Sure! I'm telling you, don't stress. We'll keep you save." She began to walk towards the door, then stopped and turned round for another addition. "You can't leave the settlement though. Dinner is in forty minutes!"

And she left Amber in the same position she was in a few seconds ago--mouth slightly open, face blank, stare absent.

"She's right." Curie, the little girl with no foot pointed out cheerfully.

"You don't have to worry. You'll like it here. We have pet pigs! We eat them sometimes...but they are cute."

"Somebody is so having a giggle up there," Amber mumbled, pointing a finger at the ceiling. "I sure hope that it's for a damn good reason."

Upon making her way from the patient room to the improvised cafeteria, Amber discovered that the facility was built underground--and pretty deep down too. They were carried upstairs in an open-wall elevator, and she watched the crumbling rock walls go past her with slight concern.

How big was this war? Not whole-planet big, obviously--considering that the rich Han and city tourists were either unaware of it or ignoring it. How were they managing to ignore it though? And who were these people fighting? What were they fighting for, and what with? Not with nuclear weapons, she guessed. Guns? Bombs? Biological warfare?

"Light grey or dark grey?"

Curie's voice interrupted Amber's train of thoughts.

They were in the line for food, and it was nearly their turn to receive their portions.

"A little bit of both?" Amber shrugged, and observed Eva —who was serving the role of lunch lady in this instance —pull a spoon out of a huge bowl of some dirt-colored murky substance.

Judging by the effort it took her, the substance had the consistency of swamp mud.

"Left is veggies and herbs, and right is meat stew," Curie explained. "It tastes better than it looks."

The girl picked up her plate with one hand and maneuvered out of the line, using her crutch for support. She didn't have a prosthetic, but she walked on that one crutch with the grace and speed of a circus dancer.

"Is Han food suitable for you?" Eva asked, filling up a plate for Amber.

"It will do." She sniffed the dish upon receiving the plate, just about prepared to give it a chance. "Is Lullaby around?"

"Haven't seen them."

212

"Here's hoping the smell of food will attract them," Amber said, leaving the line.

Indeed, Lullaby entered the area before Amber got to the middle of her portion. They came in wearing a compound robe made out of two Han outfits, their face covered in dirt and tiny pieces of plastic clippings. After some consideration, Eva handed them the entire remaining bowl. They thanked her profusely before locating Amber's table.

"Boy, am I glad to see you." Amber made way for the Rx'lng.

They needed an extra chair to sit down comfortably.

"Came to visit you before," Lullaby said. "You were not all with the world. Feeling better?"

"Eh." Her face twisted in a 'not the best but won't complain' expression. "Honestly I preferred the drug-induced half-coma."

"Hi!" Curie beamed and nearly climbed the table in an effort to extend her hand to Lullaby.

"Hi!" they replied, copying the intonation. "Amber, introduce me to your roommates?"

"Sure." She quickly accessed the two nearby tables which were occupied by her fellow patients. "Curie, sad dude, eye patch lady, granny Smith and, uhhh, Larry."

"Not quite." A small, rapidly balding Han at the next table smiled awkwardly at her.

"Barry? Terry? Jerry?"

"Hoggerfuld." He gave up.

"Close enough." Amber waved the concern away. "All Han look the same to me. All humans too, actually," she added. "I just don't recognize faces."

"Where are you from?" Curie seemed to be endlessly fascinated with the insectoid alien.

"My species is from Qst'ln," they responded. "But the home world was destroyed by a Gamma ray burst. Was born on a big spaceship, called King of Kings."

"Sorry about your planet." She frowned. "Are you a warrior?"

"An archaeologist."

"What's an archaeologist?"

"A scientist who studies ancient cultures."

"Alright." She nodded. "What's a scientist?"

"Hey Lu, you can engage in public education later," Amber interrupted. "I remember fuck-all about the previous day. Can you enlighten me?"

"Were walking through the forest together." They took pauses every other word to eat. "You started slowing down. I waited, gave you time to rest. You were very tired, wanted to have a nap. Didn't let you. Told you we had to keep walking. You stopped responding and went limp on the ground. Didn't pass out, just... lost touch. I took you and carried you out of the forest."

"You navigated out of the forest on your own?" Curie's eyes widened, as did her grin. "Wow! That's a-ma-zing! Even most locals can't do it. The forest is deceitful," she explained. "It makes you go in circles. Very easy to get lost. If you don't have a beacon, or a wire line, you're as good as dead!" she added excitedly. "People both sides the forest know that. It's an almost impenetrable border!"

"Something tells me Io knew that too." Amber was picking at the single-use table cloths. "What a bitch! And not in a good sense...hope she crushes under the weight of her ignorance really soon."

"We got out though," Lullaby pointed out.

"Out of the forest!" Amber retorted. "You've noticed, I reckon, that we're surrounded by a security wall in the middle of a war camp. I wouldn't call that fortunate."

"You're safe here," Curie said.

"I don't wanna be safe," Amber told her. "I'd stay on Alexandria if I wanted safety. I need to get to the research station, and then to the Teardrop Cluster--not take part in an involuntary historical reenactment."

"They are good people," Lullaby insisted. "They won't keep us here against our will."

"No," she agreed. "But their enemies will."

By the time the last piece of fruit was eaten and the last empty plate was returned to the kitchen, night crawled quietly into the solemn valley. Amber had been sitting next to a window for close to an hour, gasping in fresh air. Lullaby had left, off to help the villagers with construction work. A different woman had replaced Eva at the canteen and was now giving out hot drinks. There were no payments in the settlement, Amber noticed—no money, no records, no debt. Everything essential was distributed fairly among the people, and that somehow included her and Lullaby.

She didn't notice as the room began to fill with villagers once more, up until she turned around and realized that every seat had been taken. Amber watched with curiosity, confused and intrigued. One by one, the people moved the tables out of the way and made a circle out of the chairs. Then they sat down, joined hands, and began to sing.

It was a wordless, directionless song; a song of untrained, unskilled voices that nevertheless blended into a sea of heavenly sound. It was, Amber guessed, a song of love and unity and strength. It reverberated through the air, through her nerves and thoughts. It made her feel safe, peaceful. For whoever long it had lasted, she lost her worries and her sense of time. She didn't dare interrupt the singers to ask them about it; she just sat in her place by the window and listened.

The song ended with people saying a few lines--the same words, more or less, from what Amber could tell —one after another in the circle. Then some sort of powder was blown into the air. It made the room smell of spices and ground after heavy rain. Still silent, Amber watched the villagers move the furniture back to its place, exchange a few words and hugs, and leave the room in an organized line. She got up, walked out after them, and asked one of the nurses to show her back to the patient ward.

"But am I really in such a rush to leave?" Amber thought as she climbed into her bed, her mind still full of the flowing, magical song.

EIGHTEEN

Soon after coming back to her bed, Amber slipped into a short nap that turned into a long, completely un-refreshing sleep. Disturbing dreams kept bothering her, and she couldn't find the right blanket-over-face ratio that blocked out the light but allowed her to breathe. The effect of her drugs was wearing off and she was gradually becoming aware of all the scratches, bites and bruises on her skin.

She took a deep breath in. The room smelt of disinfectant liquid, a mix of artificial flower essence and ethyl alcohol that failed to cover up the subtle stench of bodily fluids and decaying organics. Combined with the low hum of electricity generators and the sterile white light, it made her feel like a lab rat locked in a plastic box cage. It was not a nice place to be in while fully conscious.

Amber tossed and turned for a few more minutes, before giving up at last and slipping out from under the pile of blankets. The rest of the patients were either absent or asleep, and there were no signs of the doctors. She stepped forward and flinched as the monitor on her wrist tugged on her skin. Removing the sticky patch with one swift motion, she wrapped herself in a spare sheet and quietly left the room.

The elevator took her upstairs to ground floor. As she now knew, the building was the only solid structure in the secure area, so it had to function as a hospital, a school, and a communal kitchen all at the same time. Amber wandered the corridors and empty halls, not sure what she was searching for. She stumbled upon a vending machine, but it refused to accept her digital currency. It didn't react to a firm kick to the side either. She yawned, traversing a particularly long corridor on the second floor, her mind filled with meaningless thoughts and worries. It was either her new drugs kicking in, or her old drugs losing their power completely.

The corridor took her to a seemingly abandoned area, where Amber found a bunch of ID-locked doors and an out-of-order information panel. As opposed to most other places in the building, this didn't have the annoying white light or the disinfectant smell. The walls were covered in newspapers, as if left in the middle of redecoration. She stepped in closer to read the titles. 'New conflict breaks out in the Bessenen region. Skia authorities declare non-interference. See crossword on page seventeen'.

"No one's allowed here."

Out of the corner of her eyes, she saw a young Han wearing a leather jacket on top of medical uniform, peeking out of a door frame on the left. She recognized his voice but not his face.

"Hi, no-one." Amber smirked.

"I work here," he retorted. "You aren't even Han."

"Well, that's just speciest. Come on." She pouted. "I'm feeling lonely. Let me into your secret hiding place."

"I'm not hiding," he said, and opened the heavy metal door to let her slip in. "I'm on a break."

He closed the door shut behind her and returned to his previous spot. Amber sniffed. As soon as she walked in, she was cloaked in water vapor and hot humid air. The room was dark and stuffy, and she could hear a loud and annoying noise somewhere nearby.

"Is this a...?"

"Ventilation unit. Yeah. I'm not hiding though," he insisted.

"Not saying you are."

"I just get...overwhelmed, sometimes."

"Yeah, me too."

She noticed a pile of what seemed to be empty potato sacks in one of the corners, and a few dried up flowers stapled to a wall near it.

"You made it homey," she pointed out. "I like it. Amber." She extended her hand in his direction.

217

"Santos," he replied after a while. "And I recognize the gesture, but as a physician I choose not to participate in such activities."

"Fair enough." She chuckled. "Santos? You're the one who treated me then."

"You're welcome."

"You ever treated a human before?"

"I've never even met a human before. Or a giant blue cockroach, for that matter."

"They're called Rx'lng," she explained. "Rare species."

"So is my clan."

He wanted to say something but stopped himself. Instead, he reached into his pocket, took out a small red pack and an even smaller cardboard box. After producing a cigarette out of the pack, he lit it up with a match, shook off the first portion of ash and inhaled deeply.

"You want one?" he suggested.

"Won't it interact with my meds or something?"

"Nah. It's pretty weak. I'm not sure it will even work on you, but it probably won't hurt."

Holding his own cigarette with his lips, he lit up a second one and handed it over to Amber. She coughed, gave her mouth some time to adjust to the heat, then inhaled again.

"Nicotine," Santos said. "Good stuff. Calms you down when you're anxious, wakes you up when you're sleepy. Also gives you lung cancer in this form."

"The Muuk can cure that," Amber told him, taking another drag. "They can cure everything, except for the common cold and male pattern baldness."

"Don't think I'll make it to baldness." He laughed. "Don't think I will make it to lung cancer either."

"Is the war that bad?"

"It doesn't have to be that bad if you're a young, healthy man. They need me so far, cause I've got medical skills, but once we're down in numbers to a critical state, that won't save me either. Unless." He shook his head.

"Unless something happens to the other doctor," Amber guessed.

"Exactly. But let's not talk about that."

They co-existed in silence for a little while, finishing their cigarettes. After one last inhale, Santos crushed his against the wall and dropped it to the ground.

"How rare is your species then?" he asked.

"Not that rare," Amber admitted. "We're past the bottleneck. And the incubators pop out babies way better than human people. You?"

"Two hundred and eighty-three in this settlement. Not the entire clan, obviously. You know, 'don't put all your revva fruits in one fruit sack' and all that. A few thousand overall."

"And your enemies?"

"Juhnwe knows. About the same, I reckon."

"But you are both Han?"

"Biologically speaking, yeah."

"So why are you fighting each other?"

"For resources, mostly." He shrugged. "Land to grow food on. Well."

"Can't you just move somewhere else?"

That question was answered with a dismissive scoff, which Amber took as a sign not to push it further.

"And you're the only people on this land? All Hans, I mean."

"There are natives," Santos replied, "but they have degraded into a very primitive state ages ago. They hang out in the swamp, do a lot of dancing and praying and such. Strange fellows--hairy, sharp claws, tails...pagans."

"Surely you're not one to judge people for their religion," Amber smirked.

He sighed, and seemingly was about to retaliate with some sort of profound tirade, but decided against it. "Doesn't matter. You tell me...what is Alexandria like?"

She wanted to tell him about the Muuk control. About the limitations on out-of-planet travel, and strict regulations, and constant interference in their plans and affairs. She wanted to complain about the irritating pompousness of her superiors and hypocrisy of the politicians. 'It's about as convenient for living as it is boring', she wanted to say... then changed her mind.

"It's beautiful." She smiled. "Most of the planet surface is for wildlife only, so we have platforms that reach many kilometers into the sky to live on and do research on. The cities are integrated with the forests. Every place grows its own fruits and vegetables. There's no pollution, no burning of fossil fuels, no ugly factories pumping carbon dioxide into the air...

"All people live well. They can find their passion, even if it takes years, and they can pick a new one when it's no longer fulfilling. Everyone's disgustingly kind to each other, at least in public, and in principle. We don't go to war with each other. We don't die unless we are ready to and willing. And children don't get bone cancer."

"Must be nice."

"It is. I wish everyone in the universe could live like us. I..."

She was about to tell him exactly how much she hated the current state of the galaxy, when something beeped in his pocket, and his expression changed from that of calm concentration to a concerned frown.

"Gotta go," he muttered, reading a message on a simple comm device that looked like a large pen with a tiny screen.

A second later he rushed out of the room. Not really thinking about it, Amber dropped her bed sheet cover and followed him outside.

Together, they ran out of the abandoned area, through a few corridors and up two flights of stairs. Amber could barely keep up. Her lungs were not at full capacity, and a sharp pain in her chest quickly became constant. By the time Santos rushed inside a room labeled 'OR' in a red marker, she was panting like a dog. She collapsed by the wall, trying desperately not to pass out. Not sure why she had to make the trip in the first place, she shielded her eyes from the blinding white light that drowned the room and listened to her heart pound in her ears.

"You took your damn time!"

Amber recognized Eva's voice. She sounded squeaky, close to panic even.

"Sorry."

Judging by the rustling and a dull hum of flowing water, he was prepping in for something.

"Why is the human girl in here?"

"Don't know, she followed me inside."

"Well, get her out!" she yelled.

"No time for that!" he yelled back at her.

"Don't mind me," Amber said, "I'm just dying over here."

"Oh, whatever," Eva muttered, and a brief loud bell filled the room for a second.

Immediately, Amber sensed a definite uptick in the disinfectant smell.

"Scrub in," Eva urged. "Before he bleeds out."

Gradually, Amber's eyes grew somewhat accustomed to the lamps, and she peeked through a gap in between her fingers. She was in an operating room, that was clear. About the size of a lecture hall, it hosted an array of fairly modern medical equipment and operating tables. Judging by the color of the walls, floor and even ceiling, it was squeaky clean and isolated from the rest of the building.

She turned her head to the entrance and saw a red light flashing above the door. Next to it was a pile of used up medical uniforms and a trash bag which, for some unknown to her reason, was made of transparent plastic and showed a gruesome mess of blood-soaked tissues, plastic packages, and single-use instruments.

"It's no good," Santos muttered, and Amber eyes were drawn to the source of sound at once.

There, on a low-set operating table lay a body of a person, their face hidden by a layer of blue fabric. Their legs were covered by camo-colored trousers, but their torso was exposed and clearly visible under the bright white light. Amber swallowed hard and couldn't help but look away for a second.

The person's stomach was cut open, blood spilling onto the table and dripping to the floor, and both Santos and Eva had their hands deep inside them. Their movements seemed rapid and harsh, and she wondered how they managed to see anything in the mess of liquids and organs, and not cause even more damage.

"Just clip the hepatic artery, for fuck's sake!" Eva was holding a long plastic tube which was sucking out blood from the person's body cavity--which, at the moment, was one huge gaping wound.

"Thanks for the tip," Santos replied, in a much calmer manner.

"His BP is below forty. We don't have any spare blood either."

"I'll clip it!"

The monitor started to beep in a particularly irritating manner, and Amber's morbid curiosity took over. She watched the doctors work with unblinking eyes.

"Give him epi!" Santos instructed. "I can stabilize him. Come on."

The monitor was still beeping.

"Santos." Suddenly, Eva stopped what she was doing and took a small step back.

"The hell, Ev? Get back!"

"Santos," she repeated. "It won't work. He's lost too much blood. We won't stabilize him for long enough to get more."

"Who says?!"

"Santos!" she yelled, and he paused to give her a look of glaring hate. "We gotta do the ceremony before it's too late."

"Great." He took his hands out of the person's body and dropped the metal instruments hard on the ground. "You do that."

And he took off his gloves in the same angry matter.

What happened next made absolutely no sense to Amber. It was difficult for her to follow a fast dialog in a language she was not fully proficient in, and she knew nothing about medicine either. Still, based on what she had heard (and seen previously in Old Earth medical dramas), she expected Eva to turn off the patient's monitors, close him up for dignity and send him off to whatever they used as the morgue. It was not what happened.

While Santos stood aside, clearly unwilling to participate, Eva did a very hasty job of stapling the person's stomach and pushed a full syringe of some yellowish liquid into the line that, Amber assumed, was supplying them with anesthesia. Then Eva removed the blue cloth, revealing a face of a young Han man. Very young, in fact. Barely an adult.

While the monitors changed their beeping into something different yet equally irritating, she took off her gloves and rushed to the opposite side of the room. From the far corner, she dragged over what looked like a large bucket, or maybe even a baby bath, carved out of red wood. Once it was situated close to the table, she rushed for other supplies--a different, distinctly not medical garment, a small wooden chest and a canister of water.

"You could help me, you know," Eva said, changing from her medical uniform into the baggy brown cloak.

"I could have saved him." Santos didn't move.

"I am saving him, you dimwit! Bloody hell, you're a doctor, Santos."

With a sigh, Santos walked towards the operating table and helped Eva fill the wooden bath with water. Amber, who had a lot of questions but didn't feel like voicing any of them, watched them from the floor with round eyes.

Then, to her absolute horror, the Han boy began to wake up. His eyes flickered open, and he whimpered in pain, trying to touch his stomach with his blood-covered hands. Eva launched to his side.

"Lem?" she said, her voice shaky. "Are you awake?"

He mumbled something that Amber couldn't understand.

"You're safe, Lem. You're home," Eva cooed, hugging the boy gently. "You did good. You won your battle."

Santos took over her duties while she opened the wooden chest and painted her face with something oily and intensely orange. She helped Santos take the boy off the operating table and lower him to the ground in front of the water-filled bath. While Santos held him up, Eva put her hands on the boy's cheeks and read something out loud in a monotonous, song-like manner. Amber couldn't understand most of it.

"Juhnwe commands," Eva said. "They who perish in his name inherit his kingdom. Iros. Estos. Vens."

"Iros. Estos. Vens," the boy repeated, barely audibly.

So did Santos, before letting go of the boy's shoulders and turning away.

Amber quickly realized why.

She watched, motionless and speechless, as Eva grabbed the boy by the basis of his skull, pushed him down and forced his head under the water. She watched while he fought against Eva's grasp, scratching the smooth floor with his fingernails and making the wooden bath rock and spill some of the water. She watched until his movement ceased abruptly, his body now limp and lifeless.

Eva took him out of the water and laid him on the floor with his head on another brown piece of cloth. She closed his eyes and gently kissed his forehead.

"Iros. Estos. Req," she whispered, and stepped away. "Find his family," she added in Santos's direction. "Tell them he is with Juhnwe."

"Hi. Hello. Excuse me." Amber forced her body off the ground and stood, wobbling, near the white wall. "I have a few questions. First off...what the actual, ever-loving fuck was that?!"

Santos escaped the room before she had time to ask anything else. Eva shook her head, evidently not eager to provide any comments. She walked over to a sink and rubbed her hands and face, washing off the blood and the oily paint. After taking off the ceremonial robe, she remained in a thin white t-shirt, the lower part of her uniform and battered up snickers covered in protective plastic.

Amber tried to make eye contact with her, but she stared at the floor the whole time. She took a few deep breaths, in and out, and a layer of wrinkles formed on her forehead. She was, Amber realized, not as old as it could seem like from her face.

"Go to your bed," Eva finally said.

"I won't."

"We'll need to burn his body. There's nothing for you to see here. Go to sleep."

"What did you do to him?!"

"Listen." She looked her in the eyes at last, and it was a fierce look of a someone who was prepared to have a fight--and win. "He received twelve close proximity shots to his limbs, chest and abdomen. He had a ruptured spleen, a shattered hepatic artery and a collapsed lung, on top of massive blood loss. I don't have a professional medical facility here and I'm not a magician. I did all I could."

"That explains nothing to me," Amber insisted. "He was beyond saving. Okay. I get that. But you couldn't let him die under anesthesia because...?"

"He was a soldier," Eva explained calmly. "A protector of the settlement. We interfered with his battle when we operated on him."

"And that's why he had to drown in a bucket while his own people held him down?"

"That's the holy law." Eva nodded. "Only the soldiers who die gloriously in battle are allowed into the sacred kingdom."

"The kingdom of...?"

"You aren't one of us. You won't understand." She was about to walk away, but Amber stood in front of the exit in her path.

"In more detail now, from that point on. This is a...religion of some sort, I guess?"

"The one true religion," Eva replied.

"Says who?"

"The sacred texts. The priests. My heart and soul."

"And according to your one true religion, you get a good afterlife if you die in battle?"

"If you're a warrior, yes. It's different for others. Look, I'm not an expert," she muttered. "Talk to our priests. They will explain."

"Na-ah," Amber disagreed. "If you follow it with that much dedication, you can explain. Go on! Tell me, who started your religion?"

"Prophets." Eva sighed, rolled her eyes, but continued. "Hundreds of years ago. Juhnwe appeared to them and said that we are his chosen people. He told only us his ancient law and the way to earn eternal reward."

"Only to you?"

"He favored us, the most righteous, the most worthy of his wisdom."

"So, you follow his law to get into a heaven of some sort?"

"When we die, we go to the land before time, where there is no pain, no suffering, and where you can reach true happiness."

"And everyone else?"

"Go to land after time, where all the world's evil resides."

"So, everyone in the galaxy will go there just because your Juhnwe didn't pick them."

"Yes."

"What kind of just and merciful god is that then?!"

Eva laughed. "Who said Juhnwe was just and merciful?! I mean, he commands to fight and kill for his word! Does that sound nice to you?"

"Well why the hell do you follow him then?"

"Cause he is the most powerful thing in the universe and I have no other choice," she spat out.

"Says who?!" Amber stomped her foot in anger. Her patience was long gone. "A several centuries-old book which, for it's own credibility, refers to itself? A bunch of goons whose job depends on people actually believing in this bullshit?"

"No." She chewed on her lip for a few seconds. "I know it to be true. I've seen it. Juhnwe spoke to us. He speaks to me too. He speaks to all who truly believe."

And she pushed past Amber, leaving the room.

"Na-ah, love, you won't get away this easy."

She lunched into the rapidly shrinking gap of the closing door and chased Eva down a corridor.

"We ain't finished."

"Your ability to speak my language is awfully good all of a sudden." Eva gave out a brief, almost forced laugh. "Were you pretending before?"

"Anger fuels my abilities." Amber dodged her attempt to change the topic. "So, tell me, this other clan you're at war with...is it because of your idiotic religion?"

"I am not affected by your words, for I am strong in my spirit, clear in my devotion, righteous in my..."

"Answer the question."

"Yes. They are the forsaken."

"Who decided that?"

"They admit that. They've left the religion a long time ago."

"Is that really your business though? Like, mighty god meanpants is gonna send them to the oh-not-so-good place anyway once they die, so why does it matter?"

"I don't pass judgment on them." Eva, who had just paused in front of an elevator, shrugged nonchalantly. "I'm not Juhnwe and it is not my place to judge. They are trying to deconvert our children and take our land though. And I won't give them our kids, or my land."

She stepped into the elevator and Amber followed.

"I understand the land part, though there are definitely better ways to settle a territorial conflict. But why are you afraid of them deconverting your children if you know your religion is true? Wouldn't they arrive at the truth naturally, even after being deconverted as kids? And wouldn't Juhnwe protect the righteous from deception? Maybe those they do manage to deconvert weren't righteous in the first place."

Eva didn't reply until the elevator dinged and opened its doors, allowing her to escape into a dark corridor and around a corner. Amber felt a sharp surge of pain in her side as she tried to catch up but didn't slow down her pace. She was determined to get a reaction out of her--if not for the sake of persuading her otherwise then, at the very least, to mightily pissed her off--which, luckily enough, Amber was pretty good at.

"What's your answer then?" she demanded.

"I don't know, okay?" Eva replied. "I'm not Juhnwe. I can't see his plan. I'm just doing what I think is right."

"You sure about that, doctor death?"

"Don't you dare!"

Within seconds, Amber was thrust against the wall by Eva's strong hands and pushed up till she had to stand on her tippy-toes to hold balance. Eva's face was now mere millimeters away from Amber's, and she was breathing rapidly, a drop of saliva stuck to her lower lip. Amber paused, not sure what she could do. If it wasn't for the fact that she felt a mix of pity and disgust towards the Han woman, she would have almost been aroused by her action.

"I've lost both my parents to disease, and my husband to war," Eva whispered. "I have no family, no friends, and likely no future. My faith is all I have. It's all my community has. If it's true, I will meet my family again and we will be happy. If it's a lie, then they're dead forever, and the same will happen to me, and to all people I know, including that boy I just drowned, and the babies that were born this year, and little Curie who is an orphan with terminal cancer. If you were in my place... what would you believe?"

And she released her grip on Amber's shoulders.

They continued to stand there in front of each other, silent, pent up, and rather lost. Amber truly considered letting it go and moving on. She almost did so too. But then another thought struck her.

"If it is true, then my parents are currently suffering in your version of hell," she replied calmly.

"I am deeply sorry about that," Eva told her, already walking down the corridor again.

"Think!" Amber plunged after her, and Eva's sigh echoed across the building. "This place."

"What about it?"

"How long have you lived on this continent?"

"Hundreds of years. Over a thousand, actually."

"And how long has Ika-Ika existed?" Amber asked with obvious excitement in her voice, now on a new lead.

"What does Ika-Ika has to do with this?"

"Just answer the question, will you?"

"For as long as we've been here."

"And that doesn't give you any ideas?"

"No. Leave me alone."

"You live alongside a parasite that infects all of you from an early age and causes hallucinations!"

"Yes, and we treat it with drugs."

"But doesn't that explain your religion visions?"

"How does it explain the fact that we all see the same thing, the same being, telling us the same things?!"

"Oh, gee, I don't know," Amber struggled to talk and walk at the same time, "maybe cause you indoctrinate everyone from before they can talk?!"

Eva stopped in front of a door, reached into a pocket of her trousers and took out a plastic card. She pressed it to a door, and, once the lock clicked, attempted to go in without Amber following.

"Uh-uh!" Amber protested.

"It's the dressing room." Eva sighed again. "Would you like to see me change?"

"Oh, yeah, like I find you even remotely attractive, with a life position of 'whatever makes me feel warm and tingly inside must be true'...please, I just want to finish the conversation."

"Whatever." She allowed her to follow her inside. "I don't buy your explanation, by the way. We've had Ika-Ika for hundreds of years and not a single other religion has appeared since."

"I'm sure that a beginner course in sociology and animal psychology could tell you why."

"Please!" Eva laughed, and Amber turned around when she began to take her t-shirt off. "Alexandrians...I've never even spoke to one before, and guessed exactly what you're like anyway. All smug, pretentious, full of yourself assholes who worship science and think they are better than everyone else. Tell me, human, do you have all the answers? To all of life mysteries?"

"No," Amber replied calmly. "I don't have to. I can be intellectually honest and say, 'I don't know'. Yet. I don't have to stick god into every empty gap in my understanding of the universe!"

"But wouldn't you want to have answers?"

"Of course I would!" She laughed. "But if we're operating on the basis of 'I believe what is nice' or 'I believe what my parents have taught me', I wouldn't arrive at the objective truth, now would I?"

"Child." Eva smiled. "I admire your spirit, but you don't understand many things...one of them being that objective truth is not something that exists, and that there are things much more important than that."

"Right." Suddenly, all fire was gone from Amber's voice. "Well, if that's what you think... I'm afraid I can't help you."

"I don't need your help," she said, in a soft, almost dreamy voice. "Go to bed and have some rest."

"You're wrong."

"Time will tell."

Amber wanted to say something so clever and so poignant as to make sure she had definitely won the debate, but missed her opportunity and had to settle for a dramatic "it sure will".

She wandered around the building for a while, trying to find the patient ward. Her entire body ached, exhausted by both the exercise and the emotions. She didn't want to talk any further. She didn't even have enough energy to make appropriate facial expressions at her fellow patients as she entered the room.

Without a 'hello' or 'good night', she collapsed onto her bed, covered her eyes with her blanket and pretended to be asleep.

She lost this battle before it even started.

NINETEEN

Amber didn't sleep that night. At all. She lost awareness at times, listening to the sound of her breath reflect from the wall and flow back into her ears, but she didn't dream or relax even for a second. Powerful emotions were brewing inside of her, and she wasn't in control of the storm. She wasn't even along for the ride. Rather, she realized, twisting and groaning in bed in the dead hours before sunrise, the feelings were threatening to drown her.

Morning didn't bring relief. Lights flickered into life and pierced through her closed eyelids and right into the pain center of her brain. Curie's excited voice announced 'breakfast' for the entire room, and the mere thought made Amber dry-heave a little bit. Still, the prospect of staying in bed even for one minute longer was no more appealing. Without even making an attempt at untangling her hair, Amber crawled out of the mess of bed sheets and blankets and placed her bare feet on the cold squeaky floor.

"Good morning, Amber!" Curie was sporting a new dressing gown, one with red flowers made from threads woven intricately into the silky fabric. "You're... not worse than yesterday."

"I beg you, piglet," Amber barked at her, "dial down the cheer, or I'll be forced to strangle you with a pillow."

"You're not as funny as you think," she replied.

"Yeah, people tell me that." Amber narrowly avoided smashing into the door frame on her way out. "Wasn't a joke though," she added under her breath.

Down at the cafeteria people were slowly starting to gather along the left side of the hall, queuing for food. The smell of butter and spices hit Amber's nose as soon as she approached the line. She suppressed a grimace. Eating didn't seem like fun, but she knew that she needed some calories to keep her body going. She sighed and took a spot at the end of the queue.

"Hi, I'd like some free-range non-GMO whole organic gluten-free deep fried snickers bars," she repeated a joke from an Old Earth movie once it was her time to 'order'.

"We've got roasted dwolli and porridge," the diner lady replied. "Pick."

"I'll have the roast version, please."

At the last section of the line, Amber picked a hefty stack of paper napkins and added three packets of sweetener to her drink. It tasted like a mix between hazelnut latte and freshly cut grass.

"I sure hope this has some caffeine in it," she mumbled. "Or heroin."

The drink contained neither of those things. It was, however, infused with a substance similar to the Old Earth drug "aspirin", which for Han was considered recreational because it caused a pleasant tingling feeling and slight dizziness.

She sat alone at the table furthest from the crowd and picked at her food, eyes focused on the floor. Lullaby had either left already or hadn't arrived. All in all, the morning wasn't absolutely horrible. The blended noise of conversation blocked out her thoughts, and the food was tasteless enough to be gulped down without much protest from her digestive system.

There were people, of course. People she hated viciously, down to the roots of their hair. People she couldn't even stab with her fork to death since, according to their stupid religion, it would make them vainglorious heroes. Therefore, all she could do was sulk.

"I need to explain."

Amber's mind was dulled down enough to stop her from flinching at the sudden sound. She raised her gaze from her plate and saw Santos. He had dark circles under his eyes and was clutching a huge mug with both hands, even though it appeared to be steaming hot.

"You really don't," she responded, looking away.

"Eva is the kindest, most compassionate person I've ever met."

"Is that why you want to get under her skirt?" she pondered, tilting her head slightly to the right. "I don't blame you, man. She's pretty hot for her age."

"That..." His milk-pale skin turned red as he mumbled. "Has nothing to do with this conversation. Listen, I..."

"If the next thing to come out of your mouth will be a religious apologetic of any sort or kind," she said, "I swear to every god people have ever made up, Santos, I will drown you in your own mug."

All of that was pronounced with stoic calm and serious manner of a math professor explaining a theorem to their students. Santos didn't react.

"Lem was taught from cradle that his only road to eternal happiness is through a winning battle," he finally said. "Do you think he would appreciate if his last thought in this life was 'I failed and I'm going to the land after time'?"

"Santos, sweetie." Amber sighed. "I don't fucking care anymore. If you think that barbaric ritual was justified, fine. Do whatever you want. You don't have to evangelize me. I'll leave the settlement soon enough, and then you can go back to indoctrinating babies and fighting your own kind over your idiotic fairy-tales."

"But the evidence..."

"What evidence?" She dropped her fork on the plate and raised her head to face Santos at last. "Life is as complex as a watch, therefore there had to have been a watchmaker? All events have a cause, the universe had a beginning therefore god was the cause?

"Without god there is no objective morality therefore they exist? It's a safer bet to believe in god and be wrong than to not believe and be wrong? My ancient book of superstition says so, and I believe it cause it says so?"

Judging by Santos's expression, he had trouble keeping up.

"I've heard it all." Amber paused. "Hundreds of arguments and apologetics for dozens of different religions, all similarly flawed."

"I don't need any arguments." He shook his head. "I have my experience and I trust my own mind."

"Well, you bloody shouldn't!" she almost yelled. "If Han brains are anything like human brains, they suck at interpreting reality. Especially in a place where, like I've pointed out to your precious Eva, you get delirium-causing infections since kindergarten."

"It's not that simple."

"I'm sure it isn't." She laughed. "Listen, Santos, I know it's hard not to trust your eyes and stuff, but I have my experiences too. And I hate how I keep telling the same story to everyone I meet but seems like I've no choice. So.

She paused to take a sip of her drink. "Remember how I've told you that no one on Alexandria dies involuntarily? Well, that was a lie by omission. There have been two documented deaths by accident, with no retrieval of consciousness. My parents. Died when I was a kid, in an explosion. I was there too, but all I got was this lousy scar."

She pointed at her face.

"I'm sorry," Santos muttered.

"Don't be," she continued. "Anyway. After they died, I became obsessed with religion and mythology. Science wouldn't give me an answer as to why this has happened to me, so I searched for it elsewhere. I went through everything in The Library, studied everything that humans have ever believed in. I was desperate. I wanted to have an explanation, a reason...I wanted someone to blame for their death.

"So, I kept looking, but man, there were so many options! So many different worldviews, different holy books and different interpretations of those books. All claiming to be true and using the same shitty logic to justify it, but contradicting each other. I wanted to believe, wanted to understand, but they were all the same at their core.

"Fictions. Powerful fictions, no doubt--they outlived their creators and made an enormous impact on the history of my people, our people, Santos, our ancestors, but they were still fictions. Don't you see? Made up things hold power, they can change lives and alter the course of history...but it doesn't make them actually real."

She stopped, out of breath and exhausted. She was sure that she made a hundred grammatical mistakes in her speech, but it hardly mattered. Santos stared at her, a blank expression on his face. Then he glanced sideways.

"What?" she questioned, following his gaze.

With a heart drop Amber realized that the whole room was staring at her, silent. She must have raised her volume quite a lot at some point. Oops.

"What?" she repeated, louder on purpose this time. "Anyone disagrees? Anyone can offer an argument I haven't heard before?"

She got up from the table. All those emotions that she had been suppressing for the last few hours had reached a boiling point and were spilling out of her, like hot steam out of a kettle. She pushed a chair out of her way, marched towards the center of the hall, and climber on top of an empty table. It was time to say something at last.

"Gods don't actually exist," she announced. "Or if they do, they sure don't give two fucks about us mortals, cause they keep giving us contradictory stories. Funny that, almost as if they're trying to confuse us, keep us in line and pit us against each other...a bit like tribe chiefs, or kings, wouldn't you say?"

No reaction.

"Truth is," she continued, "they're all made up. They only exist in your heads and in your imaginations. That might be important to you, but listen...your feelings can't change the nature of reality. You won't go to some nice place after you die, you will cease to exist as a conscious entity. And so will heretics, infidels and atheists. Your god will never actually win your battle, cure your disease or fix your problems. Only you and other people can do that."

Still no reaction.

"The universe," she said, voice increasingly shaky, "is unfair, and scary, and full of pain and misery. Bad things happen to good people and for no reason. Some things cannot be explained by science, now or ever.

"And your brains are designed to hate it, and want to invent something to make it right. Believe your fairy tales all you want, it's fine...but stop trying to kill each other, for fuck's sake!" she yelled. "Don't you understand?! We only have each other! There's no one else! The universe is bad enough as it is...don't make it even bloody worse! Your fiction, people," she was on the verge of tears, "it's just isn't worth it."

235

She stopped. The crowd was quiet. What would they do now? Argue with her? Shout profanities at her? Stomp her to the ground and tear her to shreds? Amber waited, her heart pounding, ears attuned to every breath and tiny move.

Santos blinked a few times, rubbing his forehead. Curie moved further from her table and looked down at the ground. Eva, who sat in the far-right corner, shook her head and sipped her now lukewarm drink. A few people coughed. Then, almost in unison, they turned away and resumed their chatting and eating, leaving Amber without a single comment. No one approached her, no one even as much as booed or clapped. They just quietly ignored her.

"Yeah?" Her voice trembled a little as she climbed down from the table. "Well screw you too. I hope your entire clan goes extinct," she added, and stormed out of the room.

"I almost feel sorry for her," Eva said, taking a seat opposite Santos and pushing away Amber's still half-full plate. "Too bad she's going to the land after time."

"You can't win every battle," Santos replied. "But I will pray for her to find her path."

Outside of the building, the sun was shining with broad vigor, making the stunning Skian sky look like an artificially beautified image. Amber covered her face with her hand. She hadn't been outside for a few days and had forgotten how bright and overwhelming it was. The weather was perfect--warm, windless, just the right amount of moisture in the air. As if it was mocking her, Amber thought.

Yet another reminder of the universal reality. Human emotions, thoughts, actions, lives, it didn't matter to nature. Nature couldn't tell the difference between a person and a pile of rotting leaves. She might have been mad, and upset, and desperate, but the world moved on with its beautiful sky and lovely weather.

"Lullaby!" Amber called out. "Lu, are you here?"

No answer. She shook her head slightly and set off on a walk across the village. It consisted mostly of tents and makeshift habitats, with the occasional bench or picnic table here and there. All in all, it seemed rather peaceful. Like a cute place to spend a weekend at. It was hard to believe that she was traversing a temporary refuge in the middle of a military crisis.

"There you are."

She discovered Lullaby at one of the village's boundaries, helping two Han men to fix a gap in a three meters high wall.

"Hello, Amber." Lullaby didn't detach themselves from the wall. "Am assisting with repairs. Will have breakfast later."

"Forget breakfast. Forget everything, actually. Well, not everything, but certainly whatever you're doing in here. We're leaving."

"Leaving?" Finally, they turned around and blinked their huge eyes at the human. "So soon?"

"Not soon enough. I'm sick of this place. If I don't get out of here asap, I think I'll chew off my own leg out of misery. Or someone else's."

"But do you feel okay?"

"No, which is precisely why we need to get the fuck out!"

"Alright-alright." They stepped away from the wall. "Let's discuss this rationally." They switched to their native language. "Considering your health situation and the circumstances in general, would you say it is wise?"

"I'm done being wise!"

"Have you been wise before then, 'cause I haven't noticed."

Amber pouted.

"We have to leave," she repeated, a hint of tears in her voice. "I can't stand these people and their bullshit. It's killing me."

Lullaby chirped, thinking.

"Do you know how to get to that research station from here?"

"No, but damn it, Lu, you got me out of that forest, I think you can sure as hell get us to the station as well."

"Fair enough," they gave up. "Get your things."

"I don't have any things," she replied. "And I won't take anything from them either."

"Not even water and food?"

"I'd rather starve."

"Must be serious. Okay." They glanced at the Han and switched back in languages. "Sorry, but will have to leave you. Take care."

"No problem!" one of the men said. "You've helped lots. Take care!"

And they waved as the two aliens walked away.

"Boy, would I love to strangle that cheer out of them," Amber muttered once out of their range.

"You tell me what happened?"

"No."

And they continued to walk in silence.

To Amber's relief, no one tried to make them stay by force. In fact, most of the villagers seemed similarly relieved to get rid of the aliens and return to their normal mode of living. The only person waiting for them at the gate to say a farewell was Eva. She stood next to a barely visible outline of the door in the thick perimeter wall, holding a basket in her hands, and smiled faintly as they approached.

"Keep your handout," Amber said, as Eva opened her mouth to say a greeting. "I won't accept it."

"I won't let you leave without it," Eva retorted. "It goes against my faith."

"Well according to my faith, taking gifts from deranged douchebags will lend me two extra years of boiling in olive oil after death. So, no."

"Fine." She dropped the basket on the ground, and it took her considerable effort not to throw it at someone instead. "Take this at least." She rummaged through the basket and pulled out a small plastic bottle. "One pill a day, in the morning before food, till they run out. Here." She outstretched her arm.

Amber considered it for a second. She suspected that scientists at the research station had those drugs as well, and weren't constantly in need either. On the other hand, what did she care if some snotty Han kid went for a couple extra days with visions? It would probably get them a higher spot in the looney-ranks too. Mindful as to not lock gazes with Eva, she snatched out the bottle and stuffed it in the pocket of her trousers.

"Would you also like your clothes back?" Eva scoffed, pointing at the white overalls that Amber was wearing.

"Did the person they belonged to before me die a natural death?" Amber asked back.

Eva was silent.

"Thought as much." She nodded. "Now open the fucking door."

On the other side of the wall was a site untouched by purposeful activity. A wide patch of forest stretched to the left, and to the right span a vast grassy plane. As opposed to inside the village, the wind was rather strong and sharp here, messing up Amber's hair and making her eyes water. She noticed how her boots sank into the dry soil beneath her, as well as the dusty smell in the air.

"Research station that way." Lullaby pointed across the plane.

Amber squinted. She saw nothing in the distance, except for more grass and an occasional bush. Perhaps she needed to be as tall as Lu to see beyond the horizon.

"Do you magically sense it or some shit?" she wondered.

"Not magic. Have a navset." They demonstrated a small circular device which was barely visible in their enormous palms.

"Does it say how long we'll have to walk there?"

"No."

"Oh." She frowned.

"You were the one who wanted to leave immediately."

"And I do," Amber assured them, taking a peek back at the wall. "I just hope that getting away doesn't involve sleeping on the ground with no tent. My back is already busted."

Meanwhile, Light and Darkness were floating in space, bathed in the tepid light of brand new stars. All around them was nothing but the pitch black cold of the cosmos beneath them was the same dark that was above them. And in front of them, a nebula was being born. Blinding glow in stark vivid colors spilling over the non-existent horizon and drowning the black, enveloping them like a cloud; right in the middle of a cosmic event of a millennium.

"Do you like it, dear?" Light asked, gently squeezing Darkness's hand.

"Absolutely," Darkness replied, smiled, and kissed her forehead. "You are a very good wife. This is way better than any other birthday gift I've ever received."

"I'm glad." Light smiled back. "Took me a week to find this, you know. Not recorded or discovered by any conscious being, ever."

"Ever?" Darkness arched an eyebrow. "But how are we...?"

"To your left," Light replied.

To Darkness's left was one of the newborn stars, a tiny white dwarf, spitting out helium as it burned its first batches of hydrogen.

"You mean...?" Darkness asked.

"Not discovered by any organic conscious being, I should have said," Light explained.

Darkness looked at Light, and Light looked at Darkness, and the baby born star looked at both of them.

"Damn," Darkness whispered.

"Now we just need a gift for S," Light continued. "His birthday is in a month."

"Oh. Right."

"He's your husband, you know."

"I know!"

"We can try to figure it out together," Light said.

"Yeah, I'd like that."

And so they stayed, floating in vacuum, watching the nebula and the baby stars, discussing birthday gifts.

TWENTY

Amber couldn't feel her toes.

Well, she could feel them, if she concentrated on it--which was an unusual state to be in. Most often than not, tuning out sensations was close to impossible for her. She was aware, at all times, of the clothes touching her skin, and tiny drops of sweat running down her back, and the taste of breakfast in her mouth. Without a filter, she lived in a constant state of slight overwhelm. Except for now.

Now, she was starting to go numb from the world. They'd been walking for hours, she thought, and the plane just kept stretching into infinity. The wind blew relentlessly into her face whichever way she turned and the technicolor sky shimmered the same way from any angle.

Lullaby didn't talk. She also didn't talk. Every now and then she would find a bunch of pebbles on the ground, or an occasional plant. A dead critter at one point. Apart from that, her brain had nothing to focus on. And it hurt almost as much as sensory overload.

"Is the sun moving at all?" Amber said, squinting at the sky through her palm. "Cause it might be stuck."

"Suns don't get stuck." Lullaby heard Amber's language but replied in their native tongue.

"Then why does it look like it hasn't moved at all since we've left?"

"Because you have nothing to compare it to. No point of perspective."

"Huh. Maybe you're right." She stumbled on a dried root and kicked it hard. It only rolled away by half a meter. "I don't like this place. I preferred the forest."

"It's twelve kilometers that way." Lu pointed. "Better turn round now if you want to get there in time for the mosquito happy hours."

"Lu?" Amber stopped and looked up at the Rx'lng. "Are you...mad at me?"

"A plus for Shakya."

"Wait." She had to start walking again, since Lullaby had no intention of pausing. "For realz?"

"Are you surprised?"

"Yes!" Amber confirmed. "Why would you be mad at me?"

"You know why."

"No, I don't. Explain." No response. "Explain. Explain!"

"That!" Lullaby snapped. Literally. With their mandibles. "You behaving like a bratty, spoiled child."

"What the crap?" She frowned. "I asked you a question cause I don't understand. Lu, I don't!" She had to pick up the pace, since Lullaby was walking faster and faster. "Tell me. Please."

They kept walking.

"Oh, come on!" Amber whined. "Lu, tell me, or I..."

"What, throw another tantrum?"

"Tantrum?" She blinked a few times. "Yeah, I still don't get it. Is this about me leaving the settlement or...?"

"Not about the action. About the attitude."

"The attitude?" Amber was getting more confused by the second. "Jesus, Lu, can you just spell out exactly what I did wrong so that I can, I don't know, apologize and learn from my mistakes and whatever inspirational nonsense they put in kiddie books?"

"That's exactly what I'm talking about." They nodded. "The attitude."

"What fucking attitude?!"

Amber was running out of breath, and when Lullaby stopped at last, she quietly sighed, thankful for the break.

"I've heard about your monologue at the cafeteria," Lullaby said. "From the workers. Just before we left."

"Oh." Amber couldn't help but smile a little. "You think it was good?"

"No!" they exclaimed. "It was stupid. Extremely so. They could've killed you! Didn't you notice how religious they are?"

"I've noticed exactly that." She laughed briefly. "And yeah, they could've reacted badly to it, but could-shoulda! They didn't. They ignored me. Quite empathetically, in fact."

"And you should be thankful they did. They kill other Han for deviating slightly from their interpretation of the scripture. What made you believe they would all deconvert on the spot over a passionate speech from an alien?"

"Well, duh! I wasn't trying to deconvert them on the spot. Put a seed of doubt in their minds though."

"As if."

"I had to do something!" Amber insisted. "They're all nuts. Hardcore! A full-blown cult. I've seen things Lu, but what they were doing...horrific isn't strong enough of a word to describe it."

"You'd never change their mind," Lullaby responded. "Not overnight, not in a lifetime. And it's not their fault either."

"Not their fault?" Judging by Amber's voice, she was half-appalled, half-saddened. "Of course it is their fault! Nobody has free will, but they do have will. They can change their behavior based on evidence presented to them."

"The evidence you were presenting wouldn't have convinced them —not overnight, not in a million years," they said calmly. "Not when you're that full of yourself, and exuberant over being right."

"I am right!" she shouted. "I'm right, Lu, and they're wrong. And they know it! They keep lying to themselves —cause it's easier, more comfortable, much better than ever having to question their beliefs. Damn." She chuckled. "I can't believe I've let myself feel so bad about everyone in this fucking galaxy. Dig deep enough, and you discover that almost every tragedy of sentient beings is caused by sentient beings themselves."

Lullaby paused.

"You're right and they're wrong," they repeated.

"Yes."

"And all the problems are caused by people."

"Most of them."

"And you, the wise one, know how to fix it all, if only they'd listen."

"What'cha getting at, Lk'st?"

"Maybe you could," they replied. "If you actually cared about making things better instead of proving your intellectual and moral superiority."

"Oh, I'm done being meek about it, that's for sure," Amber exclaimed. "Done keeping quiet and minding my own business."

"When have you ever kept quiet about anything?!" Lullaby produced something akin to a laugh.

Amber swallowed, looking away.

"You don't know me," she said. "You've met me two months ago. There are a lot of things you don't know about me."

"Neither do you," the replied. "Cause you never bothered to ask."

Amber paused, the argumentative spirit gone from her all of a sudden. She had nothing to reply to that. It was true. Over the time they've spent together, she hadn't asked Lullaby a single personal question. All she knew was what the Rx'lng would share voluntarily, which wasn't much.

"I know you've lost your nest," Amber told them quietly. "All of your sisters and a brother. And that you've never left the King of Kings before going on the mission. And that you have no reasons to return there."

"You can't imagine, can't understand what it's like to be away from the hive," they said. "We are one and the same. We sleep together, eat together, live together and die together. We sing in our minds, and can hear every other being in the hive. We are born into it, already singing, and we remember ones we've lost till the last person who remembered them is gone. One Rx'lng is nothing without the hive. I might be no one in it, but so is the Queen without the hive. And I've lost it."

They faced Amber, huge eyes unblinking.

"First my planet, so many years ago, and then my nest. I've lost my only meaning," they paused. "You have no idea what it is like to feel for others, to hurt for them. The empathy you humans feel is just as selfish. You reflect what others

244

experience, copy it in your body, and that's the only way you can understand why you should care about them. You will never understand what it is like to truly be a part of something bigger than yourself."

And they continued to walk in silence alongside Amber.

The wind slashed Amber's skin and picked up clouds of sand under her feet. The sun continued to move across the sky unobserved. The air grew denser, heavier, filled with vapor and dust. Amber's clothes stuck to her body, hugging it like a wet, squishy monster in the depths of the ocean. Her empty stomach rumbled and she tasted acid on her tongue. The empty world was full of sensations all of a sudden, and she hated every single one.

But not as much as she hated herself.

She couldn't tell how much time had passed in between their conversation and the moment she noticed a change of scenery. Could have been hours, could have been twenty minutes. Could have been seventy days.

First, a smudged spot popped up on the horizon. It grew as they walked towards it, spilling to the sides and acquiring form. Soon enough it became clear that they were slowly approaching an arrangement of small buildings. Amber found it hard to focus on them. 'Maybe my vision has atrophied over the three thousand years that we've spent walking', she thought. And carried on walking.

When the research station got within a vigorous spring range, Amber realized why it was so difficult to see its outlines. The whole thing was enveloped in fog. Or smoke maybe, she couldn't tell. She glanced at Lullaby, who was sniffing the air, suspicious of the situation. They didn't speak up or stop though, so Amber didn't stop either. She rubbed her eyes and took in the scenery. Granted, there wasn't much scenery to take in.

The research station consisted of five single story 'concrete box' houses, a few smaller wooden ones, and a bunch of constructions with no obvious purpose. One looked like a tall metal tower with no doors or windows. Another resembled an upside-down gazebo, with a bunch of wires and metal bits sticking out of it. There was an enormous satellite dish in sight, as well as what seemed to be an empty and rusted swimming pool.

All of it appeared to be ancient in design and not cared for--paint peeling off, rust and decay claiming the exterior, piles of junk arranged loosely close to it. Amber saw a cat sitting on an exposed water pipe, licking its paws serenely. Or maybe it wasn't a cat, she thought, as she approached closer and noticed that the creature had a monkey-like head and no tail.

It didn't change her impression though. The research station must have been long abandoned by all sentient life.

"Lu, I think we're screwed." Amber turned around, but Lullaby wasn't there. "You gotta be kidding me," she muttered, headed in the direction of the nearest building. "I'm supposed to be the one who wanders off!"

She approached one of the concrete houses and located the entrance. To her surprise, the metal door was locked, and the corresponding panel lit up when she pressed a few buttons at random. She also noticed papers stapled to an announcement board on the right. Mostly item exchange offers, as well as some scientific equipment ads. She touched the paper. It was solid, though stained by rain and people's dirty fingers. Fingerprints. Humanoid fingerprints. Not human or Han, but definitely belonging to a person.

She tried the door again and pressed more buttons, but it didn't do anything, so she moved on to the next concrete block. Same story--entrance locked, buttons unresponsive, though no announcement board this time. She circled the house, hoping to see someone through a window, but all the windows were shut down, and some were even painted black from the inside. She examined one of the constructions and found a few different screwdrivers and an empty notebook. And still she found no one alive.

The place gave Amber a feeling the she couldn't quite put her finger on. The station was an anachronism, a spot torn out of history, like a slice of the time continuum in a digital library simulation. She detected a smell coming off the rusted hull of the machine. The smell of singed wires and heated up rubber. One she remembered very well.

"What's that?"

Little Amber, who sat on the steps of a tall ladder, pointed her finger at a tall cylinder on her right.

"That is a tokamak," her dad explained. "An electromagnetic fusion reactor. It fuels the collider."

"Collider?"

"This thing." He patted the large tube he stood next to, one that was half-buried into the ground and ran a circle of about five meters in diameter.

"What does it do?"

"Accelerates particles and smashes them together."

"What for?"

"To release other particles, which I detect over there," he pointed at a large cupboard next to the cylinder, "and analyze in here." And he raised his laptop, a thick piece of transparent plastic, from his lap.

"Yeah." Amber was swinging her legs. "But what for?"

"Steady now, sweetie." Her dad smiled. "That's philosophy, not physics."

She watched him work on his project for a while, imagining tiny particles crashing into each other and falling apart into smaller ones. It must be really pretty, she thought. She wished dad would open the tube and show it to her.

"Blast it," he said, and Amber smelled burned rubber in the air. "This equipment is ancient! Almost as ancient as professor Coleman."

Amber giggled. "Can I help?"

"Well." He was fanning the smoke with his hand. "You can read to me from the instructions."

She jumped down from the ladder and took his laptop from the ground.

"But don't tell mum I let a six year old do physics with me." He winked. "Or professor Coleman, for that matter."

"Cross my heart and hope to die." She nodded. "Connect the transduction wire to the stabilizer unit..."

One of the wooden houses was further from the rest and had a path of trampled grass leading to it. Amber followed the trace and arrived at another metal door. The wooden plates around it were scorched and battered, the gaps between them filled in with some thick white glue-like substance. Amber rubbed her eyes again.

They were watering and stinging, which was not a reassuring feeling. With a slight tremble in her hand, Amber grabbed the door handle and pulled, expecting it to be locked once again. But it wasn't.

She stepped inside of a broad hallway, lit up by a few natural sunlight lamps and with rather low ceilings. It was much warmer inside and decisively less damp. Amber closed the door firmly behind her. What was this place? She saw a bunch of empty tables around, but no food line or waiters traversing the room. There were, however, some vending machines. A sort of a fully automated cafe, perhaps?

"The hell were you doing outside?!"

Amber flinched. A man--Sojhi, by the look of it--was approaching her fast from the other side of the hall.

"The gassing's still on! Oh." He stopped mid-way. "You aren't Alice."

"No." She shook her head. "Amber Shakya. I arrived here like half an hour before."

"We didn't detect any vehicles." He frowned.

"Yeah, well, that's cause we walked here."

"We?" The man walked up to her. "How many of you are there?"

He was definitely Sojhi, Amber recognized. Tall, dark skinned, middle aged. Dressed in thick fabric trousers and a stretched out jumper.

"Just two, if you count me," she said. "I had a...friend with me. Rx'lng."

"Rx'lng?"

"I guess they didn't show up then. Are they in trouble if they stay outside?"

"Depends." The man thought for a second. "We use ozone, dichlorohexane and vaporized fenoles for gassing. It's pretty toxic for Sojhi and Han, but it doesn't seem to do anything for local wildlife."

"What about humans?"

"What about them?"

"Is it toxic for humans?"

It took him a minute to realize what she was referring to.

"Not tremendously, I think," he replied at last. "But wear safeseal goggles if you decide to go outside again."

"No thanks." She wiped her feet on the doormat and moved over to one of the vending machines. "Where do I press to get like a bucket of water and something that I can digest?"

Upon reaching the nearest table with a stack of plastic containers and bottles, Amber collapsed into the beaten down seat and allowed herself a minute of unadulterated anxiety. She had barely any money left, alone on a foreign planet, on the run from the Muuk and with no certain direction in mind.

Lullaby was gone, and the station was clearly lacking in spaceships. Kidney Stone had said that it was teaming with pilots for hire, but perhaps he hadn't been here as of recent. Was there an efficient way out of this? She had no idea. That was enough panic though. Amber straightened her back, gulped down half a liter of water and proceeded to open one of the lunch boxes.

The taste of the food barely registered on her tongue as she consumed it. It was hot, salty and probably not poisonous, which was enough. She was now becoming aware of how heavy her limbs felt, the dull buzzing in her ears and a piercing headache spreading from her forehead and down her neck and spine.

"A nap would be nice," she though, and took a lid off a drink she left for last. Steam rose from the surface of the milky brown liquid. She sniffed. It smelled weirdly familiar for something being sold on Skia. Ginger. Cardamom. Cinnamon. All Earth spices.

"Curious," she said to herself as she sipped the drink.

The cup warmed her palms, and the sweet spicy taste soothed her mind. For just a moment, she forgot all about her journey and the terrifying choices she had to make. She closed her eyes.

She was in their living room, sitting on the floor in a nest of pillows and puffy blankets. Her head rested on the sofa as she turned the glossy pages. She liked reading about all the planets that used to be in the Solar System. Jupiter was her favorite. It was the prettiest.

"Hey there, ladybird." She could hear her mum's footsteps from the other side of the house. "I brought you masala chai."

Amber took the mug from her mother's hands and placed it on the floor.

"Wait for it to cool down," her mum instructed.

"Did you know that Enceladus has the highest albedo of all the objects in the Solar System?" Amber asked. "It's like a huge ice ball with an ocean underneath."

"That is fascinating." She smiled at her daughter. "You should tell your dad about it when he comes back."

"Maybe he can explain about the spot on Jupiter."

"I'm sure he will. Okay." She kissed Amber's forehead. "I'll go before David gets bored."

Amber listened in on her mum talking to doctor Nawahi for a while, but it got pretty boring. They were discussing something about the Newtonian-Cartesian revolution and the relation of science and art, and Saturn was much more interesting than that. She drank her masala chai and flipped the pages, thinking about other things she could ask dad. Everything was simple. Everything was good.

The drink was getting cold. Amber sighed, downed the last gulp and licked her lips. She didn't feel full, but she didn't want to order more food either. What was she here for again?

She turned the bracelet on her hand. Sarah hadn't been active for ages, and she had no new notifications. She turned the device on and off and searched for local connections with free access. As soon as she had a signal, her inbox was flooded with ads and news updates. She checked her personal tab. No new messages.

Were they looking for her back on Alexandria? Was Nawahi worried about her? What about her colleagues at the Novella Institute--were they concerned, or happy to get rid of their most annoying employee?

Amber covered her face with her hands and rubbed her closed eyelids. She didn't feel sad, or nostalgic even. Truth is, she was too exhausted to feel in general. Exhausted from the walk, and from the illness, and from the events of the last few days. Just drained. Done.

How did she end up here, in the middle of nowhere, on this world, in this part of the galaxy? What was she thinking when she altered their course to Alexandria? So stupid, she thought. Impulsive. Childish. Exactly in her style. She didn't want to fix it or draw any meaning from it. Mostly she wanted it to be over, whatever it was.

"Amber."

The chair opposite her moved and Lullaby forced themselves into the small, human-sized seat.

"Lk'st," she said, barely raising her gaze from the surface of the table. "You're alive."

"Why wouldn't I be alive?"

"They're gassing the place outside, god knows what for."

"Haven't noticed."

"Guess it isn't toxic for you. Where have you been?"

"Post office."

"They have a...post office."

"Tried to contact some people. Didn't work."

"I've had lunch." Amber indicated the pile of empty cups and containers. "I can buy you some as well."

"Not now. Need to tell you something." They paused. "I'm not going with you to the Teardrop Cluster."

"Okay."

Lullaby chirped and tilted their head.

"Are you ill?" they asked.

"No. Why?"

"You aren't yelling at me."

"I'm not," she said. "How's that for a change, eh?"

"Will you go?"

Amber gestured vaguely with her hands.

"Anything is possible now," she elaborated. "I've no clue. Are you going back to the King of Kings?"

They nodded.

"Good for you." Amber sighed.

"We should come up with a story. Alibi."

"Alibi?" Amber repeated. "We haven't committed a crime."

"Did, actually," Lullaby disagreed. "Broke Muuk rules."

"You think they can persecute us for it?"

"Doubt it. But there may be consequences, and they'll ask us questions. We should have matching answers."

"Fine," she said, getting up. "Let me buy you food and then I'll come up with a nice story to cover our asses. Lying is like my thing. At least the theoretical part."

Lullaby didn't protest.

Amber spoke while they ate, throwing ideas at them whenever inspiration struck, and together they concocted a semi-believable long tale. They had to go for an emergency landing on Cryptos, had their ship stolen while they were looking for help and got kidnapped in the process. Kidnappers broke their comm devices and left them without a possibility of contact. So they went to the airport, boarded the wrong ship and ended up on Skia. After that, they would finally get through to the Muuk and go home. Or Lullaby would, at least.

Overall, it was close enough to the truth to be taken as such, Amber reckoned. Besides, why would the Muuk even care?

"How do we explain getting on the spaceship after the kidnapping?" Lullaby was on their third food box.

"Say that we panicked." Amber shrugged. "Wanted to get off the scary planet. That the kidnappers were still searching for us."

She rubbed her sore eyes, thinking that the gas must have damaged something after all, and scanned the room for activity. The tables had not filled up since she first entered. On the contrary, a few people had left and were not replaced by newcomers. She counted four: two Han occupying a cozy corner table next to the drink machine, the Sojhi guy who spoke to her before, and a girl.

Strange, Amber thought. She didn't notice her before, and no one had come in through the main door for a while. The girl sat alone with her back to Amber. She wore black leather and had long, fiery red hair.

"What about time?" Lullaby asked.

"Spent it all in captivity." Amber couldn't take her eyes off the red-headed girl.

"We have no spaceship tickets."

"Who cares."

"Our purchase history won't agree with our words."

"Wipe it. Masterclean chips ain't that hard to get your hands on."

"They won't erase it from the global network."

"Does that matter though?" she pondered. "Honestly, I don't think going missing for a few weeks is a terrible crime."

"Nine days."

"What?"

"In relative time, it's only been nine days."

Amber blinked in confusion. That didn't seem right in her head. In fact, it didn't seem right even when she had said 'a few weeks'. Their journey so far, from landing on Cryptos to here, felt like half a lifetime compared to everything she had experienced before. So many people, worlds, events... and it ended so fast.

"Is this what it feels like at the end of your life?" she thought. "Looking back on everything and realizing that it all rushed past you in a blink of an eye...and realizing you cannot get it back now."

Lullaby's next words hardly registered in her consciousness. She rubbed her eyes again and focused her gaze. The red-headed girl was still there. She studied her from afar--her posture, the movement of her hands as she raised a glass from the table; her brightly painted nails.

Amber was about to ask Lullaby to repeat her question, but then...Then the girl turned around and looked directly at her. Their eyes met. Amber felt her heart skip a beat. From across the room sat the most beautiful woman she had ever seen.

Meanwhile, a young woman was tapping her fingers on the glossy surface of a cafe table, a packet of sugar nested between the knuckles of her other hand. She chewed on her lip, her eyes focused on the thin streak of vapor raising from the coffee cup. It was getting cold. She tapped on the table some more. Then, with a quick sideways glance as if to make sure no one was watching, she tore open the packet and poured the white substance into her drink.

She took the first cautious sip, savoring the bitter-sweet taste on her tongue, and pressed her index finger to the screen of her smart-phone. So much junk mail. She deleted a bunch of spam messages in one quick swipe and was about to move on to her Pinterest feed, when her finger hovered over a new message in her 'social media' tab. A Facebook notification, from her brother. Again. She didn't need to open it to know that it was another angry rant about the presidential campaign.

"Miss?"

She looked away from the screen and saw a kid standing in front of her table. He was about the same age as her Jacob, and had big blue eyes and a mess of curly brown hair.

"Do you need the other chair?" he asked, putting his hand on the chair's back. "Mum has nowhere to sit."

"Sure. Take it." She smiled.

"Thanks, miss!" He beamed and began to drag away the heavy chair.

It made a terrible scratching noise.

She chuckled, licking milk foam off her lips. Kids. They grow up so fast! And you never stop worrying about them. Jacob will go to high school soon, and he will surely want to walk there alone. Question is, should she let him? In their neighborhood?

She sighed, unlocked her smartphone once again and clicked on the e-mail.

"Immigrants are five times more likely to commit crimes than American citizens," the post read. "Why is no one talking about this?"

S stood aside, a satisfied smirk on his face, and ticked a box in his imaginary notebook.

"And that's how you win an election--winning them over one by one," he announced. "Perfect work! One bus driver's thought process tweaked, one more client for the coffee shop, one missing chair, some fake facts as a cherry on top and, voila, one worried mum's mind changed."

"Great work, genius," Darkness said, and put a hand on his shoulder. "One of your finest."

"Why the sarcasm, Darkness? Are you jealous?"

"Wouldn't dream of it." She shook her head. "Two words: wrong candidate."

"Oh." The notebook disappeared from his hands. "Well. At least it's the right country this time

TWENTY-ONE

The woman got up, leaving her glass on the table. She flashed a shadow of a smile at Amber and turned towards her. Her high-heeled shoes clanked against the floor as she walked--not a runway model, but a captain of a spaceship, graceful and confident. She was tall, much taller than Amber, and not just because of the heels. Apart from the black leather, she was wearing a tight t-shirt and a pair of skinny jeans.

"Is she Sojhi or Han," Amber thought, once she got the first good glance of her face.

The woman had a rather prominent nose, fair skin, full lips covered in pink lipstick and big, blue-grey eyes. To Amber, she looked like a Greek goddess who stepped out of an ancient painting and now stood in front of her, a cheeky smile on her lips, and took her breath away.

"Is that seat taken?" the woman asked.

Her voice was a bit hoarse but flowed like a song.

"Go ahead." Amber gestured at the empty chair.

She sat down and immediately crossed her legs.

"You're not locals," she pointed out.

"Golden star for observation," Amber replied. "My name is Amber, and that's Lullaby."

She outstretched her hand for a handshake, and the girl took it--but instead of shaking it, she raised Amber's hand to her face and placed a gentle kiss on her outer palm.

"Nina," she said, releasing her hand. "It's a pleasure."

"Likewise." Amber coughed and awkwardly scratched her nose. "Funny, I thought Sojhi couldn't have red hair."

"What makes you think I'm Sojhi?" Nina chuckled. "Seriously, tell me so that I can work on that."

"So much species-ism in this galaxy."

"Isms are kinda in my genes. I'm human."

"What a coincidence." Amber smiled.

"I've noticed that too. So," she said, leaning ever so slightly closer to Amber. "What is a girl like you doing in a place like this?"

Amber had no reason to trust this girl. After all, they had met literally two minutes ago, and she knew nothing of her except for the name that could as well be an alias. Yet she found herself telling her everything--from her job on Sereneae, to where she was going, to how she ended up in that seat. Lullaby didn't protest. They too seemed to have reached a certain level of apathy and exhaustion beyond which caution was no longer a prerogative.

"Teardrop Cluster then." Nina nodded. "Impressive. Do you think that moon is actually there?"

"It's the best lead we've had in centuries," Amber replied. "Problem is, I can't get there by foot."

"That problem can be easily solved with a decent spaceship and a daring yet competent pilot, both of which I can offer for the low price of your precious company."

"You have a spaceship? But where?"

"Where most of this research station is." She pointed downward with her perfectly manicured nail. "Underground. There's a whole fleet of ships in the hangar."

"How do you blast off from a dungeon?"

"The roof opens up. It usually is open, they just closed it for the gassing."

"Huh," Amber said, still not giving a concrete answer. "What is the gassing for, by the way?"

"De-ionizes the particle space or something," Nina replied, making it up on the go. "I wouldn't know. Science is stranger than fiction these days."

257

"I'll have to disagree with you on that." Amber raised an eyebrow in her best acting attempt at flirting.

"I'm looking forward to the debate," Nina told her. "Come."

And she got up.

Amber found herself leaving her seat, her legs moving as of their own volition. She was prepared to follow Nina to the other side of the world and back. It's not how it usually worked, she thought. Amber didn't beg, she only ever offered. She couldn't stand The Dance: the hope, the uncertainty, face flushing and palms sweating as she awaited an answer upon asking out a pretty girl. She would much rather act as if her company was a privilege, a gift that others had to compete for. She played out rejection as another person's loss and not her own. Her dignity was of higher priority, yet...there was something different about this girl.

Nina walked across the hall and halted before a wall. She made a come-hither motion, then placed her open palm on the dark polished wood. The wall clicked, hissed and whirred. A thin panel detached itself from its base and slid up, revealing an elevator cabin. She stepped inside. Amber was motionless. She'd lost all sense of where she was going, but she knew where she needed to be.

"Lu." Amber turned round.

Lk'st, who hadn't said a single word during the whole exchange, was getting out of the tiny seat.

"You go," they said. "Find the Moon. Send me video message when you come back to Alexandria."

"And you?"

"Back to the King of Kings. Helping to rebuild my world."

"Will you be okay?"

"I'll be better off than you," they joked.

Amber hesitated. She wasn't a big fan of hugs, or of cheesy goodbyes for that matter. She smiled in what she hoped was a sad yet warm manner, and tried hard to persuade herself that it was okay. They weren't going into deadly battle. They would not lose each other. Online communication existed and they weren't going to jail for their mischief. It wasn't a forever farewell...so why couldn't she believe herself?

"Thank you," Amber muttered. "For keeping me safe. For saving my life more than once. For being the best friend I've ever had."

"You're welcome," Lullaby replied, and placed their huge palm on Amber's shoulder. "Be a good girl."

"Never." Amber laughed. "You take care."

"The elevator's closing!" Nina called out. "Hurry up."

"This was fun," Lullaby said.

"Greatest fun of my life," Amber confirmed. "Well...gotta go."

And she rushed for the elevator, where Nina was pushing the 'door open' button again and again.

"Did I interrupt something important?" she asked, once Amber was inside.

"Nah, it's fine," she lied. "Take me to your spaceship."

And she watched as the image of Lullaby disappear from her field of vision. Gone.

"I'll regret this one day," Amber muttered under her breath.

"Oh, trust me baby," Nina said. "If at the end of your life you won't have any regrets, that means you haven't really lived."

The elevator whizzed down the shaft and slammed against the floor with enough force to make Amber's stomach jump up to her diaphragm.

"Level zero," a soft synthetic voice announced.

Nina yawned and zipped her jacket.

"Mind your head," she advised, ducking as she maneuvered out of the elevator.

Amber took a cautious step forward, careful as to not bump into the ceiling.

For a second or two, she thought that she was in a cave, or an actual dungeon. It was pitch black, so she couldn't see where she was going, and the air felt stiff and damp. She was beginning to worry when a sharp turn took her to a broad and brightly lit corridor. Nina was waiting for her at a tall, wryly decorated arc.

"Has this place been carved out of rock?" Amber asked.

"Yes, actually." Nina stepped through the arc and into a circular room with similarly cave-like walls. "Over here."

They traveled through a multitude of doorways, arcs, and corridors, passing by a few more empty rooms and halls. Amber couldn't decide whether the place looked abandoned or brand new. She stumbled over a pile of rocks on more than one occasion, wondering how Nina managed to walk the path on high heels. They've only met two people on their way, a male and female Sojhi in glossy protective suits. Both glanced at Nina with a frown of apprehension.

"On the right," Nina said as they passed a large door with a caution sign painted across it. "It's bio-locked, but I'll let you in on my pass."

"Huh?" Amber paused in front of a doorway.

Through it she could see a huge hangar filled to the brim with spacecrafts of all shapes in sizes.

"Just keep close to me."

Nina stopped behind Amber and gently wrapped her shoulders with her left hand. Then she pressed her right palm to the wall, and Amber heard a melodic ting followed by an 'entrance authorized' message. Nina pushed her through the arc, still gripping her shoulders. She could smell Nina's hair, the soft notes of flowery perfume, and the leather of her jacket. Together they stepped into the hangar. The arc tinged again behind them, and Nina let her go.

"Busted equipment," she explained. "Can't tell two people apart if they're close enough to each other, especially if they're of the same species."

"Uh-hm." Amber nodded, her heart racing like she was in the process of winning a hundred-meter sprint. "So." She made an effort to collect herself. "Which one's yours?"

Nina lead her through the gaps in between the parking lots, and Amber tried not to gape at the spaceships too much. These weren't commercials or cargos, she realized. Personal transport. Sport ships. Collector items. Crafts of all shapes and colors, most seemingly too sophisticated and beautiful to even take off. Some reminded her of illustrations in kid books about space travel, some looked more like figurines at the bottom of cereal boxes. She saw one spaceship with a shining gold exterior, not a single scrap on its broad (and useless) wings. She smiled.

That was the kind of fancy transport she imagined when dreaming of exploring the galaxy.

"End of the road," Nina said, and Amber span on the spot. "Amber, meet Enlightenment."

Nina stood beside a slick, polished spaceship about the size of a house transportation van. It was shaped a bit like a paper airplane, with a pointy front and a stretched out back. Like most modern spacecrafts, it had no portholes or decor, and the only thing indicating the door was a barely visible indentation on its side.

Amber whistled. "Girl...not bad at all."

"Wait here for a second." Nina patted the ship's silvery side, eyes following a distant figure. "I need to have a word with management."

"Sure," Amber replied, but Nina wasn't around to hear it.

She walked towards the front of the ship, hoping to listen in.

A few meters away, Nina had walked up to a short Han dressed in a dark uniform, his hair hidden under a protective helmet.

"When is the roof going off?" She cut straight to the business without a greeting.

"When I say so," the man responded with a fake smile.

"Does that mean you've no idea what the hell you're doing?"

"No, Miss Moon, it means the roof is going off when I say so."

"Oh, come on, Rudy." She batted her eyelashes at him. "Don't you want me gone?"

"That I do," he agreed. "But it isn't worth poisoning half the station."

"I'm sure it's already safe."

"It will be. In two hours."

"Two hours?!"

"That isn't up for negotiation," he said, ignoring her protests. "Or do you want me to do an inspection of your ship? You still haven't told me what you have in the cargo hold."

"Weapons. Drugs. Dead bodies." She shrugged. "Usual stuff."

"I'd watch my tongue if I were you," he pointed out. "You'll be hard pressed to prove that was a joke in a court of law."

"Don't worry, Rudy." Nina smiled coyly. "Even if I did some truly shady stuff, I'd never get caught."

"Two hours," he repeated, and walked away.

Nina returned to the ship, and Amber pretended to be studying her fingernails.

"It's okay," she told her. "I'm not hiding anything."

"So, you don't have dead bodies in your cargo."

"Nah. Just living kidnapped people. Oh, I'm kidding," she quickly added, forcing a laugh. "Come on. If we are stuck here for two more hours, might as well have a proper drink."

Five minutes later, the two of them entered what Amber presumed was a bar. She had already mentally prepared herself for sad rock music and depressing mood lighting, when the automatic doors slid open and let her into... what? A small patch of forest in the middle of an underground research station?

The place was rather empty and wonderfully quiet. Illuminated by warm natural light, it smelled of fresh air, damp grass and spring flowers. Amber glanced down and discovered that she was standing on a patch of actual soil. All around her were small trees and bushes, and there were no chairs or tables in sight. Nina tugged her by the sleeve.

"Keep walking," she encouraged.

"The hell is this?" Amber leaned to the floor and picked a raspberry of a shrub brunch.

"Food delivery system. The conditions outside are a bit harsh, even if you don't count spraying the soil with chemicals on a weekly basis. So, they've made the produce section of a supermarket here."

They passed by several patches of sprouting vegetables, as well as a tiny cherry tree garden.

"So by 'drinks' you meant 'freshly squeezed apple juice'." Amber smirked.

"No. By drinks I meant drinks. Actual drinks, not the watered down disinfectant that Sojhi serve."

They took a turn alongside a greenhouse and arrived at a glade in between denser fragments of the forest. It was covered by blankets and exercise mats and had a peculiar looking vending machine in the middle. Nina invited Amber to sit. She picked a fluffy white blanket next to a tree stamp and leaned her back against it.

"You're of legal age, I hope," Nina said, handing her a tall transparent glass.

"Sure am," she responded, and took a sip. "Uh, strong stuff." She almost chocked on the liquid.

"Take it easy," Nina recommended. "It'll grow on you."

For a while, they enjoyed the drinks in silence. Soon Amber felt her worries dissipate, as if they were never there. That sensation of peace and happiness was exactly why she stayed away from weed for the most part. She valued realism, wanted her mind to stay sharp. In her opinion, being content and being rational at the same time was not possible. At least for her.

"I like your nose ring." Nina set her drink aside to take off her shoes.

"It's traditional," Amber explained.

"Sweet. Mines are just for the aesthetic." She brushed her hair aside, revealing an array of rings and studs on her left ear. "Used to have one in my lip, but it annoyed me too much."

"I had my lobes pierced as a kid. Dad agreed, without telling mum. Had a huge scandal afterwords, made me take them out."

"Right." Nina chuckled. "Not everyone approves of body mods. Most of the galaxy doesn't actually. They think humans are weird for poking holes in our bodies and forcing ink under our skin."

"To each their own." Amber shrugged. "Personally, I don't understand that Sojhi thing where they bleach their hair to the roots to make them white forever, but I don't comment on it."

"Trust me, baby, that is far away from the weirdest tradition out there. Don't wanna talk about it though." She picked up her glass again. "I wanna talk about you."

"What about me?" Amber produced an awkward laugh. "I've already told you my backstory."

"Not really," Nina disagreed. "You told me how you got here. That doesn't explain why you are here."

"Oh god." She shook her head. "Who were you back on Alexandria, a shrink?"

"Worse. A philosopher."

"Damn."

"Indeed." Nina smiled. "Assistant professor at the Novella Institute."

"No way!" Amber exclaimed. "I work there as well. Ancient history. How come I've never heard of you?"

"I bet you haven't heard of many people," she responded. "I wasn't called Nina back then either."

"Is 'Nina' your pseudonym then?"

"No, I had it changed before I left. See, back at the Institute, before I quit, I was still under the illusion of being a guy."

Amber raised an eyebrow. "What, as an adult? Doesn't everyone get that scan at eight?"

"Oh, I got the scan alright," she replied. "But technology isn't perfect. That one exceptionally not perfect, actually. Eighty nine percent accuracy."

"That's rubbish."

"Indeed. The diagnostician squinted at the scan for five minutes, then told my folks I was 'gay, probably'."

"And were you?"

"Didn't get that one right either. I don't discriminate," she elaborated, "not by gender and not by race. I was even with a Bellazi once. He had impressive stamina, but he was a bit scaly down there, if you know what a mean."

Amber chuckled. She wasn't sure how much of Nina's tall tales were actually true, but she was sure loving the conversation.

"So, you didn't know you were trans?"

"Well, I knew there was something wrong," she continued. "But I didn't feel like 'trans' was an option. I was aware of it, obviously. My cousin's a trans guy. Except his scan worked just fine, and he never had to deal with years of confusion and existential crises. Maybe that's why I went into philosophy as a teen. Thought my existential angst could be put to good use. Unfortunately, it turned out that the examined life is not worth living."

"How did you figure it out?"

"I came across stories of people getting their results wrong. Started reading, talking to people. Went to a clinic for a consult.

"They didn't believe me, of course. Said I was delusional, seeking attention and all that shit. Took me a year to find a person who was willing to listen. I pretty much begged them for a re-scan. They said they believed me even without one, but I got it just in case. Didn't trust myself at all. When I got my results, all the other "specialists" didn't even apologize. Well, at least they got it right in the end. I quit the job, claimed my medsurance credits... became who I've always been. Became Nina."

"And left Alexandria?"

"Yep. Four years ago, a few months after my twenty sixths birthday. Best decision of my life."

"How?"

"Surprisingly easy." She laughed. "Got a ticket to one of those orbital tours, to the guest station, and paid some Han bloke online to hitch me off that thing. The security in there is laughable."

"And no one tried to find you later on?"

"Why would they?" She shrugged. "My folks are rather open-minded, so they didn't stop me, and it's not like I escaped from a prison. I know rares often feel like they're special and irreplaceable, but with a stable population, losing a tiny percentage of your mating pool is not an issue."

"How many of us are out there?"

"Not sure. Dozens. Hundreds maybe. We don't all keep in touch."

"That's...insane." Amber chuckled and shook her head. "I've never even heard of anyone going missing like that."

"People don't talk." Nina caught a strand of her hair and twirled it on her finger. "Maybe they're scared, or maybe they're just jealous. Don't want to admit that they want off the planet too. I mean, who doesn't at some point in their life? Except no one ever speaks up, not on a massive scale. No one wants to upset the Muuk. It's all about the Muuk, as if they own us somehow."

"They're the ones who recreated us though."

"So fucking what? Your parents made you, but that doesn't mean you are their property. You don't owe shit to the incubator machine either and it carried you for nine months."

"We depend on the Muuk for longer than nine months," Amber retorted.

"You can survive without their help just fine."

"I wouldn't call the state of this galaxy 'fine'."

"Depends on where you look, now doesn't it?" Nina responded. "I absolutely agree that there are plenty of shitholes in the universe, and even most advanced settlements aren't all sunshine and puppies. But that's what life is! It's living. With all the grief, and pain, and death. Not the censored, sanitized existence people get on Alexandria."

"You've got some interesting opinions in that pretty head of yours." Amber smirked.

"I've barely started." She smiled back and finished her last swig of the drink.

"What do you do then?" Amber asked. "On the free side."

"This and that," she replied. "Try to balance having fun with helping out where I can. I'll be taking a supply of meds and vaccines to one place, once I drop you off. Need to make money too, of course, so there's some contraband to go with it."

"That's what you have in your cargo hold then? Medical supplies? That's kinda underwhelming."

"Trust me, if people knew what it was, they'd slit my throat in no time. I'm better off with them thinking I'm a crime lord, or a narcotics dealer."

"And you just gave up that info wily-nilly." Amber arched an eyebrow. "Do you trust me?"

"Oh, baby, that's cute," Nina said. "But gangsters and criminals don't dress in overalls or take drinks from strangers."

"Maybe I'm an undercover agent," she suggested.

"Well." She paused. "That's a risk I'm willing to take."

Amber smiled and licked the last drop of her drink of the side of the glass. She felt so light, almost weightless. Her senses weren't screaming at her, for a change, and she basked in the wonderful absence of worry. A little holiday from being herself. Her eyes were drawn to Nina face--to the sunbeams gleaming in her hair and reflecting off her earrings, and the soft pink gloss on her lips. Nina was quiet and motionless, as if waiting for something. Amber felt her pulse ringing in her ears. She took a deep breath in, preparing to say something...then bailed.

"Your comm is flashing." she mumbled.

"Huh?" Nina said, having heard her just fine.

"Little green light on the side. I think you got a message or, khm, something."

Nina reached into the breast pocket of her jacket and pulled out a black plastic device about the size of a bar of soap. It looked a bit like a flatphone, Amber thought, except it was mostly solid material with a rather small screen and a bunch of buttons.

"Such a troll!" Nina read the message of the screen and shook her head in disbelief. "Opened up the roof way earlier than he promised. Someone must have complained. Someone more important than a mere human."

"So we're leaving now?" Amber guessed.

"Unless you wanna stay for another glass."

"Nah." She got up on slightly shaky legs. "I'm good."

"Well, if the first dose wears off too fast, I've got better stuff on the ship," Nina said. "Come on."

Amber nodded and returned her glass to the machine. She didn't think she would need another drink to stay high, as long as she was around Nina.

"And a parking ticket too!"

Back at the hangar, Nina located her spaceship immediately, and had just removed a sticky piece of paper off its side.

"You've got to be kidding me."

Amber regarded the paper suspiciously.

"Do you really have to pay it off? Doesn't look official."

"I do, if I wanna come back to this place." She sighed. "Wait for me here. I'll give that asshole his five units, along with a nice door slam."

She stormed off, leaving Amber to stand next to the spaceship, as if guarding it from the placement of another ticket. She leaned against the craft's slick wall and felt its cold surface, her fingers finding little scrapes and imperfections. Amber closed her eyes for a moment. Her stomach rumbled, and her legs were heavy with a dull ache. What she needed right now was a hot shower, a snack, and a warm bed to nap in…but that's not what she wanted. She sighed and opened her eyes. In front of her stood Lullaby.

"Didn't think weed could cause hallucinations," Amber said calmly.

"Not a hallucination. Me."

"Yeah, well, that's what a hallucination would say."

"Would it do this?" Lullaby asked and smacked her on the arm with significant force.

"Ow!" Amber smacked them back and rubbed the rapidly forming bruise. "Aren't you supposed to be on your way to the King of Kings?"

"No. I miscalculated."

"Miscalculated?" She frowned.

"Made a wrong assessment of my values and priorities."

"Yeah, and?"

"I'm coming with you."

Half a second ago, Amber was preparing a sassy comeback worthy of a situation. And now, instead of an opportunity to use it, she was left with something she didn't even dare try put into words.

"If you want to, of course," Lullaby added.

"You insult me, Lk'st." Amber smiled softly. "Of course I want you to come with me, doofus."

Lullaby chirped in excitement.

"Just... don't ruin my game, okay?"

"Will try to remember that."

"Parking ticket done," Nina announced, approaching the ship. "Oh, hello there. I believe we've met."

"Lullaby," the Rx'lng introduced themselves. "Do you have another place for me?"

"Do you come as a joined package or something?" She chuckled and unblocked the door. "I mean, yeah, sure. I have a spare bedroom."

They boarded the spaceship one by one, and the entrance door closed again behind them. Inside was a tidy, modern living room, with a couch, armchairs, bookshelves and even a hat stand. Not what you would expect inside of a space craft.

"Make yourself at home." Nina took off her jacket and hanged it on the hat stand. "I'll go fire up this baby. Teardrop Cluster?"

"Teardrop Cluster," Amber confirmed.

"I won't promise a super close fly-by, but I'll get you to an autopilot capsule range," she said, and disappeared behind another door.

"Like this." Lullaby fell into one of the armchairs, which squeaked under their weight. "Cozy."

"Hey." Amber took a seat as well. "One question... how did you get inside the hangar?"

"Through the entrance."

"Wasn't it security locked?"

"Yes. But it opens to anyone. Just pressed my hand to the panel, and it let me in."

"Curious," Amber muttered, leaning back into the armchair. "I wonder if Nina knew that."

TWENTY-TWO

"Dreadful, simply dreadful!" Professor Nawahi paced the room with a perfectly synchronized motion of a clockwork toy. "How will I ever explain this to the dean?"

Amber, who was sprawled across her bed, didn't appear to be so concerned.

"I'll buy him flowers," she said, and covered her face with a pillow. "I'm pretty sure he fancies me."

"The Muuk will be horrified," Nawahi whaled.

"Fuck the Muuk."

"I certainly hope you didn't, young lady."

"What, fuck the Muuk?" Amber snorted with laughter.

"No. Sleep with that fugitive girl."

She wanted to say something in protest and give mister Potatohead a lecture about breaching privacy, but when she removed the pillow, Nawahi was gone. Amber shrugged. She assumed the professor must had left in a hurry. Now was time for another coffee, she decided.

Walking through the corridor which ran in circles for a good half a mile, she somehow ended up in the kitchen of her old apartment back in Ishtar. It didn't surprise her. She reached into the cupboard for a mug and moved to the coffee machine.

"Do you drink coffee?" she asked, turning round to look at Lullaby.

"Only on Tuesdays," they responded.

Amber smirked. She wasn't sure whether it was Tuesday or not but made another cup anyway.

"You're out of milk," Lullaby reminded. "Fresh and canned."

"Of course. Sorry. Wait for me here, I'll fetch a new packet."

Amber left the kitchen and walked out into a vast, empty field. Above her was a murky, cloudy sky. Below her was a sandy wasteland of moss and dry grass. Suddenly, she was running. Wind whistled in her ears as she launched for the horizon with all her strength.

Something was chasing her. She could tell. It was getting close with every second, staring right at her, breathing at the back of her neck. She tried to speed up, but her legs refused to move. Stuck, as if enveloped by tar, or honey. She gave up and fell to the ground, closing her eyes and covering her head with her hands. Nothing happened. Slowly, she blinked one eye open, then the other.

"Hi."

A man was standing right next to her--tall, distinctly human, with jet black hair and thick square glasses perched on his nose.

"I'm S," he introduced himself. "I'm looking for the Teardrop Cluster. Can't find it anywhere on this map."

He had a map. Of course he did. How didn't she notice it before? Amber got up from the ground and approached the stranger.

"Why do you even need to go to the Teardrop Cluster?" she asked, looking over his shoulder.

The man opened his mouth to speak...

"Hey, sleeping beauty."

"Huh?"

Amber never found out what S was about to tell her. She woke up in the armchair on board of starship Enlightenment, with a streak of saliva running down her cheek and a mighty cramp in her neck. She quickly wiped her face and attempted to gather herself.

"You've been out for a couple hours." Nina stood near the armchair, her hair now tied up in a ponytail. "We're well on the course to the Teardrop Cluster."

"How the hell did I manage to sleep through the hyperspace jump?" Amber wondered, stretching her heavy limbs. "Not that I'm complaining. How long will it be?"

"Half a day, relative time. Give or take."

"Impressive."

"Thank you." Nina smiled with a corner of her mouth. "It took some tinkering to kick this ship into good shape. No offense to the ship," she stroked the wall gently, "only to her previous owners."

"You tinkered with the engines?"

"Oh, my goodness no." She chuckled and shook her head. "Only with the coding. And, on one occasion, with the plumbing system. But it's in perfect order. Don't worry."

"Right." Amber got up from the armchair. "Speaking of plumbing. Can I use the shower? I don't wanna check but I probably stink like a dead possum in a dumpster during summer."

"Colorful metaphor. And be my guest. The bathroom is first door on the left."

"Thanks." She was about to turn towards the door, when Nina stopped her with a gesture.

"Keep the overalls," she instructed, putting a hand on Amber's shoulder and picking up the overall strap with her finger. "Pop it into the washer. It will be dry but the time you step out."

"Sure. Thanks." Amber coughed.

Nina let go of the strap.

"I'll go check the settings. Wouldn't want you to be stranded in there, naked and with no hot water in the tab."

"Mm-mhm," Amber muttered, and turned her back on the room.

She couldn't fight a broad grin and a rapid heartbeat as she walked towards the door and out into the corridor.

By the time she returned to the lounge room, her body mellow from the bath and hair smelling of lavender, Nina had set up a small table by the couch. Amber raised an eyebrow. A white napkin instead of a tablecloth and a vase with a fake flower in it wasn't the height of romance, but it was certainly a sweet gesture.

"Come." Nina patted the couch cushion next to her, and Amber took a seat.

"Did you dim the lights?" she asked.

"A little bit. Didn't want to wake up your friend."

Amber looked around and soon found Lullaby, who was sleeping in another armchair, their arms hanging down from it and touching the ground.

"You woke me up."

"I have plans for you." Nina smiled coyly. "Dinner?"

She raised a tall glass of a thick, creamy liquid. Another, identical glass stood on the table next to the vase.

"Is that nutrigen?" Amber gave out a short laugh. "Cause I've had enough of that at school."

"I'm rather fond of it, actually." Nina shrugged. "Besides, it's my own recipe, not just the original formula. Less sugar, better flavor and no lumps."

Amber accepted the glass and took a first cautious swig. Compared to the memories of her childhood, she judged, it was certainly not bad.

"I've crashed a Boost tablet in mine," Nina added. "Can add one to yours as well."

"Is that how you get by in life?" Amber wondered out loud. "By pumping yourself full of pharmaceuticals, one after another."

"We're all constantly pumping chemicals into our bodies," she responded. "Oxygen, water, food, supplements. That's basically how being alive works-- taking from the universe to stop yourself from decaying."

"Careful, girl. Your degree is showing."

"Oh, I've barely scratched the surface. Enough about me though." She put the glass down and licked her lips. "Tell me, baby--what the hell is in the Teardrop Cluster?"

"Don't know yet," Amber said. "I'm on a hunt for a very old mystery. Have you ever heard of the Aquamarine Moon?"

Nina shook her head.

"Well, prepare to be amazed."

Amber had told this story at least a hundred times: to professors, students, random people, phone cameras and bathroom mirrors. At this point it was practically telling itself whenever she pleased. It was her pride. Her thing. The topic that she loved more than books, or starry nights, or quiet sunny mornings on the balcony of her apartment. Whenever she spoke of it, the world would disappear, dissolve and coalesce into a tiny yet all-encompassing bubble. A little haven where the only things that existed were herself, her passion, and the story of Nos.

"And that is what you get when you base your entire civilization on philosophy instead of science," Amber concluded and proceeded to catch her breath as stealthily as possible.

"Oh, that doesn't surprise me at all," Nina said. "If the moon does exist, I bet you'll find a bunch of old folks in badly tailored suits, arguing about, I don't know, experiential truth of the Logos while their tea gets zero Kelvins cold."

"Don't think we will find it at all."

Amber blinked in surprise. Evidently, Lullaby had woken up and was listening to the conversation from their armchair.

"Seems too easy," they elaborated. "They could have hidden it very well, stop random people from visiting."

"And that's when you tell me." Amber scoffed.

"Just a guess. Gut feeling. Might be very wrong."

"Doesn't sound like something they would do," Nina said. "Based on what you described at least. I'm getting a sense that they basically went on a planet-wide version of a meditation retreat. Left to reconsider their worldview, and who knows what happened next. Maybe they forgot about the need for reproduction and died out without noticing. Or maybe they're still in the process. In which case," she picked up her glass again, "I don't envy the poor bastards. Six years of philosophy nearly killed me. Imagine a whole millennium of that."

"What is your beef with the love of wisdom?" Amber asked.

"None!" she responded. "In fact, I think it is incredibly valuable, and I'm glad it is taught in schools, on Alexandria at least. It's a pretty useful tool when consumed in moderation. It only becomes a problem when you decide to dedicate your career to it. It almost always ends in severe burnout."

Nina paused to gather her thoughts.

"You see," she carried on, "philosophy is not something you can ever escape. Doctors, teachers, rescue officers, they all have stressful jobs, no doubt--but at the end of the day, they get to go home and relax. With philosophy, you are given no respites.

"You wake up in the morning thinking about it, and you go to bed thinking about it. You work on it with all your power and strength, and you never arrive at an answer. Sometimes it lets go of you for a while, but then you hear an opposing argument, and it knocks you off and leaves you exactly where you've started.

"I'm certain that there are people who can deal with this, and I admire their courage and self-sacrifice, but I sure as hell ain't one of them." Nina paused again and rubbed her fingers together, in what Amber had identified as the only sign of anxiety she had ever seen from her. "When you spend too much time trying to decide how to live your life, you start to forget about actually living it," she concluded.

"What is the meaning of life?" Amber just couldn't resist.

Nina laughed. "Happiness. Salted caramel. Forty-two."

"Yeah, but seriously." Amber smiled, leaning her head against the couch. "Don't you think about it?"

"No such thing as meaning." She shrugged. "Neurobiology has thoroughly demonstrated that the present experience of our consciousness is all we have, or ever have had, or ever will have. If you're anything like me, you've learned it in two-form, convinced yourself that you understand it, and never let that properly sink in.

"All we ever have is now. All we are ever sure of is the conscious experience. Once you dwell on it for a while, you arrive at certain conclusions. It begins to actually mean something. And to me, it means that the meaning of life is to enjoy your stay, not be an asshole to other people and make their lives better instead. Just that." She smiled. "No over-complicating things, no living in the past and searching for higher truth in everything--no matter how badly your human brain wants it."

"Right." Amber nodded. "Seems like solid advice. Except, by that merit, I have utterly failed at life so far."

"It's never too late to change," Nina said. "Hey. Lullaby, isn't it? What do you think?"

Lullaby attempted to turn in the armchair, but quickly discovered that it wasn't a feasible solution. Instead, they got up and rotated the armchair. Then they sat down and focused their big insect eyes on Nina.

"Am done searching for meaning and expecting anything from the universe," they began. "On the King of Kings, we were taught from birth that gods have a plan for us. That they know what is best for us and can guide us towards the best life. Everything happens for a reason. Everyone has their place in the cosmos. For worker Rx'lng, that meant protecting the nest. Spending your life subservient, being treated like garbage. Always the last to have food. Never asked or consulted when making decisions for the nest. No gametes, no value. Sisters and brothers are persons, us--just spare parts. I hated it. Always."

"No joke," Amber interrupted. "I'd hate that too!"

Lu glared at them, and she gestured "shutting up".

"Hated it," Lullaby continued, "but would tell myself--it's how it was meant to be. Then, the King of Kings took off on a course for another place. Closer to Muuk, more stable spot. In a solar system where we could build a new home world."

They paused, big insect eyes wandering the room, thinking.

"One day, ship was flying through a dense cluster, and there was a positron storm ahead. Main terminal calculated a 0.015% risk. Captain took it. Flew right into a storm. Less than one chance out of ten thousand, and they got right into it." They looked away and folded their arms on their chest, making themselves seem smaller. "I should have gone to my nest, to the A deck, when it happened--but I stayed in the D deck with another protector. The A deck got fried. D deck was spared. Two nests were wiped out completely. Mine and theirs."

"You wouldn't have been able to save them." Amber frowned. "You'd just die with them."

"Yes." Lullaby nodded. "But didn't. Hid in the D deck. Thought 'if this is meant to happen, it will happen'. What sort of cruel joke of gods is this, to kill the nest and spare the protector?!"

Amber was silent. She had never seen Lullaby like this: sad, scared... weak. It almost didn't feel real.

"The cruelest joke," Nina said, "was for creatures who personalize everything and see patterns everywhere to be born into a universe with no higher intelligence, no creator, and no ultimate purpose."

Amber had a thousand and one thing to say about it all--with references and whole-page quotes memorized from ancient books at the tip of her tongue--but she didn't. Instead, she turned slightly towards Lullaby and told them "I am very sorry about your nest." And she meant it.

Lullaby didn't reply.

"Where the spare bedroom?" They climbed out of the armchair with a quiet puff, eyes focused on the floor. "Need rest before the big day."

"Second door on the right," Nina told them. "It should be clean. Let me know if there's no..."

"Whatever."

They snapped the door shut behind them.

"Did I," Nina frowned, "upset, uh, them?"

"They'll be okay," Amber responded, and wiggled on the couch.

She really wanted to believe what she had just said.

An awkward pause lingered for a while after that. Amber wanted to talk, wanted to care...but felt too exhausted to even think. She wished the world would go away, leaving only her, Nina, and the couch they were sitting on.

"Like I've said." Nina sighed. "Better not dwell on the past too much. Still," she pushed the table away from the couch and stretched, "at least we're on our own now."

"We sure are." Amber forced herself to smile. "So...what do you wanna talk about?"

"Oh, I don't know." Nina brought a hand to her face and tucked a streak of her hair behind her ear, leaving her ear piercings on display. "You. Me. Anything in between."

She put an arm around Amber's shoulder, which made her heart skip a beat. All the heavy thoughts were gone from her mind, replaced by less civilized depictions. Fantasies. Wants. Desires. She searched her memory and concluded, with a high degree of confidence, that she hadn't been that attracted to a woman in a long while. And she wasn't sure what to do about it.

"You're bold." Amber smiled in, what she hoped, was a sexy and confident manner. "You've been flirting with me since the first minute, and you don't even know whether I'm open."

Already a pre-determined program of action was running in her head--a collection of phrases, moves and facial expressions she invoked whenever she was out on a search for a mate.

"If you have someone, I'll be better," Nina was whispered in her ear. "I'll convince both you and them that monogamy just isn't worth it."

"You don't know whether I'm queer either."

"Oh, baby, I'll be better than any man, any day." She smirked. "Just give me a chance. Besides, I can tell that you want it."

"Yeah?" Amber was about to say something equally outrageous but got stuck on the wording.

She blinked, trying hard to think of an alternative, but nothing came to mind. Immediately, she began to sweat. She could feel the anxiety crawling up her back and putting its cold hand around her neck, making her take an extra breath. She paused, breathed in slowly, then chuckled.

"You know, I was in the process of giving you my usual shtick," Amber confessed. "Acting my way through the social…bullshit. But enough pretending. I'll just be myself."

She turned sideways on the couch and looked Nina in the eyes--or, rather, somewhere in the vague direction of her eyes.

"I don't have anyone. I am gay. And I like you. A lot."

"You're bold too." Nina seemed impressed. "Autistic?"

"Uh-huh."

"I'll skip the formalities too then." She tilted her head slightly to the right and put a hand on Amber's cheek. "Would you like me to kiss you, Amber?"

"Yes. Yes, please."

She didn't wait for her to say it the third time.

Nina leaned forward slightly, covering the last few centimeters of distance between them in one swift motion, and pressed her lips to Amber's, her hand still on the girl's cheek. Amber felt as if reality had dissolved once more, teleported her away from the couch and into another place.

When their lips first touched, she felt Nina's other hand on the small of her back, noticed the delicate scent of perfume in Nina's hair. They shared a few quick kisses. Amber could no longer tell whether she was breathing at all. She put her fingers through Nina's fiery red locks, and opened her mouth slightly, letting in the girl's tongue.

Their mouths danced the dance for a while, diving out for brief gasps of air, and Amber's hands went wandering along Nina's body. The soft smooth skin of her neck, the firm outline of her breasts, the dimples of Venus on her back. When her hand ended up on Nina's inner thigh, she broke apart the kiss and paused.

"If you're wondering whether I've had The Surgery," Nina began with a slight smile, "I..."

"I'm not wondering," Amber interrupted.

"Just wanted you to know ahead what you'll be working with."

"We'll get there when we get there. For now, I don't care," Amber replied.

"You've ever been with some who..."

"No, but that wouldn't make a difference. Just for your information."

"Good to know," Nina said. "Now...would you like to continue this conversation in another place?"

"Thought you'd never ask."

Everything after that, Amber remembered more like a dream than an actual thing that happened to her. Sex was never a special occasion for her; she was good at sex, and she got it easily, on demand and whenever she wanted. It was almost a sport as far as she was concerned. A quest consisting of a search, a negotiation, and, often enough, a prize. Uncomplicated. Simple. 100% physical. It had its rules, a structure, and a goal--followed by an awkward morning conversation, followed by moving on to the next goal.

All of that did not prepare Amber for that night. It did not prepare her for sex as an art. This time, there was no structure set in stone, the rules were discussed and changed on the spot, and the only goal was to enjoy each other. They took breaks, and talked, and laughed, and the moments lingered; any sense of time was lost. Any meaningful expectations were abandoned. Nothing existed, except for the two of them, their bodies, their shared pleasure…two humans clinging to each other, lost together in the vast emptiness of hyperspace.

"Is this what sex is supposed to be like?" Amber thought, falling asleep in Nina's arms. "Have I been doing it wrong all this time?"

She didn't have an answer, and she didn't need one.

The past was a forgotten country, unreachable and rejected. The future was a fuzzy fantasy with no discernible outline.

And the present was the only thing that mattered.

TWENTY-THREE

Amber woke up to a startling kick of a spasm in her stomach and a piercing noise that seemed to be happening directly inside of her ear. Thankfully it was over in a moment. She rolled over onto her back and took a deep breath in.

The bed was cold and empty, the room was lit up only by the tranquil rays of a ceiling lamp, and they were out of hyperspace. She stretched and slipped out of the bed. Her clothes were folded carefully on a nightstand, with a long, silky bathrobe laid near it as an alternative. After a moment of hesitation, Amber put on her underwear and opted for the robe.

The artificial lighting system was emulating the early twilight hours just before a sunrise, which, together with the eerie silence, made the ship feel like an abandoned mansion in the middle of a vast, empty field. Amber walked through the corridor, past the bathroom and guest bedrooms, and into the lounge room. There was no one there. With a shrug, she crossed the room and put her hand on the control room door. She wanted to just open it, then paused and knocked instead.

"I'm here." Nina's voice was dulled down by the barrier between them.

Amber pressed her palm against the door and slid it sideways in one gliding motion.

Nina sat with her back to the door and next to a smooth white panel. Once Amber walked in and leaned against the wall, she turned in the chair and smiled at her.

"Good morning. Thought you'd sleep for longer."

"I had that nap before, remember?" Amber smiled back. "And I didn't dodge the hyperspace carousel this time."

"Coffee?"

"Yes, please."

Nina got out of the chair and moved to the left side of the room. She pressed her fingertips to the white wall and it opened up, revealing a kitchen corner, complete with a fridge, a stove and a coffee machine.

"Your kitchen is in the control room?" Amber arched an eyebrow while Nina prepared two cups of steaming hot espresso.

The room filled up with the smell of freshly ground coffee beans at once.

"Where else would it be?" Nina asked.

She handed Amber the tiny glass cup.

"It's the most secure space on the entire spaceship. That's where you hide in case of emergency."

Amber regarded the room skeptically.

"What about other bodily needs?"

She gestured for Amber to step away from the wall, then pressed another button. Just like the kitchen before it, in the place of a solid white wall appeared a toilet, a sink, and a small cupboard stocked with bathroom necessities.

"There's a bed hidden under the floor tiles," Nina added, hiding the pop-ups with another touch of the invisible button. "One time I lived here for two weeks."

Amber took a first swig of the coffee. It was a bit more bitter than she preferred, but also full of flavor.

"Problem with the law?" she wondered.

"Flew into a gamma ray burst," Nina responded. "I was fine, but it killed all of my house plants. Now I only have plastic ones."

"It's an Alexandrian thing."

"Huh?"

"Wanting plants around you," Amber elaborated. "When you grow up surrounded by trees and flowers, it's difficult to adapt to an absence of green."

"Perhaps." She drank her espresso in one go and proceeded to the control panel. As her hand brushed along it, a laser keyboard appeared on top of the white. "Personally, I prefer this view."

In the place of the solid white appeared a hyper-realistic image: a vast darkness with one bright spot in the middle. A dense cluster of stars, burning with countless shades of red, yellow and light blue, shaped like a teardrop, with its narrow end being sucked into an enormous splotch of pitch black. It was breathtaking in its solemn, sad beauty.

"It's not in real time," Nina said. "We've past that point a while ago. We're now inside of the Cluster."

"Is the ship being affected by the time distortion?" Amber pondered.

"Yes, but it can compensate for it," she replied. "Muuk technology. It's pretty much time travel, but only on a small scale and only in one direction. Basically, when we will jump out of it, for the outside world it will be as if we were only gone for a brief second."

"Huh." Amber scratched her forehead. "I always wondered how come a few weeks in hyperspace only take a couple of hours in the normal dimensions."

"I prefer not to think about it too much," Nina responded. "Makes me dizzy."

"Did you follow the coordinates I gave you?"

"Yep." She pressed a few keys and the image changed. "There's your Aquamarine Moon."

Amber raised her eyes to the screen. It blinked black for a second, then the image of the Teardrop Cluster was replaced with a different one. A planet, suspended in the darkness, perfectly spherical and completely grey. No seas, no continents, no lights or constructs on its surface. Just a solid shade of wet concrete.

"That's the Aquamarine Moon?" Amber couldn't hide the disappointment. "It looks...dead."

"It probably is dead," Nina told her. "I'm receiving no signals from the surface, and it has no source of external energy. It orbits the black hole, not a star of any sort."

"It's a moon of a black hole. Interesting."

"I've programmed the capsule to take you there and back," Nina continued. "From my perspective, the trip will only take a minute, but you can stay over for

283

as long as you need. Just don't die of old age." She smiled. "Or of anything else, for that matter. I do wish to see you again. Many times, preferably." She paused and lowered herself into the armchair. "Actually, I have a proposal for you."

"A proposal?" Amber repeated.

"Not what you think." She chuckled briefly. "I'm not that impulsive. Say... are you planning on coming back home after this? Cause if you're not, I'd love to have you on board. You and your friend. You're quite resourceful, and have valuable knowledge, and, well, us rares should stick together, right?"

"Right." Amber nodded. "Would I be like, your friend, or partner in crime, or your girlfriend?"

"Take a pick!" She shrugged. "All three, if you want to."

"That," she smiled with a corner of her mouth and felt her cheeks flush with warmth, "is certainly an enticing offer. I'll think about it."

"Please do." Nina paused. "I feel like we'd click really well. You're special. In a good way. Best way possible. And no, I don't say this to every person I sleep with," she added with a grin. "And if it doesn't work, well--you can always return to Alexandria, or pick another occupation. It's all in your hands."

Amber nodded, letting the words sink in properly in her mind. She could do Whatever She Wanted. At last.

"Hey, before we take off," Amber said, "can I send a message real quick? It will send to Alexandria, right?"

"It should," Nina confirmed. "But keep it brief, maybe. The Internet will be mighty slow in this region."

She pressed a few buttons on the panel, and the screen changed once more, now reflecting Amber's face like a mirror. A red circle appeared in the top left corner.

"Push this to start recording, then type in the user ID once it will ask you," Nina instructed. "I'll leave you to it."

Nina left the room and slid the door shut behind her. Amber took her place in the spinny armchair. She sighed, turning left and right in the chair. Once she finally settled on the words, she pushed the button and faced the screen.

"Hello, professor," she began. "I'm really sorry I didn't call you earlier. I'm alive and safe, and so is the Rx'lng. Now, well. Now I will try to explain."

The autopilot capsule was a peculiar metal contraption, shaped like a huge bean and with a completely transparent roof. It had barely any controls and two human-sized seats, which Lullaby struggled to fit into. The panel was flashing blue, indicating that the capsule was ready for takeoff. Amber patted the smooth grey metal and lingered in front of the craft.

"So, we'll be going then."

"I figured." Nina stood nearby, her hair tugged into a ponytail again.

"How long will the trip take, in relative time?"

"About forty minutes," she responded. "If you won't get into a traffic jam."

Amber forced herself to smile at the joke. She couldn't quite believe that she was that close to the endpoint of her journey. Somehow, she wasn't nearly as excited about it as she thought she would be.

"Time to fly then." She was still stalling. "Before the traffic gets busy."

"Yeah."

"I'll be off then," Amber repeated, then shook her head and chuckled. "God, I hate goodbyes."

"Me too," Nina said, then stepped forward, grabbed Amber's shoulders almost swooping her off her feet, and kissed her.

Lullaby chirped in the capsule.

"Consider my offer," Nina added after they broke apart.

"I will." Amber attempted to fix her now ruffled hair but failed. "See you in a few minutes."

And she finally boarded the capsule.

The transparent roof slid on, and Nina waved at her before leaving the area and sealing the door. Amber waved back with a soft smile. Soon the room began to depressurize. A fragment of the wall detached from its base and slid upwards, revealing a mass of deep darkness in front of them.

"Preprogrammed trajectory initiated," the screen announced, and the engines sprang to life, making the whole capsule vibrate.

Slowly it rolled out of the belly of the starship Enlightenment and slipped into the vastness of space, heading towards the Aquamarine Moon.

"Say," Amber leaned back in what was left of her seat, "is it just me, or are you also really disappointed by the fact that the Aquamarine Moon isn't even of an aquamarine color?"

"Not just you," Lullaby responded.

They watched in the rearview mirror as Enlightenment became smaller and smaller, until it disappeared from view completely and left blackness in its place. The capsule hummed and roared as it glided towards the grey surface. The moon moved closer and closer. After all this time, Lullaby and Amber really succeeded in what they set out to do.

Or so they thought.

David Nawahi took off his jacket, hung it on the back of an armchair and pressed the power button on the old office tea brewer. While the machine whirred and spitted steam, he prepared two cups, a packet of milk, and a box of sweetener cubes. He regarded the cupboard with a sigh. He hadn't cleaned it in a while, and it was starting to show.

The brewer boiled, and he poured two cups of the aromatic liquid. After moving the tray to his table, Nawahi returned to the cupboard and snatched an oatmeal cookie from an opened box. He stuffed the entire thing in his mouth and chewed, realizing that the cookie was completely dried out. He drowned it with a sip of the tea and picked up another. He could afford to do so, after all. Over the last two weeks, he had lost five kilos of weight without even trying.

Then came a knock on the door, and he lowered himself into the seat, inviting the visitor to come in. Doctor Ebele Chike--a tall, almost sickly slender man-- greeted professor Nawahi and sat down opposite him.

"How was your flight?" Nawahi asked, leaning slightly backwards in his chair.

"As enjoyable as commercial flights can be." Chike smiled and took a tea cup from the tray. "Glad to be here, professor."

"How long has it been since your last stay at the Institute?"

He shrugged. "Five years, maybe."

"And how is life at the Trinity College?"

"A bit slow and uneventful, but I shall not complain."

"Right." Nawahi nodded. "I understand. You see, Ebele," he paused, "actually, I'll say it as it is. The Novella Institute would like to hire you."

"And?" Chike asked, anticipating a follow-up to that statement.

"And," Nawahi continued, "as much as I'd love to have you on board, I must admit--I don't support the decision. Not because of you, you'd be perfect for the position. Because I don't think there should be a position."

"I appreciate your honesty, professor, but I'm afraid I'm not getting it."

"They're looking for a replacement for Amber Shakya."

A moment of heavy silence lingered in the air. This was a topic that you weren't supposed to discuss, yet everyone who knew of it was eagerly discussing nonetheless.

"Do you think that she will come back?" Chike suggested.

"I believe she will."

"But has that ever happened before? You know, has any escapee ever changed their mind and returned to Alexandria?"

Nawahi didn't answer. He lowered his gaze to the ground and brought the tea cup to his lips.

"I am no final authority," he said. "I can't stop the board from doing what they think is the right thing to do in this situation. But I also have a certain amount of emotional investment in this."

"Of course, professor." Chike folded his arms on the table. "She was your adopted daughter, wasn't she?"

"Is," Nawahi corrected. "She is my adopted daughter, regardless of what she'll decide."

"Does that mean you won't hire me?"

Nawahi took a deep breath in.

"No," he responded. "And if Amber will return, I won't fire you either. But I will ask of you to pick different subjects to teach, and a different office too."

"Absolutely no problem." Chike beamed. "Oh, sorry." He wiped the smile off his face. "I didn't mean to...didn't want to upset you or..."

"It's fine," Nawahi assured him. "Now, let's talk technical details."

Half an hour later, professor's unfinished tea had gotten cold, and Chike was about to sign his papers. He carefully read through the contract--including the small letters, and even smaller, psychic transference letters--and pressed a fingertip to the designated field. The device confirmed his fingerprint, consulted with his chip and concluded the operation. Chike smiled, and okay-ed his bracelet's suggestion of sending a letter of resignation to the Trinity College.

"Thank you, professor." Chike shook the man's enormous palm.

"See you in six weeks, Ebele."

He got up and placed his half-empty cup onto a reheating panel by the brewer. "Professor?"

Evidently, Chike wasn't ready to leave just yet.

"Feel free to stop me if you'd rather not talk about it," he said, "but my archive search didn't yield much results--Muuk block, I'd guess--and," he paused, trying to gage Nawahi's reaction, "well, could you tell me what the Aquamarine Moon actually is?"

Nawahi suppressed a sigh. He picked up the reheated cup and returned to the table.

"A myth," he replied to his question. "A fairy tale."

"What sort of myth?"

"You want the whole story then?" Nawahi pondered.

"If you could be so kind as to tell it," Chike confirmed. "In broad details."

"Fine." He didn't seem happy with the answer but chose to comply. "This story is considered a late addition to the Nos mythos, and it exists in several different versions and translations, but this will give you the general idea."

Chike nodded and took a seat.

"Well," Nawahi said. "This is how it goes. A long time ago..."

A long time ago in a valley at the other side of the world lived a young man named Janas. He was strong, smart and talented, and eager to accomplish many great things. Unfortunately, he didn't have many opportunities in his town. He didn't fancy any particular job, and got terribly bored waiting for something better to come around. So he packed a bag, gathered a group of other young people and set off into the wilderness--to start his own village.

For decades, things went well in the village. More people came to join them, and many children born chose to stay as well. Janas was a good leader. He always made the right decisions for his people, and he cared for them deeply. Whenever there was a problem, he would work hard to solve it, and he put the needs of his people above his own. And everything was good, but the people weren't happy.

"The food isn't good enough," they complained. "Houses are better at the other village," they said. "We work so much for so little rest," they moaned. "We will find a different leader," they threatened.

Janas felt deeply saddened by their troubles. He searched for a meaning, a higher purpose, something that would give his people a clear goal and make them happy. He asked everyone he met and read all the books he could find, but no one would give him the answer. He grew old in his village, and still he could not find what he was looking for. So, he sat out on a journey.

First, he climbed to the top of the tallest mountain, where in a cave lived a wise hermit.

"How do I make my people happy?" Janas asked.

"They must abandon all their possessions and live in silence for seven years--then they will reach happiness," the wise hermit replied.

Janas wrote it down and moved on.

Second, he went to the greatest ocean, whereby the seaside lived a prolific writer.

"How do I make my people happy?" Janas asked.

"They must find their passion and follow it with all their heart--then they will reach happiness," the prolific writer replied.

Janas wrote it down and moved on.

Third, he went to the biggest city in the middle of a desert, where in a tiny house lived a famous philanthropist.

"How do I make my people happy?" Janas asked.

"They must be kind to each other and do their best to help each other--then they will reach happiness," the famous philanthropist replied. Janas wrote it down and returned to his village.

He told his people about the answers and prepared to see them finally reach happiness. Alas, it didn't help.

"We did everything you told us to do," the people said, "and yet we aren't happy."

Janas cried. He didn't know how to fix it. He felt like he had failed at being the leader. So he packed a bag, left his people a note and set off to one final journey--to meet the gods of the Aquamarine Moon.

He crossed seas and oceans, forests and deserts, valleys and mountains. He walked for years until he reached the great peak--the stairs of a million steps. For many days he walked up the steps. He walked until he couldn't feel his legs anymore. He walked until his feet got scraped to the bone by his shoes. He walked until he had no more food or water left. And finally, he reached the Aquamarine Moon.

Up there, on the Aquamarine Moon, the gods were already waiting for Janas. He fell to his knees in front of them and begged.

"Great gods," he said, "you've created our universe, and you watched us crawl out of the mud. I am your servant. Can you make my people happy?"

"We understand your wish," the gods said.

Then Janas collapsed on the ground, closed his eyes and thought no more.

He woke up in his bed the next morning, back at his old village, young and with no memories of anything that happened. He got out of bed, made breakfast and thought "I feel so bored in this village...I should pack a bag and start my own."

"That's it?" It took Chike a few moments to realize Nawahi had come to the end of the story.

"Yes."

"And we're sure that we have the entire tale?"

"Quite certain. There are some variations in different sources, but it always has the same beginning and the same ending."

"Huh." Chike frowned. "And what is the moral of the story?"

"Nobody knows." Nawahi shrugged. "Some scholars believe it is about the futile search for perfection, like a reminder that there will always be suffering. Others say it is a poetic interpretation of the cosmic cycles theory--the universe expands, then contracts, then expands again, and so on. Some words in the story can be interpreted to suggest that it was not Janas's first quest. And there are many other ideas."

"That is one strange myth."

"Indeed," he agreed. "Nos homeworld didn't even have a moon, as far as we can tell. They knew about such things, of course--but it isn't clear why they chose to include it. We also aren't sure which gods they were talking about. The dominating religion of the time did not include any deities with corporeal presence, only spirits of nature and such."

"And did the recent discovery explain anything?"

"We were hopeful at first," Nawahi responded, "and Amber's preliminary translation indicated that the Aquamarine Moon was an actual, physical object. The research team even decoded the coordinates and adjusted them for spacetime distortion. But when the Muuk sent a probe there, it turned out that the place was empty. No objects there--planets or moons. The plates are genuine, but the coordinates appear to be made-up."

"That doesn't seem right." Chike scratched his chin thoughtfully.

"Many things in this universe don't," Nawahi told him.

"Okay." The young man got up. "Thank you for your time, professor."

He lingered by the door.

"I do wish professor Shakya would return," he added. "I'm awfully intrigued by this occurrence, and I do have expertise in the time period. We could do great work together."

And he left Nawahi's room.

This day, like many days before it, David Nawahi worked till the sun hid behind the horizon and almost everyone in the Novella Institute returned to their homes. He brewed another cup of tea and selected a book from his digital library.

Taking the last cookie from the cupboard, he lowered himself into the chair and began to read.

He wasn't sure what hour it was when someone knocked on the door of his office. Rather startled, he got up and walked over to the door--but didn't open it. The knocking repeated.

"Who is it?" Nawahi asked.

"David, it's me."

He recognized the voice at once and opened the door. On the other side stood Lucy Franklin--a shawl draped over her shoulders, hair a wild mess.

"What is it?" Nawahi rubbed his tired eyes and stepped sideways, allowing her to come inside. "But be brief, because my mental capacities are not at their sharpest."

"There's a message on the Institute account. It was sent to you but got stuck in the spam filter."

"A message?" he repeated.

Lucy paused and tugged on a strand of her hair.

"What is it?" Nawahi urged.

She bit her lip. "It's from Amber."

Meanwhile, a heavy stack of paper materialized out of thin air in front of Gena's face. No, not materialized--was placed there with a surprisingly loud flop by his colleague and fellow grad student, Fedya.

"All yours." He smirked and poured a handful of paperclips on top of the stack. "Hey...Gen? Are you daydreaming again?"

"No," the young man responded before he had a chance to understand the question.

He raised his head and regarded the stack with a frown.

"All from professor Lebedev," Fedya elaborated. "Most of it is useless, I'm sure--but there might be some hidden gems."

Gena shrugged and began to sort out the papers. As everyone in the department knew, he was the only person, other than Lebedev himself, who could decipher the old professor's handwriting.

"This is kinda sad, really," Light pointed out, swinging in an invisible hammock.

"It's the death of Pompeii," Darkness replied. "It's supposed to be sad."

"Well, at least it was quick."

"It wasn't. They suffocated slowly under a pile of ash."

"Well..." Light struggled to find a silver lining. "At least we didn't cause it."

Darkness didn't argue with that.

"Where's S?" she asked. "I haven't seen him for a while."

As if summoned by her words, S's figure shimmered into being in place of thin air.

"Someone said 'big volcano eruption'?" he beamed.

"Why are you two so excited about volcanoes?" Darkness asked. "It's horrible."

"Doesn't your planet have volcanoes?"

"It has too many. Which is why I don't appreciate them."

"Well," S continued, "you have to admit though--they have a certain fatal grace."

Back at the Moscow State University Theoretical Physics Institute, Gena Sazhencev had just zoned out over a half-sorted stack of papers.

TWENTY-FOUR

"This isn't as bad as I anticipated," Amber said to herself.

The automatic capsule was on a smooth, tranquil descent into the Aquamarine Moon's atmosphere. It moved with a ridiculously low speed, like a luggage pickup line at a spaceport, with no turns and no changes in acceleration.

Amber had discovered a seat arrangement which allowed Lullaby to stretch out their legs and was now gazing at the world outside of the thick plastic. The starry skyline was growing fewer, gradually replaced by a thick white veil of the Moon. It swirled and danced like a streak of milk being poured into coffee.

Amber wondered where all the light was coming from. There were no stars in the immediate vicinity of the Moon, and the Black Hole sure didn't help the matter either. Was the Moon's surface artificially illuminated?

"Can you see anything below the clouds?" Amber asked, her nose pressed into the window.

"No." Lullaby searched through the control menu but didn't find what they were looking for. "No downward-facing camera either."

"Guess we'll have to be patient."

Eventually the blackness of space disappeared completely, leaving the creamy whirs of clouds in its place. Amber moved, trying to lean against the cold plastic with the back of her head, and sighed. She felt like a kid on the backseat of a bus, dying of boredom on her way to a museum of some sort. School trips weren't really her thing.

"Let's play 'I spy' or something," she muttered, and was about to go first, when her blood froze up in her veins.

Just a second ago, they were bathed in the warm glow of the Moon, then, with no warning, they were thrown into absolute, unrelenting darkness. No, it wasn't even darkness--it was nothing. Amber's heart echoed in her ears. This wasn't the first time she had seen this. She had a sharp, visceral memory of this void--but she couldn't for the life of her recall where that was. A dream, perhaps?

She wanted to call out, but no sound came out of her mouth. She reached out to grab onto something and realized that she couldn't feel anything in her body. All of her senses were gone. The only thing that remained was her consciousness. Amber screamed.

And the world returned, as suddenly as it had disappeared.

"Was it just me or..." Amber whispered in a hoarse voice.

"Wasn't just you." Lullaby's voice, on the other hand, sounded even more high-pitched than usual.

Almost in sync, they turned towards the windows and gazed outside. The clouds were gone. The air seemed still and clear, almost like they were moving through a liquefied crystal. Above stretched a blended, even line of a creamy, swirly sky. And below...below, was a city.

"The hell?!" Amber exclaimed, squishing her nose against the window once again.

They were too high up to see the exact details, but she had no problems catching the shapes and outlines. The capsule was descending towards a magnificent metropolis. Enormous buildings of exquisite artistic design, surrounded by perfectly straight roads and perfectly square squares.

Dark-green and ocean-wave blue swirls of gardens and forests, woven into the city's structure. Vast empty fields with cute tiny houses placed in delightfully symmetrical patterns. It looked more like a cardboard model than a physical place. It seemed too perfect to be real.

"It's definitely their architecture," Amber said. "If you believe the textbooks, that is."

"Don't see any cars or planes," Lullaby commented.

"No, me neither. Actually," she detached herself from the glass and rubbed her nose, "I don't see any movement in general. It looks..."

"Dead," they finished for her.

Amber didn't think of 'dead'. She thought 'empty', 'abandoned', 'new'...but the closer they got to the surface, the more she got convinced that Lullaby was onto something.

The capsule touched down with a gentle thump, and Amber's hand lingered over the control screen before initiating an atmosphere diagnostic.

"Bit too much oxygen for my liking," she concluded, skimming through the readout. "And some not so nice gasses too. But I think I'll survive. You?"

Lullaby didn't even glance at the screen.

"I'll be fine," they said, and opened the roof.

Amber attempted to climb outside and stumbled out awkwardly instead. Her legs felt like pins and needles, and half of her joints cracked as she stretched her arms and back. She blinked a few times, taking in a deep breath of Aquamarine Moon air. It lacked a smell and seemed to be at a perfect temperature to go unnoticed by her senses. The ground underneath had a soft bounce to it, indicating a lower than standard gravity. Just like the upper layers of the atmosphere, the world seemed fixed and unmoving.

"Light generators." Lullaby pointed at the bright, round, snowy white structures that lingered high above ground.

Amber counted seven of them in her field of vision.

"There's a village of some sort over there." She turned towards a smooth plain road that lead to a bunch of single-family houses. "Shall we?"

Lullaby nodded, and secured the capsule before heading towards the village.

They didn't hear or see a single living thing while they walked. Amber paid attention to her surroundings, searching desperately for any signs of activity. Yet there was nothing: no tiny creatures crawling in the dust, no footprints or forgotten things, not even a discarded chocolate package.

"Maybe they're just really tidy," she wondered out loud.

Soon they reached one of the houses. Like many things on the Aquamarine Moon, the building seemed fake in its pristine decor and evenly mowed grass. The windows were low, and the doors were a bit too tall, but it was, otherwise, a normal human house--complete with benches and flowerbeds and a doormat that read the Nos language phrase of "welcome".

Amber swallowed hard and knocked on the door. No answer. She knocked again, which yielded the same result. Glancing over her shoulder at Lullaby, she shrugged and pushed the door open.

Inside was a perfectly clean room complete with perfectly situated furniture. No dust on the shelves, no dirty spots on the carpets, and, yet again, no signs of sentient activity. Amber couldn't help but shudder as they explored the house. The place was too new, too quiet, too empty--it scored ten on her creep-out meter. And what she had found in the kitchen made it ten times worse.

"Lu." Amber breathed out, freezing on the threshold.

In the middle of the perfect kitchen, by the round table covered with a frilly tablecloth, sat a Nos woman. She had leaned backwards in the chair, her hands folded on her knees, her eyes opened and unmoving.

Amber had only ever seen Nos on hand-drawn pictures, not even photographs. They followed the universal humanoid body plan, with upright posture and four limbs and a head on top of their shoulders. To Amber they looked basically human, except for their body and faces being ever so slightly out of proportion, compared to her own. Arms a bit too long, nose a bit too small, forehead a bit too tall. They also lacked hair, including eyebrows and eyelashes. But that wasn't really bothering her. Definitely not as much as the woman's clear, unblinking eyes.

"Is she dead?" Amber asked.

"Is she real?" Lullaby responded with a question.

The two of them approached the table almost on tiptoes and Amber prepared for a jump scare of some sort, but it never came. She stopped in front of the woman's body and cautiously placed a fingertip on her hand. She was definitely real, but the body wasn't cold. In fact, apart from the total lack of movement, including a heartbeat, the woman appeared to be well.

"I think she's dead," Amber concluded. "But it's weird. She's like, warm, and she hasn't decayed at all."

297

She tried raising the woman's arm, then gently placing it back on her knees. Nothing happened.

Lullaby went around picking up objects in the kitchen. They checked out the fridge, and found food--untouched and unspoiled. Amber took a mug out of the washer and sniffed it. It didn't have a discernible smell. She rotated it in her hands, then, in an unexplainable feat of curiosity, dropped it on the ground. The mug shattered--but instead of breaking apart into several chunks of ceramic, it fell apart into fine dust, which too vanished completely.

"Have you seen that?!" she exclaimed.

Lullaby nodded slowly. Amber grabbed a piece of cutlery of some sort from the washer and slammed it hard against the table. Both the cutlery and the table disintegrated into nothing.

"What the hell is going on in here," Amber muttered.

"Don't know," Lullaby said. "Let's check another house."

The story repeated in the next house--and the next, and the next. Wherever they went, they found clean and tidy homes, untouched by rust or decay. And in those homes were people, frozen in time. Sleeping on a couch. Resting in an armchair. Laying down next to an opened wardrobe. Slumped down a wall in a bathroom. All perfectly preserved--and perfectly dead.

"I don't like this." Amber's hand went to her mouth, fingers picking on her lips--a nasty stress response she had ditched a long time ago.

"You're not the only one."

She glanced at Lullaby, who was studying an arrangement of books and random trinkets on a coffee table in another living room. Their massive shoulders slumped, mandibles twitching slightly. This was, Amber supposed, the first and only time she had ever seen the Rx'lng visibly, profoundly scared.

"Let's go," Amber insisted. "Nothing else to see here. We should try the city next."

The city wasn't any different. There they found more dead people--lying by the roadside, sprawled out on benches, frozen in their seats in cafes and restaurants. Amber had lost count of how many they had found. Older men with their heads resting on a table, interrupted in the middle of a board game. A young couple holding hands on the grass, even now. A mother, presumably, laying on the pavement, surrounded by two children and a baby in a stroller. A small fluffy animal of some sort, frozen forever in the hands of its owner. And not a sound, or a flash of light, to be seen anywhere.

"Hey. Look."

Amber flinched at the sound of Lullaby's voice. She searched the street and saw the Rx'lng standing by a wall of some building, pointing to a poster that hanged on the said wall.

"What does this word mean?" they asked once she was close enough to read the poster.

"'Ending'. Like," she snapped her fingers, struggling for words, "a culmination of some sort. The finished product of an action. Grand finale."

"Grand finale of what?"

Amber read the text for herself.

"Fuck knows. That," she pressed her finger to the paper, mindful not to push too hard and dust the entire thing, "must be the place, and that is the date. But I've no idea what a 'sioulaike' is, or why it's ending."

"Third time I see this poster," Lullaby said. "You think we can find that place?"

"Well, we can try," Amber replied. "Not much to do otherwise."

After a thorough search of the nearby train station, they've discovered a directions table in the arrival-departure lounge. It consisted of a huge map and a stack of books with addresses and postal codes. While Amber flipped the pages, Lullaby studied the map.

"This place is a bit...analogue." Amber pointed out, carefully picking up a page corner with her nail. "For a civilization that crossed the whole galaxy and settled on a planet that orbits a black hole, they sure don't use modern technology that much."

"Seems in line with what they believed," Lullaby disagreed.

"Well, maybe. But still--a yellow pages book? I think that's pushing it too far."

She was beginning to get frustrated with the book, when her eyes caught a familiar arrangement of letters.

"Got it!" Amber exclaimed even before she verified her guess. "That's the address, right?"

Lullaby read the word a few times, then crossed the hall to consult one of the posters.

"Yes," they confirmed, returning to the table.

"Now." Amber grasped the page in between her fingers and gently tore it out of the book. "How do we get there?"

They went down the stairs and into a deep dark tunnel of the metro system. Like everything on the Aquamarine Moon, it was in ideal condition and perfectly functional, if not for the profound sense of dread that it inflicted.

While Lullaby studied the directions panel, Amber walked up to one of the trains and pushed the button that was supposed to open the door. The first push did nothing, nor the second. She sighed and poked it a dozen times more. Surprisingly, it was the fourteenth try that did the trick.

"Well, that's the only time in the history of ever that this worked," Amber muttered, stepping inside the train.

Lullaby joined her soon enough.

"No bodies in this cart," they pointed out.

"Yeah, and I'm not complaining." Amber crossed the empty cart and stopped in front of a glass door that separated it from the next. "That's the control cart, wouldn't you say?"

Through the glass, they saw a woman slumped in a chair next to a wide desk and a huge dark screen.

Amber tried the door, meaning to slide it sideways, but pushed a bit too strongly. The door--along with the wall that separated the carts--fell apart into dust. Luckily it didn't destroy the entire train.

"Let's say problem solved," Amber muttered, a touch of embarrassment in her voice.

She approached the panel and put her palm on its cold smooth surface.

"It's working." Lullaby watched the dark screen blink into life.

"Looks like it is pre-programmed." Amber was already trying some controls. "Guess they couldn't risk a person-operated transport. Good for us."

The train twitched and buzzed, making both Lullaby and Amber grab the panel for balance, then took off its spot and began to accelerate.

Amber gave out a sigh of relief.

"Thought it might dust itself, poor thing." She checked the screen for instructions. "All set. Four clicks till arrival. That's like, an hour and a half, I think."

They took a seat in the first cart and watched the walls of the tunnel flash in front of their eyes. They were moving with an astonishing speed, but the train was quiet and steady. If not for the blur seen through the window, it would be hard to tell it was moving at all.

"Was it difficult to find the right train?" Amber asked, taking off her shoes and sprawling across three seats.

"No," Lullaby replied. "Not at all. They were all going to the same place."

The next two hours were a strange mix of awkward silence, awkward attempts to start a conversation and even awkwarder conversations. Both knew exactly what they wanted to talk about and neither had the courage to bring it up. Just a few minutes before the train began to decelerate, Amber sat up in her seats and said:

"I think we shouldn't have come here."

She expected Lullaby to nod in agreement, but the Rx'lng said nothing.

"Something killed all of those people in an instant," Amber continued. "And then preserved them for hundreds of years in this...state. Whatever it was, it can't be good."

"Don't know whether it was hundreds of years."

"Well, it has been hundreds of years, actually. Thousands even."

"Black Hole orbit," they pointed out. "Time distortion. Might have been only a few hours for them."

301

Amber shivered and felt a twitch of the cart as it slowed down to a halt. She leaned forward and put her shoes back on.

"You have a local map?" she asked, stepping towards the exist, then paused.

Outside of the train was a platform, just like the one they'd come from. With one exception--it was chuck full of dead bodies.

"Lovely," Amber muttered, hesitant to leave the train. "Just...lovely."

The two of them crawled through the sea of corpses, trying hard not to step on any, and made their way to the surface. It wasn't much better upstairs.

"Fuck, this must have been a densely populated planet." Amber wrinkled her nose as she maneuvered through the thick--and completely dead--crowd.

"Or they all came here for the event." Lullaby had even more trouble navigating the scene.

"You think that's what killed them? The Grand Finale of whatever?" She stopped, catching onto the implications. "And we're walking straight into it?"

Lullaby didn't reply to that question. Instead, they took out the map from the pocket of their robe and pointed towards a peak of a skyscraper.

"Must be that building," they said. "Come on."

As they walked through the city's packed streets, Amber realized that she had since gotten rather desensitized to the sight of dead bodies. It was relieving and disturbing at the same time. She stopped herself from imagining the moment every single person on the planet dropped dead from, well, something, but she also couldn't help but notice that the people's faces didn't look scared.

They didn't even look surprised. Instead, she thought to herself, they seemed rather...peaceful.

The crowd in front of their point of destination--a tall, plain building of some sort--was packed even denser. Amber cringed as Lullaby forced their way through piles upon piles of bodies. Many of them blew away into dust with almost no effort.

"I thought I'd feel nauseas," Amber admitted once they've made it to the entrance hall of the building. "But I don't. Actually," she frowned, "come to think of it, I haven't felt anything since we've landed. I'm not hungry, even though I've barely had a breakfast. I'm not thirsty, and I haven't had a sip of water in hours. And I'm not tired, even after all this walking. You?"

"Don't feel anything either," Lullaby replied, but they didn't seem nearly as concerned about it as Amber. "Not important right now."

"Everything's important," Amber disagreed. "This is a mystery, a puzzle-- and we need all the pieces."

"Let's go get the pieces then."

So, they got through the last stretch of the corpse crowd, up the steps and into the mysterious building.

TWENTY-FIVE

The building was huge, with ceilings several stories high and arches wide enough to let Lullaby walk through comfortably for a change. It reminded Amber of Old Earth universities, like Cambridge and Oxford. The two of them explored the place for a while. Thankfully they no longer had to skip around through a field of corpses.

"I think this was an institute of some sort," Amber said.

It was the third time she had opened the door into an empty lecture hall.

"Seems likely," Lullaby replied. "But where's everyone?"

"Waiting outside, probably." Amber had discovered the announcement board and was now studying it. "Or so they were. Aha." She poked her finger into the board. "They were supposed to have the big reveal at the aula. Have you found a map of the place?"

"There was one at the entrance."

"Let's go check it out then."

They located the aula with the help of the map. Like all the lecture halls they visited before, it was empty--but clearly set up for a big event. The projector screen which span the height and width of the entire wall was lowered down, the seats were labeled with names and surnames, and the stage was prepared for a speech.

Amber walked down the steps towards the stage and climbed it. A chair by the lecturer's desk had someone's jacket left in it, and there was a stack of papers on the desk itself. She picked up the white pages.

"Esteemed guests, welcome to the event we've been anticipating for generations," Amber read out loud.

"What event?" Lullaby skipped down the steps as well and joined Amber at the stage.

"Uh, there's so much pompous nonsense in here. Five pages of introduction," she complained. "Typical academic event."

She sat down in the chair and put her feet up on the desk.

"Bla-bla-bla, thanks to ten thousand esteemed people, more jibber-jabber… here." She paused, frowning at the page. "Well. I might be wrong about this, but I think they were about to reveal the results of some very long experiment. No, wait, not an experiment. A calculation. Yes, a computer has been calculating for, oh, years, apparently. Thousands of years. Impressive. And it was about to finish and reveal the answers."

"Did they?" Lullaby hovered over her shoulder. "Reveal the results?"

"I don't think so. Based on this speech," she flipped through the pages quickly, "I'd say they were planning to do it a few minutes after that. Get the cameras rolling and shit. But it doesn't look like it happened. Or maybe it did, I don't know." She got up. "I think this supercomputer of theirs is in this building."

"Back to the map?" Lullaby suggested.

"Back to the map."

After what felt like a whole day of making the wrong turn and getting lost in underground corridors, Lullaby and Amber pretty much stumbled upon the right door. Amber regarded the sign with a furious glance, as if it had just told her to go fuck herself. She placed her hand on the door handle, then removed it and turned around to face Lullaby.

"I'm scared," she said, and her hand went to her lips once again.

"Me too." Lullaby replied. "But it's good. Means I'm alert, and strong, and can protect you."

"Thanks." Amber forced a smile. "Do we have to do this?"

"No. We can walk away, get on train, and go back to our capsule. Leave and never find out what happened here. Move on with our lives and always wonder…"

"Yeah, okay, I get the point," she interrupted, and put her hand back to the door handle. "Well, here goes."

Behind the door was an airy conference room. It was painted the most boring beige color imaginable, and, for an underground facility, it was surprisingly well-lit. Though, considering that the entire planet required artificial illumination, perhaps it was not that surprising after all.

Amber took first cautious steps inside the room and took in the details. Her eyes went immediately to a long and narrow table on her right. By the table sat eight, no, nine people, all dressed in what appeared to be formal attire. She approached the table cautiously.

"What a surprise," Lullaby muttered. "More dead people."

"Hey." Amber smirked. "Leave sarcasm to the masters."

She studied the gruesome scene for a while, then stepped towards one of the chairs and gently leaned the body against the chair's back. After one glance at the person's face, she proceeded to do the same to everyone else.

"That's...interesting." She was pretty much thinking out loud by that point. "Maybe I just suck at interpreting facial expressions--which, admittedly, I do--or maybe theirs just differ from human, but. They look distressed. Profoundly. Terrified, and sad. All the people before had calm expressions. Could they...Hey, Lu." She called out. "I think these poor fuckers were the only ones on the entire planet who knew what was about to happen. Lu. Hey, Lu?"

She looked around, but the Rx'lng wasn't there.

"Lullaby?" she repeated, her heart already speeding up.

"Over here."

Their voice came from somewhere far away, and it took Amber a few moments to locate them. Lullaby had found another flight of stairs which led to even deeper levels. Downstairs was a small patch of space which lead to a door. It was dark, and Amber had to strain her eyes to read the door sign.

"Input-output center," she read. "Is that where they keep the supercomputer?"

"The whole planet might be the supercomputer," Lullaby replied. "This should be where they communicate with it."

"Do you think," Amber changed her mind mid-sentence, then changed her mind again, "do you think the computer killed them?"

"Didn't look like they were struggling. Also, what could even kill them so fast?"

"I don't know." She shrugged. "Like a brain frying ray of some sort. Something did kill them."

"But we're still alive," they pointed out. "If computer wanted us dead, we would be dead."

"Fair enough." Amber nodded and opened the door.

Inside, was mostly empty space--a large area with plain walls, a plain floor and a plain ceiling. The only spot that had any furniture was the far right corner, where stood a one-person desk surrounded by book shelves.

"That's a tad bit underwhelming," Amber said, approaching the desk. "Is that the interface?"

"Doubt it," Lullaby responded. "Look."

They walked towards one of the empty walls, and suddenly Amber noticed that the wall was gleaming, reflecting its surroundings like a mirror. When Lu brushed their palm against it, white light flashed in the room, and Amber realized that it wasn't a wall at all, but a giant computer monitor.

"They went all out with this piece of tech, huh?" she said.

The screen was white and blank, except for one line of text--a question followed by two options.

"Continue displaying calculation results?'", along with "yes" and "back to the menu".

"Don't touch anything," Amber warned.

She noticed a large sheet of paper laying on top of some object on the desk in front of her. A sheet of paper with a message on it. She squinted at the paper, picking it up.

"Curiouser and curiouser," she muttered, taking a seat. "I think they were expecting guests."

"What?" Lullaby joined her at once.

"It's in Esquerte," Amber explained. "Considering they have likely written

307

this a couple million years ago, this was a good bet for communicating with alien races."

"Watch this if you find the Aquamarine Moon," Lullaby read. "Watch what?"

"This." Amber reached for the object which lay underneath the paper--a black plastic brick of some sort, which turned out to be pretty heavy. "A memory storage...thing, I presume."

She found a device that had a similarly shaped hole in it and put the black brick into it. The wall next to the desk flashed white like the wall and an image appeared on the screen. A Nos man in formal attire, facing the camera. Shivers ran down Amber's spine. She recognized him as one of the people they've found, sitting by the table upstairs.

"Press play," Lullaby prompted, and Amber located the button with ever so slightly shaking hands.

"Greetings." The man on the screen pressed his palms together in a traditional gesture. "If you are watching this tape, it means I am dead."

"Predictable." Amber said, and Lullaby shushed at her.

"It also means you have located the Aquamarine Moon. Maybe it's been a few days since my death, or a few billion years. Maybe the Nos disappearance has been a mystery for your civilization, in which case congratulations for solving the mystery. Before you watch further, you should know this.

"The planet is enveloped in a stasis chamber. Inside of the stasis chamber, entropy has been paused. It means that nothing on here will rot or decay, unless a strong force acts on the object. So, it can stay like this till the end of the universe. It also means that you are completely safe. Your metabolism has been slowed down, and you can stay here safely for up to a few months. You could also leave at any moment. The black hole orbit is stable, and you'll have no problem exiting the stasis chamber."

"That's fascinating," Amber told the screen, "and answers a few of my questions, but it's not what I wanna know right now."

"Can't hear you," Lullaby reminded.

After a pause in the tape, the man spoke again.

"If you are still listening, you probably want to find out why we have all died."

"Hell yeah I do." Amber scoffed.

"Shush!" Lullaby hissed.

"I'll start from the beginning," the tape said. "My species has been searching for the ultimate questions of life since the dawn of our civilization. For many centuries and many generations, we studied the world and ourselves, trying to get to the truth. But it didn't help.

"So we embarked on our most ambitious project--the quest for the Aquamarine Moon. We created this planet from scratch, placed it on the orbit around a black hole to harness its energy and created the most powerful computer the universe had ever seen. It takes up the planet's entire core, and it has been calculating for countless generations. It had finished the calculations this morning."

"Will you please cut to the chase." Amber was picking on her lips once again.

"Now I must warn you," the man continued, "if you don't stop watching now, you'll have no way back. I am about to reveal some of the answers, and after you learn them, you won't be able to unlearn them. So, I'll give you some time to turn off the tape and leave."

"Duh!" Amber laughed. "I'm a human. Morbid curiosity is in my blood. He might have as well said 'watch this right this instant'." She paused and turned around. "You?"

"Keep it on," the Rx'lng replied. "I need to know."

A few minutes of excruciating silence passed by, and finally the man spoke again.

"You are still watching then. Fair enough." He sighed. "The first question we asked, and the first that was answered was," he paused and rubbed his eyes," is life worth the suffering it brings." His voice was breaking down now. "The computer's answer was unambiguous. It said no."

"Right." Amber nodded. "That I did kinda suspect."

"We did not read any more answers."

"What?!" Amber's eyes were round with shock. "Are you kidding me? You didn't read any further?!"

309

"As of our initial agreement," the man continued, "we were forced to initiate plan two point two one. As life was determined to be not worth the suffering it brings, according to our convention, we had to stop the suffering."

"But you didn't even learn whether there's life after death!" Amber yelled at the screen. "What the hell?"

"All life on the Aquamarine Moon has been eliminated with the least suffering possible," the man said. "We are free now."

"I can't believe this." Amber shook her head. "That is ridiculous! They could've just, I don't know, stop everyone from procreating and let them live out their lives in peace?"

"They would die eventually," Lullaby said.

"They have god-like technology! They could've lived till the end of the universe!"

"They would find out that life isn't worth living."

"Says who? The stinking computer?!"

Amber was about to run headfirst into a mighty rant when the man spoke up again.

"All the questions and answers are still there. You can read them if you wish. I did what I had to do." He closed his eyes for a second. "We all did what had to be done. Goodbye."

And the tape ended.

Amber sat there, staring at the black screen, fuming silently. She slowly breathed in, then out, letting the anger fizzle out. Screaming and shouting wasn't a good response.

"All those people," she muttered, and shook her head. "This is horrible. Just horrible."

"They were at peace," Lullaby said. "Like you've said, they had calm expressions. They didn't know what was coming. All died instantly and at at the same time. Left no one to grieve. Eliminated all suffering."

"Are you defending this now?" Amber couldn't believe her ears.

"Not defending. Trying to understand. They did succeed, you know."

"What, doing away with pain and misery by the means of instantaneous genocide?" She gestured vaguely, then let her arms drop by her side. "That's like getting rid of ants by burning down the house. It will work, sure, but is it really worth it?"

"Computer said it was."

"Fuck the computer!" Amber jumped out of her seat and began pacing the room. "I don't care how much data it processed or whatever. It can be the most intelligent thing in the universe for all I care, but it's still not self-aware. It can't understand what it's like to be conscious. Frankly, I don't even care if it's right. Maybe it is. That doesn't mean it should choose for us whether we should live or die. I am one perfectly conscious and self-aware bitch, and I can tell you, even if life is not worth living for those who haven't been born yet, it sure is worth sticking around for as long as you can."

"It didn't choose for them," Lullaby disagreed. "It only gave them the answer to a question. They killed themselves. Besides, life isn't always worth living even for those who are alive. What if you're suffering from a terrible, incurable disease that is making you suffer?"

"There are exceptions to every rule." Amber shrugged. "But even then... we've got Emmerson devices. And that's not even that advanced! If these motherfuckers managed to build a whole planet and put it into the Teardrop Cluster, I'm sure they could figure something out."

"Still. Was their choice to end it."

"Yeah, well. Doesn't mean they were right."

She stopped her furious pacing and rubbed her eyes and forehead.

"God, I'm so stupid." She chuckled softly. "When we were going down in the capsule, Lu...I thought we were about to discover something amazing. Something that would blow your socks off. I've studied the Nos for years, and I've tried to stay academic, but I had my guesses. And I thought--or hoped, rather--I hoped..." she paused and laughed again, "that they transcended their physical form in some way."

"Transcended their physical form?" Lullaby repeated.

"Yeah, like uploaded themselves to virtual reality and became one with the universe or some shit. Evolved into beings of pure thought. They had so much ideas! Such a rich culture. All that knowledge, and art, and stories...all gone."

She sat down on the grown, leaned against the wall and covered her face with her hands. She wasn't crying. She wasn't even that upset, really. Just severely disappointed.

"Do you think life is worth living?" Lullaby asked a few minutes later.

Amber sighed and removed her hands from her face.

"I don't know," she said. "The computer...it might have answered the question for them, but it doesn't mean it is true for everyone. They might have different psychology, or different neurology in general. And it might not take everything into account. I think...I think that there are things more valuable than total absence of suffering. Discovery. Progress. Knowledge. Ideas. Stories. There's more to life than just, well, life."

"That thing has all the knowledge." Lullaby pointed out. "All the other answers they never bothered to read. Should we?"

Both of them looked at the dark screen and exchanged glances.

"No such thing as forbidden knowledge?" Amber suggested.

"They did warn us."

"That just means this is informed consent."

"If you'll look, I'll look too."

"Same."

"We won't be able to un-learn this."

"Well," Amber said, getting up from the floor, "if it's really depressing, you can knock me on the head real hard and hope I'll forget all about it."

Together, they walked towards the screen in solemn silence. Both hesitated, unwilling to be the one who activated the screen. Amber jumped the gun eventually. She raised her hand, moved it towards the screen, then poked it with the fingertip of her index finger. The screen displaced its message. Amber swallowed hard and pressed "yes". The next question popped up on the screen.

"Is there an afterlife?"

"You gotta be fucking kidding me." Amber snorted with laughter and shook her head before pressing 'display results'.

For the next half hour, they slowly went through the computers entire data read.

'Why is there something rather than nothing?'

'Is there any physical possibility for free will?'

'What is the best system of morality?'

'What does actual objective reality look like?'

'Is math an invention or a discovery?'

'What is art?'

'What is the meaning of life?'

And so on, each with a well-defined, concise answer.

"Display last piece of data?" the screen read, and Amber gave out a deep sigh.

She felt like leaving the holiday table after a disgustingly big meal--but instead of a full stomach, she had a full mind. She glanced at Lullaby. The Rx'lng archaeologist was staring at the wall, eyes unblinking.

"A lot to think about, huh?" Amber said. "Some of these were rather predictable. Mind you, the Scientologists..."

"What do we do with these answers?" Lullaby interrupted.

"I don't know. Use it, I guess."

"Do we have a responsibility to communicate this knowledge to everyone?"

Amber shrugged, rather nonchalant for someone who had just absorbed the full entire wisdom of the universe.

"We can always ask the computer," she suggested. "It is the most intelligent thing in the world after all. Though it didn't answer some of my more pressing questions, like, when you go to a movie theater and it's the sitting down kind, which arm rest is yours? I wonder if you can ask it new questions. Also, I'm not sure I agree with it on everything," she added. "Like the meaning of life thing... maybe it's the best answer for the computer, but I've always thought that meaning is more of a jumper you have to knit yourself. And..."

"Stop talking, Amber," Lullaby spoke up. "This is the most important moment in the history of sentience, and you're ruining it."

"No, I'm not!" she protested. "I mean, come on, we need someone to verify all of this stuff first. It might be wrong, or just slightly incorrect, or it can be a prank. Like, it's been fun, sure, but I'm still gonna take this with a pinch of salt. Maybe even a whole kilo of salt. I didn't program this thing, so I ain't gonna trust it completely."

"There's one question left," Lullaby pointed out.

"There is," Amber agreed. "Shall I?"

Lu nodded, and she pressed the button.

"Was the Big Bang initiated by a sentient entity?" the question read.

Amber asked it to reveal the data. The screen halted for a few seconds, before blinking black and displaying, in the now familiar neat font:

"Yes".

Meanwhile, Light, Darkness and S were playing ping-pong on top of the mountain called Kilimanjaro. Or, rather, S and Darkness were playing, and Light was keeping the score. S prepared for a throw in and twisted the non-existent plastic ball in between his fingers.

"This is gonna be a good one," he promised, and prepared for the move.

"Less talk, more action," Light urged. "Go on, show us some talent."

S extended his arm, pressed his lips together and closed one eye for good measure. Then he threw in the ball, hitting it with the racket and sending it flying off the table.

"Missed," Light announced, delighted.

"No, it didn't!" he protested. "She could've gotten that one. She missed."

"Na-ah." Light shook her head. "Eleven to nine. Darkness, you can serve."

"Oh, come on!" S was still not over it. "Who even made you the referee?"

"I did." She smirked. "Darkness. Serve. Darkness?"

But Darkness didn't seem interested in serving. She stood a step away from the table, her hands in front of her face, fingers dancing in the air. S frowned, and the ping-pong table vanished. He moved towards her and put a hand on her shoulder.

"What is it?" S asked.

Darkness watched the events flicker in front of her eyes some more, then waved them away.

"It happened," she explained, and looked him in the eyes. "The veil has been lifted. We are needed."

"So soon?" S's shoulders slumped. "But we were having so much fun!"

"We're professionals, S." Light reminded. "And we have a job to do."

She spent one last moment enjoying the Kilimanjaro view, then flickered out of existence. Darkness soon followed.

"We'll be back," S said to no one in particular, and disappeared as well.

"Well, shit." Amber was still trying to process the answer. "Checkmate atheists. Who was the unmoved mover then? Zeus? Allah? Santa Claus?"

"I wouldn't jump to conclusions if I were you."

Amber turned around and sighed. Her world had just gotten even more confusing, if that was at all possible. In front of her stood three people: a dark-skinned girl who seemed to be human, a tall, pale bloke, also human in appearance, and another girl with grey-ish skin and silver hair. Amber couldn't identify her species.

"And now I'm hallucinating," she said.

"No." Lullaby shook their head. "Can see them too."

"You aren't hallucinating," the grey-skinned girl assured them. "I'm Darkness, that," she pointed at the presumably human girl, "is my beautiful companion Light, and that," she pointed at the bloke, "is S."

"Nice to meet you." Amber scoffed. "Are you holograms then?"

"That is irrelevant right now," Darkness continued. "We have a protocol to carry out."

"Protocol?"

"You've revealed the answer." She pointed at the screen. "And that violates the experimental conditions. We have to de-brief you immediately."

"Now hold on a second..." Amber began.

But Darkness clicked her fingers, and the room around them disappeared. Instead, Amber and Lullaby found themselves inside a temple of some sort. It was made of shimmering dark stone and looked new and ancient at the same time. Amber's head was dizzy. She sat down on one of the stone beds and took a few deep breaths in and out.

"Sorry," Darkness apologized. "The transportation process isn't always pleasant. So." She clapped her hands together. "You've worked it out. The greatest mystery of science: the universe had a creator. Congratulations. Now." She paused. "As the representatives of conscious life in the universe, I'm afraid you'll have to make some decisions on life's behalf."

Amber and Lullaby exchanged glances.

"And I thought this couldn't get any weirder," Amber muttered, and made S smile.

"Wait till you hear the details," he replied.

Back at the input-output room of the Aquamarine Moon computer, Lullaby and Amber just collapsed on the ground unconscious next to each other.

TWENTY-SIX

Amber sat on one of the stone benches in the far corner of the temple, swinging her legs absent-mindedly. The setting was making her queasy. It was bright and sunny, yet there were no windows or artificial sources of light. It was rather cold, yet she wasn't shivering, and white puffs of vapor didn't appear whenever someone spoke. And, worst of all, she could swear there was a dreamy, ambient music playing in the background--but every time she tried to focus on the sound and identify its source, it slipped away from her.

S stood in front of them, a heavy volume in his grasp. Amber wasn't sure where he got the book from. She read the title on the cover. "So, you've just discovered that the universe had a creator," the title read.

"Shall we begin?" S asked and cleared his throat.

"You might as well." Amber shrugged. "It's not like I can get any more confused than I already am."

She glanced sideways at Lullaby, who was seated at the next bench. The Rx'lng seemed to share her sentiment.

"Okay then." He smiled. "First of all, on the behalf of my masters--thank you for participation."

"Your masters?" Amber repeated. "Who are your masters?"

"They don't have--and cannot have--names."

"The Unnamed then," she suggested.

"No, they can't have names."

"Well, if they can't have names, I'll name them the Unnamed."

"No, you don't get it," S hissed, losing his patience. "By definition, my masters aren't able to possess a name."

317

"Exactly." Amber nodded enthusiastically. "The Unnamed. Ones who can't have a name."

S removed one hand from the book and covered his eyes with his palm, breathing in slowly through his nose. At the other side of the temple, Light snickered quietly.

"She's just messing with you." Lullaby explained.

"Thank you!" S took his hand away from his face and flashed a sarcastic smile. "I've noticed."

Amber gave him a nasty grin.

"Where was I?"

"Thanking us for participation on the behalf of the Unnamed."

"Right. Yes." S was hard to derail. "Thank you for participating in the experiment. So far, it has been a very successful run, but like I've said, it has to end now. You have breached the non-disclosure, so, according to the protocol, I have to de-brief you, and then we'll discuss our options. First..."

"The Unnamed are the creators then?" Amber asked.

"You guess correctly."

"And the experiment is the universe?"

"Indeed."

"So, they were the ones who pushed our four dimensions out of the other dimensions before the Big Bang?"

"Yes."

"And they exist in those other dimensions?"

"They do," S confirmed, "which is why they cannot have a corporeal presence in this world. We are their representatives. We speak for them."

"What, like priests?"

"Pretty much," it was Light who spoke up. "Except we actually tell you the truth, instead of making shit up on the fly."

"They all say that." Amber pointed out. "How can I trust you? How do I know you aren't lying to us too?"

"Well," Light walked over to the stone benches, "they are all-knowing, so

318

you can ask them any question and get an exact reply."

"Not really a good test, is it?" Amber said. "If I ask you about something I don't know yet, I have no way of verifying it from inside this magical dungeon. And if I ask you about something I do know already, well, I might just be dreaming, or hallucinating."

"Am seeing this too," Lullaby reminded.

"Might be hallucinating that too."

They leaned forward and pinched her hard on the arm.

"Rude!" Amber exclaimed. "Might still be hallucinating that!"

"Is it always this tedious?" Light whispered to Darkness, who had just joined the party.

"I've never done this before either," she replied.

"Look," Light continued after the interruption, "like I've said, they're omniscient, so they know exactly what to tell you to make you believe."

"Yes, and..." Amber prompted.

"It's done. Go on, look inside of yourself."

Amber wanted to call bullshit on it, but the words got stuck in her throat. She frowned, thinking hard about everything. She had received a message from Them, and she was in Their temple. Of course. It all made perfect, logical sense. It would be foolish to even try and argue against it. She rubbed the bridge of her nose.

"These aren't the gods I've always believed in," Lullaby said. "But I know they are the true gods."

"Splendid!" Light smiled. "S. Continue."

"Who are you then?" Amber pondered. "How can you speak for them?"

"We are the basic building blocks," S explained. "We represent the core components of the universe. Light is energy." The girl made a theatrical bow. "Darkness is matter." The other girl waved her hand. "And I am everything else. Time. Information. Entropy."

"Doesn't mean he's the coolest one," Light pointed out.

"Why are you called S?" Amber wasn't done with the questions.

319

"S stands for entropy," he explained, looking rather disappointed that she didn't get the reference. "At least it used to, on Earth in the 21st century. That's where I am from."

"How can you be from the 21st century Earth if you're here, in fuck knows which century and on the Aquamarine Moon?"

"Well, technically," Darkness began, "we aren't here at all. We are projections. People have different names for us--travelers, shadow-walkers, muses...ghosts."

"You can't be in a parallel universe." Amber smirked. "There is no exchange of matter or energy in between the universes."

"There isn't," S agreed. "But there is an exchange of information. We don't actually exist," he elaborated, "we can't interact with your world in any way, except for one. Through the exchange of ideas."

"We can appear to people," Light added. "They can see us, hear us, touch us, and so on. But no equipment can ever detect us."

"So like hallucinations?"

"If you prefer." Light shrugged. "Mind you, the vast majority of hallucinations aren't caused by us. We interfere very rarely, and when we do, we don't usually straight up appear out of thin air to tell someone to invent the light bulb. We're more subtle than that."

"When do you interfere?"

"When our masters tell us to," S replied.

"Or when you mess something up," Light said, and S elbowed her to make her shut up.

"And you're all from different universes." Amber ignored it.

"Correct." S confirmed. "Also different times and places. I'm from Earth, Light is from Elipsia, and Darkness is from Cartthrain."

"Okay. Got it" Amber nodded. "One last question before you move on. What is the relationship between you three?"

"She's my wife." Light pointed at Darkness. "And he's my wife's husband." She pointed at S.

"Right." Amber chuckled. "So, you're a queer, polyamorous, inter-species, cross-dimensional throuple? Guess some things never change."

"Enough distractions." S picked up the heavy book again. "We have a lot of bases to cover, and not a lot of time. Well, actually we have all the time in the universe, but that's not the point. Okay. The Unnamed. I mean, our masters. So. Here's the story of everything."

The Unnamed have always existed.

Their world didn't have a beginning, nor would it ever have an end. It didn't have matter either, or time. The Unnamed did not get born and didn't have to die, they did not feel happiness or grief, and they existed purely and peacefully. Free of doubt, free of ignorance, free of suffering. For ever and ever, they just were.

We don't know when, as the Unnamed have no time, and we don't know why, as the Unnamed have no desires, but somehow they realized that there's more to the world than their twelve dimensions. Or, rather, they discovered that they could create more. More worlds. More place to exist in. And so, they joined their forces and pushed at the edges of their being, until it spilled over and created the first ever universe.

They experimented with dimensions. One wasn't enough, and five was too many for a material universe, but everything in between worked. They tried different combinations of conditions. Matter couldn't exist without energy, and energy couldn't exist without matter. And, whenever they combined the two, entropy would appear--and entropy was good and bad at once.

With entropy, the Unnamed could inhabit the world, but entropy also made it rot and decay, until it couldn't be used any further. Entropy meant action. Entropy meant past and present. Entropy meant knowledge. Entropy came with the universe, and entropy would end it eventually.

The Unnamed discovered many places where they could live. In the very fibers that wove the universes. In the elaborate atomic structures of crystals. At the edges of black holes, and inside them. In the polymer chains of complex molecules. In the patterns of stars in the sky. Even in the sounds and electromagnetic waves. But most of all, they liked the black holes, as every black hole would itself create a universe.

So, they tweaked the universes, each of them starting from a singularity of condensed matter and energy, adjusting the initial conditions to produce universes with more black holes. They found just the right combination of forces and constant values and kept repeating it again and again.

When the universe would run out of usable energy, they would bring it back to a singularity and start the process all over again, with the exact same position of atoms at Big Bang. A perfect copy. A closed circle of births and deaths. That's how they approximated what was most natural to them--eternity.

The Unnamed continued to make more worlds with the same principle, and they would do it forever, but then, something happened. Something amazing indeed. Life appeared in one universe. The first ever material life. Defying the terror of entropy, taking in from its surrounding to sustain order. To live and proliferate for as long as it could fight the chaos.

They didn't notice it at first, and when they did, they thought nothing of it. For the Unnamed, life was just another pattern, a material phenomenon they didn't take much interest in. But then it happened again, and again, and again —until life evolved something that they thought only they could have. Consciousness.

The moment the first creature gained consciousness, and saw in itself the world and their unique perspective, a spark went on across the dimensions. And so, the Unnamed discovered that it wasn't just them who could be self-aware.

More and more conscious creatures appeared all over the universes, and the Unnamed watched them grow and progress and explore their condition. Very quickly they realized the terrible circumstance these creatures faced. Being conscious, they knew of death, and were capable of experiencing profound suffering. Born into a world with time, with endings and the ultimate triumph of decay. Speeding up the rotting of the universe with their own existence.

And the Unnamed thought it was unfortunate. But the Unnamed also knew

322

this: these creatures were both material and conscious. Therefore, they could carry them. They could be their home. They could keep them better than anything else. Better than black holes. Better even than their own dimensions. And so they went back to planning.

This time the Unnamed tweaked the conditions to ensure as much conscious life in the universe as possible. It still wouldn't yield a high percentage, since life was fragile and self-awareness was rare, but they certainly improved it. More and more planets would now give birth to self-aware materials. More conscious minds for the Unnamed to live in. And entropy would turn them all to dust eventually, and the cycle would repeat.

Just like the creatures themselves, the Unnamed competed and evolved. Ideas which were shared more proliferated. Ideas that no one wanted to share would die off. Certain ideas were especially effective at proliferating. Useful knowledge, like how to start a fire or how to carve a wheel out of stone. Powerful knowledge, like family secrets and outrageous claims that made people talk. Infectious knowledge, like silly jokes or ridiculous phrases that people just had to repeat. And sacred knowledge, like myths and legends and religious texts.

The best knowledge was not one that was true, or useful, or entertaining. The best knowledge was that which protected itself. Knowledge that discouraged doubt. Knowledge that asked for it to be spread around. Knowledge that formed your very identity. Those were ideas that would stick around--in ancient books, and carved images in temples, and people's minds for thousands of generations. Never have the Unnamed seen a better place to live than the minds of others.

They continued to tweak the initial conditions of the universes until they discovered all possible variations that would lead to conscious life. A big number, but a finite one. An unimaginable but limited number of universes, blinking in and out of existence, running its course for trillions of years then collapsing back into their beginning.

Each time atoms set in exact same places, events running smoothly according to the same scenario, same story. People living out the same lives, repeating all the same mistakes over and over again and never finding out they've done it so

323

many times before. Blissfully unaware. Thinking themselves authors of their thoughts and masters of their fate. And the Unnamed thought it good.

But the Unnamed also saw the creatures suffer, and they saw them aware of their suffering. They thought it sad, and came together to find a solution. Together they decided that whenever a creature would discover the true nature of their being, they would give it a choice. Allow it to decide the fate of its world —whether to continue the experiment, restart it or cease it. They would give them a choice, but only if and when the creatures would work it out for themselves.

And so it went on. Creatures gaining consciousness. Creatures spreading ideas. Creatures discovering the greatest truth. Creatures making their decision. Over and over again, in a loop of life. A circle of the same events. The perpetual story.

The world of the Unnamed.

A sudden rush of silence hit Amber's ears like a gush of cold wind. She opened her eyes and blinked, staring at S. The book in his hands was now closed, and he smiled at her in a polite and ever so slightly patronizing fashion. She wanted to scowl back at him but felt too tired to get the facial expression right.

"That's it?" she asked, making eye contact for a split second, then turning her attention to her shoes. "That's the end of the story?"

"Yes."

"Are you sure?"

"Quite sure."

"But that's hideous." Amber wrinkled her nose. "You mean my whole life, and the whole history of my species, we've just been...hosts, for these masters of yours?"

"It's not as bad as it sounds." Light interfered. "Ideas and stories are kinda nice, eh? Don't you like movies and books and stuff?"

"I do!" she replied. "I used to at least. Loved them more than anything else.

Except that was back when I used to think that they were our creation, and not some other-dimensional parasite setting up a cozy habitat in my synapses."

"I know it is shocking," Light continued, "I mean, I remember finding it out for the first time, but once you do learn it, it all starts to make sense. For example, you know how sometimes ideas just come to you? How you get inspired and words start appearing on the page as if of their own volition?"

"Yeah," Amber nodded, "that's called flow. It's coming from your brain, from the subconscious part. It just happens so quickly that you don't have time to form the illusion of consciously thinking of it."

"Well, no, actually," Light said. "It's Them. Popping into your head out of their twelve dimensions."

"That's disgusting."

"But true," S assured her. "It also explains why the universe is fine-tuned for life."

"The fine-tuning argument is bullshit." Amber told him. "There are billions of parallel worlds, each with their own set of conditions. We don't have a perfect environment for life, we just evolved to fit it well."

"That's partially true," he nodded, "but like I've read to you, the Unnamed actually do focus on creating universes that are good for life to exist in. They pretty much maximized it for your particular world."

"Why is most of the universe immediately lethal for me then?" Amber smirked.

"They aren't magicians." S shrugged. "There has to be a limit. Additionally, now you have an answer as to where the universe came from in the first place."

"We've known that it was pushed out of other dimensions for a long time." She didn't seem impressed. "We just didn't know why it happened, and that never really bothered me. Point is, it did happen. That should be enough."

"Not to millions of souls in the past," Darkness pointed out. "People who've spent their lives trying to work out the exact conditions before the Big Bang. Not to your father."

Amber was on her feet even before Darkness finished that sentence. She

325

leaped forward and reached with her arms, eager to grasp Darkness by the lapels of her ceremonial robe. Her fingers went right through her shoulders.

"Don't you dare mention my father," she hissed. "I swear to god, if I figure out the way to put my hands on you…"

"You wouldn't do such a thing," Darkness said calmly. "I've watched your entire life. I know you."

"Fourteen years," Amber told her. "Fourteen years I've been looking, searching for the one responsible. If you think I won't do what I've wanted to do all these years, then you don't know shit about me."

"You're threatening the wrong entity." S walked over and stood between them. "We had nothing to do with your parents' death."

"Don't you try telling me he did it to himself," she began.

"Technically, he did," Darkness said, and Amber clenched her jaw. "He ignored the safety protocols. He was aware of what he was doing wrong."

"And he had no choice in doing it," S reminded before Amber had a chance to retaliate. "It can all be calculated from the initial conditions of this universe." He paused, wiggling his fingers in front of his face. "Specifically, the position of particle number 18973335. And the reactor exploding is due to the initial position of particle," he wiggled some more, "number seven. I'm truly sorry," S said, and Amber reluctantly admitted to herself that he sounded genuinely empathetic. "It was meant to be."

"What about my nest?"

Amber turned around. Lullaby hadn't said anything in a long time, watching the scene play out from the stone bench. Now they were on their feet, shoulders wide, back straight, and looking rather menacing. S seemed to have picked up on that, as the next words that came out of his mouth were a little bit shaky.

"That's a bit more complicated." He forced an awkward smile. "You see, uh, Lk'st, we say that the universe always runs the same course, but it's only true overall. There are…complications. We call them quantum fluctuations, and they tend to mess stuff up a bit.

"And the Unnamed, well, they don't really like it. They want order, the want their universes to work the way they intended them to. So, they use us. We come from other, parallel universes, and we make sure that things stay on track. Tweak a thing here, change a line there, plant the right ideas in the right minds. Help keep it tidy. And your nest..." he sighed, "it wasn't crucial for the preset course of the universe per say, but, eh, it was, well, let's call it collateral damage."

Amber couldn't wipe a nasty grin off her face. She expected Lullaby to lunge at them and snap their necks, the way they did with their kidnappers back on Tenebris. But they didn't. They just made a few steps back, took a seat at the stone bench and went quiet again. Defeated.

"I still don't get it," Amber said after a short break. "You're the priests, yeah?"

S nodded.

"And you come from a parallel universe, which is supposed to be impossible, but works somehow."

"Exchange of matter or energy between universes is forbidden," S explained. "Doesn't mean you can't exchange ideas."

"So, you're what," she continued, "just...imagining stuff?"

"Basically." He shrugged. "It feels a bit like daydreaming, but more real. Mind you, the people who see us in this universe--which doesn't happen often--they are either imagining or hallucinating as well. We would never be able to create a physical apparition. We can only interact with your mental realities, not physical realities."

"But doesn't that mean you have breached the secrecy for your own world?"

"Oh, no. No no no." S chuckled. "You see, it's not true knowledge. You can't have true knowledge moving in between universes. Only some knowledge. I know the greatest truth, but I don't have definitive proof."

"Like religion?" Amber guessed.

"If you wish to call it that, yes." He nodded. "Although I'd like to point out that, by definition, no religion can ever get it right, so to speak. It's information coming from the Unnamed, and they can't spoil their own experiment, now can they? People do have brilliant guesses from time to time, but it's not the same as definitive evidence."

"Buddhists got pretty close," Amber pondered. "With the whole Dharma thing, and the Wheel of Sansara. Do you escape the cycle if you reach Enlightenment then?" she asked.

"I'm afraid not," S responded. "Like I've said, nothing more than a brilliant guess. You, on the other hand, have the calculations to prove it."

"We don't." She laughed briefly and shook her head. "The Nos have crunched the numbers, or rather their supercomputer did. But they offed themselves before they got the chance to read the results."

"Which makes you the representatives," Darkness spoke up, "since the computer wasn't a sentient being."

"So how long did it take us to work this out?" Amber was beyond anger or grief at that point.

"Fifteen billion years." S told her.

"That's it?" She blinked. "Our universe is only fifteen billion years old? But that means it's only been a billion and a bit since humanity first evolved."

"A billion is a long time though."

"We were all unicellular for more than a billion!" She laughed. "That's insane. And it makes no fucking sense! I thought Earth existed trillions of years ago. If all that was a billion and a bit ago, Sun might still be around."

"It's not," S replied. "You've consumed it and the rest of the Solar System in the twenty sixth century."

"Where are all the stars then?" Amber continued. "We thought the universe is very old and has expanded so much that the gap between the galaxies is too big."

"It hasn't." S had that sad smile on his face again. "You, along with some other races, just consumed most of it a long time ago. Left a few galaxies alone for the sake of it. The prettiest ones, and the most precious."

"That can't be right." Amber shook her head. "Humanity has gone extinct fuck knows when. There are Han, and Indigos, and Alexandria, but Alexandria was created by the Muuk."

S frowned, and looked kindly at her, as if trying to explain something sad and complicated to a child.

"Where do the Muuk come from, do you think?"

Amber frowned as well, thinking hard.

"No," she said and covered her mouth with her hand. "No. You've got to be kidding me."

"Look into your heart," Darkness said, and Light elbowed her in response.

"But they don't look anything like us!" Amber was waving her arms around now. "Not that Han or Indigos look exactly like us either, but still, you can see the family resemblance. The Muuk are octopus monsters!"

"Evolution works in mysterious ways." S shrugged. "Especially over eons."

"All that power then," she whispered. "All that might. And they still weren't the ones to work it out."

"Well, you did," S said. "Or you found out anyway. And as much as I'd love to keep discussing this for longer, I think it is time to talk about your options. So, take a seat, please."

Amber obeyed, taking a spot on the bench next to Lullaby. S walked over to them and cleared his throat before making the book appear in his grasp once again.

"You've breached the conditions," he said. "You've discovered the greatest truth. And as the representatives of conscious material life, you now have to make a decision on their behalf.

"You can," and he outstretched his palm to count on his fingers, "end the cycle now and forever. Everyone will die instantly and without pain, and this universe will never repeat. You can end this cycle at the end of the universe, as in let this run continue naturally till it reaches maximum entropy but prevent the next Big Bang. You can restart the cycle now, but, like you now know, it will just end in the same place, so that's more of a 'buying you some time' option. Or you can do nothing--wipe your own memory, replace the knowledge with something else and continue on with your lives. If someone else discovers the greatest truth, we'll have this talk again."

"It won't happen soon, even if it will," Light said, and Darkness gave her a weird glance. "The Muuk are terrified of the greatest truth. They lied about the plates and they're planning to destroy the Aquamarine Moon. Until someone else thinks of it, this story will just be that--a story."

"Let's recap then," Amber sighed, "my options are--multiple genocide, delayed multiple genocide, or allowing this meaningless nonsense to continue, knowing that we're nothing more than hosts for these twelve dimensional parasites who find our suffering unfortunate but don't give a single flying fuck about it."

"You won't know it," Lullaby reminded. "They'll wipe our memories."

"We can replace it with whatever you want," S added. "A nice story in place of..."

"Truth?" Amber suggested.

"Well, yes."

"Splendid." She chuckled. "So many options, and all terrible!"

"Can't they fix the world?" Lullaby asked. "Remove the suffering?"

"Technically, I think they could," S replied. "Stop entropy, I mean. But you see, this world would be useless for them. Entropy equals information. A universe without entropy is a universe they can't live in."

"Omni-benevolent my ass," Amber said.

"No one said they were omni-benevolent." Darkness pointed out. "Or omnipotent, for that matter. Just omnipresent and omniscient."

"As far as gods go," Light shrugged, "they kinda suck, to be honest."

"Yeah," Amber scowled. "I've noticed."

"Is this the first cycle?" Lullaby tilted their head at S, blinking their big black eyes.

"Can't tell that, sorry."

"If it's not the first one," Amber said, "then we automatically know what every single Amber and Lullaby before us have decided. At least we know they didn't end it."

"Aren't really deciding," Lullaby told her. "No free will."

"You have free will in here," S disagreed. "Just not in the real world."

"How is that even possible?!" Amber scoffed.

"Magic," Darkness said. "Don't question it."

"You should get to work then," S told them. "Gotta make up your free mind. Oh, and one more thing--the decision has to be unanimous. No voting. You have to agree with each other."

"Oh, right," Amber shook her head, half-scowling, half-smiling, "you are asking two persons to make a decision on behalf of trillions, and the two of us have to agree. A-ma-zing."

And before Amber could add something intensely sarcastic, S blurted out 'call me if you'll have any questions' and vanished into thin air along with Light and Darkness.

"I should have stayed put on Alexandria," Amber mused, swinging her legs again. "Be nicer to people. Find a research project. Keep my mouth shut and mind off things. So many things I could have done differently."

"Coulda-shoulda-woulda," Lullaby teased. "Should have died with my nest."

"Yeah, right."

"If you were to leave... what would you do?"

"Don't know. Either go back to the Novella Institute, or take Nina's offer."

"She gave you offer?"

"I didn't tell you?" Amber raised an eyebrow. "She wants us to join her. Fly across the universe, help people out, have fun. Be gay, do crimes. Forget about this nonsense."

"Could you do it?"

"Of course I could, if they were to wipe my memory."

"Now, I mean. Could you let the world suffer to have that good life?"

Amber shrugged. "Half a year ago, I'd say 'sure, what do I care about the world'. But after everything I've seen...I don't know anymore. So much suffering that, apparently, isn't even worth the happiness."

"You said fuck the computer."

"Oh, I said many things." She got up and began to pace the room. "I hate

331

this, Lu. I hate how all the options are the bad ones."

"If they are all bad, does it matter what we choose?"

"Well, we gotta choose the least bad option, right? Ugh, I hate this." She stomped her foot. "I know rationally what I should do, but emotionally." She stopped and smiled. "The computer might be right, but it's not alive. It's not conscious. Cause god knows Lu, I've suffered in this life and," she paused, and a sob escaped her lips, "I love it too... and I don't wanna die."

She sat down on the ground, and a single tear ran down her cheek and dropped to the ground. Lullaby got up from the bench and walked over, taking a seat near her. They put an arm around her shoulders and chirped.

"Let's talk about this," they said. "We've got this far, right? We'll work this out too."

"Yeah." Amber wiped another tear from her eyes and smiled. "Yes, Lu. Together, we'll work this out."

The starship Enlightenment stayed absolutely still, bathed in the shimmering dull glow of dying stars as they descended gracefully beyond the event horizon of a ravenous black beast beneath them. Inside, it was similarly tranquil, a low hum of the idle engines filling its rooms. Nina glanced at the digital clock. Just a quarter of an hour had passed, and already she was getting impatient. She leaned back in the pilot's chair and listened for any minuscule changes in the familiar hum. As soon as she heard the metallic click of a docking capsule, she was on her feet and walking.

The docking bay was already depressurizing when she approached the door. Through the thick transparent plastic, she could see first Amber and then Lullaby stumbling out of the capsule and onto the cold floor. Both waved at her cheerfully when she stepped over the threshold. Both looked exhausted: stretching, signing, and rubbing their aching muscles and joints.

"Well, that was quick," Nina smiled, eager to hear their story.

332

"Quick?" Amber half-scoffed, half-coughed. "I feel like I've been down there for a week! I need the bathroom, a three course meal, a stiff whiskey, and then the bathroom again, all at the same time."

"Three course meal is good start," Lullaby muttered, and was immediately off in the direction of the food cupboard.

"Leave some for the rest of us," Amber shouted at their back. "Jeez," she twisted her head to the right and heard something crunch in her neck, "this capsule is pure murder. It should come equipped with a chiropractor. Or a tissue repair kit, perhaps. Would still prefer this to a commercial flight, mind you, cause let me tell you, the people on commercials..."

"Amber?" Nina interrupted the inevitable rant.

"Yeah?"

"Well? What did you find down there?"

"Oh." Amber appeared pensive all of a sudden. "Right. That. The short version is, there was nothing down there. And the long version is, well," she scratched her eyebrow thoughtfully, "there was nothing of historical or scientific interest down there. A breathable atmosphere and a lot of dust, and I mean, a lot. I'll be getting that out of my shoes and my underwear for the foreseeable future."

"You mean," Nina frowned, "it was the wrong place, or...?"

"Fuck knows!" Amber beamed. "Wrong place, or wrong time. Maybe they've all died out and left no trace. Maybe it was a decoy. Maybe we got those coordinates wrong after all. I mean, come on, that moon isn't even blue! Point is, we'll never know."

"And you're okay with that?"

"I will learn to be. Anyway, never mind that place, that quest is done. What is it next for us then, medical supplies or contraband?"

It was clear from Nina's expression that she was far from satisfied with this answer, but she got Amber's hint alright and stopped pushing.

"Contraband," she replied. "It's on Gellavan. Ever been there?"

"Nope," Amber responded cheerfully, "I'm sure it is a lovely place. Thing. Crime-ridden hole. Whatever, Lullaby will find something to appreciate there, and I can always just appreciate you," she smiled with the corner of her mouth. "I'm ready to go. Almost. Need to call my dad first."

Already, the spaceship was on the move, taking them further away from the swirl of the black hole and the moon orbiting it. Amber watched it get smaller and smaller from a porthole in a bedroom. And far from Amber and the spaceship, the Aquamarine Moon was rapidly turning to dust. The atmosphere had been breached, the stasis effect disturbed; now the forces of entropy were taking hold and reducing to atoms every object on its surface--including the giant supercomputer.

Lullaby entered the room almost on tiptoes (as much as a Rx'lng could), unwilling to disturb Amber. They took a few steps towards the porthole, then took a seat on the unmade bed.

"You okay?" Lullaby asked.

"Was going to ask you the same thing," Amber responded, eyes still fixated on the tiny dot of the moon.

"Will live," was the answer.

"Same. So," Amber said, then took an awkward pause. "Do you remember, like, anything?"

"Not a second of it."

"Right. Me neither. I think," she began, turning around to look at Lullaby, "I think we were down there for a while. Like, a whole day or something. But my memory is just blank. That is so freaking weird."

"May have wiped our memories."

"Oh I bet they did," Amber smirked. "I bet there's a whole ass civilization down there and they gave us a huge tour with sight-seeing and everything and told us all their secrets, then wiped our brains clean so that no one would disturb them again."

"Could have spent many months there," Lullaby mused. "Years, maybe."

"Nah," Amber wrinkled her nose, "I don't feel older. I think it was like an extended weekend. Also," she took a seat on the bed near Lullaby, "I feel different. Peaceful. Mellow. But also very determined to just, I don't know...get out there and do things."

"Can feel that too," Lullaby confirmed. "Could be a gift to us, of some sort."

"Maybe we will remember one day," Amber said. "When we're very old or something. Or it will come to us in a dream. Or a really good story that we'll never know the inspiration for."

"Yes," Lullaby chirped. "Yes. A dream sounds nice."

"So, overall," Amber concluded, getting up again, "I'd say this was a pretty decent outcome."

And Lullaby had nothing to add to that thought.

They all gathered together in the piloting room--Nina in the pilot's chair, Amber standing close with a hand on Nina's shoulder, and Lullaby sitting on the floor, their head nearly bumping into the ceiling--as the ship processed its new coordinates. The black hole and its moon were too far to see now; in front of them, the space was pitch black and utterly empty. The engines were kicking into gear and sending a gentle vibration through the walls. They were almost ready to blast off into hyperspace.

"How did your dad react then?" Nina asked. "To your sudden change in living arrangements and career directions."

"Honestly, I'm not a hundred percent sure," Amber replied. "He was either really angry or strangely proud. Possibly both. It's fine though," she assured Nina and Lullaby (and also herself), "I'll keep in touch with him, maybe even visit sometimes. Maybe he'll decide to join me, who knows," she joked.

"I am not taking your entire family on board," Nina chuckled. "Though I am pretty close to repairing that smart band of yours, so maybe you'll have your assistant back, if that counts."

"It does," Amber smiled. "Thanks. Anyway, just because I've left Alexandria, doesn't mean I have to stop being a historian. I bet there's way more history I can find in situ. You know, history in its natural habitat, not just in old books. And something better than a dusty old moon."

"Can be rogue historian and archaeologist," Lullaby suggested. "Have our own secret special science."

"That's right, my dudes," Amber agreed. "Go off the grid. Start our own thing. Be gay, do crimes. Hell yeah."

"You're weirdly enthusiastic about this," Nina smiled with a corner of her mouth, "have you gone through my booster supply by any chance?"

"Maybe I'm just excited about Gellavan," retorted Amber. "Come on then. Press the button."

"As you wish," Nina shrugged, and initiated the first stage of hyperspace jump.

The spaceship shook, creaked, flashed its cabin lights for a split second, then dived into the curved dimensions, making their stomachs twist. "Will I ever get used to this sensation?" Amber wondered, gripping onto Nina's chair for dear life. To her left, Lullaby was chirping in excitement, and to her right, Nina watched the Rx'lng dance on the spot with a smile on her face.

Amber smiled too. She did not feel particularly certain about her future, or her decisions, or even her own sanity. She also did not think that she would feel sure, one day. But, in that shaky, bubbling, blurry moment, she did feel in the right place; and she felt loved.

And for now, at least, she did not have a need for anything more.

Meanwhile, S climbed a few more steps up the steep, grassy hill and poked the ground with the tip of his boot. Having found the location satisfactory, he took a seat on the cold grass and leaned against the hill's slope. Soon Light and Darkness followed suit.

"The air is so fresh up here," Darkness said, breathing in to the full capacity of her non-existent lungs. "Untouched by dirt and dust and pollution of civilization."

"Cherish it," S told her. "Cyanobacteria worked hard to produce that air."

"So simple," she continued, ignoring S's remark. "Some clean air and a great view. What else can an ephemeral projection of a conscious being want?"

"'A great view'?" Light arched an eyebrow.

"What?"

"Just 'great view'?" she repeated. "It's not just great. It's gorgeous."

They turned their eyes towards the horizon where, in bright iridescent strokes of crimson, ruby and amber, burned the most beautiful sunset you could ever imagine.

No tourists were bothering them with tacit remarks and camera flashes. The birds weren't singing in the distance. No clouds obstructed the flaming sky. Even the air was completely still.

"I guessed what they would choose from the get-go," Light mused, running her hand across the grass.

"You did?" Darkness asked.

"Uh-huh. It was kinda obvious, for someone who followed their lives since one."

"I was surprised, actually," S said. "I know I'm not supposed to judge and all that, but it's hard to stay objective with these things."

"It's their choice," Darkness told him. "That's how it works."

"I know, Darkness." He smirked. "It's not my first day."

A pause took hold, full of thoughtful sighs and gazing longingly at the blazing line of the horizon.

"And what did they choose again?" S asked.

"No clue," Darkness replied, and Light nodded in agreement. "And honestly? I don't care. It doesn't really matter."

They talked for a while, exchanging stories and ideas, until there were no words left to be said. And so they ceased the conversation with an understanding nod and a few soft sighs.

Down the hill, tiny creatures crawled in the mud, basking in the setting sun's warmth, about to start a long path towards a mighty civilization. Species would evolve and die out. Cities would be built and reduced to dust. In one family, billions of years from that moment, a girl would be born, and the girl would be named Amber Shakya. But not now.

Now, the sunset burned, and the three of them watched as the last rays of the sun touched the skies and died out.

Night descended on the world.

Everything was at peace.